SEQUOYAH REGIONAL LIBRARY
3 8749 0053 6660 7

THE DAUGHTER-IN-LAW

Also by Diana Diamond in Large Print:

The Babysitter

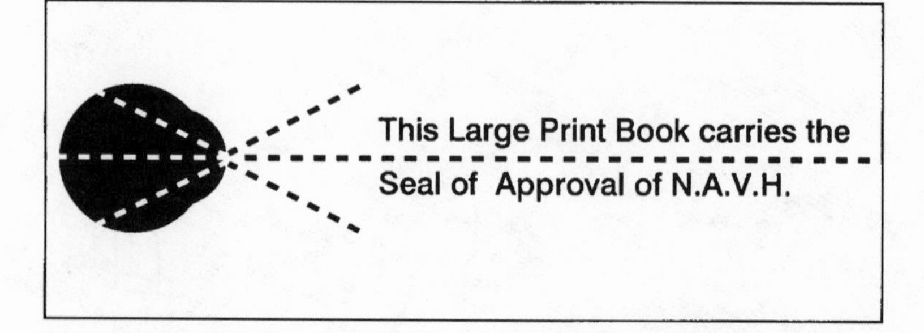

The Daughter-in-Law

DIANA DIAMOND

Thorndike Press • Waterville, Maine

Published in 2003 by arrangement with
St. Martin's Press, LLC.

Thorndike Press® Large Print Basic.

The tree indicium is a trademark of Thorndike Press.

The text of this Large Print edition is unabridged.
Other aspects of the book may vary from the original edition.

Set in 16 pt. Plantin by Ramona Watson.

Printed in the United States on permanent paper.

Library of Congress Cataloging-in-Publication Data

Diamond, Diana.
The daughter-in-law / Diana Diamond.
p. cm.
ISBN 0-7862-5825-X (lg. print : hc : alk. paper)
1. Accident victims — Family relationships — Fiction.
2. Daughters in law — Fiction. 3. Mothers in law — Fiction. 4. Rich people — Fiction. 5. Widows — Fiction.
6. Large type books. I. Title.
PS3554.I233D38 2003b
813′.6—dc22 2003056432

With thanks
to my readers,
Rena and Marge

National Association for Visually Handicapped
serving the partially seeing

As the Founder/CEO of NAVH, the only national health agency solely devoted to those who, although not totally blind, have an eye disease which could lead to serious visual impairment, I am pleased to recognize Thorndike Press* as one of the leading publishers in the large print field.

Founded in 1954 in San Francisco to prepare large print textbooks for partially seeing children, NAVH became the pioneer and standard setting agency in the preparation of large type.

Today, those publishers who meet our standards carry the prestigious "Seal of Approval" indicating high quality large print. We are delighted that Thorndike Press is one of the publishers whose titles meet these standards. We are also pleased to recognize the significant contribution Thorndike Press is making in this important and growing field.

Lorraine H. Marchi, L.H.D.
Founder/CEO
NAVH

* Thorndike Press encompasses the following imprints: Thorndike, Wheeler, Walker and Large Pr int Press.

ONE

She was frightened. Maybe even terrified. Jonathan could tell from her expression. Staring eyes focused on empty space. Lips pulled into a tight line. The way she rolled her head to crack the joints in her neck.

"First jump?" he asked in a soft voice that was just for her and not intended as a public announcement to the others.

"What?" It took her a few seconds to realize that he had spoken to her.

"Is this your first jump?"

"No . . . well, yes. First time without my instructor."

He nodded.

"Is it so obvious?"

"Not obvious. It just seems that you're thinking too much. Like you're trying to make damn sure you haven't forgotten anything."

She flashed a quick, darting smile. One that was pure formality without any trace of joy. "Have I?"

"Have you what?"

"Have I forgotten something?"

Jonathan looked her over carefully. A brand-new helmet without even a scratch, the dark plastic face mask pushed back. A blue nylon jacket fitted with elastics at the wrists, waist, and neck. A parachute on her back with the packer's tag hanging from the ripcord and a smaller emergency chute across her belly. A wrist altimeter. Skintight black pants tucked into the tops of soft, suede boots. Some outfitter had sold her the high-price package.

"You have your AAD set?"

She nodded confidently. "Automatic activation at three thousand feet."

"Then you haven't forgotten anything. You're allowed to relax."

She smiled again, this time more easily and with a hint of genuine pleasure.

Jonathan checked his wrist altimeter. "I'm setting the alarm for thirty-five hundred. By then I should see your main chute deploying."

"Thanks. That's what my instructor does, not that he's ever had to remind me. I tend to let the chute go early."

He smiled. She laughed at the absurdity of her situation. When you jumped out of an airplane you generally didn't forget when it was time to pull the chute, unless you knocked yourself unconscious leaving the plane or flying into another jumper. That was what the AAD — automatic activation device — was for.

"I'll be okay," she said. "Once we get started. It's the standing around that gets to me."

He held out his gloved hand. "Jonathan Donner."

"Nicole Pierce," she answered. She shook his hand with more strength than he had expected. Her eyes smiled for the first time, shining arcs of blue above high cheeks. "I don't know why in hell I do this. I spent the last half hour in the ladies' room upchucking my morning coffee."

"It gets easier," he assured her. "And the thrill never goes away."

"You've been jumping for a while," she said, putting words to the obvious.

"Yeah! Nearly ten years. All over the world."

Her eyes widened. "High altitude?"

"All kinds of altitude. Out of balloons. Jets."

"Then why are you making this dinky jump?"

Jonathan laughed. "There are no dinky jumps. And no matter how many times I go up, I still toss up my coffee while I'm getting dressed. I just don't let it bother me anymore."

She held eye contact, her expression accepting his friendship. "Thanks," she said. "I'm going to be okay."

The pilot sauntered out of the shed, bouncing to the beat he was hearing through his CD headset. He didn't look up at his customers until he was right on top of them. "All set?" he asked, and without waiting for an answer he jumped into the doorway hatch of his De Havilland Twin Otter. His passengers climbed aboard behind him.

There were six making the jump. Nicole was the only woman. Jonathan was jumping with a close friend, Ben Tobin. The other three were oversize Navy SEALs, treating themselves to a postman's holiday. They talked quietly in a language all their own. The SEALs strapped themselves into the sling along the airplane's right side. Ben Tobin was nearest the door on the left side, then Jonathan, and finally Nicole closest to the pilot. The only sounds were the safety harness buckles snapping closed.

The pilot clicked on the intercom. He started a word, paused, and then clicked off. When he returned, he had his script in hand. "We're climbing to ten thousand feet, which shouldn't take more than twelve to fifteen minutes. Then we'll cross downwind over the jump area so you can find your marks, saunter back, and then make a jump run. Okay?"

There were grunts of approval.

"Anyone changes his mind," he added, "can ride back with me at no extra charge." He laughed at his own sense of humor. None of his passengers cracked a smile.

The left propeller began to turn cutting blinking shadows in the morning sunlight that was streaming through the round windows. The pitch of the turbine whine eased up the scale until the roar of ignition drowned it out. Then the right propeller started to swing.

"Anyone ever flown this crate before?" one of the Navy men asked.

Ben nodded. "It's a good jump plane," he said to no one in particular.

"Is he kidding?" the SEAL went on. "Ten thousand feet in twelve minutes? Looks more like it could take twelve weeks."

Jonathan had logged dozens of jumps out of Twin Otters. They were quaint-looking planes with spars supporting the wings and a landing gear that didn't retract. But they climbed quickly and turned on a dime. "It's a big door," he answered the cynic across the aisle, "easy to get out of, and once you jump the plane doesn't make a lot of difference."

Nods from the SEALs. What did it matter if it took a few extra minutes to get to altitude? Once you went out the door no plane was better than any other. They settled into an anxious silence.

"You all right?" Jonathan asked Nicole, leaning close so that it was their private conversation.

She nodded. "As soon as we get out. It's the waiting that scares me."

"Why don't you go ahead of me," he offered. "I'll follow you down."

"I'll be fine," she insisted. But within a second she suggested, "Maybe I will go ahead of you."

Jonathan nodded. Then, just to reassure her, he reached over and squeezed her hand. She squeezed back gratefully, but she didn't look at him. Her eyes seemed fascinated with the toes of her boots.

With both engines growling, the Otter bounced across the grass and out onto the gravel runway. The pilot didn't pause to check anything, but simply pulled the throttles to a melodic howl. The plane rushed ahead and within a few seconds lifted into the air. The SEALs exchanged approving glances. They were impressed.

"He doesn't waste any time," Nicole said, nodding toward the pilot. Her fear was leaving her as the plane climbed. Like she had said, it was the waiting around that made her nervous.

"Where are you from?" Jonathan asked, trying to start a normal conversation.

"New York. I'm a stockbroker. Well, at least I'm going to be a broker. Right now I'm a broker's assistant who gets to talk to customers."

"You're in the market? That would scare me more than jumping out of airplanes."

Nicole nodded. "You know, now that I think of it I get sick getting dressed for work. I guess it's the same dread of putting your life on the line with every move you make."

"Well, when the market crashes and it's time to jump out the window, you'll already know the routine."

She laughed out loud, and then put her hand over her mouth as if she had caught herself laughing in church. The three SEALs were looking at her with disapproval. Skydiving was serious business. Leave it to a woman to trivialize it, they probably thought.

The plane banked into a tight turn and continued climbing into the heading that it had just come from. The pilot was carving his own switchbacks, like climbing a road that turned back and forth up the side of a mountain. The Otter was holding its steep angle and going up fast, promising to beat the twelve-minute estimate.

Jonathan thought she might be attractive, but with the parachutes she was wearing and the straps across her chest and thighs, all he could do was guess. She had a nice smile and very expressive eyes. Her voice sounded a bit like music. The shape of her legs was obvious in the skintight pants and she seemed to be on the slim side of curvaceous. But he had to fill in the rest from his imagination. Her hair was probably light given the complexion of her cheeks and the color of her eyes, but it was hidden beneath her helmet. Her figure was probably good. Great legs generally went with a well-turned butt, and if all that worked then the rest couldn't be too shabby.

"What do you do?" Nicole suddenly asked, resuming the conversation that Jonathan had started.

"Jump out of airplanes," he answered with a mischievous grin. "Race sailboats, do some scuba diving . . ." His tone indicated that the list wasn't all-inclusive.

"And what do you do to support all these adventures?"

He shrugged. "As little as possible. I have a job . . . in banking. But that's what really makes me sick."

Now Nicole had the mischievous smile. "You don't look like a banker. At least none of the bankers I've met."

Jonathan preened his shaggy mustache. "You mean this?"

"I suppose so. Aren't bankers supposed to be painfully shaved and completely buttoned-down? I thought displays of personal affectation were considered fiscally irresponsible."

"That's why it makes me sick. But I give it five days a week and then I escape on the weekends."

She looked suspicious. "This is only Tuesday."

"True, but a drive into New Jersey for a quick dive out of an airplane isn't what I mean by escape. This is just like taking a long lunch. Escape is when I really get away. Fly someplace on a Friday and come back on Monday."

"So, let's see" — Nicole calculated on her fingers — "four day weekends and one day for a late lunch. That sounds like a two-day workweek."

"Like I said, as little as possible . . ."

The plane banked into another turn, still climbing to altitude. It was laboring more in the thin air, its propellers working harder to get a grip.

"We're at eight thousand now," the pilot's voice reported, "turning downwind over the drop area."

Ben Tobin twisted in his seat and leaned into the door opening. The western New Jersey horse country was familiar to him, as was the distinctive bend in the Delaware River. He elbowed Jonathan and then the two of them pressed toward the doorway. Across the aisle, one of the Navy men turned his face to the window, his nose to the glass. The other two leaned close to Jonathan and Ben so they could see out the door. Nicole was the only one who didn't seem curious.

They climbed slowly out past the jump area. When they finally leveled off they were thirteen minutes from takeoff, just about what the pilot had predicted. The plane began a wide turn to the left, banking so that the open door gave a perfect view of the ground they were turning into.

"Okay," the pilot announced. "I've told them we're ready. Once you see the smoke you can go anytime."

The smoke appeared instantly, a crimson cloud generated by a burning flare at the beginning of the runway they had used for takeoff. It rose straight up for a few hundred feet, and then began to tail off to the east with the prevailing wind. The plane leveled at the end of its turn, and headed straight for the smoke signal.

The three Navy men unbuckled, closed the dark visors over their faces, and gathered at the doorway for an exchange of high fives. Then they dove out into space on a quick count, right on one another's heels. Jonathan and Ben unbuckled and pulled down their face masks. Ben went to the door. Jonathan waited for Nicole to get to her feet and let her step around him. Then he reached out and touched Ben's shoulder. Instantly, Ben was out. Nicole went right behind him without a moment's hesitation, and then Jonathan dove after her.

They were hit with the air blast, a cold slap delivered at better than one hundred miles an hour, and then spun in the turbulent wash of the propeller. Before they could orient themselves, they were already arcing down toward the earth, beginning their acceleration into the breath-stealing speed of free fall. Ben was the first to get his bearings, stretching out his body and then extending his arms like wings. From his head-down position, he pivoted until he was lying parallel to the ground, stretched across the wind that his fall was generating.

Jonathan found his position across the wind and then turned his head to find Nicole. She was just below and a bit to his right and she was in perfect position, a human airfoil generating lift by her extreme angle of attack to the rushing air. He checked his fall next to her and then steered over close enough to touch her. Blonde, he announced to himself confirming his guess. There was a length of blond hair streaming from the back of her helmet.

They maneuvered by controlling the angle of attack, the presentation of their bodies to the wind stream generated by falling. Their bodies moved in the opposite direction of the wind. Lie flat, and the force of the air would slow their descent. Lean right, so that the air bounced off to the left, and they would turn right. Lower their heads and they would accelerate ahead. Raise their heads and they would drift backward. There was also the fabric that filled the space between their extended arms. It made them bigger airfoils and gave them that much more control.

By combining these movements, they could fly anywhere relative to one another. Away, widening their circle, or back together again where they could link up and hold hands. They could dive under one another, or fly circles around each other. They could cavort like swimmers in three dimensions. The only difference was that all the while they were falling at about a hundred and twenty-five miles per hour.

He touched her hand and she grabbed onto him eagerly. Ben glided up to them carefully and took hold of her other hand. It wasn't smooth. The slightest movements of their bodies eased them in different directions, straining at their grips. They held together for a few seconds as they fell several hundred feet, but then exploded apart. Nicole was suddenly fifty feet above the two men who were soaring off in different directions. She watched Jonathan tuck like a platform diver and begin tumbling head over heels. Ben, with his arms extended, was spinning like a windmill. Far below, between her and the red smoke signal, were the Navy SEALs, flying like a formation of ducks. She was soaring above them all.

She could feel the adrenaline filling her with a wild euphoria. In part, it was the release from her natural fear of jumping and the wild abandon of plunging downward toward her own destruction. And there was the frantic intoxication of the moth banging against a lamp to get to the consuming fire. At this instant, flying through space, she was fully in touch with herself, trembling with the joy of simply being alive, and yet mesmerized by her flirtation with death. She was in total control of her own destiny, able to command changes in direction with a simple turn of her hand. She was risking her life in order to live it more completely.

She fell through five thousand feet, riding on the bubble of air that was compressed under her body. Far below, the SEALs had changed their formation and were soaring through the highest traces of the red marker. They would have to open their chutes soon. You could fall one thousand feet in just a few seconds and they were nearing the three thousand foot safety level.

Off to her left, Jonathan had turned back toward her, keeping himself a few hundred feet below. He would watch her chute open before he let out his own, just so that he wouldn't be hopelessly hanging in the air if she needed help. Instructors did the same thing, staying ready to steer themselves to a student in trouble. Ben was coming in from the right at about the same altitude as Jonathan. Both of them seemed to feel that she might need help. But Nicole knew better. She was queen of the universe, flying with abandon that only expertise could justify. She glanced at her wrist altimeter: forty-two hundred feet, the digits blinking down too quickly to count.

She was in the tracking position, head down and arms by her sides, moving toward the smoke marker at more than half the rate that she was falling. Jonathan eased in to within fifty feet, adjusting his body angle to hold position on her. He was pointing at his wrist altimeter, reminding her to watch her height. She checked the flashing digits on her own wrist: four thousand feet. Time to pull the release on the small pilot chute that would drag the big, steerable wing out of her backpack. But Nicole didn't want to end her free fall just yet. She still had plenty of time.

TWO

Jonathan's wrist alarm went off. He was at thirty-five hundred feet, which meant that the young woman he had just met was already past four thousand feet. And she was still flying, making no move to deploy her parachute. It was no problem for an experienced jumper. But the frightened novice who had gone out the door ahead of him shouldn't be pushing her margins. She ought to start popping the chute.

Nicole laughed to herself. She didn't need saving, but she welcomed his concern. Stay with me, she thought. Watch me fly like a goddess.

From below, she seemed to be in a trance. She wasn't acknowledging his signals and still wasn't reaching for her ripcord. Jonathan couldn't see her face through her tinted face mask, but her body language said that she was either an expert or a novice locked in an adrenaline high, so thrilled with flying that she had forgotten she was falling. He gestured broadly, to the point where he threw himself out of balance and began to roll.

"Damn it," he screamed uselessly into the deafening roar of the air, "do something. Pull the chute." He checked his altimeter. He was at three thousand feet and the girl wasn't far behind. He couldn't stay below her more than another few seconds without putting himself in jeopardy.

Ben Tobin could see his friend's signals and, glancing upward, he could tell that the girl was ignoring them. Either that or she had pushed over the edge where the euphoria blinded her to the danger. He changed his angle, adding air resistance so that he seemed to move up toward Nicole. He mimicked Jonathan's gestures and signaled to his wrist altimeter. He noticed that he was at twenty-nine hundred feet, which meant that the woman was falling through three thousand with no apparent concern. Where had she set her AAD?

Jonathan watched her parachute bag, waiting for the pilot chute to pop free. She had set her automatic activation device for three thousand feet and the instruments had a very narrow margin of error. Another few seconds and he would know if the safety system had failed. And that would leave him only five seconds to get to her and pull her chute out. Even in her horizontal tracking position, she was falling at better than two hundred feet a second.

Nicole could see the ground rushing up to consume her. What had been nothing more than a patch quilt of earth colors was now a very detailed landscape. She had no trouble defining the roads, the trees and even the furrow lines in the fields. She could see the gravel landing strip and the trace of red smoke that was still rising from the dying marker flare. It was intriguing to watch more and more details coming into focus. She knew she had never flown so low before. Always, she had been riding safely in her wing-shaped parachute when the hard reality of the earth was this close. She knew she should pull the release.

He was out of time. He had five seconds to get to her, five seconds to deploy her chute, and five seconds for the chute to open and break her fall. Anything more than that and she would still be traveling at a deadly speed when she hit the ground. Jonathan canted his body, felt the wind angle off and struggled to control his direction. He seemed to move up to her even though he knew that she was really coming down to his level. He had simply slowed his own speed so that she was falling faster.

The air, angling off his tilted body was pushing him to the right. He was moving at her too quickly, closing at a dangerous speed. But there was no time for precise adjustments. The seconds were rushing past.

He crashed into her with a jolt that would have knocked her down had they been standing, and grabbed her harness to keep her from bouncing away. His hand groped for the release on her parachute but he couldn't see. The midair collision had turned them face-to-face, banging their visors together. He was pressed against her, reaching over her shoulder to find the end of the ripcord. How many seconds did he have left? There was no time for an error. Maybe he should hold on to her and deploy his own chute. It could easily carry them both down. But could he hold her when his chute opened and jerked him upward? Her momentum could tear her completely out of his grasp. He had to decide, but there wasn't a second left to waste.

Ben Tobin was steering at them from the other side but his aim was too high. He reached out to catch them as he fired past but only succeeded in banging his hand against the side of Nicole's helmet. Then he was on the other side, moving away from them. He tried to stop, but he was out of time for maneuvering. They were past two thousand feet. He was only ten seconds from a grizzly death, maybe twelve seconds from a crippling landing. He pulled his release cord.

The small pilot chute popped out behind his head and filled. It began dragging the folded wing parachute out of its container, building resistance that jerked Ben out of his free fall and sent him flying upward, away from his friends. He could clearly see Nicole and Jonathan, still locked together, plunging away in their death spiral.

He saw a pilot chute pop free. A main chute began unraveling. Then the two bodies broke apart, one snatched away from the other by the tug of the white cloth wing as it filled. It must be the girl! Ben knew the bizarre colors of his friend's parachute, but the wing that formed far below him was pure white. So where was Jonathan? He caught sight of the small black form tumbling in the air, seemingly out of control. "Pull it, damnit! Pull the fucking cord!" He knew he was screaming but he couldn't hear his own words.

Jonathan knew he had popped her parachute. His fingers had found the release, and as soon as he pulled it he felt her being dragged out of his arms. He felt the container on her back collapse and then his hand was knocked away by one of the control stalks. He saw her fire up above him as if she had been shot from a cannon. His instincts told him to deploy his own chute, but there were already two chutes above him. If he suddenly stopped falling there was the risk that the parachutes could get tangled. He knew he should try to move out of the way.

He was already in his tracking position when he checked his altitude. He was passing through one thousand feet, only five or six seconds from death. But he was slowing, and at the same time moving out of the paths of the chutes above. Could he wait one more second to get clear?

His AAD snapped inside his parachute container. The pilot chute blew out and then the large wing began unfolding above him pulling him to a vertical position. He looked up. The wing was unraveling, fluttering as it tried to fill. Five seconds, four, three . . . he was still falling at a deadly speed.

The parachute snapped like a whip as it deployed across the wind. Jonathan recognized the tug on his harness. He reached up for the steering toggles, hoping to clear the row of trees that was clutching at him. But there wasn't time. The parachute swung him through the top branches, turned him over, and dropped him unceremoniously on his belly. Then the wing dragged him for ten yards along the ground before it doused.

He got to his knees and pulled the D rings on his harness. The parachute rig came free and then the cloth, deprived of its resistance, settled gently into a patch of bushes. Jonathan pushed up his visor and looked up. The girl's white parachute was settling easily into an open area of what seemed to be a newly plowed field. A hundred feet above her, Ben was flying down for a controlled landing.

They came running toward him, first Ben who had steered himself in close, and then Nicole who was hobbled by her hard landing. Jonathan climbed to his feet just in time to fall into his friend's arms.

"You scared me, buddy," Ben said, as they rocked each other like lovers.

"Not as much as I scared myself."

"You should have pulled sooner."

"I didn't pull at all. It was the AAD that saved me."

Nicole's voice pushed them apart. "You're all right. Jesus, tell me that you're all right." She rushed into Jonathan's arms and took up the embrace that Ben had started. Their helmets banged together as she forced her mouth against his, kissing him, talking, and sobbing all at once. "You saved my life! Are you hurt? Can I help you?"

"You can let him get some air," Ben said, easing her away. Then he looked at Jonathan, "Unless you'd like me to leave the two of you alone?"

Jonathan wasn't amused. His eyes blazed into Nicole's. "What the hell happened up there?"

She sobbed deeply and shook her head. "I don't know. I was lost until you hit me. And then I thought we had collided. I must have . . . lost it."

He reached out angrily, grabbed her shoulder harness, and pulled the AAD out of her pack.

"What are you doing?" She was shocked by his violence.

"What did you set this for?" he demanded.

"Three thousand. It's always at three thousand . . ."

Jonathan studied the device and then pushed it in front of Ben's face. Ben read the gauges. "Holy shit . . ."

"What's the matter?" Nicole looked from one man to the other. Ben handed her the activation device.

Nicole's hand went up to her cheek. "Oh, my God." Her eyes came up to meet Jonathan's. "How could it have happened?"

"One thousand feet," Jonathan snarled. "You know how close that puts you to dying? A second. Two at the most. Only experts cut their margins that thin."

"No, I didn't set it at a thousand. Do you think I'm crazy? It's always at three thousand."

"Did you set it this morning, or were you too busy throwing up?"

She hesitated. There was a flicker of doubt in her eyes.

"You didn't check it," Jonathan concluded. "You figured it was always set for three thousand feet so why bother to reset it and recheck it."

"I . . . I never change it. Just the base altitude depending on where I'm jumping. But the safety margin is always the same: three thousand. I swear. I'd never set it for one thousand. Do you think I'm insane?"

"No," Jonathan said as he stormed away from her and began gathering up his chute. "Not insane. Stupid, maybe. And careless, without a doubt. But not insane."

She followed after him, waving the AAD in his face. "I don't know how it got this way. Someone must have changed it."

He wheeled on her. "Or it changed itself while it was bouncing around with all the other gear in the back of your car. But either way, you would have caught it if you just bothered to check."

She started to protest but she had no voice. He was certainly right. She should have checked. You should always check. "I'm sorry," was the best she could do.

Jonathan rolled the chute under his arm, his anger stiffening every movement and gesture. "What I'm sorry for are the people who'll be with you on your next jump. I wonder how many of them will get themselves killed."

The van from the jump center turned from behind the trees at the end of the field. The school owner, a former paratrooper who identified himself as Willis, got out and walked around the front. The SEALs emerged from the sliding side door. Willis walked toward his errant jumpers. Jonathan led the humiliated procession across the field toward the van.

"You're being a bit of prick," Ben whispered to Jonathan.

"She's an idiot," Jonathan snarled. "She could have gotten us all killed."

"It was a mistake. She said she was sorry."

"Well then I guess all is forgiven. So why don't you go back up and jump with her?"

"What in hell happened to you guys?" Willis demanded as he drew close to them.

Jonathan answered. "We had equipment trouble. One of the chutes was screwed up." Ben smiled. Jonathan had conceded his point that the girl didn't deserve to be skewered over one mistake no matter how serious it was. He was covering for her.

"It was my fault," Nicole confessed.

"It was equipment," Jonathan contradicted, and he led his group right past Willis.

The SEALs were all leaning back with their arms folded. "Nice flight," one of them snickered.

"You two were really getting it on up there," another added.

"Equipment problem," Jonathan lied for the third time.

"What happened?" a Navy man leered. "Your fly get stuck?"

"He saved my life, jocko," Nicole snapped. "While you Boy Scouts were working on your merit badges, these guys were bringing me down."

She pushed past them, tossing her unfolded gear into the back of the van.

"Hey, I'd like to bring you down," one of the three offered. The others laughed in agreement.

Nicole wheeled around and found Willis. "You know what? If these three apes are riding, I'd rather walk." She stormed away from the car and began marching down the road.

"They came out here in case you needed help," Willis called after her.

Nicole never looked back. Her answer was a middle finger raised into the air.

"So what happened?" a Navy man asked Ben as they were getting into the van.

"Her AAD failed. Set for three thousand and the damn thing never went off."

The SEALs looked shocked. "You're kiddin'," one said.

"Those damn things never fail," another added.

"Just don't bet your life on it," Ben answered. Jonathan sat silently, his eyes locked closed.

They passed Nicole on the road and persuaded her to climb in. She took the place up front next to Willis, who kept stealing glances toward her. The group rode home quietly.

At the center, which was little more than a corrugated steel warehouse with a storefront, they all climbed down. Nicole went directly to the back of the van, hauled out her chute, and dragged it to her Volkswagen hatchback. She spread it out like an unmade bed, and then rolled it into the back.

One of the SEALs lifted a cooler from the back of an SUV and began tossing iced beer cans to his friends. "Join us," he said to Jonathan and Ben and handed each of them a beer.

Another SEAL walked after Nicole. "Have a beer with us, babe. I'd like to hear about your jump." His tone was polite, even professional. Sharing tales was part of the sport and by jumping out of the plane she had paid her membership dues.

She looked uncertainly at the gathering and spotted Jonathan's scowling face. "Thanks, but I've got to get back," she said. She tossed her helmet in the trunk.

Then she unzipped the jump jacket and pulled it off over her head.

Wow! Jonathan thought. Nicole was no fashion photographer's emaciated imitation of a woman. She was the real thing — a firm breast line, slim waist, and hips that actually flared out into graceful curves.

Her skintight jump pants revealed an ample butt and muscles down the backs of her legs.

The SEAL made no secret of admiring her figure. "You're sure you can't stay just for one?"

"I never stay just for one," she answered. She slammed the trunk closed and slid in behind the wheel. Their eyes never left her as she shifted into gear and accelerated away.

THREE

For the first few days after their meeting, Jonathan held fast to his just anger with Nicole. Her carelessness had nearly killed him, and he had been completely within his rights to tell her so. Skydiving was an inherently dangerous sport, and if she couldn't handle a dressing-down then maybe she should get into something more timid. But by the end of the week he had become more forgiving. Sure, she had made a dumb mistake in not checking her equipment. True, she had compounded it by not watching her jump partners. But she was just a beginner, and very good for a beginner. She had realized the gravity of her error and had apologized profusely.

"I wonder if that airhead girl will be here today," Jonathan asked absently as he and Ben headed back to the jump center for their weekly flight.

"What girl?" Ben asked from the passenger seat of the Mercedes convertible. His attitude was all innocence; he knew which girl. Jonathan had mentioned her several times, at first fuming over his near-death experience, and then explaining his change of heart.

"Nicole, or whatever her name is. The one we had to rescue last week."

"You're going to jump with her?" There was a smile playing at the corners of his mouth. "But I thought you said —"

"Yeah, and I don't regret what I told her. But what the hell? She's a novice and probably deserves another chance." He kept his eyes fixed to the road, knowing that he would blush with embarrassment if he glanced at his friend. "I mean, it takes balls for a woman to cut it in a macho sport."

"Oh, she's got balls, all right. I really loved the way she gave those Navy guys the finger." They both laughed at the memory of Nicole, boiling mad, putting the Navy SEALs in their places.

They turned off the interstate but Jonathan didn't cut back on the speed. He enjoyed testing the car against the narrow roads that wound through New Jersey horse country, and racing along the miles of white paddock fencing that bordered the lush green fields. It was the thrill of speed in his overpowered sports car that had made him search for the new and more pleasant highs in jumping. He found nearly erotic excitement in the few minutes of free fall and then a narcotic euphoria in the glide down to earth after the parachute had deployed.

"You've been talking about her a lot," Ben said, restarting the conversation they had let lapse.

Jonathan shrugged. "I guess it's not easy to forget a near-death experience."

"Or a woman who nearly suffocated you with kisses when she found out you were alive."

"I think she was just relieved she hadn't killed me."

Ben snickered. "Why don't you ask her when you see her? To me, it looked like she was after your body."

But when they reached the jump center Nicole wasn't there. Jonathan asked if she was coming when they were making up their jumping order.

"Called in this morning and canceled," Willis answered nonchalantly. "Asked me who was going to be flying. I went through the list, six people in all, and she said it sounded too crowded."

"So, when is she coming?"

"I don't know," Willis answered. "And I don't really care. Wasn't she the one who got tangled with you guys?"

They made their jump from eight thousand feet, joined hands with three of the others to form a star, separated and released their chutes at thirty-five hundred and steered themselves to perfect landings.

"Glad she didn't make it," Ben announced as they were packing up. "She could have spoiled a beautiful day."

Jonathan nodded, but he begged the girl's address and phone number from Willis. "Just to get a few things off my chest," he explained.

He phoned twice and when she didn't answer he hung up without leaving a message. "You don't apologize to a machine," he said, explaining his perseverance to Ben. But on Friday morning, just before he left for a weekend dive in the Florida Keys, he did just that. He called, hoping to catch her before she left for work, and when her answering machine clicked on, he left his invitation.

"Hi! This is Jonathan Donner, your jump partner from a few weeks back. I'm calling to apologize for being so tough on you. I'm not always that uptight, and I guess I was a bit of an ass. Put it down to the excitement of the near-death experience. I wasn't quite my lovable self. At any rate, I'd like to see you to tell you I'm sorry. Maybe we could have dinner or something. I'll be away for the weekend, so I won't get back to you until Monday. If you want to leave me a message, my number is . . ."

He left both his office and home numbers, said he hoped that they would talk soon, and drove up to Westchester County Airport where his company's charter jet was hangared.

The weekend of scuba diving was breathtaking and the company was exciting. The diving conditions were perfect with sunlight sparkling on the Florida reef and illuminating a wreck that was forty feet down. He played in and out of iron hatches, chasing a school of snappers that had settled into the pilothouse, and coming face-to-face with a moray eel that lived in the boiler. The captain's assistant turned out to be a marine biology major from Miami who returned with him to his hotel in Marathon and made love as if it were an endurance sport. But even so, Jonathan found himself remembering flashes from his skydiving experience with Nicole, and looking forward to Monday when he hoped to talk with her. He realized that she had been on his mind off and on since he had told her what a careless lightweight she was.

He was disappointed when he got to his apartment on Sunday night and found that she hadn't returned his call. Logic told him that she, too, would have returned that evening even if she were away for the weekend. She must have gotten his message, so it was obvious that she wasn't all that anxious to talk to him. In the morning, he passed up the opportunity to call her, fearing she might put him in his place for his rude behavior. He reached his office at Sound Holdings early, hoping she might have called his office number, but again he was disappointed. When his telephone rang promptly at nine, he answered in his business voice.

"Jonathan Donner?" It was her.

"Yes . . . yes it is."

"*The* Jonathan Donner?"

"Well, maybe. There are two of us."

"The principal partner at Sound Holdings?"

"That's the other one. I'm just an ordinary partner."

"But I think you're the one I'm looking for. This is Nicole, the one who nearly killed you and several other skydivers out in New Jersey."

"*The* Nicole. The one who gave the finger to the Navy frogmen?"

"I'm afraid so. And I can't tell you how happy I am that you called. Really, I wanted to call you . . . to apologize for being such an idiot. I remembered your name was Jonathan Donner, and of course I know about Sound Holdings. But I didn't make the connection until I got your call. Your business number was already in my computer."

"Well, if we both need to apologize, maybe we should meet. How does dinner sound?"

"Fine, but only if you let me cook it. That's the least I can do for someone who saved my life."

"Is your cooking as good as your flying?"

"Hell, no. Not nearly as good."

Jonathan sighed. "Then why don't I just let you buy me dinner?"

He was so excited when he hung up that he knocked his morning coffee across his desk. Typical of his luck, his father walked in at just that moment to see if his son had made it back to work.

Nicole arrived in a little black dress of perfectly cut satin with spaghetti straps that showed her flawless neck and shoulders and gave a generous hint of cleavage. Her hair was an off-platinum blond, shoulder-length and casually styled. Her eyes were a deeper blue in the dimly lit restaurant, and the smile that she had shown so reluctantly in the airplane now came easily. She was a flawless dinner companion.

The setting was appropriate, an intimate French restaurant on the West Side that catered more to neighborhood diners than to Midtown credit cards. There were only a few items on the menu, and the chef had been democratic enough to give the French offerings English subtitles. Jonathan had obviously been here before, and ordered a wine without looking at the list.

"You look different without your flying gear," she said as soon as the waiter left.

"Disappointed? I know that some people mistake me for Captain Marvel when I'm wearing my helmet."

"No, relieved actually. You look . . . softer. Less imposing. I remembered you as being like a . . ." She was grasping for the word.

"Like a nazi," he said, completing her thought. "That's what I want to apologize for."

"A nazi? I wouldn't go that far. Maybe like a school principal . . ."

He did look different. His face was

rounder than she remembered. The helmet had pinched in on the sides and made it look longer. While his mustache was full, his hair was thinning in front, something she hadn't noticed before, even when he had taken the helmet off. But the mischief in his eyes was the same, as was the smile that pulled one corner of his mouth higher than the other. His complexion was as she remembered — light and even a bit wind-burned.

His shoulders weren't quite as square, nor was he as tall as she had thought, though he was still a few inches higher than she was. Certainly not tall, dark, and handsome, but still quite attractive in his requisite Manhattan-black jacket over a dark shirt. He might not be every woman's first choice, but when you added the fact that he had a few hundred million in pocket money, it was amazing that no woman had ever been able to take him down.

Nicole made her apology. Her mistakes had been grave, she admitted. "Even if I didn't kill myself, I was a danger to everyone around me. Isn't that the first rule of a team sport — watch out for your team-mates?"

Jonathan nodded, but his eyes were fixed on hers, and a smile was playing on his lips. It was plain that he wasn't interested in discussing team sports.

"Anyhow, I was so glad that you were okay that I . . . well, I was more affectionate than I usually am with strangers. So, when you chewed my ass out, I felt like a complete fool. I suppose that's what turned me into a total bitch."

"You don't always throw the bird to our naval heroes?"

"Oh, God, I really did that, didn't I? And then what did I say? That I never stop at just one?" She dropped her face into her hand to hide her embarrassed laughter. "But then I came to my senses. How could I be angry with a man who had saved my life? Just because he gave me a tongue-lashing that I probably deserved. So that's when I began looking up Donners in the phone book. But, I couldn't even be sure what book to look in."

"It's Manhattan, but I'm not listed."

"To avoid telemarketers who are hawking yachts?"

"No, just to deter unsatisfied clients who want me dead."

The wine arrived, and she watched as it was uncorked, tasted, and approved. Then they got into the brief versions of their life stories.

Hers followed a well-traveled path, a Midwestern prom queen who left junior college and came to New York to take the world by storm. "I could sing and dance. I wasn't bad looking. The folks back in Muncie, Indiana, thought I couldn't miss. The problem is that there are about a million attractive girls who can sing and dance who come to New York because they can't miss. There are new ones arriving every day."

There were no folks back in Muncie. Her mother had died when she was in high school. Her father, who clerked in a hardware store, died while she was in college. There had been an older brother, but he had gotten himself killed in his teens, racing a train to a crossing. "He was just a passenger. The driver, another teenage immortal, walked away without a scratch. He said he was sure he had the train beaten by a mile. But it ended up in a tie."

She had avoided getting involved with drugs. "The pot put me to sleep and the pills were too dangerous." Instead, she had found her identity in her high school's theater club, where she did the lead in two musicals. "The school orchestra hasn't been on-key since the school opened, so I really didn't know how I sounded. But all the teachers said I couldn't miss. Except for the guidance counselor. She said I needed a bit more polishing and talked me into junior college. In truth, she probably knew I was just ordinary and feared that I'd end up on the streets of New York."

She came to the city eight years ago, and wasted two years going to tryouts, modeling at trade shows, and paying for voice lessons. During that time she had realized how much talent was sitting on the bench, and that her chances of making the big leagues were slim at best. "And that was what it was all about: making the big leagues. I probably could have eked out a living in the chorus of traveling productions, or maybe become a regular with a small-town theater company. But I was bitten by New York, and New York is all about making it big."

So, she had started over with a clerical job in an insurance company. "Dead-end, but it did pay my share of the rent and put me through a secretarial school. I switched to Wall Street when the Dow shot past eight thousand, started my savings plan, and took the internal brokerage course to earn my license. So here I am. A New Yorker and making enough money to stay in the game."

Ballsy, Jonathan thought. This was one tough young lady who wasn't about to step out of the way for anyone. "And then you decided to kill yourself by jumping out of an airplane?" he said, as if that were the logical next step in her story.

"Not kill myself. Just add a little excitement. It's been eight grinding years, ten if you count the two I spent in college."

"Why not a houseshare in the Hamptons? Or rollerblading in Central Park?"

"Did that," Nicole answered. "Neither quite do it for me. I took up golf down at Chelsea Piers, and tried sailing out of City Island. Then I saw an ad for a weeklong jump school upstate and I gave it a try. You can fill in the rest. You know what it's like. An adrenaline rush that goes on and on, assuming you don't have to stop to rescue some stupid girl."

They were well into dinner when his turn came up. He tried to pass. "Nothing nearly that interesting about me," he confessed. "I'm still exactly where I started."

"And where was that?"

"Well, let's see. I was born in Rhode Island where my parents have a summer house."

"On the beach?" she asked pleasantly.

"In a way. It's on the cliff at Ocean Drive."

She blushed. “I was thinking of a bungalow with a screen porch.”

“Think of a castle on the Rhine,” he advised. “You’ll be a lot closer.”

“You grew up in a castle?”

“Yes, but not that one. There’s another castle out on the Long Island Gold Coast in a place so exclusive that not even squirrels are allowed to live there. That’s where *I* found out that hashish made me sneeze. Of course, pills were another thing. They were expensive, but we owned a couple of drug companies.”

His voice took on a cynical tone. The words might be taken for boasting but instead Jonathan seemed ashamed. He was apologizing for his life of privilege and hinting that having everything can be just as debilitating as having nothing.

He had been tutored at home, then moved to a boarding school where the teacher addressed ten-year-olds as “gentlemen.” Then on to a New England prep school with alumni that smiled out of the pages of corporate annual reports all over the world.

“College was the first time I broke the mold. My father wanted one of the military academies. He thought my spine needed a little stiffening and he had enough congressmen in his pocket to get me an appointment. Mother wasn't big on the academies. She thought uniforms were for doormen and preferred one of the Ivies. My grades weren't that good, but the family could always promise to donate another building."

"And you?" Nicole asked.

"I wanted a small college in Florida. They had a wide-open curriculum, and the only athletic team they fielded was in beach volleyball. I wanted to study oceanography. I'd had all the academic courses I could stand, and I thought if I saw one more building with leaves growing up the wall I might become an arsonist."

"What was it like?"

"The school in Florida? How would I know? I went to Dartmouth."

Nicole had to put down her fork while she stifled her laughter. Jonathan was certainly bitter, but he had decided to laugh at his fate rather than rage against it.

"From there it was business school at Columbia and then right into Sound Holdings. Mother couldn't stand to have me start at the bottom and Dad was too smart to put me anywhere near the top. So they compromised and put me in the middle. That way only half of the company is pissed off at me."

What was his job? He told her that he didn't really know. "I manage a small fund that represents a very small part of the family's holdings. The only clients are businesses that we control, so there isn't a hell of a lot of bitching. Basically, I watch it go up and down with the market. Every now and then I sell something that has really tanked, and buy something else to replace it. Oh, I also have to write very imaginative quarterly messages. Things like 'The market went down because it stopped going up,' or 'We had unexpected losses with International Freightways because a wheel fell off their truck.' Sometimes I think I took up skydiving because I was hoping the chute wouldn't open."

Nicole turned down dessert, lying about the difficult time she had zipping up her dress. But they lingered over single malts for another hour, and moved from the past to the future. Jonathan wondered what she hoped to get out of a career as a stockbroker.

"I think a healthy portfolio is essential if we're going to bring fresh milk to third-world countries," she said, imitating the teary-eyed idealism of a Miss America contestant. After they laughed together, she rephrased her answer. "Who was the bank robber who said he went where the money was? I think Wall Street is the fastest road to riches."

"Rich is overrated," he allowed, as he raised his glass to his lips.

"Maybe," she said. "But I won't know until I get there."

She seemed dead honest in defending her choices. She wasn't impressed by the American dream, not because she thought it was too materialistic but because it was the wrong material. "I don't want to spend my life paying down a mortgage," she said at one point, and seconds later added, "I won't let myself get so tied down that I can't just pick up and move to another opportunity."

She turned to Jonathan. "And what about your future? Is it possible you could come to terms with the Sound Holdings investments?"

"Not a chance," Jonathan answered. "I'm not working there because I think there's hope. The fact is that I haven't yet gathered the courage to leave. A hundred times 'I'm outta here' has been on the tip of my tongue. But Mother would be suicidal and my namesake would be disappointed. And of course there's the fact that I probably couldn't make a living without it."

Nicole wouldn't believe that a man who jumped out of airplanes could lack self-confidence. He couldn't be worried about making a living. There must be some sort of escape plan. She asked him point-blank.

"I have a modest trust that I could probably keep if I decided to walk. And there are things I could probably devote myself to. Doesn't one of the Kennedys sail up and down the Hudson, trying to save the river? So maybe I could take my money and devote my life to saving the fiddler crab. Or head a committee to return Manhattan Island to the Indians."

"How about a dive boat?" she asked. "Or maybe open your own jump center?"

He shook his head. "It would have to be something that sounded very idealistic. Something that the family could lie about to explain my failure."

"So, find something. You can't go on doing something you hate."

Jonathan shrugged. "I'm like you, I guess. You went to where the money is. That's where I am, and I'm a bit hesitant to leave."

They finished their drinks and made their exit. Then came the awkward moment on the street when any future they might have together was on the line. If there were no future, Nicole would say something like “Thank you for a lovely evening.” And he would explain, “I’ll be busy for a while, but I’ll give you a call.” But if they were taken with one another, then one of them had to make a move.

“You realize of course that I belong to you,” Nicole announced.

He was taken off-guard. “You do?”

“Certainly. I was in the process of killing myself when you butted in and saved my life. That means you’ve assumed responsibility for me. I’m like the baby left in a basket. Once you take me inside, I’m your problem. My life is in your hands.”

He squinted suspiciously. “Is that an invitation to come up to your place for a nightcap?”

“Certainly not,” she answered immediately. “Just the opposite. It’s your duty to protect me from cads who want to come up for a nightcap. So you’ll have to stay very close to me to safeguard me from men with evil intentions.”

Jonathan smiled. “Sounds like the kind of work I’ve been looking for.” Then he asked, “Do you like baseball? I’ve got some tickets for the Yankees. I think Baltimore is in tomorrow night. Or maybe it’s Cleveland. I don’t really keep on top of it.”

"I'd love to go. I was a catcher in Little League."

When her cab pulled up, Nicole held out her hand. Jonathan used it to pull her close and kissed her gently on the cheek. He stood like a statue, with one foot off the curb, until the taxi turned out of sight.

FOUR

"She's terrific," he told Ben the next afternoon while they were at the bar waiting for their table. Jonathan had begged his friend to join him for lunch, promising him "big news." Now he was delivering on the promise.

"You should see her in a dress. An absolute knockout." He described her from head to foot, providing details of her hairstyle, makeup, and attire that he didn't generally use to describe the women in his life. Then he took Ben line-by-line through the conversation they had shared. In his recital, Nicole came off as intelligent, witty, sympathetic, honest, ambitious, and courageous.

"Our table has been ready for twenty minutes," Ben interrupted. Jonathan awoke from his dream and they carried their drinks to the table.

"So, how was she in bed?" Ben asked as soon as they were seated.

Jonathan seemed shocked at the audacity of the question.

"Usually, that's the first thing you tell me about a date. Generally in more detail than I really need to get the picture. I don't think you've ever begun with a description of a dress, unless the zipper got stuck when you were taking it off. And you've never run through the Girl Scout rule in describing a date's good character. So I assume that you are really taken with Nicole and are keeping the best for last. I've heard enough of the preliminaries. I want to hear about the main event. How was she in bed?"

"She wasn't. We didn't spend the night."

"She turned you down?" Ben was stunned.

"Yes . . . well, no, not really. I didn't push the point. It just didn't seem right at the time."

"It didn't seem right?" He couldn't believe what he was hearing. "Jon, how many times have you told me that it always seems right? Don't you preach that even bad sex is better than sitting up with Letterman? What went wrong?"

"Nothing went wrong," Jonathan snapped, showing annoyance at his friend's teasing. "It was just different. Everything went right."

They passed on lunch and simply reordered their drinks. Then they hunched together over the table like conspirators as

Jonathan gave a step-by-step and word-by-word rendition of his final ten minutes with Nicole. He was particularly factual in explaining Nicole's analogy of the baby in the basket. "I couldn't be sure if it was an invitation. Was she saying, 'I owe you one. Your place or mine?' Or was she saying, 'This was fun. Let's do it again'? So I asked her if it was an invitation."

"You asked her? Jon, you know better than to put the question point-blank. You're supposed to act like it's just for a nightcap, and that you were swept into bed by an overpowering emotion."

"I didn't want to play any games with her," Jonathan insisted.

Ben leaned back and studied his friend across the table. "Let's think this through, old buddy. You were with a lovely lady in a black dress, recently wined and dined, and you didn't want to play any games with her? And she's with Manhattan's reigning playboy, whose picture is on her American Express card, and she didn't offer her body in sacrifice." He paused dramatically. "This is bad, Jon. Very bad. You may need a psychiatrist."

Nicole's mind wasn't really on her work. Not that she wasn't functioning well. She fielded customer calls with unfailing grace, answered complex questions with unflappable composure, and suffered in silence through the outrage of customers whose recent purchases were bleeding. But she was operating on remote control. Her mind was on the clock.

She had lingered at home until the last possible moment expecting Jonathan's call. He had invited her to the baseball game, but he had left the invitation hanging. It was still possible that despite the obvious interest he had shown last night, he might well change his mind in the bright light of day. In the office she had checked her voice mail but he hadn't called. Then she went to her e-mail. It was a long shot that didn't pay off.

Her phone had been ringing all day. The market had been up at yesterday's closing bell, but opened in the morning with a swan dive. Yesterday's buyers were irate. People who had sold up were now lining up to buy back in. Each time the phone had rung, Nicole cleared her throat, trying to sound attractive in case it might be Jonathan. Each time she had been disappointed.

She thought that she had played it perfectly. Intelligent conversation with hints of admiration and sympathy, promising that she would never be boring. Enough show of flesh to make the sexual side of a relationship appealing. A frank statement of her desire to get closer to him. A polite refusal of his invitation to bed, proving that she wasn't for sale no matter how much he might bid. Obviously, he had been interested enough to make another date right on the spot. Did she blow it by not inviting him to take her home? Had she let him slip away, or had he simply broken the line?

Maybe she should call him. "Hey, if we're meeting at the stadium, you better tell me the gate number." Or, "Just checking. Did you say tonight, or did I get the date wrong?"

She stepped out of the elevator and crossed the polished marble floor to the revolving doors. In the street, she nearly missed her name when it was flashed in front of her. It was lettered on a white sign in the hands of a chauffeur: "NICOLE PIERCE." She stopped and did a double take.

"Are you looking for me?"

"Are you going to Yankee Stadium?"

"Yes, I am."

He stepped back and opened the rear door of a Lincoln Town Car, letting her slide onto the seat. Next to her was a corrugated cardboard box tied in a bow. The card read "To Nicole, from Jonathan." She pulled the ribbon away and opened the box. Inside, she found a catcher's mitt and mask.

FIVE

The limo pulled into the VIP gate, and Jonathan was waiting to open the car door. Nicole jumped out wearing the catcher's mask, which sent him into hysterics and gave them an excuse for a swinging embrace. They went to the Sky Club elevators and snickered like children when the other passengers tried not to stare at the mask. Jonathan explained that the lady covered her face because she was so ugly.

Nicole had expected to be sitting in a box, but Sound Holdings' private box was more than she could have imagined. It was as big as her apartment, with one wall a pane of tinted glass that looked out over the field from behind first base. There were half a dozen swivel loungers for those who took their baseball seriously. The bar was against one wall, with a high-definition television filling the space over it. A dining table with silver and white linen was set for four. Beside it was a grouping of leather furniture, with two small televisions popping out of the cocktail table, and then a card table that could seat six for poker. The kitchenette had a two-burner stove, microwave, refrigerator, icemaker, and a small sink. And, in a small alcove, doors led to a powder room and a gentlemen's room. The three men waiting inside were in white shirts and ties, and one looked suspiciously like the former mayor of New York.

"Dad, this is Nicole," Jonathan said casually. It was at that moment that Nicole realized she was still wearing her catcher's mask. As she eased it up over her head one of the men, with the short, stocky build of a linebacker broke toward her. He had a fringe of red hair that was fading to gray, mischievous blue eyes, and a jaw like a bulldog.

"A pleasant surprise," he said. His grip locked on her hand like a vise, and his eyes swept her from head to toe, lingering at every curve.

"Nicole Pierce, Mr. Donner," she answered softly.

"Jack," he corrected. When her eyes widened he explained, "That's my name. 'Jack.' " He was already walking her to the other two. "You've probably seen the mayor in a police lineup," he said as Rudy Giuliani flashed his best smile. "And Joe

Tisdale," as he turned her to the other man, "is the biggest slum lord in the city." She remembered Tisdale's face as soon as she heard the name. Next to Donald Trump, he was the city's biggest real-estate developer.

"Help yourself," he said pointing to the bar. "If it's not there, we can get it."

Jonathan shook hands with the other two guests, asking after names that she guessed must be significant others. Obviously, he was at home in this company. When he reached his father he whispered, "Sorry, I didn't know you had guests."

"It's Boston," Jack Donner answered. "I always have guests for the Red Sox."

Jonathan nodded weakly. "I thought it was Cleveland." He went to the bar to help Nicole.

Tisdale joined them. "Is that what the attractive women are wearing these days? Catchers' masks?"

"She works on Wall Street," Jonathan answered.

Tisdale doubled over. "Did you hear that, Rudy? Things are so tough on the Street that you have to wear catcher's equipment." The three of them laughed, which eased Nicole's embarrassment and toned down the blush in her cheeks.

Jack Donner reigned supreme even in the company of dignitaries. He ordered everyone about, telling the mayor and the developer where to sit, what kind of snacks they should eat, and what they were going to have for drinks. "I'll send down for steaks. Medium rare. With Heinekens all around," he shouted as he picked up the phone. Then he remembered there was a newcomer. "You drink Heinekens?" he yelled at Nicole.

"Could I have wine?" she asked.

"Sure!" His eyes flashed to Jonathan. "Open up one of those reds." The red turned out to be an eighty-dollar cabernet.

When the game started, the elder Donner began his commentary, generally unflattering to the players and poisonous toward the managers. When they had all finished their steaks, he announced cheese-cake for dessert. "From Myron's. It's the best!" He poked Jonathan. "Pour us a round of brandy."

There was no middle ground with Jack Donner. If you were around him enough, you learned to avoid the jagged edges, ig-nore his rudeness, and enjoy his excite-ment. If you did business with him, you started out fearing him and ended up hating him. His personality was too strong to tolerate indifference.

He had been born in a South Boston Irish enclave of a German father and a first-generation Irish mother. His red-headed features favored his mother, but his drive and determination were definitely Teutonic. A public school education earned him a scholarship to a Jesuit high school, where he lettered in three sports and finished as valedictorian. That record won him a scholarship to Boston College. He was a mediocre guard on a mediocre football team, but once again at the top of his class academically. His classmates graduated with Jesuit inspired ideals and set out to remake the world. Jack Donner set out to make a fortune.

He toiled in a money-center bank during the day and in Boston University Business School at night. By age twenty-seven he was a junior partner in a small investment bank, by twenty-eight he had several accounts of his own, and by thirty he had his own portfolio. That was when he changed his letterhead to his proper name, "John."

John Donner Partners caught the minicomputer wave that swept down Route 128, put money into DEC, Data General, and Prime, and emerged with his first one hundred million dollars. On his letterhead, the

"John" became "Jonathan" even though his friends still called him Jack. The day Jonathan first understood the microprocessor, he dumped the minis and put his huge profits into Hewlett-Packard, Apple, and a software outfit headed up by a nineteen-year-old nerd named Bill Gates. When everyone else jumped on the minicomputer train, Jack moved to New York and named his expanded operations Sound Holdings after the view of Long Island Sound he had from his living room. He diversified into blue chips when the Dow was at thirty-five hundred and left his bets on the table all the way up to ten thousand. Shares in his funds cost too much for the average investor, but to the very rich and very famous, Jonathan Donner was a sure thing.

He screamed an obscenity in the sixth inning, when the Yankees scored four runs to put Boston out of reach. There were more brandies for the seventh inning stretch, and then Jack, the mayor, and Tisdale left when Boston went down in the eighth.

"We're going to beat the traffic," he told his son, and then with a glance toward Nicole, "Great meeting you!" He was already through the door while Giuliani and the slum lord were saying proper good-byes.

Nicole and Jonathan sat quietly until the voices disappeared in the direction of the elevators. "That's my father," Jonathan said, his tone indicating that she had seen the unadorned version.

"Wow!" Nicole answered. "He certainly is . . . energetic."

"A regular ball of fire."

"Do you think he remembered my name?"

"Did you give him a million dollars to invest?"

She laughed.

"Then he didn't remember you at all. Next time I'll introduce you as Mother Teresa. He won't know the difference."

"You don't get along very well, do you?"

Jonathan pursed his lips. "For a while we didn't. He was disappointed when I joined the company and didn't catch fire. But then he realized that the things I did had absolutely no effect on his net worth. So now he doesn't waste his time being disappointed."

"But how do you feel?" Nicole asked.

"I'm not disappointed in him either."

They shared a nightcap while they were waiting for the fans to empty out of the stadium. Then he escorted her down to the gate, put her in the limousine that had apparently waited the full nine innings, and gave the driver her address. For an instant, Nicole thought that she had struck out with Daddy, and for that reason Jonathan was simply sending her away. But before he closed the door he said, "You free over the weekend?"

She was, but she didn't want to leap at the invitation. "I may be working Saturday."

"I'm going up to Newport. I think you'd like the place so, if things free up, give me a call." Then he added, "Dad won't be there. He stays in the city until August."

SIX

Nicole begged off Friday night. Togetherness, she had learned, was best in short sessions. Three days together and St. Francis could get on your nerves. But she promised to free up on Saturday morning, and that was when he pulled up in front of her Village apartment in the Mercedes convertible. They were an hour getting into Connecticut, and an hour and a half more reaching Rhode Island. It was well after noon when he turned off the Jamestown Bridge and sped down to Ocean Drive. They passed behind the mansions; Vanderbilt's Breakers, Château-sur-Mer, and a summer home that had been converted into a university.

"The neighborhood seems to be holding up," Nicole teased.

"My father thinks they should be knocked down and turned into townhouses. Much more efficient . . ."

He paused in front of an iron gate that groaned open when he touched the car's sun visor. Then they drove on a Belgian block driveway through manicured gardens and broke out on a cliff that looked straight down on Rhode Island Sound. The house to her right was a three-story weathered clapboard, with a covered porch that saw water on three sides.

"We'll have to take our own bags," he apologized, lifting both hers and his out of the trunk. "There's no staff until mid-June."

"What a bother," she said in a pouting voice. "Who's going to draw my bath?"

"I will," he volunteered.

Nicole smiled coyly. Things were looking up.

It was clear, as they settled in, that someone had been there. The windows had been wiped to an invisible finish. The living room, with its grand piano and two furniture groupings, had been dusted and polished, and the fifty-foot oriental had just been shampooed. The dining room table, long enough to seat a score of guests, had been set with two places at one end. The kitchen was stocked with all the essentials, and several bottles had been brought up from the wine cellar.

Jonathan led the way up the sweeping staircase, pushed open a door to a bedroom suite done in pale yellow with green accents, and stepped aside to let her enter.

"Will this be satisfactory?" There was a mint on the pillow.

She went to the window and saw that she was looking across the porch roof and out to sea. "It will be fine, unless there's a very high tide."

He led her on a tour of the house and grounds, pointing out himself in short pants in one of the family photos, and then in a sailor suit with his baby sister, Pam, on his lap. His mother was always sitting with the children while Jack stood behind, as if he needed to make a quick getaway. Mrs. Donner was thin and attractive in the earlier pictures, and lean and authoritative in the later ones. Nicole thought that when Jack and his wife embraced it would be like flint striking iron.

There were different pictures in Jack's study. In a black-and-white news shot he was standing between Joe Kennedy and his son, the president. In a color photo he was sharing a golf cart with Jack Nicklaus. There were cover portraits from *Fortune* and *Business Week*, a candid from the *New York Times* that showed him and Alan Greenspan testifying before Congress, and a campaign photo with his arm around George W. Bush. And there was a framed letter from Windsor Castle thanking him for his assistance to the queen.

"No wonder he wouldn't remember my name," Nicole allowed.

"He doesn't remember any of their names either," Jonathan said, gesturing to the photo display. "The people are eye-wash. The money is real."

They toured the grounds, stood by the edge of the swimming pool that was still topped with its winter cover, crossed the tennis courts that needed rolling, and walked through the formal gardens that were filling with spring flowers. "This is my mother's joy," he explained casually. "This one, and the garden at the Long Island house. Out there, she just about lives in the greenhouse."

"I love flowers," Nicole said.

He nodded. "Then you and Alexandra will get along just fine."

"Alexandra?"

"My mother," Jonathan explained. "Like the late czarina."

Back at the house, he made martinis, apologizing because he couldn't find the olives. Then he decided that the stove was too complicated and drove Nicole down to the harbor for a lobster dinner.

Over the appetizers she asked him how he fit into the family. "I mean, there's so much for you and you don't seem to want any of it."

"It's not my style," he answered with a shrug. "They see money as a way of life. The business, the estates, the celebrity galas . . . that's the center of their world. For me, it's just an opportunity to live the way I please. An opportunity I don't take lightly because I know that most people would die for it. It's been given to me and I don't intend to waste it."

While they were trying to pry the meat out of the shells, Jonathan turned the tables on her. "What would you do if you were part of the family? Do the social scene, or get the hell out?"

She swallowed hard. It was a question that needed a careful answer. "I'd do the things that I enjoyed, and then spend some time with things that are important."

"Like what?"

Careful, she reminded herself. "Oh, maybe open a first-class restaurant. Or put together some funding for would-be actors and musicians. I'd like to be close to theater, even though I don't have serious talent."

"So you'd do the charity balls. And the opera auctions . . ."

Nicole could hear a hint of disgust in his voice. "No," she said. "Not the 'for-show' events. Not the new dress for every affair. I'd do things privately, and in my own way, because I thought they were important. Not because of what anyone else would think."

Did she sound too much like Miss America? She studied his face for a reaction.

"That's what my sister would like," he said, without looking up from the claw he had locked in a pair of pliers. "She's like Jack. She does her own thing for her own reasons. She has no time for charity balls."

"Well, why does she let herself get sucked in?"

"She's still under my mother's thumb. What she needs is an infusion of courage. You may be just what she needs."

They walked along the harbor front, which was already buzzing in anticipation of the summer season. The bars and restaurants were open and there was a decent crowd even though it was only June and the air was still chilled by the winter water. "How about a nightcap?" he asked.

"That sounds nice." Her glance was coquettish. "Your place or mine?"

"Mine is closer."

He gave her a head start to her bedroom while he locked up and turned off the downstairs lights. She was sitting at the vanity in a nightgown when he closed the bedroom door. "Shall I draw your bath now?"

"Why not?" she answered, smiling into the mirror.

Nicole waited until she heard the water stop running. When she opened the bathroom door, he was already in the tub, his knees poking through the surface of bubbles that reached to his chin.

"It's a bit crowded in here," he warned her.

"I'll find a way to squeeze in . . ."

Nicole eased the nightgown up her legs and then pulled it over her head. She paused with the gown wrinkled across her face to give him her best view. Then she tossed the gown behind her and stepped over the edge of the tub.

SEVEN

The sheets still felt wet when she woke up. For an instant she was puzzled, but as soon as she recalled the night's romp she smiled deliciously. They had used the bath for foreplay and then rushed to the bed still dripping wet. She opened her eyes into sunlight that was streaming through the window. A lovely day, she thought pleasantly, but sat up with a jolt when she realized how late she had slept. She was alone in the bed.

She looked around for her nightgown and remembered how she had tossed it away in the bathroom. Her robe was still in her suitcase, across the room next to the vanity. She tugged on the top sheet, trying to wrap it around her, but then shook her head at the absurdity of modesty. She bounded up and walked naked to the vanity where she gathered her toiletries and put on a silky black robe.

The bathroom was evidence of their abandon. The water was still in the tub, last night's playful bubbles wilted to an oil slick. There were puddles on the tile floor, one of them soaked up into a bath towel, another blotted into the corner of the bathmat. Her nightgown was bunched up like a wet wash rag, and one of his socks was behind the toilet. Nicole smiled as she took in the damage. Jonathan had either had the time of his life or he was a much better actor than she was.

She dressed quickly, hoping to be ready before he returned. She didn't want him finding her near naked and getting ideas about a rematch. New underwear, a pair of jeans, and a light cotton sweater went on first. Only when she was decent did she re-apply her makeup, touch up her hair, and put on her sandals.

Nicole poked her head through the door. It didn't seem that Jonathan had retired to one of the other bedrooms. She crept down the stairs, stealing glances over the banister. There was no sign of him in the living room and the dining room was in darkness. "Jonathan!" she called softly, and when there was no response she tried a full voice. "Jon, where are you?"

"In here!"

"Where?"

"The kitchen. I'm fixing your breakfast."

She walked across the living room, into the dining room, and pushed open the swinging door. He was standing at the counter, lifting doughnuts out of the box and spreading them on a decorative plate. Paper coffee cups still wore their plastic tops.

He pointed to the elaborate espresso maker at the other end of the counter. "You have to be a computer genius to work that damn thing."

"I can make coffee," she said, moving up close for her morning kiss.

He pecked at her cheek.

"That's it?" she asked. "Some come down after last night."

He blushed, then chuckled. "You had a good time?"

"Incredible!" She was still holding her head back with her eyes closed. This time he brushed a kiss across her lips.

"Well, that's a little better. But it's still a long way from last night."

He carried the doughnuts to the kitchen table. Nicole followed with the two paper cups of coffee.

"I hope you found me worth saving," she said when they were seated. "I'd hate to think that if you had it to do all over again you wouldn't bother pulling my parachute."

He looked at her sheepishly. "Skydiving

is like a walk in the park compared to you. First I thought I was going to drown in the tub. Later, maybe die of exhaustion. Plunging to the earth isn't nearly as dangerous as getting into bed with you."

"Does that mean that you don't want to do it ever again?"

"Only if I'm wearing a parachute."

Jonathan was quiet on the drive back to the city, and Nicole knew enough not to interrupt his deliberations. There were several paths he might be pursuing and she was anxious that he choose the right one.

They all began with the same premise that Nicole Pierce was a terrific woman. She was attractive, an adornment on any occasion, and personable, a center for any gathering. She, like he, was a free spirit, determined to live her own life in her own way. She wasn't trying to break into the charity balls, but anxious to be his coconspirator when he found a way to break out. She had a healthy respect for money — she had easily admitted that money was the reason for her switch from theater to Wall Street — but it didn't seem to leave her breathless. As with him, Nicole saw wealth as an opportunity to do the things she wanted. And the things she liked were the same things that interested him. He had met her while skydiving, and she was keenly interested in his scuba diving ventures. It was unlikely that she would die of fright at the sight of an octopus.

But that premise could lead Jonathan to any number of conclusions. The most likely one — the one that Nicole was desperately hoping for — was that this was a woman he shouldn't let get away. This was the one he ought to marry.

The thought must be playing in his mind even while he was hurtling in and out of Sunday night traffic. After all, he had already presented her to his father, if the encounter at the baseball game could be called a presentation. He had introduced her to his family when he walked her through the photo gallery, commenting on each of the relatives. He had grilled her to detect whether she was genuine, and she had passed the test, apparently with flying colors. Hadn't he suggested that she could be the dose of courage that his sister sorely needed? And then there was the physical compatibility. Jonathan had been wildly thrilled in their Saturday night rumble, and had been trembling with delight when they made love again in the early afternoon. That wasn't something that most men could simply walk away from.

But there were other possibilities. Men could string along even the most perfect woman for years and sometimes even decades. She was a wonderful companion and lover, but she had already demonstrated that he could have her in either capacity without any commitment on his part. Wasn't that the perfect arrangement for a self-confessed free spirit? Jonathan wasn't the kind to take on obligations. So, there was every chance that he would shower her with attention just to encourage her to keep giving free samples.

Another possibility: maybe he was sensing that his freedom was in jeopardy and, in his moody silence, he was looking for ways to cut and run. Simpleminded lovelies and giggling debutantes were no threat to him. He could enjoy them and discard them the same as he would a good Cuban cigar. But this woman could easily become intoxicating, an addiction that would be torturous to break. Best not sniff the stuff in the first place. Or, if the drugged illusions had been wonderful, remember that delight was the beginning of every craving, and make damn sure that he never used her again.

They were on the tangle of ramps and bridges that led into Manhattan when Jonathan finally revealed his thinking. And even then, there was no clear-cut decision.

"My sister's graduation party is next weekend. A dinner dance on Saturday night, and brunch on Sunday."

"Sounds lovely," she answered, thinking of an intimate family affair at a club that had a dance combo on the weekends. "Where is it being held?"

"At the Long Island house. Probably a few hundred people. Her friends, family friends, and the required celebrities. A lot of them will be staying over."

"It must be a very big house?"

"More like a gated development. There are several very big houses."

"Are you inviting me?"

"Yeah . . . well, sort of. But I have to warn you as well. The dinner dance is formal. Alexandra really does these things up big! The celebrities are stuffy and Pam's friends are rowdy. I was just going to bring her a present, wish her luck, and skip the party. But it would be a chance for you to meet the rest of the inmates."

"I would like to meet your sister," she said, and she knew instantly that she had given the perfect answer. But she also knew there was one more test looming: she had to pass muster with Alexandra, the lean authority figure in the photographs. And she had to show that she could fit in with the society page characters that apparently populated Jonathan's life.

Bold as he liked to sound, Jonathan Donner still had his coattails caught under the same family thumb that kept his sister in place. He might enjoy his moments of liberty, falling from airplanes, diving on old wrecks, and running through the gears on his convertible. He could put down his father's business, and make jokes about his mother's reign in society. But all that was show talk, played with great style to disguise the fact that he was still a member of the orchestra, still taking direction from his mother's baton.

Nothing could be simpler than to walk into his father's office in the morning and say, "I quit!" His father might even admire him for it. But that would cut off a generous flow of cash that he might not be able to replace. Or, he could simply make an announcement at table and say that he was heading down to the Caribbean to run a dive boat. Except that would end his life as a pampered child, and thrust him into an adult commitment where he might possibly fail.

The fact was that Jonathan had prepared himself for just one thing: exactly the life that he was presently living. So, if Nicole were to share his life, it would have to be on the same terms that he had accepted for himself. Those terms were dictated by his mother. And she would have to join him in his lifelong ruse, pretending to be venturous and independent while always keeping peace with a higher authority.

"If you don't think I'd be an imposition," Nicole answered.

"No, I'm generally the imposition. You'll be a breath of fresh air."

EIGHT

The dress had to send just the right messages. Taste! It had to be fashionable, showing her sense of style, but not so trendy that she seemed not to have a mind of her own. Quality! She wanted to show an appreciation of the better things, but not something overly expensive. Only pretenders confused price with quality. Sexy! She had a good body and the dress should show it without making a point of how much it was showing. Modest! The dress had to make it perfectly clear that nothing was for sale.

It had to talk to several audiences. Jonathan's mother was the most important and she needed to be assured that Nicole was worthy of the family and a good fit to her social circle. Jonathan's father, she had been told, wouldn't remember her. But she suspected there was nothing that escaped his notice and little he didn't remember. He had seen her playful side in her baseball outfit. The dress had to show him her womanly assets, which had seemed to be his center of interest.

It had to make Jonathan proud to have her on his arm. She had to be the belle of the ball without seeming to try, and he had to know that every man in the room envied him, that they all wanted her, but that they all understood that she was his alone.

And then there was his sister. It was Pam's party, and Nicole had to be very careful not to upstage her. But still, she had to be the older sister that Pam would want to emulate.

It was quite a bit to ask of one evening dress.

Nicole wangled a day off so that she could devote the time to shopping, and made an uptown pilgrimage, starting with the small boutiques and finishing with the major department stores. By lunchtime she had visited twelve stores and tried on eight dresses. During the afternoon, she added seven more stores and tried on another eight. The range had run from church supper to Academy Awards, with cleavage everywhere from her Adam's apple to her navel. She was completely exhausted and still without a dress when she met Jonathan for dinner.

"I told the folks you were coming," he reported.

"And?"

"Oh, they were delighted." Then after a pause, "Jack even remembered you. He called you Jorge Posada. And Pam thought you sounded like fun."

"What did your mother think?"

"My mother doesn't think anything on hearsay. She likes to see for herself."

The damn dress was going to be even more important than she thought.

She took a long lunch hour the next day, revisited one of the boutiques to try on a dress she had tried the day before. It looked even worse. She raced through two more small stores. "What are you looking for?" a frustrated sales clerk asked.

"I haven't got any idea at all."

By Thursday she was desperate. She had bought new lingerie in case she spent Saturday night with Jonathan and a cute pair of pajamas in case she was asked to bunk in with one of the other girls. But still, she hadn't seen the perfect dress. She closed down an East Side department store, leaving three possibilities in the dressing room. Her standards were beginning to drop, but still she had found nothing.

On Saturday morning, certain that she had seen every dress in the city, she returned to the boutique where she had tried the same dress twice. It was wrong for a hundred reasons, but since she had gone back to it there must have been something about it that she liked. When she reached the shop, the owner was pinning a dress onto a window mannequin. It was a black, floor-length raw silk sheath with pewter accents at the neckline and a single line of pewter across the hips. The front was high with crossover straps disappearing behind the neck for a very modest, conservative first appearance. But the back was bare all the way to the hips, creating an exit that would leave them screaming for more. And, just in case they never got behind her, there was a center slit that would show leg to the thigh with every step she took.

She tried it on, liked the fit and then moved in front of the mirror. It was exactly what she needed. Tasteful and respectable, with flashes of sensuality as she walked and turned. Ordinary as she stepped to the dance floor, and then wildly exciting when she moved to the music. The perfect blend of hot wife and respectable daughter-in-law.

Jonathan was in a white dinner jacket with a passé plaid tie and cummerbund. "Lovely," he told her when she opened the door. "Alexandra will fall in love with you." Then she turned and led him into her apartment, and he confronted her back and the hint of her breasts that moved under her arms. "Jack will try to take you on a tour of the wine cellar. You look absolutely delicious."

"Is it too . . . bare?"

"No, just about perfect. You're completely dressed and totally naked at the same time. It just depends on the point of view."

He was talkative as they drove over the Triboro Bridge and fought the traffic on the Long Island parkways. He loved the house they were heading toward and knew that she would like it, too. But at the same time, he hated the house and hoped she wouldn't find it too pretentious. He enjoyed driving the country roads on the North Shore. He hated driving in the continuous Long Island traffic jam. He enjoyed his mother's parties. He wouldn't be going at all except to have Nicole meet his family. Clearly, he was nervous, for some reason dreading the encounter with his mother. He babbled endlessly to avoid discussing what was frightening him.

There was a security officer at the entrance to the property who recognized Jonathan and saluted him through. Nicole saw the name of the estate, Rockbottom, engraved into the gateposts.

"Rockbottom?" she laughed. "Rock-bottom?"

"Jack's idea. It's sort of a tribute to his meanness. He buys everything at rock bottom."

They drove for several minutes on a landscaped road that toured through well-tended trees. There was a sunset shaping up ahead of them, and whenever they caught glimpses of the Sound, the water twinkled with fiery highlights.

The house that was suddenly visible ahead seemed quite modest, a square brick structure with a few white-framed windows. But then she realized that it was simply a gatehouse, probably a perk for the groundskeeper and his family. They drove between stone pillars and continued to the northwest, keeping the sun in front of them. And then, without any real warning, they were in a circular driveway, with a lawn in the middle that could have accommodated a football game.

The house at the end of the driveway was an English manor house, Tudor in design, with multiple bays of brick, stone, and split-timber stucco. There were two stories below the eaves, and then a third story that showed among the sharply peaked roofs. Most pronounced were the groupings of huge, mullioned bay windows, some two stories high, one bank topped with a balcony. There were a half dozen clusters of chimneys, hinting at dozens of fireplaces within. The facade, rising from a simple stone wall and broken up into a major entrance bay with five adjoining bays, was at least a hundred and fifty feet long.

To the right, set back at the end of its own driveway, was the garage, a two-story replica of one of the main house split-timber bays, with five overhead doors on the ground level.

Jonathan continued driving past the garage entrance and turned off on a road that ran past the east side of the house. A new building loomed ahead, this one two stories of stone and brick with archways instead of windows. There was a glow of light coming through the arches and a musical beat rose above the trees. The fleet of cars anchored on the lawn indicated that the party had already started.

It was a pool house, with a dozen cabanas on the ground floor, and half a dozen apartments above. Beyond it was a broad terrace where the eight-piece orchestra had set up. A few of the younger couples were already dancing. Then came the pool, a perfect sixty-foot square with an infinity edge where the water seemed to vanish into Long Island Sound. The round guest tables were set up beside the pool, each with a white tablecloth and service for ten. The floral centerpieces matched the flowers that were floating in the pool.

There were probably two hundred guests, all the men in white dinner jackets, and the women in a full spectrum of colors. The older people, presumably Jack and Alexandra's friends, were to the left side, already seated at their tables. Pam's friends were to the right, a tornado of activity that whirled from table to table, and at times threatened to toss some of the young people into the water.

As they came down the cabana steps, Nicole could feel the eyes turning to her from both sides of the water. She kept up an animated conversation with Jonathan, pretending to be oblivious to the fact that she was on display. Jack Donner came darting toward her, a smoldering cigar thrust from his jaw. "Nicole, isn't it? The one at Yankee Stadium?" He took her hand and pulled her away from Jonathan and toward the table he had just left. "You look better without that mask," he said, and then laughed at his own joke.

The slim woman from the photographs turned her head toward them, but made no effort to get up. Instead, she extended her hand and waited for Nicole to reach out and take it. "I'm Alexandra." Her face, like her figure, was long and thin with a prominent straight nose and a pointed chin. The dark hair in the photographs at Newport was now silver-gray and pulled back into an elegant chignon. Her good looks were still there but it was more an aura of command that made her unforgettable. Her authority radiated from her eyes, large and liquid blue. They focused instantly and locked on permanently, seeming to take in everything for storage in a database.

"Wonderful to meet you, Mrs. Donner."

"Alexandra," she repeated. "And may I say that you are breathtakingly lovely."

Nicole mumbled and blushed.

"Your dress," Alexandra went on, "is absolutely gorgeous. Where did you ever find it?"

Nicole told her about the small boutique, making it sound as if they were her personal designers.

"You'll make them famous," Alexandra said.

Jonathan eased past her and kissed his

mother's cheek. "Well, was I exaggerating?"

"Not in the least," Alexandra answered. "She's very beautiful." She glanced down at her guest list. "You're at table six." She rattled off the names of the others at the table. Nicole recognized the name of the conductor of the City Opera, and Tisdale, the real-estate developer who had been at the ball game.

She spotted Pam instantly, a young woman with her mother's long face and piercing eyes, slim and energetic in a pastel gown that used a lace pattern to enhance her small breasts. She was coming toward them, walking too fast for the lines of the dress so that it seemed she might step right out of it. "Jonny," she said to her brother and lunged into his arms. "I got your present and it's perfect. I just love it." She wheeled out of the embrace and reached for Nicole. "And you're Nicole. As beautiful as he's been telling everybody."

Nicole again mumbled and blushed. "Congratulations on your graduation," she said. "It must be a big relief."

"More like breaking the chains of slavery," Pam told her. "An MBA was Dad's idea. I hated every course."

They gushed back and forth for a

minute, fawning over one another. Then Pam excused herself, promising to see them later, and Jonathan led Nicole along the pool's edge to their table. She recognized Tisdale, who introduced a Wagnerian wife, and the conductor who was with a young tenor from the chorus. The other couple was the county supervisor, an overweight man with a politician's smile, and his wife who introduced herself as "his better half."

"Ben is late, as usual," Jonathan said, and Nicole remembered his jump partner, Ben Tobin, who apparently was going to complete their table.

The whole party walked down to the far edge of the pool to take in the sunset over Manhattan. From the top of the cliff, Nicole could look down at the miniature harbor below, with its own seawall and lighthouse. At the dock was a fifty-foot cruiser, bristling with fishing poles, and a forty-foot ketch with roller-reefed sails.

"Your navy?" she asked Jonathan.

"Part of it. The battleships are in Newport."

A cannon fired when the sun disappeared behind the skyscrapers. The trumpet from the band sounded colors. Then the caterer's carts rattled into place.

Ben showed up with the appetizer, wearing a collarless black shirt under his dinner jacket. The young lady who trailed after him was an Asian of indeterminate age, wearing a white sheath that set off her skin perfectly. "You look much better without a helmet and parachute," he told Nicole. And later he allowed that "Jon was keeping what he saved," reinforcing the notion that Jonathan was planning a long relationship. The evening was going better than she could have ever hoped.

It was a grand affair. The younger crowd from across the pool jumped into every rock number, filling the dance floor with their arm-waving and stamping. The big band numbers drew from her side of the pool, following the lead of Jack and Alexandra who rose for every fox-trot. Jack danced mechanically, moving with the precision of a balance sheet. Alexandra moved to the music with an intrinsic grace as if she, too, were an orchestral instrument. Tall and slim, her coloring was perfectly complemented by a deep gray sheath that flared outward at her thighs. In her heels, she was an inch taller than her husband.

"Your mother is terrific," Nicole said as she and Jonathan danced near his parents.

"I think she likes what she sees."

"Me?" she asked.

"Us," Jonathan answered. "She can tell you're good for me because it's nearly midnight and I haven't embarrassed her yet."

"How could you embarrass her?"

"Well, at her last affair I got blind drunk and walked into the pool. She told me frankly that for a few seconds she had hoped that I would drown. She was really ticked off at the people who jumped in to save me."

Nicole answered, "You said she was difficult, but she couldn't be more pleasant."

"She'll be just as pleasant when she's blindfolding you in front of a firing squad."

Tisdale made a pass at Nicole, offering to show her the design for one of his new buildings. The politician asked her to dance and ground his crotch up against her belly while blowing into her ear. Ben came to the rescue by suggesting that they spend some time with the younger set that was a better fit for their ages.

Nicole sat for several minutes with Pam, whose date seemed to have vanished on his way to the men's room. She was impressed to learn that Pam had graduated from Columbia and ranked high in her class. "I'll be starting as assistant manager of the

New York Philharmonic," she said. "It sounds important, but really I'll be just another bookkeeper." She didn't seem enthused.

"Any romantic interest?" Nicole asked, nodding her head to a gathering of young studs.

"Sure," the new graduate answered. "They'd all like to get laid in the boathouse. But if I were trapped in a burning building there isn't one of them who would risk scorching his jacket, if you know what I mean."

Nicole nodded.

"Alexandra sees through them all," Pam continued. "None of them measures up."

Nicole felt a brief stitch of anxiety. No one seemed to measure up to any of Mrs. Donner's children. Did Alexandra see through her the same way she saw through Pam's suitors? Had the warm reception been nothing more than polite society babble?

"I really admire the way you've gone out on your own and taken your chances," Pam said with overtones of envy. "Jonathan said you were a struggling actress, sort of living in a garret."

"It was a tenement walk-up with old plumbing," Nicole laughed. "Like *La*

Bohème without the music. I got out as fast as I could."

"I'm going to try something on my own," Pam said with conviction. "I was thinking that I'd like to run an art gallery, maybe a place for undiscovered artists."

Nicole and Jonathan got up for the next rock number and danced energetically. Ben used his date's trip to the ladies' room as an excuse to dance with Pam, and kept her on the floor through three numbers. The Asian lady kept her smile, even though her eyes were angry. At one point Nicole noticed Jack, standing off with another man, leering at her, a cigar grinding in the corner of his mouth. She stole a glance to his table where Alexandra had turned her chair to watch the dancing. Alexandra was looking right at them with a pleasantly blank expression, giving no hint of her reaction. It was hard to tell whether she was more concerned with her son or with her daughter.

By midnight, the entire party was tipsy, sleepily on the adult side of the pool and raucously on the other. Then the inevitable: one of the younger crowd missed a step and toppled into the pool. As his friends gathered at the edge, another was pushed in. Like a salvo of battleship fire, another dozen plunged in together and then screaming women were pushed in on top of them. In a matter of seconds, half of Pam's friends were in the water, standing chest deep and gyrating to the music. Ben was wringing out his jacket over Pam's head.

Word passed quickly that Jack was serving brandy back at the main house, which gave the elders a chance to pick up and leave before Pam's friends turned on them. Nicole and Jonathan joined the exodus, and drove back to the manor.

The entrance foyer of Rockbottom looked like a museum, with armor displayed in the corners, and heraldry banners hanging from the surrounding balcony. A left turn brought them to the reception room that could have been the lobby of a Ritz-Carlton. There were a half dozen casual furniture groupings, any one of which would have sufficed for a typical family home. A portable bar had been rolled in with a dozen bottles on display. At the other end of the room was a coffee service with a three-foot-high silver urn.

Jonathan got Nicole a coffee and left her with Ben's abandoned date while he went to find the housekeeper. He returned with keys to the gatehouse where the two women were supposed to spend the night. Minutes later, a soaked-through Ben and his icy lady left for the city, which told Nicole that she and Jonathan would have the gatehouse to themselves.

NINE

It was a delicate situation. Obviously, she wasn't going to lock him out, but just as obviously there were proprieties to be observed in his parents' house.

"Is this a good idea?" she asked an hour later when he closed the gatehouse door behind them, and turned on the light in the well-furnished parlor.

"You mean I'm not up to it?"

"I mean right in front of your family."

"They know we were together in Newport. Alexandra gets daily reports from the maintenance guy."

"They weren't with us in Newport."

He had already kicked off his shoes and was lifting wineglasses and a bottle of sauterne from his suitcase. He had told the front-door porter exactly where to put them when he had stolen them from the cart.

"Nicole, we're not fooling anyone. Alexandra knew damn well that Ben wasn't staying when she set this place up for you and his girlfriend. Ben and Pam are sort of a thing but neither of them want to announce it. The girl wasn't staying, and if Ben were staying anywhere it would be out on one of the boats with Pam. All Alexandra wants is a bit of deniability and a way to get you out of the house while Jack is around."

"Your father?" She was startled at how casually the implication was presented.

"Jack can be a bit of a lecher when temptation is thrown in his path. So Alexandra always hides the cookie jar."

He led her up the stairs to a huge bedroom that took up most of the second floor. "You'll like this better than the cabana," he said.

"The cabana?"

"That's where you'd be sleeping if you were just one of the single ladies. But Pam did the room arrangements."

"Does everyone in your family know that I'm sleeping with you?"

He slid the zipper down the back of her dress. "They will in the morning when they see the smile on my face."

She awoke to the sound of Jonathan's voice as he whispered into the telephone. "Just getting us some coffee," he said when he hung up. "I also asked for toast. They don't stock doughnuts in the kitchen."

They showered separately, dressed quickly, and were downstairs when the porter, Raymond, arrived bearing the coffee on a covered silver tray.

"What time did things finish up?" Jonathan asked. It was apparent that he and Raymond had long been coconspirators within the household.

"The people inside were gone by two. Pam's friends went on all night. There are two young men in wet clothes asleep on the lawn. There are also two evening dresses floating in the pool. God knows where the young ladies are or what they're wearing."

"Is Pam okay?"

"Asleep in her room," Raymond answered, "although no one saw her come in."

"Sounds like her party was a great success."

"I think it will be talked about for some time."

Over coffee, Jonathan filled her in on the day's schedule. Brunch at the cabana, which would start at ten and run until there were no more guests to feed. Boat rides for any that wanted to cruise the Sound. The pool was open, of course. For serious, adult conversation, Jack would be holding court in the library. And Pam would be opening gifts in the reception room.

"I didn't bring a gift," Nicole confessed.

"I signed your name on mine."

"What did we give her?"

"Well, she's becoming business manager at the Philharmonic . . ."

She reacted with horror. "Oh God, not a fountain pen, or a briefcase?"

"I stressed the art over the business," he answered. "I got her a CD set of all last year's concerts."

It seemed like a relaxing, pleasant schedule. Nicole hadn't brought a swimsuit so she was leaning toward a sail out on the Sound.

"Oh, I told Alexandra that you liked flowers. She wants to show you her garden."

Nicole felt her heart miss a few beats.

TEN

The gardens could have been the botanical center for a city. In terraces that fell down the hill to the south, away from the water views, there were fields of perennials and fresh rows of brightly colored annuals. Interspersed were collections of grasses, tall and green now, and destined to ripen to golds and ambers as the summer progressed. There was a miniature bamboo forest that Alexandra feared might not survive a full year. And there was a huge greenhouse hidden behind a decorative wall that was devoted to epiphytes. The orchards were sensational. Below the gardens there were potting sheds filled with tools, plant feed, and sacks of aromatic soil. The way Alexandra handled the plants on the workbench showed that she wasn't just a spectator. She liked to get her hands dirty.

Nicole strolled up and down the pathways at Alexandra's side, oohing and aahing, asking questions and, in general, trying to sound impressed. It was quickly obvious that Nicole's knowledge of flowers was limited to a florist's window, but her love of plants seemed sincere. They were passing in front of a row of rose bushes when Alexandra got down to business.

"Jonathan is quite taken with you. He talks about nothing else."

"That's flattering. He's a wonderful person."

Alexandra stopped walking. "Do you really think so?"

The question was a shocker. "Of course," Nicole answered. "You know he saved my life."

Alexandra's expression said she didn't know, so Nicole told her the story of their first meeting. "I hated him for chewing me out like that," she explained with a laugh. "But then I realized that it was for my own good. I could easily have been killed. So, when he called me a week later —"

"He called you?" Mrs. Donner seemed surprised.

"Yes, and asked me to dinner."

"When did you find out he was a Donner?"

A key question, Nicole realized. Did she find she liked Jonathan before or after she learned of his millions? "When he left me his phone number. I'm in brokerage, so I know about Sound Holdings.

Jonathan Donner rang a bell."

"When did you know that you loved him?"

Another mine in the minefield. "That's hard to say. I liked him right away, when we were in the airplane. He could see I was nervous and tried to be encouraging. And he took responsibility for me during the jump."

"And now your feeling for him is more than just 'liking'?"

"Yes," she said softly. "Much more."

Alexandra nodded and resumed her walking tour. "That's very important to me. There have been several women who wanted to marry my son. But none of them loved him. They were all very enthusiastic about learning skydiving, and helicopter skiing, and some of his other hobbies. But when it came right down to it, none of them ever jumped out of an airplane just to be with him."

A few more steps and then Alexandra stopped again. "What do you see in Jonathan's future?"

Nicole shrugged. "I haven't looked that far ahead. We've only been together for a few weeks."

"Long enough for you to have discovered that he's flawed."

"Flawed? I don't understand, unless you mean that he's very nonchalant. But I like that better than someone who is grimly serious."

"I mean he's a frightened child with a death wish. That isn't a description of the ideal husband."

Nicole was speechless. Her eyes blinked and her lips moved, but there was no sound.

"Jack Donner is a dreadnought," Alexandra said in a tone that was flatly factual. "He leaves a wake that swamps all the other boats in the harbor. Jonathan has been sunk so many times he's waterlogged."

"At times he seems a bit . . . resentful," Nicole agreed.

"He's been castrated! He doesn't have the balls to stand up and fight. Not even with me. I've been propping him up against his father for so long that now he waits for instructions from me."

"How can you talk about him like that? Your own son —"

"Because I love him. And I don't want to see him marry a woman who will caress him and console him, and make his decisions for him. He has me to do that. What he needs is a woman who will pour some steel into his spine."

"He seems strong to me . . ."

"If he was strong he would have told his father off years ago. And he would have put me in my place as well. He would be out on his own, not sniffing around the table for the scraps that Jack throws him to keep him from barking."

"Mrs. Donner, I've seen none of this in Jonathan. He thinks for himself."

"Thinks, maybe, but does nothing about it. Because he's afraid that if he stands up Jack will kick him out. He's too content on the family dole to risk a confrontation. So he stays in a job he hates and puts up with the ridicule. And he jumps out of airplanes because in his case dying can't be much worse than living."

They were walking up the steps from the garden to the house when Alexandra said, "I guess that's what I'm asking you. Are you the woman who will get him up on his feet even though it will cost him — and you — the family fortune? Do you love him? Or do you love his lifestyle? Some young women have thought they went together. But they don't. His lifestyle is what his father pays to keep him on a leash."

"I want a husband I can respect," Nicole answered after digesting the question.

"Good," Alexandra said, "because that means you'll be giving me a son I can respect."

Jonathan was waiting at the top of the steps. "Talk about smelling the roses. I thought you two would never come back."

"There's a lot to talk about in a garden," his mother answered. "But now I have to spend some time with my other guests."

The two boats had already sailed, so they wandered down to the cabana building, ordered drinks, and then sat and enjoyed the illusion that the pool was pouring out into the Sound.

"So, you survived the third degree. Hopefully Mother didn't resort to the rubber hose. What did she ask? Insanity in the family? Any sexually transmitted diseases?"

"She asked if I loved you."

"Oh!" They looked at each other for a moment before he continued, "And did you tell her?"

"Yes, as a matter of fact."

Another pause. "So tell me. I'd like to be the second one to know."

"I told her I did. Very much."

"Did she believe you?"

"Is that important to you?"

Now it was Jonathan who recognized the mine waiting to be stepped on. "I suppose it is. I'd like to have Alexandra on my side."

"And if she isn't? If she decides I'm not right for you?"

"Don't be silly. She's already bragging about you."

"Jonathan, if it came down to me or your mother, or me or your father, would I stand a chance?"

His eyes darted off into space. "That isn't a fair question, Nicole. I'd like to think that we'd all get along. It doesn't have to be one or the other, does it?"

She set down her drink. "Do you know that's the toughest question I've been asked all day?"

Neither of them answered the other, and they let the conversation drift off into other areas. When the sun began to fall in the west they went back to the gatehouse and gathered up their things. They were both very quiet during the drive back into Manhattan, lost in their separate thoughts. The gauntlets were down on the table. Jonathan had to decide whether he would defy his parents, if it came down to that, in order to marry Nicole. Her decision was less complicated. Would she marry Jonathan at the cost of the Donner family fortune? Neither of them was anxious to make the difficult choice.

ELEVEN

Jack wandered into Alexandra's bedroom, still wearing his trousers and shirt, but shuffling in bedroom slippers. "Great party. You really outdid yourself. Pam and her friends seemed to have a marvelous time."

She was sitting up in bed, reading a magazine article. "Thank you," she said, responding to the compliment.

He sat on the edge of her bed. "Did Pam mention our gift?"

"She was thrilled. She's trying to get one of the girls to go with her. And she's hoping she can change the itinerary. She'd like to change the week in Russia for an extra week on the Riviera, if that's all right with you."

He shrugged. "Fine with me. I wouldn't go to Russia myself if it weren't on business."

They sat quietly, until Alexandra asked what he thought of Jonathan's date.

"Great looker," he answered. "She really knows how to shake it on the dance floor."

"Did you talk to her?"

He seemed taken back. "Why would I talk to her?"

"Because she and Jonathan are quite serious."

Jack smirked. "Jonathan? Serious? The only thing he's serious about is getting into her pants."

"No, I think they've passed that stage."

"Well, good for him. It's nice to see him finish what he starts." He leaned over, kissed her cheek, and started to take his leave.

"Jack, do you ever wonder what it would be like if we had bombed on that minicomputer company? If it had failed and dragged us down with it?"

"Data General? It did fail. But we were off the deck long before it went under."

"I mean if we hadn't made all that money. If we both just went to work like everyone else . . ."

"We would have found a different winner. I told you the first day you came to work for me in that little office above the savings bank. I had no intention of being like everyone else."

"I never had any doubts about you. But what if you hadn't made it so big? If each of us didn't have so many things to take care of?"

"You mean if we were losers? Hell, I never thought about that. It's not something I ever want to think about." He smiled. "Why are you asking? Did you bet it all on a horse?"

"No, nothing like that," she laughed. But then her expression became serious. "It's just that today I asked a young woman who says she's in love with my son whether she loved him or his money. Isn't that a hell of a question to ask someone your son cares for?"

Jack chuckled. "Oh, I wouldn't worry about it. Today Jonathan is in love with the girl. Tomorrow he'll be in love with a new motorcycle. The next day it will be something else. How long does he ever stay involved with anything?"

"Still, I wonder if you should have Lambert find out what he can about her?"

He looked at her sternly. "I've got more important things for Lambert to do than check out Jonathan's latest bimbo. Hell, she'll be old fish by the time he finds out anything."

"I don't think so. This time it seems to be different."

"Okay," he conceded. "If it makes you happy, I'll put him on it. Just leave me a note with everything you know about her."

He stopped in the doorway and called back to her. "Don't let the housekeepers clean up the room where she's sleeping. Remember when I wanted to check on that bond salesman who slept in the cottage? Lambert said the place was as clean as an operating room when the housekeepers got through with it. He couldn't even find a fingerprint."

TWELVE

Nicole let the romance cool a bit. Not to the extent that her conduct announced rejection, but enough so that Jonathan Donner couldn't quite take her for granted. When he called on Monday for dinner on Wednesday, she lied that she was already committed with something at the office. Thursday? She hemmed a bit. Sure, but it would have to be early, a way of telling him that there would be no nightcap. Then on Thursday, when he mentioned a Block Island sailing race, she let her face fall with disappointment. "Oh, I wish you had mentioned it sooner. I'd love to, but I have plans for the weekend. Nothing exciting, but it's a commitment to a dear friend and I can't really break it."

The following week he called Monday and suggested a quick bite and maybe a movie to her answering machine. She didn't return the call until Tuesday, explaining that she hadn't gotten in until "real late." Then she surprised him with news that she had scheduled a sky dive for the following Saturday. Maybe he would like to join her.

"Sure, but I'd like to see you before the weekend," he pouted.

She paused long enough to seem like she had been glancing at her appointment book. "Well, we could do the dinner and movie on Wednesday, if you're free."

Then, on Wednesday, when he was about to dismiss his limousine at her front door, she begged off the implied nightcap. "I've got a hell of a day tomorrow. The auditors are in."

The message was clear. He didn't have an exclusive on her time, and she didn't expect one on his. If he wanted to have her on call, he was going to have to make a commitment. One that was binding no matter what his father said or how his mother felt. And Jonathan picked up on the message: Nicole Pierce was different. Other women might throw themselves in front of his car just to get his attention. And they might wait up all week for his phone call. But Nicole wasn't all that awed by his fame and fortune. She didn't come free.

She was just stepping out of the shower, a towel wrapped around her head and another tucked in under her arm, when her telephone rang. She had no intention of answering it until she heard the voice on the machine.

"Answer the phone, Nicole. I know you're there. I just saw the limo drop you off. Very impressive! I just want to offer my congratulations. So pick up the phone before I go up there and kick down your door!"

She stood staring at the machine. He wasn't going to hang up, and the one thing she knew about Jimmy Farr was that he didn't take "no" for an answer. He wouldn't hesitate to kick down her door. She picked up the receiver.

"Hello, Jimmy."

"Nicole! Great to hear your voice. It's been a long time."

"How did you find me?"

"Your picture in the paper. On the society page of all places. Most of my friends never get past the police blotter. But there you were at a very uppity party, with about a billion dollars hanging on your arm. You've never looked more beautiful!"

"What do you want, Jimmy?"

"Just to see you, Nicole. It's been too long."

"Our business is finished," she snapped. "We're all even."

"Nicole, would I call you over the nickels

and dimes you still owe me? We're both onto bigger things. You seem to have latched on to one of biggest pigeons in New York, and I just wanted to offer my services."

"No thank you. I'm on a new page now Jimmy, and it's not about you. In fact, you're not even in the book."

Jimmy Farr's polite tone was suddenly menacing. "Don't even think like that. With all I have on you I'm always in your book. Don't make me remind you."

She felt a long forgotten pang of fear — the fear that he could cause with just a look or a gesture. "You don't scare me," she lied. "I've gotten over that."

"Well, then, maybe I'll have to scare you again. Real soon."

"I'm hanging up, Jimmy. And then I'm disconnecting the phone." That was exactly what she did. But she took her cell phone with her and sat with her back pressed against the door of her apartment, waiting for him to come pounding. She was still sitting there when she woke in the morning, and breathed a sigh that at long last she seemed to have faced him down.

THIRTEEN

On Saturday Nicole and Jonathan met at the jump center, and formed up into a team with two other men. Nicole stood directly in front of him, and had him watch every step of her preflight safety checks. He verified the packing of her backup parachute and her main canopy. He checked the settings on her AAD, making sure it was calculated to the specific altitude of the runway. Then he went over her harness, testing all the clasps and rings.

"Now you," she said. "I'll go over your gear."

"I'm checked out."

"Sure, but it can't hurt. And it will help me review the checklist." They went through all his equipment just as thoroughly.

They formed their plan on the ground with the other jumpers. Follow the leader down to six thousand. Then, on the leader's signal, they would come together, grasp hands, and form up into a star. At three thousand, they would break up and open into a box fifty yards square. Deploy the main canopy chutes at eighteen hundred. Then fly down to the landing flare.

They went to ten thousand feet, toured the jump area, and then crowded to the door. The plane banked and they went out one behind the other with less than a second interval between them. Quickly, each of them found the tracking position and steered into a place in line behind the one they had appointed leader.

He proved to be a good flier. He shot off in a straight line back toward the landing area, then pulled into a climbing turn. The second man and Jonathan were able to stay right with him. Nicole was wide in her turn and then too abrupt in her climb, stalling out and falling back. But she kept them in sight, regained her forward speed, and was able to cut across their circle and get back into position. The leader went into a left turn and then a dive. This time it was the second diver who turned too wide. Jonathan and then Nicole flew by him. They leveled off, went flat to reduce speed. Then the leader signaled, flipped so that he was facing the line behind him, and held out his hands. Jonathan closed on him immediately. Nicole oscillated a bit before she was able to reach out and catch on. The fourth jumper had a difficult time joining up, at first unable to close on them and then overshooting his mark. They were all electric with adrenaline by the time they were able to form the star, and they were past their target altitude of three thousand feet.

The leader let go, raised his head and backed out of the formation. The others did the same, flying away from one another as they passed through two thousand. Just enough time for one quick stunt, Jonathan decided, and he did a tuck and spin like a diver off a springboard. Nicole watched for an instant, and then popped her pilot chute. She was the first to deploy.

They were still falling away from her when her main chute filled, stretching its broad wing over her head. She used her toggles to turn slowly until she picked up the smoke signal, and then steered upwind of the landing area. She had nothing fancy in mind, just a well-controlled descent and, hopefully, a running landing.

Two chutes were filling below her. She felt an instant of panic when she couldn't find Jonathan. He was tumbling when she last had him in sight, probably falling through the eighteen-hundred-foot deployment altitude they had agreed on. He was cutting it close. Where was he? She pulled a toggle, dumping air from one side of the wing. Immediately, the chute turned, swinging her out like an amusement park whip.

There he was, a hundred feet below her. His chute was filled and he was steering up wind, right into the haze from the marker flare. She completed her turn, found herself too far to the north, but still over wide-open field. To hell with hitting the landing marker, she decided. She'd land away from the others. Nicole watched as Jonathan adjusted his glide path, and touched down dead center in the box. She settled down a hundred feet away, stayed on her feet, and doused her chute. And suddenly she was able to breathe again. They were both down safely.

"You scared the bejesus out of me," she scolded Jonathan when he came over to help her.

"Did you see that landing?"

"Great! Wonderful! But why in God's name did you start doing spins?"

"I had plenty of room."

"We were supposed to keep an eye on each other." There was hurt in her voice.

He shuffled. "I didn't want to open until I saw you deploy. You know, if you were late, I didn't want to be sitting up there watching you fall."

"But I lost you," she countered. The hurt was gone and now she was near tears. "I didn't know if you were okay . . ."

"I knew for both of us."

She reached out to him and once again their helmets banged together. "I love you," she told him.

He seemed surprised, and for an instant even confused. Her admission required a response. A joke, making light of it, like, "Of course you do. I'm very lovable." A simple acknowledgment that might be, "I know, and there are some things we ought to talk about." Or a dismissal, "You don't mean that. You're just happy to find me still in one piece." But before he could decide, he simply blurted out the truth: "And I love you."

He took her hand and they walked back to the shed. They didn't stay to celebrate their dive with the other jumpers.

FOURTEEN

It was just a week later when Nicole found out that Jack and Alexandra were investigating her. Harold Lloyd, her boss, called her into his office, shut the door, and asked her if she were planning on leaving the firm.

She was agape for an instant. "No, of course not," she managed, and then with more conviction, "I'm doing very well here. I'm planning on doing even better. Why would I be leaving?"

"For a government job?"

"Government? You can't be serious."

"Something that requires a security clearance?"

"Harold, if it were after lunch I'd swear you had too many martinis. What are you talking about?"

He laughed and shook his head. "It didn't make sense, but I had to ask. An FBI investigator was in last week. All very hush-hush. But he wanted to know a lot about you. I thought it was none of his business so I asked if you were under investigation for anything. And he told me it was just a routine security clearance."

"Security clearance? What for?"

"That's what I asked. He told me he wasn't at liberty to say. Just that you had applied for a security clearance, and that a background check was mandatory."

It didn't take her long to convince him that she wasn't planning a job change. Nor had she joined anything or applied for anything that would require a security clearance.

"I suppose I should have called his office," Harold apologized. "But he looked like a Fed. Plain suit, no jewelry, his hair styled by his wife. And he had credentials."

Nicole asked him to call the local bureau office right then and there.

"No, I believe you. Like you said, it doesn't make sense. Probably some credit bureau that wants to lend you money."

She made it a point to call the FBI uptown office, and pressed ahead until she got someone in authority. As she suspected, the Feds didn't know what she was talking about. They hadn't run a security check on anyone. But they wanted all the details she could provide. The FBI didn't like normal citizens impersonating its agents.

Two nights later a friend from her brief

theatrical career called. They had kept in touch and met for lunch once a month. "Do you have some big news to share with a friend?" the young woman teased.

"Now how did you find out?" Nicole asked, assuming that somehow she heard about her serious relationship with Jonathan.

"This guy from your firm called me. He said it was a routine check, but when I said I needed to know more before I'd say anything, he told me you were in the zone to become a partner."

"Partner?"

"Yes, partner! Were you keeping it from me just because I've stooped to doing commercials?"

Nicole insisted that she was not up for partner, and asked about the person from her firm. There was no one with the name he had given. Then she pressed about his questions.

"Sleazy stuff," her friend told her. "Like, did you do any centerfolds or men's magazines. Did you sometimes work for an escort service?"

Nicole dialed other friends. Two of them had been interviewed by investigators. "Don't worry," one of them said. "I made you out to be Martha Stewart. I didn't say a thing about that bachelor party we did together."

Someone was looking, with lots of detectives, into every phase of her life. This career, her earlier career, maybe even back to her cheerleading days in Muncie. She called the high school music teacher who had encouraged her into the school musicals. "What a coincidence," the teacher shouted into the phone. "I was just talking about you. I hear you're up for a big promotion, and I couldn't be happier for you . . ."

It had to be Jonathan's parents. She thought of phoning Alexandra at the house on Long Island. "If you want to know, just ask me," she wanted to challenge. "You don't need idiots pretending to be government agents." But she could almost hear Jonathan's mother reply in a bored voice, "My dear, what on earth are you talking about? If I were hiring detectives, they would be the very best. You wouldn't know anything about it."

Or, maybe she should storm right into Jack Donner's office. Everyone else might founder in his wake but she had heard that he really respected a fighter. "Jack, when your detectives send you the report I'd like to have a look at it. I'll be happy to fill you in on anything they miss." Except there was always the possibility that he would explode into one of his legendary rages. "Get your ass out of here before I kick you all the way out to the elevator. And take my wimp of a son with you."

But the snooping had to stop, and there was one person who might be able to stop it. Nicole phoned Jonathan making no attempt to hide the anger in her voice, and demanded a lunch date the next afternoon. "In fact, make it a breakfast date," she said. "If I wait until lunch I'm apt to kill somebody."

"Me?" he asked in surprise.

"Among others," she snapped.

At eight in the morning, he was waiting by the maître d' stand at the Plaza dining room. He smiled as he saw Nicole approaching, but realized from the determination in her stride that a smile might be dangerous. Instead, he greeted her with serious demeanor and a brushed kiss as if she were a distant cousin at a funeral. They followed a waiter to a table with a single rose in a silver vase, set for two. Then they waited quietly while coffee was poured.

"Did you know your family is having me investigated?"

"No . . . well, yes, I suppose. I mean I

don't know but I'm not completely surprised."

"You're not surprised? Does that mean you approve of them pushing their noses into my private life?"

"No, of course not. I don't approve. I didn't approve when they investigated a girl I was dating in college, or when they ran background checks on Ben Tobin. But they're protecting a ten-billion-dollar estate. They think anyone who comes near them is a potential kidnapper —"

"I'm a potential kidnapper?"

"No, it's not about you. You remember the suits at the gate to the house? They were screening everyone arriving. And I'll bet at least three of the waiters were really with the security firm and had guns down the backs of their pants."

Nicole's eyes were widening. "Doesn't that strike you as a bit paranoid?"

"It did, until last October, when a fake deliveryman tried to drag Pam into the back of his truck. He had already mailed the ransom note."

The waiter came with the menus, and then fled under Nicole's fiery gaze.

"I'm not a deliveryman," she hissed at Jonathan as soon as the man was out of earshot. "I'm someone you say you love, and I expect that your mother and father are planning on loving me, too. If you trust me, then they should trust me . . ."

"They do. You're taking this too personally. They —"

"It is personal," she snapped, cutting him off. "So far their investigators have suggested to my boss that I'm looking for another job, which could well get me fired. They've asked friends about my career as a porno star, and even called my high school teachers. They're digging for dirt and getting mud all over me in the process. I —"

"Nicole, they did the same kind of research on Pam's college boyfriend. The works — right back to his childhood when it turned out he had been an altar boy. Joyriding in a borrowed car when he was in high school. Drunk and disorderly at a frat party after a football game. When they added up all the crimes of his youth he turned out to be just a normal kid, not nearly as dangerous as I was. But by the time they gave him a clean bill of health, Pam had changed her mind. The guy wasn't ambitious enough for her."

"Is that what you're saying? That none of this will matter because you'll probably change your mind?"

Jonathan exhaled deeply in his frustration. "Of course not. I'm just saying that my parents are very defensive about everything. Their house has more security than the White House. It's not about you any more than it was about Pam's boyfriend. Or Ben Tobin, because he's been showing an interest in Pam. For them, it's just business as usual."

"Business as . . ." She stopped, her voice choking in her throat. Her eyes flooded, not with rage but more with despair. She shook her head, then jumped to her feet and darted for the door. He bounded up after her, hesitated for an instant to wonder what he should do about the check, and then walked rapidly across the lobby. When he reached the top of the steps, he saw her running past the fountain toward Fifth Avenue. By the time he reached the street she was already into a taxi.

Jonathan took his own cab downtown to her office building and searched the lobby. Then he rode up to her floor and inquired politely. She hadn't come in yet. He waited until almost 9:30, and then went back down to the street and hailed another cab, this time to her apartment.

He pressed her doorbell and heard her voice on the intercom.

"It's me —"

The intercom clicked off but the door didn't unlock. He rang again.

"Let me come up. We have to talk —"

It clicked off again. He was ringing it for the third time when the lock buzzed, letting him into the lobby. He punched the elevator button for her floor, and found her door ajar when he reached it. He passed the tiny kitchen, crossed the living room in three strides, and found her in the "L" that she used as her bedroom. Her suitcase was on the bed, and she was dragging four seasons worth of clothes out of the bulging closet.

"What are you doing?"

She kept packing. "Getting out of here. What does it look like I'm doing?"

"You can't just . . . leave. What about us?"

She pulled open a dresser drawer and began loading stacks of underwear into the suitcase. "I'm in way over my head, Jonathan," she said. "I'm running for my life."

"Then I'll run with you," he announced.

She stopped abruptly and looked up from her packing.

"I mean it," he continued. "You pack what you need and then we'll go to my place while I get some things together."

"Pack for where?" Nicole asked suspiciously.

"Anywhere you say. Just as long as it's a place where we can get married tomorrow."

Her eyes narrowed.

"I'm serious," he insisted. "I'm asking you to marry me. Right now! Tomorrow at the latest."

Nicole took a deep breath. "I can't do that. I don't want to live under surveillance. And I can't let you do it. It would cost you your family." She went back to her packing.

Jonathan waited until she had turned away and then slammed the lid down on the suitcase. "I'm not going to let you go. You asked me at the party what I would do if I had to make a choice. Well I'm choosing. I'm going with you to get married. And whatever happens, happens. Nothing at home is as important as you are."

Her eyes filled again, but this time with a glow of joy. "You really mean that, don't you?"

"Let's go," he said. "Forget the packing. We'll buy whatever we need."

"Don't you need to call your father?"

"We'll send him a postcard."

FIFTEEN

They spent the morning at City Hall and then the afternoon shopping while they were waiting for their license to be processed. They spent the night at his apartment where he ignored two calls from Alexandra that were on his machine, and then went back down to City Hall in the morning. A Marine and his girlfriend stood up for them, and then they changed places so that Nicole and Jonathan could witness their marriage. On the steps, Jonathan reached into his pocket, pulled out a handful of rice, and tossed it in the air over their heads. Then he rushed Nicole into the waiting limo that pulled away without any instructions from him.

"Where are we going?" Nicole asked.

"On our honeymoon." He pulled her into an embrace.

She resisted. "Where's that?"

"In heaven . . ." He turned her face to his.

"No, tell me. Where are you taking me?"

"I told you. Straight to heaven. Non-stop . . ."

The car climbed the ramp to the Brooklyn Bridge.

"Jonathan, am I being a brat?"

"No, you're being impossible. I'm trying to consummate our marriage and you keep pushing me away."

"I mean, have I dragged you into this? Because that's not why I was packing. I wasn't trying to force a proposal."

He pulled back. "You mean you would have settled for an ordinary proposition? I could have just thrown your suitcase off the bed and pulled you under the covers?"

"No, I mean are you sure that this is what you want?"

He slid his hand under her skirt. "You know exactly what I want."

She grabbed his wrist, keeping him well short of his goal. "Can we be serious for just a minute?"

"I'm dead serious," he said, tugging at the edge of his mustache and trying to look villainous.

The car came down in Brooklyn and turned onto the expressway that ran east toward Long Island. Jonathan reached for her but Nicole slid away across the sofalike seat. "I love you, Jonathan," she said in a factual, businesslike tone.

He laughed. "Well, I should hope so. We

haven't been married long enough for you to start hating me."

"Your mother doesn't think I love you. That's why she's investigating me. She thinks I'm in love with your fortune."

He feigned despair. "Ah, the curse of being rich. Does she love me or my money?" He slid across the space that was separating them. "Fortunately, I don't give a damn as long as you hurry and get out of your clothes."

"I want you to give a damn. I have to know that you believe me."

Jonathan turned away. "Okay. I'll renounce my inheritance so that we can be filthy poor. Let's get out of the limo and take a cab. Or better yet, he can drop us off at the subway and we'll honeymoon in a rooming house on Rockaway Beach."

"Don't make fun of me," Nicole snapped. "Do you think I like being investigated? Am I supposed to ignore your mother's suspicions?"

"Nicole," he said, serious for the first time since they left City Hall, "I come with the fortune. I spend money like there's no bottom to the barrel because I've never seen the bottom. So, instead of spending it on foolish things, I'll be spending it on you. Why does that make you mad?"

"Because even if you didn't have the money —"

He put a finger to her lips. "If I didn't have it I'd probably throw myself off a tall building, because I wouldn't know how to live without it. So, you'll just have to take me the way I am . . . filthy rich . . . strikingly handsome . . ."

She laughed genuinely and leaned back into his arms.

"Good," he said. "This is where you belong. Now, can we just forget all this talk about taking a subway? I have bigger plans for the rest of the day."

Nicole recognized LaGuardia Airport ahead, and saw the driver moving to the exit lane. "We need a plane to get to heaven?" she asked. But the car turned away from the passenger terminal and took the road that curved around the field and led to the private plane gates. The driver jumped out and began handing their luggage to a porter. Jonathan led Nicole through the waiting area and out onto the taxiway. A twin-engine jet, much bigger than an executive jet, was waiting.

"What is this?" she asked suspiciously before she started up the steps.

"An airplane," he deadpanned. He started her up toward the open door where a waiter in cutaway attire was standing. The waiter greeted her with a slight bow. "Mrs. Donner," he said, showing that she was expected. "And Mr. Donner. I trust the drive over wasn't too difficult."

"Better than the subway," Jonathan answered. Then he ran into Nicole who had stopped short as soon as she turned into the cabin.

"Oh, my God," she breathed.

"Like it?" he asked.

The plane, normally fitted out with seats for a hundred passengers, had been turned into a luxury suite for just a few. There was a full kitchen, a stocked bar with swiveling stools, a media area with theater seats in front of a five-foot television screen, a bumper-pool table, an intimate dining room, and then a cluster of soft chairs and ottomans that formed a living room. There were flowers on every table, champagne in ice buckets, and a wedding cake hung from the overhead so that it wouldn't be tipped during the takeoff. The windows were covered and the lights were dimmed. Strings were playing over the sound system.

"I don't believe it," Nicole stammered.

He took her arm and led her through the cabin. "Wait until you see the bedroom!" He opened a door to the last third of the plane.

The bed was round, set in the center of the space, beneath a matching mirror hung from the ceiling. It was at least eight feet across, and covered with a white satin comforter and oversize black pillows. A black negligee, invisible except for the seams, was tossed casually at the edge. There were two night tables, one rigged with enough electronic controls to pass for the mixing board in a recording studio. The walls were a brocaded white fabric, and the floor a black shag.

"How cozy," she chided. "Is this your debut as an interior decorator?"

"Is it too subtle?" Jonathan wondered.

"It looks like an altar for sacrificing virgins."

He went to the control panel. "Watch this!" The lighting dimmed and then went through a range of colors. Stereo sounds seeped through the wall coverings. The bed rotated so that it could face any one of three television monitors, and a nicely stocked bar rose up from the floor.

Nicole lifted the nightgown and held it up to herself. "I don't think this will fit," she said.

"Does it really matter?" he asked with his eyebrow arched. Then he pushed past her and opened a door that was hidden by the brocade. "The bath," he announced.

The Jacuzzi was nearly as big as the bed, a black tub set into white tile. Shower nozzles aimed in at it from every angle. The wall above the double sinks was entirely mirrored. The toilet and the bidet were behind a privacy wall.

She looked at him curiously. "Is this one of your toys?"

"What? The Jacuzzi?"

"The whole flying whorehouse. You couldn't have done all this since yesterday."

Jonathan began to laugh. Then, while trying to control his hysteria, he assured her that he wasn't the owner. "It belonged to some Hollywood guy who did porno films. He ran into prostate problems so he had to sell it."

"And you bought it?"

"No. I leased it just as it was. The only change I made was to remove the video cameras from behind the mirrored ceiling." She looked skeptical. "Honest," he assured her. "Business tycoons rent this thing for executive travel. Getting there is half the fun."

"They bring their wives?" Now Nicole feigned skepticism.

"Whatever," he answered. "I just thought that you'd never had a proper courtship.

So I wanted to do something . . . extravagant!"

Nicole laughed, wrapped her arms around his neck, and kissed him. "You succeeded. This is wonderfully extravagant."

"You're sure you wouldn't rather have a rooming house in Rockaway? A squeaky old bed with a john at the end of the hall. Because I could just cancel this . . ." She kissed him full on the lips, her mouth open and eager. He pulled back. "We could just pick up our luggage and find a subway station . . ."

She covered his mouth with hers.

They got serious during the takeoff, and kept their seat belts on during the climb-out. But once they were at altitude, the honeymoon began. Their waiter popped a cork and poured champagne, served with caviar. Then he led them to the table where he served sautéed Dover sole and poured a chilled Graves. He returned with fresh strawberries and a sauterne for their dessert.

It was while she was tasting the sugary berries and the sweet wine that Jonathan produced the small pale box from Tiffany. He went down on one knee just as the cabin filled with the heartbreaking strains of a gypsy violin. "Nicole, will you marry me?" He popped the top of the box. "Before you answer, I want you to know that this ring is not intended to influence your decision."

Her eyes flashed childlike amazement.

"In fact," he went on, "if it's too big for your populist taste I'll take it back and get something smaller."

It was a blue-white five-carat diamond, oval cut with a dozen facets in a solitaire setting.

"But it has to be returned in twenty-four hours, so we'll have to turn this thing around . . ."

She silenced him with a kiss, and then led him to the bedroom. Nicole lifted the negligee from the bed and carried it into the bathroom. "Don't go away," she said as she closed the door. Jonathan tore off his clothes and left them where they fell. He went to the control panel, dimmed the lights adding just a hint of red, and turned the bed so that it was facing the bathroom door. Nicole stepped out modeling the gown that provided just enough coverage to be wildly provocative.

"What do you think?" she asked, doing her best imitation of a runway model.

"I think we can sell a lot of those." His voice cracked as if he were about to choke.

"Do you like the way it moves?" She pirouetted, letting the bottom hem spin over her legs.

He swallowed with difficulty. "I'm not sure. Do that again."

She did, spinning in the other direction. "Maybe it's too revealing. Do you think I should send it back?"

He groaned. "I think if you don't get into bed right now, I'm going to start without you."

Nicole slid under the comforter and took Jonathan in her arms. "Oh," she whispered. "You did get a head start."

His hands slipped up along her body and then poked out from under the bedcovers. The negligee landed softly and vanished into the black carpet.

They were entwined in the Jacuzzi when the butler tapped on the outer door and cleared his throat.

"Come in!" Jonathan offered.

"No, don't!" Nicole yelled. She started out of the tub and then thought better of it. Instead, she slinked down into the water until it covered her up to the chin.

Jonathan laughed at her modesty, climbed out and wrapped himself in a towel. He crossed the bedroom and peered out around the edge of the door.

"The pilot wishes to inform you that we're in the landing area. He wonders when you'll be ready to return to your seat."

"Tell him to take it around a few more times. Maybe another half hour."

The butler nodded. "Very good, sir."

Nicole was still under the water. "What did he want?"

"Oh, the landing gear is stuck. We have to get into our parachutes right away. No time to dress and dry off."

For an instant she looked shocked. Then she began to laugh. "Wouldn't that do it? Parachuting into Manhattan stark naked. I can see the pictures of us wrapped in the chutes as the police drag us out of Central Park."

"We're not back in New York," Jonathan told her.

"We're not? Isn't this the heaven you promised me? I thought this was a flight to nowhere?"

"No," he answered. "I think we're somewhere . . ."

Nicole scampered out of the tub. "Where?"

"I don't know," he teased. "I'll have to ask the pilot."

They landed in the darkness. During the

descent Nicole had picked out a few pinpoints of light, and one cluster that might have been a small city. But when they touched down there were no runway lights that she could see, and when they rolled to a stop there was no sign of a terminal. Her first hint came when she stepped out onto the ladder that had been rolled up to the plane's door. She felt a blast of heat and a heavy dose of tropical humidity.

"Africa?" she asked. Jonathan didn't answer.

They were loaded into an old van and driven down a short road to a seawall, where the few lights she could find were matched by rippling reflections on the surface. A workboat bobbed at the dock, more a lifeboat than a cruiser, with a cuddy cabin too small to house comfortable amenities. Nicole let herself be helped onto the dock, took off her shoes, and stepped aboard in her stocking feet. Jonathan helped cast off the lines before he jumped aboard and snuggled up next to her.

"Quite a comedown from your earlier efforts," she teased.

"The *QE2* was already taken," he answered. They turned out to the open water and headed into the darkness.

"The Amazon?" Nicole asked.

"No, but you're getting closer."

It was half an hour later when the engine slowed. The captain stood with his hand still on the tiller, and stared over the port bow. Nicole followed his gaze, but could find nothing.

"We're there!" Jonathan announced

"Where?"

"Heaven. Just like I promised."

"I don't see anything . . ."

He pointed. "That faint white line. It's the surf. The water lapping up on the beach."

She squinted. And then the line emerged as the boat drove closer. The engine sound dropped another few decibels. Off to her left, a red light blinked. Then, behind it, came the outlines of a dock, actually a line of pilings with a boat bobbing alongside. She watched as the scene came into focus. They were making a landing at an open wooden dock and a walkway that connected to the beach. Jonathan jumped over and fastened a bowline. The captain handed up their luggage. Then he came ashore and helped carry the luggage up to the beach. Halfway along the gangway, Nicole spotted the cottage that was set back no more than fifty feet from the water's edge. Another wooden walkway crossed to the cottage porch.

The captain did a bellboy routine, lighting the oil lamps and throwing open the French doors. As the rooms came to life, Nicole found herself smiling.

"Like it?" Jonathan asked, anxiety sounding in his voice.

"I love it."

The porch was bare wood planking, with a hammock hung between the posts that supported the roof. The sitting room was decorated with driftwood, with dark rattan furniture and sea grass accents. The bathroom had an outdoor shower, and the bedroom, again furnished in dark rattan, had a deep, soft bed, as big as two king-sizes put together.

Jonathan sighed with relief, pressed a handful of bills into the captain's hand and waited on the porch until he saw the launch pull away. Then he joined Nicole who was in the process of learning the kitchen. "It's wonderful," she said. "You thought of everything."

"They did," he admitted. "All I did was order the honeymoon package. A week of undisturbed privacy with just enough provisions so we don't starve to death."

She came close so he could put his arms around her. "It will only take me a second to find that black negligee."

"It doesn't have to take that long," he suggested.

She awoke to find that her honeymoon cottage was on a tiny cay, a sandy beach edged with a mangrove forest. There was a dive boat bobbing at the dock.

"Belize?" she said when he told her where they were. "We're in Belize?"

"No, this is part of the barrier reef off the coast. Not only is it the world's most private place for shameless sex, but it's also the scuba-diving capital of the universe."

"I don't scuba dive," she said in a tone that indicated shameless sex was another matter.

She was resting in the crook of his arm as they swung gently in the porch hammock. They were both exhausted from lovemaking that had been wildly physical and imaginatively varied. Even though their hands were exploring, neither of them was anxious to start over again.

"Alexandra and Jack will never find us here," she allowed.

"Oh, yes they will. Jack could find the Holy Grail."

She sat up abruptly. "You didn't tell him where we were going?"

"No, but I told him that I was going and wouldn't be back for quite some time. Just in case he noticed that my office was empty."

"When did you tell him?"

"From the plane, while you were getting dressed. I just said you and I were married and that we were on a charter flight bound for heaven. Oh, and that you were a better piece of ass than he's ever had . . ."

She poked him in the ribs. "You did not. But what did he say?"

"Oh, all the usual things. Congratulations . . . good luck . . ."

"That doesn't sound like your father. What did he really say?"

"You want his exact words?"

"Yes! Every word."

He did a fair imitation of Jack's crackling voice. " 'Damn it, Jonathan, how stupid can you get? You screw a girl like that. You don't marry her.' "

"That sounds like your father. And what did Alexandra add?"

"Just that she'd call her lawyers right away and have them get working on the annulment."

She punched him again. "You're lying. She never said that. That's probably what she's doing but she'd never tell anyone. What did you call it? Deniability?"

"You're right, I'm lying," he admitted.

"She had already gone to bed and Jack didn't want to disturb her. He's probably telling her right now."

"Wouldn't you like to be a fly on the wall? What do you think she's saying?"

"Something not too committal. 'That money sucking little bitch,' or maybe, 'If he'd just use his brain instead of his pecker.' "

"Are you beginning to have doubts?" Nicole asked.

"After this morning? How could I have doubts? I'm too tired to have anything."

She twisted out of the hammock, setting it rocking and nearly dumping him out. "I'm going for a swim." She tossed off the oversize T-shirt she was wearing and raced across the hot sand.

"Didn't you bring a bathing suit?" Jonathan called after her.

"We're the only ones on the island," she shouted back, and plunged into the crystal water.

SIXTEEN

"Last night, about eight-thirty. He was calling from a plane he had chartered."

"A plane to where?"

"He didn't say, but it will be easy to find out. It won't take Greg Lambert long to run down all the charters that left New York yesterday."

Jack and Alexandra were having breakfast on the back terrace, looking down the hill to the cabana, and then out to the Sound. A huge market umbrella shaded their table.

"You should have awakened me."

"Why?" Jack asked. "If they're really married there's nothing we can do about it. And if they're not, there's no reason to care."

He went back over the details of the telephone call he had received from his son. Jonathan had started by announcing that he wouldn't be at work on Monday, and Jack had asked cynically how anyone would know whether he was there or not. "It's not as if people were depending on you."

"Well, then if I take the whole week it wouldn't put you out of business?"

"Take a month," Jack had answered.

"Okay, a month. Or maybe two. You see, I'm on my honeymoon and I don't want to rush it."

"Your honeymoon? Who in hell would go on a honeymoon with you?"

"My wife, Nicole. We got married this morning."

"The one in the catcher's mask?"

Alexandra shook her head slowly. "I was afraid of something like this. I knew that girl was different."

"Different? She must be out of her mind."

"Or else very, very shrewd. I just hope that she checks out."

SEVENTEEN

They moored at one of the marked diving trails inside the reef, a mile-long canyon of pristine coral in ten to twenty feet of water.

"Are you sure I'm ready for this?" she asked. Nicole had once taken lessons in the swimming pool of a fitness club, and Jonathan gave her a day's worth of training just off their beach.

"Just stay with me, and breathe the way you did yesterday. If you have a problem, get your hand in front of my face and point up."

She still wasn't convinced. "But I've only been in six feet of water . . ."

"This isn't deep. And there's sunlight all the way to the bottom. You could read a newspaper down there."

He did a final check of her equipment, fitted her mouthpiece, and watched her take several breaths from her tank. Then he bit onto his own mouthpiece, dropped his mask, and took her hand. Together, they dropped backward over the side.

She was instantly lost in a cloud of bubbles, something she hadn't experienced when they practiced in shoulder-deep water. It took her just an instant to get herself righted, and one kick with her flippers to clear the boat. She descended quickly, down into an explosion of color animated by ridiculous looking fish. Then she let go of Jonathan's hand, and took up the same tracking position she had learned in skydiving: her head down slightly, her arms by her side. With just a gentle kick of her feet she moved effortlessly, down into the canyons of plants and waving grass that grew between the spires of coral.

Jonathan was in and out of her sight, slightly behind her where he could watch her every move. She kept getting lost in her adventure, once following a ray as it swam away from the reef, and then tracking a turtle that moved among the spires and led her out of the preserve area. Twice he had to cut in front of her and turn her back in the general direction of the boat.

She gushed with excitement when they were back aboard, begging to return as soon as they had filled their tanks. Scuba diving was suddenly the most important calling in her life. Jonathan had bought extra tanks so that they wouldn't have to go back to the mainland every day to get air for their ventures. By midweek, he had weaned her out of the underwater park and out into deeper water beyond the barrier. They dove off Half Moon Cay, skimming by the jagged coral heads and over the soft coral gardens. Eagle rays, menacing to behold but playfully curious, glided by them. They had gone to the Blue Hole, a four-hundred-foot-deep cistern of eerily blue water with hundreds of caves in its sides. Then they had motored to a shelf where there was an old wooden wreck lying in fifty feet of water. By the end of the week, Jonathan had booked their island cottage for an additional three weeks.

Nicole had used a trip to nearby Ambergris Cay to call her office. "Married, that's what I said. So I'm going to take a few weeks. I'll apologize in person as soon as I get back." Harold was screaming mad until he learned that she had married Jack Donner's son. Then he warmed up to his affable old self. "Why do I think that in a few weeks I'm going to be working for you?" he asked. He chuckled, but he wasn't really laughing.

Jonathan called his mother at the house to tell her that he was extending his honeymoon.

"Honeymoon?" she said with mock surprise. "I don't recall you telling me that you were planning to get married."

Pam jumped on the line. "This is great! When are you coming back so that I can throw you two a party? I think Nicole is terrific. It will be such fun to finally have a sister."

Jonathan was relieved. No one seemed to be very angry with him.

But as they got through their second week, he noticed a change in Nicole. Nothing dramatic. She was still thrilled when they were diving and enthused enough to review the day's events each evening as they motored from the sunset to the dark intimacy of their island. And she was still an eager and exciting lover, in their midnight swims from their dock as well as in their oversize bed. But increasingly, and at the oddest times, there were sudden bouts of anxiety.

"Don't be silly! What could be bothering me?" she told him each time he asked. But on two occasions he had awakened and found her standing on the porch, her arms folded across her chest, her face set and staring out to sea. "Go back to bed," she had told him. "I'll be right in."

She had snapped at him when he was checking her expansion valve. "Leave it alone. I know what I'm doing." Later, she apologized, saying that she had just been nervous about the dive. Her explanation didn't ring true.

Over the last few nights, Nicole had seemed ominously quiet. She hadn't really been part of their conversation, but more of a spectator, answering with nods and grunts and proposing few topics of her own.

"Why do you keep asking?" she had demanded when he raised the question again. "There's nothing wrong."

"You're worried about the reception we're going to get when we get back to New York, aren't you?"

Nicole launched into an angry denial, but then broke it off in mid-sentence. "A little, I suppose," she admitted. "Eloping seemed very romantic at the time. Now, it seems inconsiderate. They're not going to be happy with me."

"I'm happy with you," he shot back. "Besides, we didn't have much choice. As I remember, you were packing to leave me when I came up with the idea. It was either marry you or lose you, and I couldn't bear losing you."

She nodded to accept the compliment. He was right. She hadn't given him a lot of options. But her expression remained grim. Nicole seemed more and more troubled as the time of their return grew nearer.

EIGHTEEN

"She has a lot to explain," Alexandra was telling Jack as they lounged in the shade of the cabana. "And the investigators aren't nearly finished."

He grunted. "Everyone has a lot to explain. When you dig for dirt, you find dirt."

"Do you know what her profession was before she got into finance?"

"Sure," Jack cackled. "She was a catcher for the Yankees."

"That I could handle," Alexandra said. "But I think her actual title was 'hostess.' "

He sat up abruptly. "A hooker? No kidding?"

"I didn't say 'hooker,' I said 'hostess.' But, one of her responsibilities was jumping out of cakes at stag parties."

He exploded into laughter. "Well that's a first. Maybe you can hire her for one of your symphony openings."

Alexandra found herself laughing. Whatever else it might be, that would be an opening everyone would remember. "That's about the only way she would get into the hall," she said. "Her career in theater was a complete bust. She didn't get a single part. Not even in a touring company."

She went on with her recitation of the detectives' preliminary report. When Nicole arrived in New York she had lived in a women's hotel for a few weeks, and then found an apartment with another aspiring actress. "Not really an apartment, but half a flat in Hell's Kitchen. The building has since been knocked down with no loss to the city's architectural heritage. They waited tables in a coffee shop and then in a Midtown restaurant. In their free time they took dance classes and acting lessons."

"Half the actors in New York are waiters," Jack said, already losing interest in his wife's report. "The other half are bartenders."

"And a few of them are apparently opportunists," Alexandra added. "After a few months Nicole left her girlfriend and moved in with an aspiring director. David Hanna, to be exact. He's gone on to great things, but he didn't take Nicole along with him. He doesn't even remember who she was."

Jack was paying attention again. "Why

should he? Last thing he needs is an old bed partner showing up with a brat. Only thing he can do is swear that he never heard of her." He sat up and threw his legs off the chaise. "But none of this surprises me. Lots of young people make bad starts. The important thing is that she got her act straight. I wish I could say as much for Jonathan."

"She's still friends with a call girl. One of the women they interviewed had nothing but good things to say about Nicole. But it turned out that the lady was turning tricks in an Upper East Side apartment. She even has her own Web site."

Jack had started toward the pool but he stopped and turned back. "One of my boyhood friends is doing life for murder. Does that mean I'm a murderer?" He turned and dove in, creating a shock wave that splashed up on Alexandra.

He was right, of course. All she knew was that in her first few years in New York, young Nicole Pierce had done some questionable things in the company of some seamy people. Nothing shocking or criminal. All it proved was that not every young woman went straight from the family home to the altar. Suppose she had done some exotic dancing to pick up rent money? Or maybe modeled lingerie in storefronts? It might be embarrassing if someone turned up erotic photos of her new daughter-in-law, but it wouldn't be devastating. And her live-in affair with the director could be laughed off; lots of young people give married life a try without the benefit of clergy.

Give her credit. As Jack had said, she had certainly gotten her act together. The people at her brokerage firm raved about her. She was on the way up to handling bigger and more promising accounts. If her theater career had been a failure, her budding business career showed every sign of success.

But still, Alexandra was anxious. Nicole had arrived on the scene too suddenly and become deeply involved too quickly. She was just a bit too perfect, and much too blasé about the staggering fortune she had married into. Certainly you could fall deeply in love with someone who had Jonathan's millions. But you couldn't pretend the money didn't matter. Money always mattered.

She was also concerned about the gaps in Nicole's background. Two years were missing between her exit from junior college and her arrival in New York. There was a whole blank year between the end of her theater career and her first appearance on Wall Street. And then there was the contradiction that still had to be explained. Nicole had told Jonathan at their meeting that it was her first solo jump without her instructor. But she had been certified by a school upstate in the Adirondacks two years earlier. Why pretend she was a novice? There were many questions about the new Mrs. Donner. And where her son was concerned, Alexandra was determined to find the answers.

NINETEEN

Nicole wasn't sure what she had heard. The far end of their tiny island was a mangrove forest, alive with birds during the day, turtles and gators at night. There were constant noises. The air was never truly silent. But something had caught her attention as she lay wide-awake in bed, her head resting on Jonathan's rising and falling chest. It was a water sound — a gentle splashing coming from the direction of the dock. A wave, she thought. The wake of a distant boat or a ripple pushed by a change in the wind, breaking against their boat.

But then she heard it again, and this time it seemed closer, as if someone was quietly paddling up to the beach. She nudged Jonathan.

"Someone's coming," she whispered. He snorted and turned. "Jonathan, there's someone out there."

"Can't be," he mumbled. "There's no one else on the island." He had answered without really waking up.

She slipped out from under the sheet,

found her T-shirt on the floor and raised it over her head. Another sound, this time like something sliding over the sand. She let the T-shirt fall over her shoulders and pulled it down as she stood.

There was moonlight, not bright and full, but certainly enough to set the water sparkling and draw the outline of the beach and dock. If anything were there, she certainly would have seen it. She stepped off the porch and out onto the sand. From her new vantage, she could look up and down the beach. There was nothing but the curve of the sand, marked with a tiny line of surf and disappearing into the mangroves at each end. Whatever she thought she had heard wasn't there. Nicole walked out on the dock to check the lines on their powerboat. It was tied securely and floating easily. She turned back to the cottage, scanned once more to reaffirm that she had heard nothing out of the ordinary, and then stepped through the front door.

A hand whistled through the air toward her face. She sensed the motion just in time to flinch, and the fist ricocheted off her forehead. She fell against the doorjamb and tried to scream, but another hand clutched her throat. A form stepped from behind the door, grabbed her flailing arm and twisted it up behind her back. As she twisted away from the grip on her neck she was able to get out a muffled scream. Then she was flying, hurled by a powerful force through the open doorway and out onto the deck. She landed on her face and felt the air rush out of her body. She tried to pick herself up but before she could move she was kicked. From the corner of her eye she caught a glimpse of black legs with bare feet. The foot rose and slammed down on her back pinning her to the deck. And then her arms were pulled over her head and she was being dragged. She managed another scream, this time loud and long. Then she was hit again, now on the side of her head. Her vision faded and her mind went blank.

There were sounds. Someone running, perhaps two people. Then Jonathan's voice shouting. She felt herself being lifted, then dragged. Jonathan was saying something. Then the darkness washed over her again.

It was still dark when she awoke, alone in her bed. There was a cloth across her face, ice cold and dripping water down onto her neck. Outside, Jonathan seemed to be yelling. Then there were other voices.

She sat up just as her husband came through the door. Two men in white shirt-sleeves followed. Jonathan came to one side of the bed, and the two men went to the other.

Jonathan took the wet cloth from her and carefully brushed back the hair that was matted to her forehead. "These men are police officers from San Pedro Town. They've been checking the beach and the mangroves. There's nobody here. You're perfectly safe."

"We'll just stay on guard," one of them said in English that was only slightly accented. "The detectives will come from the city."

Nicole nodded and smiled. She was grateful that they were going to let her get back to sleep.

She was up in the morning, dressed in shorts and a blouse, with just a few bruises on her forehead to show for her ordeal, when the detective arrived. She sat on the sofa, her husband at her side, while the mustached officer made himself comfortable in an open chair. He wore a jacket over an open collar. The rental agent, in slacks and a golf shirt, sat off to one side. Both men listened without interrupting to every detail she could remember, and then the police officer asked Jonathan for his thoughts on the attack.

"I heard nothing. My wife says she woke me and that I spoke to her, but I honestly don't remember." He glanced at Nicole. "I'm sorry, hon. I wish to God you had poked me or something." Then he went on, "I heard Nicole scream, and I jumped up. There was a commotion out on the porch, and I yelled that I was coming. When I got to the doorway, Nicole was lying on the deck. Not so much lying as down on all fours. There was a man — a black man — running away."

He described a big man, tall and muscular, dressed in shorts and maybe an undershirt. Because of the darkness, he couldn't provide a detailed description. No, he regretted, he certainly couldn't pick the man out of a lineup.

"Neither of you got a look at him?" the detective asked. Nicole repeated that she was on the ground before he had emerged from the darkness inside the cottage. Jonathan had been more concerned with tending to his wife.

"Did you see a boat? Did you see him leave the island?" Nicole hadn't. She had been in a daze, maybe even unconscious. Jonathan had been busy carrying her inside. His first thought had been to get the police. He had used the small radio that had come with the house to contact the rental agent. He was amazed at how quickly the police had come. "If he was in a boat rowing back to Ambergris Cay, then the police boat went right by him."

The officer went back to Nicole's story. If she had heard something outside, why had she gone out?

"I don't know. I looked first to be sure no one was there. Then I thought the boat might be breaking loose so I went out to check on it. I suppose when I didn't see anyone I thought that everything was all right."

"In your nightshirt?"

"Yes. Well, we have the island to ourselves. At least, I thought we did . . ."

"And you say there was enough moonlight so that you could see the beach and the water from your doorway? Even the dock?"

"Yes. Not enough to identify someone. But certainly enough to know if someone was there."

"So, then the man who was inside your house could have seen you out on the beach and even out on the dock?"

"I suppose so," Nicole answered.

The man wrote in his notepad, moving his lips slightly with each word. Jonathan took Nicole's hand and squeezed it.

"Have there been other intruders out at these cottages?" Jonathan asked the rental agent.

"No, never . . ." The officer glanced over at him. "Well, yes," the agent corrected himself. "But it was a long time ago. More than a year. Burglars came out while the guests were touring over on the mainland. They took money and jewelry. It was just a petty theft. No one —"

The detective didn't wait for the man to finish. "Is it possible that someone down here would want to harm you?" he asked Nicole.

"Me? I don't know anyone down here."

He repeated the question to Jonathan who said that he had made very few contacts in Belize.

"May I ask if either of you work for a large company? Could you be a key executive? Or an owner? In some way connected with a large amount of money?"

Jonathan's eyes widened. "Well, yes, I suppose so." He explained his relationship to Sound Holdings. While he was talking, he realized the direction that the interrogation was taking. "You think this may have been a kidnap attempt?"

"No. I have no idea. I'm just looking at everything."

But, as he explained, the evidence was confusing. The intruder seemed to have come in an inflatable boat, a fairly large one judging by the drag marks at the end of the beach. He had pulled the boat up against the mangrove where it couldn't be seen and then made his way through the edge of the underbrush around to the side of the house. Up until then, he was just a thief trying to take a wallet from a night table or jewelry from a dresser.

He had apparently entered from the shower room, which was outside the cottage and connected to the bathroom. Since Nicole was awake, it was unlikely he had gotten into the house while she was still inside. In all probability he entered while she was on the beach or walking out on the dock. Jonathan was asleep, his wallet on the dresser along with Nicole's diamond ring. "A burglar would have had that stuff in his pocket and been back outside in a split second," the officer reasoned. "I mean, if he came for money, then he could have had what he came for."

"How do you know all this?" Nicole asked.

"Because the man was wet and sandy coming in from the beach. He left tracks on the wooden floor, which the first police to arrive noted. According to the sandy footprints, the intruder hadn't entered the bedroom."

Then there was the question of the moonlight. The man could have seen Nicole coming back across the beach, obviously to the porch and front door. So then why wouldn't he have retraced his steps back through the bathroom and made his escape into the mangrove underbrush? Instead he waited inside the front door for Nicole to return, where he surprised her and dragged her back outside. "Suppose his punch had knocked you out. He could have had you over his shoulder without a sound, and carried you to his boat."

The rental agent was shocked by the possibilities being discussed. All his clients were wealthy Americans and Europeans. He couldn't have the island cottages portrayed as the ideal place for a kidnapping. He protested vigorously. "It makes no sense. If the intruder wanted to kidnap the lady, he would have taken her right from the dock."

The officer shrugged. "Just walk after

her on a moonlit beach? She certainly would have fled him and screamed for her husband."

In the end, nothing was certain. The police would, of course, make inquiries. They would round up the usual suspects. But in the meantime, it might be good for the honeymooners to exercise a bit of caution. Join with other groups for diving. Lock their doors at night. The police would keep an eye out, but that really wasn't very helpful when they didn't know what they were looking for. Maybe the booking agent should consider hiring a security guard.

Jonathan vetoed the idea. They wanted privacy, not company. He was sure that the whole affair was simply a botched burglary.

Nicole went along with him, but she wasn't nearly as certain. The memory of being thrown out the door and dragged across the porch was still with her. She also knew that there were people who might well want to hurt her. Jack Donner, who might send a message if he thought she might be after his money. And Jimmy Farr, who would certainly want to remind her that she still had good reason to be afraid.

They became very cautious. Jonathan bought a revolver that he admitted he didn't know how to fire, but maybe just the noise would scare off an intruder. It was better than nothing. They took their own boat over to San Pedro Town so they could join with other divers. That way, they wouldn't be alone when they were cruising out beyond the barrier reef. They planted oil torches out on the beach and lit them at night so they would have no trouble seeing the water's edge. But because they were on their guard, the freedom of honeymooning on their own tropical island lost its appeal. After two days they moved to one of the resort hotels on Ambergris Cay.

The move helped, but it didn't really end their anxiety. The sense of violation still hung over them, casting a pall on their pleasure. They found that they could talk of little else. Jonathan tried to make a joke of it. "Can you imagine the poor idiot who kidnapped me and then sent a ransom note to my father?" He roared at the idea, and Nicole found herself smiling. "The guy would want five million to give me back. Jack would make a counter offer — six million if the kidnapper kept me."

"Hey, I was the one he was dragging out the front door," Nicole reminded her husband. "What would your father pay to get me back?"

"More than he'd pay for me. You make money. I just spend it."

The jokes were just a case of whistling in the dark. They were both concerned. Nicole kept wondering if it were really a kidnap attempt. "Do you think that someone might, maybe, just want me dead?"

"Don't be silly. My parents aren't killers."

"I didn't say your parents . . ."

"But that's who you were thinking of," Jonathan said, and Nicole didn't contradict him. "Look, if they wanted to be rid of me they'd just make me head of a startup in Mongolia."

"That's you. How would they get rid of me?"

"Maybe an office in Tibet?"

"Be serious. Someone came close to killing me."

Jonathan sighed. "I am being serious. No one in my family would do anything to hurt you, or get rid of you. That's not their style. If they wanted you out of my life, they'd just make things very difficult for you. You'd get the message."

She changed the subject, but only slightly. "Do you think someone might want you dead?"

"Who? One of the women I've disappointed? Or some investor who lost his shirt? The people I deal with don't tend to be violent. At worst, the girls might scratch, and the investor might launch a lawsuit. But hiring a hitman in a foreign country? That's not something I need to worry about."

"Well, what then?" Nicole persisted.

"A common thief," he said. "People who rent islands probably have a lot of money, and by definition, they're careless with it. We were an obvious mark."

Nicole shook her head. "The police officer said it didn't look like an ordinary robbery."

He sighed in frustration. "Nicole, for God's sake, the man is the night-duty detective in Belize City. It's not like he was flown in from Scotland Yard. All he was saying was what the sandy footprints seemed to imply. Hell, they were probably my footprints. You didn't see them scraping samples into evidence bags."

But his stance was tainted with the bravado he was putting on for Nicole. He didn't want her worrying, although he still had anxieties of his own. Either of them could be a mark for kidnappers who would certainly figure that Jack Donner would pay anything to get his son or daughter-in-law back. And, in truth, he had made some serious enemies by both his social arrogance and his business ineptitude. Someone might want to pay him back. Finally, there was his father and mother. If Jack and Alexandra thought that Nicole was interested only in their money, and if she seemed to have cut herself in for a large share, they would come at her from every angle. Jack wouldn't want her hurt, but he sure as hell wouldn't hesitate to scare her off.

He found that he was looking around during the day to see if anyone might be taking an interest in them. At night, he quietly made the rounds of his suite to lock all the windows and doors.

TWENTY

"Well, here goes nothing!" Jonathan turned off the road and slowed at the first gate. The security guard stepped out sternly, then bent to peer through the windshield.

"Oh, Mr. Donner. Good to see you." He glanced down at his clipboard and then quickly flipped a page.

Jonathan had lowered the window. "We're not expected. Thought we might surprise them."

"A pleasant surprise indeed!" He stepped back into the guardhouse and the iron gate swung open. At the same time, tire spikes retracted into the ground.

They were on the road through the woods that Nicole remembered from the party, a mile of Belgian blocks flanked by perfectly trimmed trees.

"Nervous?" Jonathan asked.

"Scared out of my wits."

"They'll love you."

"Not if they're the ones who tried to have me killed."

He laughed. The small gatekeeper's

house that they had shared appeared in front of them. He reached down and squeezed her knee. Then they turned onto the circular access road and came quietly to a stop at the front door. "Leave the luggage," he said as he opened her door.

"You think they'll throw us out that quickly?"

He led her up the path, tried the door handle, and then rang the bell. Raymond, the front hall porter, opened the door instantly.

"Well, Mr. Donner. Welcome home. And Mrs. Donner," he added without missing a beat. It was as if he had been greeting her by that name for years.

"Nice to see you, Raymond," Jonathan said in a full voice. Then, in a more confidential tone, "Are they at home?"

"They are. Out on the patio having a cocktail. They'll be delighted to see you both."

The two men exchanged glances confirming that they were both aware of Jonathan's peculiar status. Raymond asked, "Shall I get your things out of the car?"

"Better wait until we find out where we're staying."

"*If* we're staying," Nicole whispered to

Jonathan as they crossed through the living room.

Jack seemed genuinely pleased to see them. "Glad you survived Belize," he said as he shook his son's hand. "Snakes and crocodiles . . . hell of a place for a honeymoon." He paused awkwardly in front of Nicole, not sure whether he should shake her hand or take her into his arms. She stepped close for a kiss on the cheek. "And you," Jack said. "You must be crazy about him to follow him into the jungle. Wonder you didn't come down with a poison dart . . ."

She laughed and called him "Mr. Donner." He reminded her that he was "Jack." Then he pushed the newlyweds toward the chair where Alexandra was sitting, a perfect martini standing proudly on the table beside her.

"Congratulations," she said to her son as he bent to kiss her cheek. She reached out to Nicole and brushed a kiss on her as well. "You're certainly the easiest child I ever had. A very short pregnancy and a painless delivery." She gestured that they should pull up chairs, and ordered Jack to get them both drinks.

When he had fixed a martini for his son and a margarita for Nicole, he lifted his own drink and proposed a toast. "Best wishes for a happy marriage." They drank, and then he said directly to Jonathan, "Hope you're better at this than managing a portfolio." They all laughed as if he hadn't really meant it.

"We wanted to get married, and we didn't want to wait while you put together a gala wedding," Jonathan said to explain their elopement. "We just said, 'Let's do it!' and that's what we did." He didn't mention that Nicole was about to leave him. They had decided it was best not to mention that she knew they were investigating her.

They talked about their idyllic honeymoon, the charms of a private island and the joys of diving together. Again, they had agreed to skip the intruder who had battered Nicole. She had wanted to lay it all out so that Jack might include them under his shield of security people. But Jonathan had prevailed. Kidnapping was a stretch from what was probably an amateur burglary. Finding time for themselves would be enough of a problem without hired busybodies.

Alexandra was completely frank about her disappointment that she had not been told. "I could have gone to City Hall, you know. If that was the way you wanted to get married, I still would have appreciated being there." It was obvious that she intended to do a good deal of pouting. "I have only one son," she reminded Nicole. "Now, all I can do is have a cocktail party in your honor." The implication was that Nicole had been directly responsible for ruining her life. Nicole might be accepted into the family, but there was still going to be a time in purgatory.

They decided to move into the gatekeeper's cottage. That would give them a bit of separation from the affairs of the main house, and keep Nicole from confronting Jack and Alexandra at every turn. And they would keep Jonathan's apartment in the city as a base for the workweek. But the arrangements were only temporary. Jonathan had ideas for a resort hotel on Ambergris Cay, tied in with a flight service out of Miami. He needed some time to work up the details into a solid financial presentation, and then he planned to offer the idea to Sound Holdings. It was an escape plan that merged financial proprietary with a career in a diver's paradise, appealing both to his father and to himself.

Nicole's presentation was just three weeks later, at Rockbottom. Alexandra had considered scheduling for Newport, in the height of the season. But she had reasonable doubts about how Nicole Pierce might be received. Better to do it quickly without too much fanfare. Just a simple Sunday afternoon gathering of the absolute minimum of family and friends — certainly not more than two hundred. Perhaps heavy hors d'oeuvres and a top-shelf bar. Maybe a jazz combo. Something big enough to get Nicole introduced, but small enough to provide deniability if the marriage crashed.

The invitations carried news of the wedding, and the vultures gathered instantly. The first appraisal was that, "She must be pregnant, but in this day that's hardly a reason to get married." Close friends who knew the family situation sympathized that Jack and Alexandra must be mortified. "Why else would Jonathan marry a nobody other than to embarrass them?" And there were those who simply couldn't believe it. "Who? Not the girl he brought to Pam's graduation? I never found reason to speak with her!"

The gentlemen's explanations were snickered in the locker rooms. "She looked like one great piece of ass to me. No matter what the settlement, little Jonny will be getting his money's worth." Followed by, "Jack ought to get a shot at her. He's the one who's going to be paying the bill."

The post-debutantes, many of whom regarded Jonathan as a prime catch, had other thoughts. "Who is she? Why would Jonathan Donner saddle himself with a nobody?"

Alexandra dreaded the gathering even as she planned it. Not that she really cared what most of the charity set thought, but she knew how skillfully they could inflict pain on an outsider, and that would mean pain and embarrassment for her son as well.

Jonathan wanted his wife to be a smash hit, and thought in terms of an elaborate dress and heavy-duty jewelry. Nicole simply wanted a repeat of the classy but sexy number she had worn to Pam's affair. "I don't really care what they think," she told her husband. "None of them is going to move in with us in Belize."

The reception, as Alexandra intended, was minimal. Everyone made a point of speaking to the newlyweds, and then sympathizing with Alexandra because she had been cut out of the wedding. Then they gathered in small groups and talked about the downfall of the Donners. "Jonathan could have done so well," was the shared regret of family and friends.

When it was over, Jonathan brought Nicole back to the cottage. "They all loved you," he said.

"They all hated me and pitied you," she answered.

At the main house, Jack ventured into Alexandra's room to get help taking off his tie. "I thought everyone seemed to like her," he said.

"They hated her," Alexandra informed him.

TWENTY-ONE

It was two days later when Nicole stopped by the main house to thank Alexandra for the party. She was surprised when her new mother-in-law invited her for another walk in the garden. There were a few moments of pleasant chatter until they cleared the house. Then Alexandra rolled out the artillery that her investigators had assembled.

"Well, you made good on your ambition: you really did marry the richest man in the world. Or, at least one of the better financed." Nicole looked stunned, so Alexandra explained, "That's what you wrote in your high school yearbook as your ambition in life. 'To marry the richest man in the world.' Surely you remember."

"That was in high school," Nicole answered softly. "Ten years ago. We were trying to be funny. I think one of the girls wrote that she wanted to be Tom Cruise's cleaning woman."

"Yes, I saw that one, too," Alexandra agreed.

They walked a few more steps before

Nicole asked, "Where did you ever find a copy of my high school yearbook?"

"At your high school, I suppose. I asked some research people to find out all that they could about you. After all, you've just become my daughter."

"You could have asked me. I'd have told you anything you wanted to know."

"Well, as a matter of fact, there are a few areas that I'd love you to fill in. For instance, you said you went to a junior college. Which one was that?"

"A community college. In Muncie. Part of the state system. But I didn't graduate. I knew what I wanted to do, so I left early."

"And that's when you came to New York. To be an actress?"

"To Chicago, first, to get some experience. And then to New York. Looking back it seems ridiculously starry-eyed. But at the time I thought I had talent."

"Did you?"

"Apparently not. I took all the lessons, got an agent, and made all the casting calls. I never even got callbacks."

It was a quiet exchange, in conversational tone, spoken as they meandered from plant to plant. But despite the setting, the words were without warmth. Alexandra was probing, and Nicole was answering, almost as if it were a job interview. Nicole was seething with resentment, but knew she had to keep her cool. In a way, she was applying for a position.

"That must have been very disappointing. How did you manage to make ends meet?"

"Waitressing. Odd jobs. A few modeling shoots. And I shared expenses with a girlfriend, another actress who never got any callbacks."

"It's the odd jobs and modeling assignments that interest me. What were they like?"

Nicole stopped and turned to face her. "I'm sure you already know. If your 'research people' found my yearbook, I'll bet they gave you a complete list of my publishing achievements."

"Yes, I do know. But does Jonathan know? Have you told him about your modeling career?"

Nicole sighed and looked her adversary in the eye. "No, I was hoping that was a part of my life that he would never know." Then she asked, "Will he know?"

"Not from me. And if you were just another couple he probably wouldn't hear about it from anyone. But you've stepped up in the world, girl. Like it or not, you're in the limelight. It won't be long before some society writer pushes your pictures into his face."

Nicole blushed noticeably. She nodded. "I suppose I have to tell him."

"But where will you stop? Once you get started, you'll have to tell him everything. Your career as . . . what do they call it . . . a *hostess?* And your year with that director. What were you trying to do? Sleep your way to stardom?"

"I did a lot of stupid things," Nicole snapped, her anger suddenly breaking through. "Lots of people make mistakes. But usually no one turns the dogs loose to dig them up."

"It didn't take much digging," Alexandra answered, running right over Nicole's implied insult. "And I suspect you knew that it wouldn't. Isn't that the reason for the speedy elopement?"

Nicole took a step back. "My God, there's no limit to your cruelty. You think the worst of everyone: your husband for bullying your son, your son for taking it. And now me."

"It's not cruelty. It's honesty. But the truth can be very cruel to those who would rather hide it."

"The elopement was Jonathan's idea," Nicole said, sounding a note of triumph.

"At the moment he suggested it, I was packing to get out of the city and get out of his life all together."

Now it was Alexandra's turn to seem surprised.

"And let me tell you why I was leaving. Because I learned that your *research* people were investigating me as if I were some sort of criminal. I didn't want to be around when you dropped your findings on Jonathan."

"It would have been so much better for everyone if you *had* just left," Alexandra said. "Even better for you." Then she changed the direction and turned back toward the house. She had disclosed the problem while they walked in one direction. Now she was going to consider a solution.

She claimed that she understood the difficulties a young actress can face when she comes to New York, repeating Jack's comment that they were all waiters or bartenders. She knew why they put themselves into unsavory situations, and she could understand why they might become easy prey to "the worst kind of men." Obviously, these were years that were better forgotten. But the fact was that the family reputation, its social position, and even its business couldn't survive the kind of scandal that Nicole's past would surely bring. Sound Holdings couldn't very well be married to a "hostess."

"Jonathan and I were thinking about some sort of career out of the country," Nicole began to explain. "You know that he has little interest in the family business. He was thinking —"

"He has a great deal of interest in the family money," Alexandra interrupted. "Your presence makes it very unlikely that he'll ever get his hands on any of it."

She had a few thoughts on a solution to their problem. Nicole should confess all, including the fact that she had been skydiving for two years, and that her meeting with Jonathan wasn't the stroke of fate she pretended. Then it would be Jonathan's decision to make. He and Nicole could exile themselves into one of his hobbies where they wouldn't be around to embarrass the family. Naturally, there would have to be some sort of suitable financial arrangement. Or, perhaps they would agree that the marriage had been a mistake. Then there would be a quiet annulment with a generous settlement for Nicole.

"You know," Nicole concluded when Alexandra had ended her presentation, "what you're doing is much more obscene than anything I've done."

Alexandra considered the indictment. "It may be," she answered. "Using the power of money to direct other people's lives is not something I enjoy. If it's not obscene, it certainly isn't playing the game fairly. But if I let this go on, you'll have nearly as much money to fight with as I have. I'll lose my advantage. And the things I'm defending — my son, my family's reputation — are dear to me. I can't risk losing them."

Alexandra turned and climbed the steps to her front door. She didn't ask Nicole to join her.

TWENTY-TWO

Nicole returned to the guest cottage, packed the essentials, and drove off in the convertible that Jonathan had left for her use. She nearly spun the security guard around as she flashed past the gate, and seconds later she merged into the parkway headed for Manhattan. She let herself into Jonathan's apartment, called him at his office, and told him she needed to see him right away. She paced in front of the window until he stepped out of a taxi in front of the building. She was in his arms the second he stepped through the door, sobbing so deeply that she couldn't even speak.

"What's the matter? What is it?" he kept asking.

She couldn't answer. Finally, when her wracking had calmed to a shiver, she managed a broken sequence of words between her deep breaths. "Your . . . mother . . . wants me . . . to . . . leave."

"Leave the house?"

She nodded. "And leave you."

"Leave me? Don't be ridiculous, Nicole.

Why would she want that?"

She tried to answer, but began crying again. Jonathan led her tenderly to the living room sofa, seated her, and then went for a glass of water. He watched her struggle as she sipped, and then moved around behind her where he could massage her neck and shoulders. "Don't try to talk," he whispered when she began a fumbling attempt to string a few words together. It was nearly half an hour before she could try an explanation.

"Your mother found out things about me. Awful things. Things that I never wanted you to know."

"Then I don't want to know . . ."

"But I have to tell you. I don't ever want you to hear about me from anyone else."

He started to disagree, then stopped. "Okay. Whatever you want to tell me." He settled into a chair across from her.

She began in a faltering voice. Her high school introduction to the stage had captivated her. She had gone to community college to prepare for a business career but her heart had never been in it. She had worked nights and weekends until she saved up a nest egg. Then she had gone to Chicago where she had a better chance of getting cast than she would have in New

York. "People told me that I'd need professional credits in New York. That's why I quit school and went to Chicago."

Jonathan nodded. It sounded sensible to him. But he knew there would be more to the story so he didn't interrupt.

She had spent two years there, and had gotten only one small part. A New York touring company had taken all the leads on tour, filling in the minor parts with locals. She was a dippy chorus girl with just two lines.

But in all the months of frustrating casting calls, she had learned all the ways that an attractive young woman could make money. Lots of money. She could pocket a thousand a week dancing in an adult nightclub. One night was worth more than a month of waiting tables. She could model clothes for visiting buyers. The manufacturers tipped lavishly if their sales went well. She could pose for men's magazines and for the porno Web sites. Maybe a thousand dollars for a four-hour session. Sure, all the men were hitting on her. The club owners, the buyers, the photographers. But that was nothing new. In high school it was the football players. In college it was the teachers. Waiting tables it could be the owners as well as the customers. One thing a good-looking girl learned was how to deflect leering propositions. Never say "no." Just tell them why it would have to be later.

"There was this English professor who called me in to tell me that with a little more effort I could get a really good grade. 'Maybe with a little tutoring over the weekend . . .' I stalled him through the marking period, always strapped this weekend, but maybe next weekend. He gave me an 'A,' and then I told him that I just didn't have the time for his personal attention. And the photographers, with their promises of photos for my book . . ."

Jonathan had no trouble visualizing the maneuvering involved in holding out hope without ever actually delivering. He began feeling rage against the creeps who would use a young woman's desperation to take advantage of her. But then he remembered how many women he had led along just by flaunting his wealth.

Nicole moved on to the next phase of her career. She had moved to New York and found a comfortable situation with another aspiring actress. Their days were spent taking acting and voice lessons and going out on casting calls. They had both been overwhelmed. There were hundreds of aspirants for even the smallest roles, and the level of talent was incredible. Nicole had sneaked out of one tryout without even auditioning. From the wings she had heard three girls toy with notes that were far beyond her range.

"I knew within a month," Nicole confessed to her husband, "that I had no future in musical theater. But I thought that it's not always the most talented player who gets the part. Mediocre talents get fantastically lucky. So, I was hanging around hoping for a break."

She had done some modeling, she went on, and not all of it for name brands. There were poses for the kind of calendars that hang inside gas stations. The dividing line between leg art and the subtly pornographic wasn't always plain when an agent booked a shoot. Sometimes she simply picked up her things and walked out. But other times, when she needed the fee and the photographer was persuasive, she did poses that she would never want to put in her book.

She had also been a hostess, she admitted, shilling prospects at trade shows, and filling in as a companion for a big buyer in need of a dinner or theater companion. "But that was the extent of it," she swore. "I was never a call girl. I never turned a trick in my life."

Jonathan tried to stop her. He had never asked about her past because he didn't think it mattered. He was sure she had reasons for whatever she had done, and he was well aware that he had sins of his own. "None of this matters to me," he assured her.

"But it does to your mother. She doesn't think the family would survive if someone got wind of my past."

Then she led into the topic of David Hanna, a Broadway and Hollywood director whose name Jonathan recognized. She had met David briefly at a party where she was on the arm of a Pittsburgh buyer. Just a few minutes of small talk. But three days later, on an open casting call for a new musical, Hanna was sitting in the audience. She had done a song and dance number, one of Gwen Verdon's numbers from *Damn Yankees*. The voice out of darkness had called "Thank you," and advised her to leave her name with the stage manager. It was the standard kiss-off. She was going out the stage door when Hanna had stepped in front of her.

"Miss Pierce!"

She pulled up and drew a breath.

"Or is it Heather?" he asked. "When I met you the other night, weren't you Heather something or other?"

She blushed. "That was just for the gentleman I was with. I didn't want him to know who I was."

"Then why were you with him?" David Hanna knew perfectly well why she was with him and he mellowed into a broad, toothy smile that said he understood her predicament and was enjoying her embarrassment.

"A favor to a friend," she lied.

He nodded. Then he said diffidently, "You don't really want the part you just auditioned for. It's chorus line behind feathers."

She didn't want to say that she would kill for any part. "It sounded like a lot more when my agent described it."

"Agents," he groaned. "They'll take ten percent of anything." Then he got to the point. "Do you have a few minutes? Maybe time for a drink? There's something I'd like to toss out. Just a suggestion, but you might find it attractive."

Nicole had known perfectly well where his suggestion would lead, but he was a rising power broker in the theater, and she was desperate for a break. Even the crumb he might toss her would be better than what she had been able to get on her own.

Jonathan held a finger up to her lips. "You don't have to tell me about this," he said.

"Someone will tell you about it. David might even remember me when he sees my name in connection with yours. I don't want you to read about him bragging in some tabloid that he had me first."

"Nicole, what will it matter when we're living somewhere where there are no tabloids? Maybe a thousand miles away from anyone who wants to talk about us?"

"It's not 'us' that your mother is worried about. It's the reputation of the family. The integrity of Sound Holdings. She wants that 'deniability' you told me about. She wants to be able to say that it doesn't matter anymore because I'm no longer in the picture."

"We'll talk to her," he promised. "We'll make her understand . . ."

"Jonathan, I can't go back into that house. I couldn't stand her looking down her nose at me as if I were some kind of trash."

He took her in his arms again, and stopped her just as she was about to fall back into her hysteria.

"Nicole, why don't we just go back to Belize? I have a lot of things to put in the works down there. We could leave tomorrow. Certainly by Friday."

"But I don't want you to lose everything just on my account."

He shook his head. "I won't lose everything. There are millions in my name, and I could put up one hell of a fight before they could take any of it back. There's more than enough for us to live on forever. Probably enough to start a small version of the resort hotel I was thinking about. If they don't need us, then we don't need them."

He spent an hour trying to explain to her why they were financially independent and why Alexandra couldn't control their lives.

She protested several times that she didn't want to know about his finances. She didn't care about the Donner billions or any portion of it that might be his. "All I want to know is that you love me," she told him. "Maybe some day your family will see me for who I am and not for the things I had to do."

Jonathan settled in his father's office the next day, and refused to leave until Jack canceled his appointment and told his secretary to hold calls.

"Now, what's so damn important that the world of finance has to stop spinning on its axis?" he demanded.

"I'm resigning," Jonathan said.

"Resigning? Quitting your job? For what? If there's one thing I know for sure it's that no one in his right mind would be giving you a better offer. What are your plans? A hotdog pushcart? Or a soft ice-cream stand?" Jack chuckled at his own wit. He was used to people laughing at his jokes.

"I was thinking of a dive boat in the Caribbean, or maybe a charter-boat business in the Mediterranean."

"You think you can make money out of one of your hobbies? What makes you think you'll be any good at running your own business?"

"I can't do much worse than I've done here."

Jack laughed. "Look, I don't have time for this. Why don't you and your baseball player take a couple of more weeks off? Then, when you get back, we'll sit down and talk."

"That's what we're doing now, Jack. We're talking, and I'm telling you what I'm going to do." He stood, replaced his chair, and started to the door. "I'll keep you posted on how things are going. Who knows? Maybe you'll want to invest in me?"

Jack stood and came around the desk after his son. "And what are you planning on using for money? Because the second you step outside that door your salary stops."

Jonathan laughed. "I was figuring on using all that money you banked in my name to avoid taxes. I know it's not much to you, but it should keep me rolling for quite a while."

"You can't touch that money," Jack snapped.

"Why not? It's *my* Cayman Island bank account. I paid the bank fees."

Jack started to sputter. Rage rose in his face from his collar line until the red tint reached his eyebrows. "Don't get smart with me," he snarled. "You're way out of your league."

Jonathan held out his hand. "I know that, Dad. You're the best. No one can touch you."

Jack waved away the handshake and stormed back to his desk. "You be in here in the morning, or your things will go flying out the window." He was already on the telephone when Jonathan closed the door behind him.

TWENTY-THREE

They landed in Belize City the next night, just in time to catch the Beech Baron that flew them up to San Pedro. Their hotel arranged a car to meet them and they were quickly delivered to a three-room cabana with shuttered doors opening out onto the pool.

Jonathan had decided that they should get the lay of the land before moving out to the isolation of one of the island cottages. "I'm not thinking about the intruder," he had insisted to Nicole. "But I'm going to be meeting with real-estate brokers, bankers, and probably a couple of local lawyers. So, I'll need to be here on Ambergris Cay or over on the mainland for a few days. Once that's done we can go back out in a honeymoon bungalow."

He made a point of calling home. "Might as well save them the trouble of finding out where we are," he told her. "They will, whether we want them to or not."

He talked to his mother. "Of course I'll

be coming back. A couple of weeks, maybe a month at most. No, don't send anyone down. If there are contracts to be signed, I'll sign them up there. I won't have time to meet with your attorneys. I'll be too busy getting things started here."

Then to his father: "No, I'm very serious. I was working up a formal proposal on the idea, and when I see you I'll have hard numbers to show you. No, I don't need one of the consultants. As I told Alexandra, I expect to be flat-out busy for the next few weeks."

His sister got on the phone. "Pam, baby, this place is heaven. Line up a couple of friends, and buy the skimpiest bikini you can get your hands on. It won't be long before I'll have a place down here that you can visit."

He recapped everything for Nicole. Alexandra wanted to send down the family lawyers with a bunch of legal documents that would establish his financial basis. She was annoyed that he was so casual about critical family affairs. Jack had reneged on his threat to throw Jonathan's desk out the window. He'd hold the job open for a while, and keep paying salary. And if Jonathan needed any help, consultants or accountants, he'd send them down right away. And Pam had bubbled with excitement. Nicole was just the best thing that had ever happened to the family. She had encouraged Jonathan into this exciting new adventure in Belize, wherever that was. Pam wanted to talk with her about some of her own ambitions.

"What does it all mean?" Nicole asked.

"Oh, some property transfers for me, a nuptial agreement for you, and probably my father's meddling in whatever operation we start."

He kept her up late, filling her in on his thinking. He would start with a simple dive boat operation. There were a lot of small cramped boats run by waterfront captains and dock rats. Great for skilled divers who just wanted transportation out beyond the barrier reef, but there was nothing for tourists. His idea was a luxurious boat with the amenities that vacationers would demand. Hot showers, private rooms, classrooms for lessons, and a cocktail bar for after-dive relaxation. He would team up with the resort hotels, start guests off in the hotel pools, move them out to the underwater parks, and finish up with dives on the outer reefs. "For vacationers and beginners — maybe even families with kids — the resorts will be able to offer a full diving package. They get the room rates, and I get the diving dollars."

Nicole praised the idea. It would start slow, in cooperation with the resorts that presumably knew the markets.

"But I want the land right away. Something on the water where we can eventually build our own resort. I won't build right away, of course. But the cost of land down here will be out of sight in another couple of years. I want to buy it now, before anyone knows that I want it."

He kissed her goodnight and made a few forced attempts to be affectionate. He fell asleep with his head on her belly. But when he tossed awake in the middle of the night, Nicole wasn't in his bed. He whispered her name, and then called it in a raised voice. There was no response. He got up, walked through the small kitchenette, and found her in the sitting room. She had the plantation shutters thrown open so that she could look across the pool out over the starlit water. She was leaning on the edge of the doorway, her arms folded across her T-shirt, her legs bare. She was startled when he came up behind her. "Something wrong?" he asked.

"No, just thinking. A lot has happened in the last couple of days. Maybe more than I can handle. I've been toasted as the new bride and then told that it would be better for everyone if I'd just leave. Then I've been flown down to a place where I was nearly murdered. And now I learn that I'm going to be living aboard a dive boat for the foreseeable future."

"And you don't like what you're hearing?" Jonathan asked.

"I don't know yet. It's only been a few weeks since I was a New York career girl, trying to break through at a brokerage house. You get whiplash when you turn around that quickly."

He wrapped his arms around her waist. "You said you wanted to get away from everything. So, that's what I'm trying to do. Build the kind of world that we want to live in."

"I know," Nicole said, squeezing his hand affectionately. "But it's all so confusing. Like these legal papers your mother wants you to sign. Is she disinheriting you just because you married me? Am I being cut off from your money? Where do we stand?"

"Nicole, no matter what they do we'll still have enough to get a start down here," he laughed in her ear. "It's not as if you're going to have to get a job cooking hamburgers."

She turned on him abruptly. "Don't make a joke out of this. How much is marrying me going to cost you?"

"Millions," he answered, still wearing a sly grin. "I plan to let you work it off in personal services."

She pushed him away. "You're losing your whole fortune on account of me, aren't you?"

"Nicole, I don't care what I'm losing. We're together, and we're both making a fresh start. Isn't that what we want?"

"Do we know what we want? What does either of us know about starting a business? And in Belize? Do we really have any idea of who's who down here?"

He pulled her close and kissed her neck. "Not a clue. But we'll figure it out. Come to bed."

He started to close the shutters, but Nicole stopped him. "You go back to bed. I need to just stand here and think for a while. There are things I have to decide for myself. Adjustments that I'll have to make."

Jonathan nodded and padded off back to the bedroom, yawning on the way. Nicole resumed her brooding vigil, almost as if she were waiting for a light signal from a distant ship.

She had plenty of time to think during the next few days. Jonathan was off making the rounds of banks and real-estate agents. She was left to lounge by the pool and order lunch in the cabana. He returned each night brimming with exciting tales of his ventures. He had visited all the banks in the city and decided on one that was really a branch of a Chicago bank. His opening deposit had been two million dollars. Then he had been looking over land maps. Property could be had inexpensively at the northern end of Ambergris Cay, but that struck him as too far from the action. "Maybe in ten years the whole cay will look like Cancún, but in the short run I think we need to be at the southern end." There was a property he was going to visit within the next few days and he wanted her to come along with him. "It won't be much to look at, so I'm going to need your imagination," he told her. And then the boat! That might prove to be a problem. The local boats were basically workboats, and there wasn't a shipyard he would trust to do a conversion. But there was one old yacht over by Belize City that might need nothing more than refurbishing. He'd like to see what she thought about it.

They had romantic dinners by the edge

of the pool, or in a small dining pavilion that was right on the beach. They sipped a bottle of wine through dessert and then for another hour as he talked and she listened. Each night, when they returned to their cabana, there were telephone calls waiting, from Alexandra, Jack, Pam, and now even from Ben Tobin. Jonathan made quick work of all of them, but still it seemed to take over an hour before he could join her in the bedroom. He would brief her while he was undressing. Alexandra had to have legal papers signed right away. Either he had to go back or someone would have to come down. Jack had noticed the funds transfers to the bank in Belize. "Those places aren't any better than hock shops," he had complained. Pam wanted pictures. Where were they staying? What were they doing? Would they mind if she came down for just a weekend? Ben had been skydiving up in the Adirondacks with a guy who claimed he knew Nicole. Did she remember Harry Gillman? He said he used to jump with her?

She didn't want to play hostess to Alexandra's lawyers or accountants or whatever they were. She would love to have Pam come and join them for a few days. And no, she didn't know anyone named

Harry Gillman, and certainly had never jumped with him. And then they made love, passionately and aggressively, but not with the same joy they had experienced on their honeymoon. Both of them were nervous and edgy.

Nicole spent an afternoon in San Pedro, browsing in shops that were either too primitive or too touristy. The next day she rode a dilapidated ferry to Belize City looking for down-and-dirty work clothes that would be more suited for exploring land parcels and climbing down to the bilges of old fishing boats. On the ferry, she noticed a man in a tropical sport shirt who had been in some of the San Pedro stores. Then she noticed him again in Belize City. Alexandra's people, she thought, envisioning the Donners' private army of security guards. But she became annoyed when he seemed to dog her every movement.

"You're following me," she said, turning on him at the entrance to a sidewalk café. He protested, in New York–accented English. "You're working for the Donners, aren't you?" More denials. "Then who, Sound Holdings?"

He pushed a card into her hand. "Call him! He'll explain." She glanced down at Jimmy Farr's name.

"I don't want this," she said, pressing the card back into his hand.

"Just call him," he repeated, and then he bolted away.

Nicole settled down at a table and ordered lemonade. Then she thought better of it and switched to a vodka tonic. Jimmy Farr's name was frightening in itself. The fact that he had known about her romance and then her escape to Belize was terrifying. That was why he had sent someone to stalk her. He wanted to demonstrate that he was watching her every move, and that he had the muscle on the scene to punish her transgressions. She had come into a great deal of money and Jimmy was trying to cut himself in. He wouldn't be easily dissuaded.

It was time to run again. Except that Jimmy wasn't easy to escape. For the past two years he had been lurking silently in the background, only to step forward as soon as she had something he wanted. This time, she would have to get farther away. But as she sipped her drink, Nicole had another thought. Maybe she should call him. His hold on her was the threat of revealing the seamier activities of her past. Wouldn't he be shocked when he learned that Alexandra Donner had already dug up all the dirt? There was nothing left that he could use as blackmail. And wouldn't he be devastated to learn that she was probably going to be disinherited. "We've been kicked out, Jimmy. The Donners giveth, and the Donners taketh away."

TWENTY-FOUR

The land agent picked up Jonathan and Nicole at the hotel and drove them in a battered Jeep out to see what he called "The perfect parcel. High priced, but a tremendous value considering the location." They bumped through underbrush, kicking up swarms of mosquitoes, and sending snakes slithering off behind trees. They splashed through stagnant marshes and sunk into fields of mud. When they reached the water, there was no beach, just tangles of mangroves and thickets of water lilies. The agent kept referring to the ease of "draining some of the swamps," and "digging canals so that the muck could be used to build up the land." He clearly envisioned the access roads and the great resort hotel rising out of the jungle. Neither Nicole nor Jonathan could rise to his level of enthusiasm. They agreed to try again and look at different sites.

"I didn't think we'd get out of there alive," Nicole said when they were back at their hotel. "It was the first time I ever thought seriously that I might get swallowed up in quicksand."

"It would cost a fortune just for infrastructure," he answered, passing over her comments about impending death. "We need something more solid to start with."

The neglected yacht was an even bigger disappointment. The hull was shabby, flaked with sea growth and rust. The permanent halo of oil that she floated in was an unmistakable indication of leaky bilges. Inside, the cabin plan was attractive even though the spaces were stained with mildew. But the insulation on the wiring crumbled in his fingers, and the twin diesel engines had obviously been pirated for spares.

"I suppose we could tow it up to the Gulf Coast and put her in a yard for a year," Jonathan mumbled, looking to find some hope for the boat.

"Tow it?" Nicole laughed. "Out into the open sea? I'll bet she sinks the minute you untie her from the dock."

Jonathan went off to meet with another yacht broker who claimed to have found "exactly what you're looking for," in Galveston.

"Probably an old oil tanker," he told Nicole when she seemed aghast at the idea of going to Texas. "I'm sure it's nothing. Why don't you stay here while I look her over?"

She was back in San Pedro shopping for a straw hat when she felt a hand on her shoulder. She started to turn, but the hand held her rigid. "You don't need to see me. You know who I am."

She did. It was the American who had given her Jimmy Farr's phone number. "You didn't call," he said from behind her.

"I've been busy," she answered, trying to sound more confident than she felt. Her knees were unsteady and she knew she had no chance of running.

"This is your last message. Call before you annoy the man. He's just trying to make you rich." He reached down and pressed another card into her hand. "Just in case you lost it, here's the number." The grip relaxed on her shoulder. She turned, but all she saw was the colorful shirt disappearing into the stream of shoppers. Nicole found a telephone in a hotel and dialed the number. Maybe she could convince Jimmy that she and her husband had gone into exile. But when she heard his voice, she couldn't manage even a word. She hung up in despair.

Jonathan returned with a dismal report

on the boat. "You think the one you saw was a wreck," he chided. "This one is in the yard. They're afraid to try and put her in the water."

To break through the cloud of gloom that was enveloping them, they decided to devote a day to diving. He made the calls, rented equipment, and the next morning brought her aboard a charter boat with three other divers. Two hours later, they were skimming the soft coral gardens inside Half Moon Cay, and plunging down along the coral walls of the Blue Hole.

They went outside the Lighthouse Reef and dove at the very edge of the shelf. They were in twenty feet of water, peering down over the edge of a cliff where the depth fell off to three hundred feet and the light from the sky vanished long before the bottom could come into view. Even the beam from the dive master's searchlight was swallowed up in the indigo mist before it could find the end of the cliff.

They were rejuvenated on the ride back to their hotel. The diving had brought them back to the fanciful world they had talked about, and let them forget the harsher realities that awaited them back on land.

But when they entered their cabana, the

telephone messages were waiting. Alexandra had someone on the way down with important papers for both of them. Jack had found a better bank that Jonathan should transfer funds to. Pam was planning on coming down the following weekend.

"Let's move back out to the cottage we had on our honeymoon," Nicole suggested. "There aren't any telephones out there and there's no cell phone coverage."

Jonathan argued that he still had business on the mainland.

"Then let's hire our own boat. Like we did last time."

He could tell that it was important to her, so he went down to the front desk and hired one of the island cottages. When they checked out, he left instructions with the desk clerk that their new address was to be kept confidential, and sealed the bargain with a twenty-dollar tip.

TWENTY-FIVE

"Victor can't find them," Alexandra told her husband over the telephone. "They checked out of their hotel."

"Victor Crane is a lawyer, for God's sake, not a detective. He can't find his own ass with both hands."

"Then we'll have to get security people down there. They have to be found."

Jack sighed in exasperation. "What's the great rush? They'll be coming back in a few days. A week at the most. Jonathan will run out of socks and he'll need you to tell him what he ought to do about it."

"I doubt it," Alexandra snapped. "He has his wife to make the difficult decisions for him, and I don't trust her. She's already made too many decisions for him."

"Like what?"

"Like rushing out to get married as soon as she learns we're investigating her. And then taking him to Belize as soon as I tell her that I know all her dirty secrets. We need to get matters settled before she persuades him to turn over his checkbook."

The thought of Nicole or even Jonathan writing checks got through to Jack. "Okay, I'll get someone down there. Tell Victor to stay put and find out where he can be reached. I'll put Lambert on it."

Jack sensed that he was losing control, and the downside risk was too big to ignore. His attorneys had taken him through the present state of Jonathan's funding, and reminded him that unless his son transferred back certain assets that had been hidden at his Cayman Island address, he was worth about thirty percent of the family fortune. Jonathan's last will, written while he was single, made no specific provision for his wife. Nor had there been any prenuptial agreement. Should he die, his wife would automatically get half of what he legally owned, and she might be able to make a case for the other half. So, if Jonathan died, Nicole would own somewhere between fifteen and thirty percent of the family's assets. "That might end up being more than you own outright," the briefing had concluded.

He had discussed the situation with Alexandra and it wasn't a chance that she was prepared to take. She had all the corrective papers prepared. A new will that specified a modest bequest to Nicole and a financial settlement that limited her future claims on the fortune. She had them ready for their signatures when she heard that they had left the country and gone to Belize. Now, they had left the resort hotel, and her lawyers couldn't find them.

It would be worrisome enough if her son's greatest danger was clogged arteries. But Jonathan swam with the sharks and fell out of airplanes. One little mistake was all that it would take.

TWENTY-SIX

"Where are you?" Pam shouted into her telephone. "Dad has his militia out looking for you."

"Back on our honeymoon island," Jonathan laughed, "where their legal eagles and pencil pushers can't get at us. The only one we want to see is you."

He had motored across to San Pedro to meet with a realtor who claimed to have the land he was looking for. When he had come into signal range, he had placed the call on his cell phone.

"How do I get there?" Pam asked.

He gave her the name of an airline out of Miami that had a daily flight to Belize City. "I'll meet the flight tomorrow. Be on it."

He docked at the dive boat pier, figuring that his father's detectives would be watching the resorts and the yacht club. Then he slinked into town, wearing sunglasses and a straw hat as a disguise. It was only a matter of time before Greg Lambert would find him. The bribe he had laid on the desk manager to keep his whereabouts secret was nickels and dimes next to the hundreds that Lambert would offer. But still, he was enjoying the thrill of the chase.

When he docked on their island, Nicole was sunning by the cottage. She followed him inside to hear his good news. The real estate was promising, a smaller plot but with a better location. "No quicksand and no snakes," he told her. Then he mentioned Pam, and she was delighted that her sister-in-law was coming to visit. Jonathan suggested that he could get her a suite at the resort, and that they could use the suite for the inevitable meetings with Alexandra's lawyers. But Nicole wouldn't hear of it. "She'll stay here with us. I can fix up the sofa. Then I'll have someone to talk with when you're off meeting with land barons and yacht brokers."

One of Lambert's people spotted Jonathan the next day at the Belize City airport, and then followed him down to the waterfront. But he lost contact when Jonathan and Pam sped away in the powerboat. Guessing that they were headed out to one of the cays, Lambert focused his search and soon came up with the location. "I can bring the lawyers out to the island," he told Alexandra when he made his report, "but they don't have electricity or communications out there. It's not much of a location for business discussions." Alexandra agreed it would be better to have the meeting at one of the mainland hotels. "And are you aware that your daughter has joined them? She flew in this afternoon."

Pam had immediately made herself at home, ecstatic over the island paradise they had found. She had gone through the house wild with enthusiasm, admiring the decor, the facilities, and even the comfort of the sofa that would be her bed. "It's the perfect honeymoon hideaway," she gushed, and promised that when she got married, this was the spot she would choose.

They sat out on the porch, sipped cold beer from their ice chest, and talked until the sun turned the sea into reds and purples. "You're never going to be able to leave this place," Pam said when the last trace of fire had spilled into the water.

"We're not planning to," Jonathan said, reaching down from the hammock to take Nicole's hand. "This is home."

Pam was shocked, even though she knew all about her brother's scheme for starting up some sort of business. She had just never thought that he would carry through with the idea. In the past, few of his plans had ever made it through a weekend. Nor had she realized that a business in the tropics would mean living in the tropics. She had fully expected that no matter what became of his newest venture, he and Nicole would be coming home. Maybe not to Rockbottom or Newport — she was aware of the coldness between her mother and her sister-in-law — but certainly to the city. That was where all the family business activity was centered.

Pam smiled and gushed as Jonathan and his wife outlined their still sketchy plans. The charter boat, leading to arrangements with the resort hotels, and finally their own resort for vacationing divers. "I saw the land yesterday," he said, and described the plot that fronted the water on the east side of Ambergris Cay. "It's more than I planned to spend," he allowed. "And it looks as if we're going to have to design and build the boat we need, so that's another small fortune. Maybe you'll want to buy in when you get your trust funds."

"That's five more years," Pam answered. She held up her bottle. "We'll be out of beer by then!"

They all boated over to San Pedro the next day, and docked at the dive boat pier. Pam needed to shop for scuba gear, and she took their air tanks to be refilled.

Nicole and Jonathan went into town for a meeting with a yacht broker who might put them onto a yacht designer and a builder. In the process, they let themselves be seen at the bank where they knew Greg Lambert's agents were watching, and then found themselves meeting with Greg and Victor Crane for lunch.

Jonathan apologized for the runaround he had given his parents' agents, but didn't see why it was so important to have a few papers signed. "We'll be back up to New York in a few weeks and we can take care of it then. Right now, there are a hundred other things on my mind."

Patiently, the attorney explained that Jonathan's marriage to Nicole had thrown the family's financial structure into disarray. "You can't marry without making provisions for your wife," he explained with a deferential nod to Nicole. "A man of your wealth can't leave these things up in the air." Then he focused on Nicole and explained delicately that her call on the assets of the Donner family had to be defined. Otherwise she or her heirs could wait years while their inheritance was tied up in court proceedings. "If anything should happen to your husband . . ." He tried to continue, but Nicole nodded that she understood. If Jonathan died, a limited amount would be paid over to her immediately. But if she inherited all his claims on the estate, then those claims would be fiercely contested.

"They want me to sign a prenuptial agreement after the wedding," she said to Jonathan.

He shrugged. "Is that a problem?"

She shrugged. "Not to me."

Crane produced several documents from his briefcase. He began unscrewing the cap of his fountain pen, but Jonathan didn't reach for it. Instead he scooped up the documents. "We'll read these and get back to you," he said, and he stood and offered his hand.

"Tomorrow?" Crane asked hopefully.

"Not tomorrow," Nicole interrupted. She looked at Jonathan. "We're taking Pam out diving tomorrow."

Jonathan agreed. "We'll get back to you in a few days. Why don't you go home and we'll call you in New York?"

Crane frowned. "Your mother was quite specific —"

"Well then wait down here at the hotel," Jonathan answered. "But get yourself some shorts and sport shirts. You'll die in your suit and tie!"

They walked back to the boat where Pam was loading the newly filled air bottles. Jonathan took over the loading, bringing aboard the provisions he had ordered, while Pam showed Nicole the wet jacket and diving gear. "All set for tomorrow," she announced happily. Jonathan threw off the lines and headed back to their island.

TWENTY-SEVEN

They spent the evening sitting on the edge of their dock, their feet dangling into the water. Pam recounted her dives in the Cayman Islands, the Florida Keys, and off the Blue Coast of Turkey. She was clearly proficient, and looking forward to trying the Belize barrier reef. Nicole admitted she was still a bit timid about going deep, but it didn't matter because there were so many shallow areas that she could enjoy. Jonathan praised his wife's progress and assured her that she was ready for anything.

The subject strayed back to the family problems. Nicole wondered if Alexandra had softened a bit in her opinion of her new daughter-in-law.

"Mother? Soften?" Pam looked at her brother and they both broke out laughing. "Don't get me wrong," Pam finally managed. "Mom's great. But not soft. She's a driver and a motivator. But if she has a tender side, she never shows it."

"Alexandra will get to love you," Jonathan added. "But don't expect flowers.

She'll say something like, 'For a scheming little guttersnipe, you certainly have developed some remarkable qualities.' That will be your cue that she's crazy about you."

"One of my boyfriends used to call her the drill sergeant," Pam said through her laughter. "Every time she saw him she'd order him to 'stand up straight,' and 'walk as if you know where you're going.' And he was the one she really liked."

But then they put the joking aside, and Pam agreed that Nicole was in for a long and difficult battle. "Once she gets an idea in her head she protects it as if her brain were a vault." She told about her own efforts to pursue her interest in art. Her father regarded artists as "flakes," who could do more good by painting some of the houses they lived in. Her mother thought that real art was hanging in the museums she sponsored, and that all genuine artists were already dead. So Pam had taken the business and financial courses that her father selected, gone to the schools her mother chose, and taken a job as a financial manager for one of Alexandra's orchestras. She wouldn't be able to make her own decisions until she got her hands on her trust fund. "I've talked with Ben about ways that I might be able to start a gallery. Any scheme that gives me enough money involves having Jack as a partner, or at least as a backer. I'd hate to see the kind of art that he'd hang on the walls!"

They were all a bit tipsy from the margaritas they had been sloshing and the conversations began to lag.

"Guess you two want to get to bed," Pam said so that her brother and sister-in-law could make their getaway.

"We usually go for a swim first," Nicole answered.

"Skinny-dip?" Pam was enthused.

"Well, when we're alone —" Jonathan started, but Pam was already up on her feet and pulling her T-shirt over her head. She stripped off her shorts, stepped out of her clogs, and dove off the edge.

Jonathan and Nicole waited until her face broke through the surface. "C'mon . . . it's fabulous." They looked at one another, shrugged, and then stripped to the skin. A second later, the three of them were bobbing in a circle, talking enthusiastically about their plans for the next day.

TWENTY-EIGHT

They left very early, ghosting over the flat water at near idle speed so that they wouldn't shatter the morning. As the sky brightened, Jonathan pushed the throttle until the boat was just skimming the surface. It was a ten-mile ride out to Lighthouse Reef, and they made it in half an hour. Nicole pulled out their matching blue wet jackets, and Pam began untying the red-and-black jacket she had just bought.

He steered away from the coral to the sandy bottom inside the reef where he could anchor. They all put on tanks, adjusted their masks, and tried breathing through the mouthpieces. Then, one by one, they dropped off the swim platform into fifteen feet of water, alive with stingrays that were rippling across the bottom. Jonathan paused an instant to check the anchor line and then pointed to the reef, its wildly colored life clearly visible in the distance. The water was warm and crystal clear with enough sunlight slanting through so that they could see their shadows on the bottom. When they neared the reef they were greeted with dense schools of ridiculous looking fish. As they flew among the coral spires, sea turtles scattered, and barracuda eyed them uneasily. The divers were ecstatic. They kept poking one another and pointing out the underwater sights, then swimming crazily from one point to another in order to see it all and take everything in.

When they were back aboard, they sat together on the swim platform, laughing together as they stumbled over descriptions of what they had just experienced. Then they peeled off the tanks and motored over to the shore where Jonathan beached on a narrow spit of sand. They hauled out their coolers into the shade of a few sparse trees, downed the soft drinks they had chilled, and nibbled on the seafood sandwiches that Pam had helped Nicole put together.

"Are you sure you don't want to buy into our plans?" Jonathan teased his sister. "Just put up ten or fifteen million. I promise you an office with a window."

"Where do I sign?" she answered. But then her eyes became serious. "In five years maybe, if there's anything left when you get done."

"We'll take a note," Nicole said, trying to keep things light. She looked over at Jonathan. "We're really going to make this work, aren't we?"

He remembered her brooding mood when she stood in their room by the open door, and he was thrilled by her change in attitude. "You're damn right we're going to make it work. And Pam, if you want in, you're a full partner."

"A full partner in a patch of rain forest and a rusty boat," Nicole said, and they all rocked in laughter.

In the afternoon they were back in the water exploring other miles of wildly alive coral, and bumping noses with fish of every description. When they surfaced, they were several hundred yards from their boat and took a long, tiring swim back to the platform. It was afternoon, with the sun now high in the sky, and they gathered under the canvas top to find shade.

"Quite a day," Jonathan said, still amazed at all they had seen.

"One more dive," Pam urged.

Jonathan looked skeptical. "We've been down a long time." He checked his watch. "More than three hours underwater . . ."

"We were only at thirty feet," Pam argued. "Most of the time less than that. As far as our bodies know we never got out of the boat."

He turned to Nicole. "You up for it?"

"Sure," she said. "I'd like to go back down to the wreck."

"Okay," Jonathan agreed. He was on his feet quickly and pulling up the anchor. "We'll anchor on the ledge and then swim out to the edge of the trench." He started the engine and pointed the bow to the southern edge of Lighthouse Reef.

Nicole went forward and brought back new tanks. They began getting into their gear while they turned the reef and headed north along the seaside shore. Jonathan studied his charts to bring them opposite the wreck. The depth finder, pinging merrily at thirty feet, assured him that he was on the edge of the barrier. He maneuvered slowly to a bearing off the lighthouse and then killed the engine. He dropped the anchor and kept checking its hold while he slipped into his wet jacket. The women were already dressed and helping one another with their equipment. Pam had connected the regulators and equalizers to the new tanks and Nicole was lifting one onto her back.

They ran their final equipment checks. Pam dropped over the side. Nicole was about to put on her tank when Jonathan remembered his underwater lamp. They both set down their tanks while they went forward to look. Then they helped each other on with their gear, and fell over together. Jonathan lingered a minute to play the light on the anchor, made sure it was set, and then kicked off in pursuit of the women.

TWENTY-NINE

Within seconds he was over deep water. The longest barrier reef in the Americas ran parallel to the Belize coastline. It had formed over the ages along the edge of a continental shelf, where the ocean floor dropped precipitously from the North American landmass into the Cayman Trench. Lighthouse Reef was an outcropping of the barrier. Leaving it was like stepping off the edge of the Grand Canyon, moving from the security of water that was only thirty feet deep and entering a sea that was nearly bottomless. He could see the cliff wall in the beam of his light, but it fell steeply into the darkness with no end in sight.

The ship had run aground on the reef, tearing out its bottom on a highpoint in the coral formation. Most likely it had settled with its masts still showing above the surface. But gradually, over the years, it slid down the cliff wall, catching on a ledge about fifty feet down. There it broke open, spilling its contents in a debris field that stretched down the wall and into the depths. Salvage divers had picked up all the valuables long ago, but there was still an exciting trail of artifacts.

Jonathan saw the women below, swimming one behind the other toward the skeletal remains of the wreck. For an instant, he had them squarely in the beam of his light. Then he lost sight of them, unable to keep the lamp aimed. He found them again, but his mask seemed cloudy. They were vague shapes, coming in and out of focus. Then the lamp turned and slipped out of his hand. He grabbed for it, missed, and watched the light fall away, the beam wandering as the lamp twisted. He kicked down in his effort to catch up with it.

Nicole had fallen behind Pam. She hesitated when she saw the light fall, seemingly confused as to whether she should swim toward Jonathan, or try to catch up with Pam. She checked her gauges, fussed with the mouthpiece, and pulled on the hose that pumped air into the bladder of her wet jacket to keep her buoyancy neutral. Then she kicked up and headed back to the surface.

Pam turned to look for Nicole. She saw a distant figure swim upward, struggle, and then discard the weighted belt. At the same time she saw the lamp falling freely, growing dimmer in the depths. Jonathan, she decided, must have run into difficulty, and shed the lamp and weighted belt in order to get back to the surface. But then where was Nicole? Pam turned in a circle, looking both up into sunlight and then down into the darkness. Get the lamp, she thought.

Jonathan couldn't find either of the women. He had gone down below the wreck chasing the lamp, but had been overcome by fatigue. His arms and legs suddenly felt leaden, and he was having difficulty keeping his mind focused. It was as if he were out of air, falling into a coma of asphyxia. But his gauge showed plenty of pressure, and he could taste the air coming into his mouth. Forget the damn light, he thought. Find the girls and signal that he was going back up.

But they were gone. He couldn't find either of them. The darkness enveloped the wreck and the sunlight was fading. For a moment he was disoriented, uncertain which way was up. He felt panic welling up inside him. Jonathan shook his head, trying to clear the cobwebs. He reset his mouthpiece and reached for the clasp on his belt. Relax, he told himself. Take a few slow, deep breaths. Then swim up easily. You've been down much deeper than this. You know you can make it back.

Pam, too, gave up on the flashlight. It was falling too fast and taking her too deep. She turned and kicked back up along the wall of the cliff. Get back to the wreck, she thought. That's where Nicole would go. Once she knew she was separated she would head for the wreck. Pam swam along the debris field, able to see much more clearly as she rose into the sunlight. The sunken ship appeared directly ahead of her and she swam to it rapidly, scanning left and right. But there was no one — not even the telltale bursts of bubbles that mark a diver's position with each breath.

She noticed a trace of air bubbles off to her right. It was a continuous stream as if someone's air hose was venting directly to the sea. Pam looked down along the trail of rising air but could see no one. She turned and headed back down knowing that the bubbles would lead to a diver.

As soon as Nicole broke the surface, she tore off her mask and gulped hungrily for air. She could see the boat, still a good distance away, bobbing in the light sea. But now, on the surface, the compressed air tank weighed her down, and there was no air in the bladder of her jacket to keep her afloat. She unbuckled the straps and slipped them over her shoulders. Just get closer to the boat, she told herself. Once she was up over the reef she could just drop the tank. It would be easy to retrieve her equipment in shallow water. But the tug of the tank's weight was more than she could overcome. She was laboring and getting nowhere. She let go of the straps, caught a few deep breaths and then set out for the boat.

Pam followed the airstream but she was getting no closer to the source. The water was murky and the bubbles came up from the depths. Had Nicole discarded her tank and gone to the surface? Perhaps when she saw Jonathan having difficulty she went up after him. There was no sign of her, and the source of the escaping air was far below the depth that Nicole would try. Pam turned around and headed back up, this time slowly. She had gone deep and rushing back up to the normal pressure at sea level could be very dangerous.

Nicole pulled herself up onto the swim platform and unzipped her jacket. Then she sat panting, her feet still dangling in the water. The effort to get back to the surface had been tiring. Then the swim to the boat, even without the weight of her scuba gear, had drained her. She scanned the water out toward the sea. There was no sign of either Jonathan or Pam. Slowly, she pulled herself to her feet and rolled over the transom.

Pam exploded out of the water right behind the boat, and looked up for a helping hand. She called to Jonathan to lift the tank from her shoulders but there was no response. She unbuckled the straps, pushed her tanks up onto the swim platform and climbed aboard.

"Jonathan?"

"Pam?" Nicole appeared, looking down from the cockpit. "Where's Jonathan?"

Pam looked up, her eyes suddenly wide with fright. "He came up earlier. I saw him. He was having some sort of equipment problem."

Nicole shook her head. "No, that was me. He must still be down at the wreck."

"I saw Jonathan," Pam nearly screamed. "He dropped the lamp and shed his belt."

"Then he must have gone back down. He wasn't in the boat when I came aboard."

"Oh, my God," Pam said. "Help me. Quick!"

She slung her tank over one arm and then turned so that Nicole could lift it onto her shoulders. “I’m sure he’s okay,” Nicole said as she adjusted Pam’s gear. “He knows what he’s doing.”

“He wasn’t on the wreck,” Pam said. “I looked all over . . .”

She pulled the mask over her face and then bit down on her mouthpiece. Then she stepped off the platform and disappeared under the surface.

Nicole moved instantly to the forward locker and lifted out another compressed air bottle. But then she remembered that she had lost her regulator and harness when she shed the extra weight of her tank. The new air supply was useless. She lowered into the seat at the helm, and stared out over the water, beginning an anxious vigil.

What could she do? Pull the anchor and motor out closer to the wreck? That would put her nearer the divers but move her away from where they would expect the boat to be. Best to stay put, she decided.

Maybe she should get on the radio and call for assistance? But there was no emergency. Despite the frightened look in Pam’s eyes, Jonathan had been down for less than half an hour. She couldn’t declare an emergency just because she had aborted her dive and come up early. She lifted the binoculars and searched for air bubbles that should be trailing Pam as she searched the bottom. She could see nothing except the relentless churning of the sea. All she could do was wait.

It was twenty minutes before Pam reappeared at the bow, holding onto the anchor chain. "Is he back?" she called.

"No! No sign of him."

Pam tore off her mask. "He has to be up. I searched everywhere."

"I'm going to call for help," Nicole shouted back.

Pam nodded. "Good! Get on it. I'm going back down for another look."

"Do you need more air?" Nicole yelled. But Pam had already dropped under the waves.

Nicole fumbled with the radio. What was the emergency channel? Jonathan had told her but she didn't remember. Then she saw that it was marked. "RESCUE SERVICE — 18." She turned on the power, keyed in the channel, and pushed the "talk" button.

"Mayday! Mayday! Diver lost off Lighthouse Reef. Please come quickly. He's my husband."

THIRTY

She kept calling, her voice ever more frantic, until the police responded and promised that a patrol boat was on the way. "I need divers," she screamed. "He's down there somewhere. He's running out of time."

Pam pulled herself up onto the platform and pushed up her mask. Her eyes flashed panic as they searched the boat and then locked onto Nicole.

"The police are on their way," she said. But there was already resignation in her voice. She expected the worst.

"He has to be —" Pam began. She interrupted herself and picked up the binoculars. "Maybe he's on the reef." She panned the glasses across the shoreline. "Jesus, where are you?" she said almost in prayer. She was frantic when she lowered the glasses. "He's alive! He has to be alive," she shouted. Then she told Nicole, "He's a great diver. He knows how to get out of trouble." Nicole turned her head away.

The police were alongside their boat in twenty minutes and put a diver into the water. Minutes later a helicopter circled and two divers dropped out to join the search. Nicole sat on the deck of the police boat, wrapped in a blanket, sipping hot tea from a mug. She stared out blankly, her eyes searching the sea but seeing nothing. Pam was rolled up at the bottom of the cockpit, her chin on her knees, a blanket thrown over her head. She rocked gently, mindlessly, her eyes staring into space. She couldn't bring herself to watch the rescue efforts that were in progress all around her.

"You were out here all day?" the police officer asked.

"Yes. We were diving inside Half Moon. And then down in the Blue Hole. We decided on one last dive over the wreck before we headed home. We switched to fresh tanks and we all went down together."

"Down over the ledge?"

"Down as far as the wreck. Except I never got there. I had trouble with my tank and I came back up."

"Which tank were you using?"

"I had to let it go on the way up. It sank out there."

"You checked it before you put it on?"

"Of course," Nicole snapped.

"And it was full? Working properly?"

"It seemed to be, until I got down a

ways, and then it stopped working."

He nodded, and then knelt down next to Pam. She told him that she had thought it was her brother who had gone back up. He had dropped his light, and she dove down past the wreck to retrieve it, but it sank too fast. When she came back to the wreck she couldn't find the others. Thinking her brother had gone back to the boat, she thought she was looking for his wife. When she couldn't find her she figured that her sister-in-law had gone back to the boat, too. But when she surfaced Nicole was alone. It was her brother who was missing.

"I went back down," Pam said, her eyes still fixed on her futile search rather than present events. "I looked everywhere. There was nothing."

"He's an experienced diver?" the policeman asked.

"He should have been able to get back up no matter what went wrong." Pam suddenly jumped up and went to the rail where the police diver's ladder hung over the side. "Jesus, where is he? Doesn't anyone know something?" Suddenly she was crying hysterically.

Nicole tried to calm her but Pam wouldn't be consoled. "You have to find him," she cried to the inspector. The police made her comfortable in a canvas chair and wrapped her in a blanket. Nicole brought her hot tea. Then they sat staring out over the water, oblivious to the divers who broke the surface occasionally, received instructions from the circling helicopter and then dove back down. No one spoke what they all knew for certain. Jonathan had run out of air at least half an hour ago. This was no longer a rescue operation. They were looking for a body.

They searched until the sun faded behind the horizon. It was dark on the water when they started back with Jonathan's boat in tow. Nicole saw the lights twinkling along the shoreline when they made it back to Belize City. The police delivered them to the care of a trusted rooming house operator, and promised that their things would be brought over from the honeymoon island the next morning. Nicole dozed in a chair, her eyes slowly closing in exhaustion. It was nearly dawn when she finally fell asleep in the landlady's bed.

She awoke to voices in the parlor. She recognized the police officer's voice, and then the Americans that she and Jonathan had met in San Pedro. As she stood, she was aware of the strangeness of her surroundings. And she was in her bathing suit, wrapped in a terrycloth robe. Hesitantly, she eased open the door. The conversations stopped immediately. The woman, whom she recognized as the innkeeper, lifted a piece of luggage that was near the door and gave it to her. "Here's the bag you wanted brought from your cottage," she reminded Nicole. "Take your time, dear. There's no reason to rush. They'll wait for you." Then she steered Nicole into a bathroom that had an outdoor shower, found her some towels, soap, and shampoo.

"Will you wake Pam and tell her we have company?" Nicole asked.

"Your sister is already up. She said she needed to walk. She should be back in a few minutes."

When Nicole finally appeared, her hair was brushed and she had made an attempt at makeup. But her face was gaunt and her eyes still dead. She was in a blue shirt with white slacks, and sandals that didn't coordinate with anything. The officer was stunned that she seemed twenty years older than the woman he had delivered to the boardinghouse the night before.

Pam came through the front door at the same time, still in her bathing suit and shorts. The only thing she had taken from the clothes that the police brought to her was a gauze beach top that she wore as a blouse. The women embraced for a moment while the visitors stared down at the floor.

Victor Crane, the lawyer, then embraced each of them with a brief word of sympathy. He was still in the suit and tie that Jonathan had advised him to shed. Greg Lambert, the Donners' security chief, took their hands.

Crane alluded to the papers that had seemed so urgent only a few days before. "Under the circumstances, these can certainly wait. But I thought you might need some help with the legalities of the tragedy."

Greg Lambert was more at ease than the lawyer. "The police have everything under control," he said with a nod to the police officer. "But if I can help you in any way . . ." They all waited for the ladies to sit and then sat in a semicircle in front of them.

"I regret that your husband's . . . body . . . has not yet been found," the police officer began with genuine sympathy. "But the search continues. We are bringing in a miniature submarine that can go to the bottom with powerful lights. We will certainly recover . . ." The words tailed off as inconclusively as the search.

Then the officer read back the information they had provided the night before. Both women nodded as he repeated their words even though the words seemed different. The facts were bare and cold with none of the emotion that each of them had felt.

"Now just a few more points, if I may," the officer said, taking a pen from his shirt pocket. He asked where the tanks had been filled, who brought them aboard, and how they were stored. He noted their responses and concluded, "Then they were always in your possession. Never out of your sight except when they were stored in your boat during the night."

"Yes," Nicole said. Pam nodded in confirmation.

He asked Pam why she had thought it was Jonathan who had run into trouble and gone back to the surface. "I guess because he had dropped the light." She was having a difficult time reciting the events without breaking into tears.

"That's all, that's all," the policeman assured her. He turned his attention to Nicole who was much more composed and asked her to describe the problems that had brought her back to the surface.

"Trouble drawing air," she answered. "As if the line were blocked, or the regulator was malfunctioning. I had air, and then I didn't."

Why hadn't she brought the tank and the other gear back to the boat when she reached the surface?

"I couldn't swim with it. It was weighing me down. So I dropped it when I thought I was back over the reef. I thought that Jonathan would simply dive down and retrieve it."

He pressed for details. Why hadn't she alerted the others when she decided to go back up? Wouldn't it have been safer if the others came along with her? When she knew there was a problem, why didn't she take fresh equipment and go back down?

Nicole's words broke up as she started to answer. She was fighting to hold back the tears. Victor Crane asked if the questioning might not be postponed. "I think, for the present, our main concern should be locating Jonathan's body." The officer nodded and closed his notebook. When he left, the Donners' attorney and security officer repeated their offers of help. Victor

Crane would take care of their local accounts and make arrangements for Jonathan's body, should it be recovered. Greg Lambert would stay on top of the police to assist the search and answer open questions.

The main issue, they both stressed, was to get the two women back home.

THIRTY-ONE

Alexandra wasn't buying any of it. "An accident? How convenient for her! Just hours before Jonathan would have signed a new will and had her sign a financial agreement."

Jack was deflated, showing none of his boundless energy. He was wearing a white shirt over the trousers from one of his business suits, a combination that he generally wouldn't tolerate. "There's nothing to implicate her. Nothing to suggest that it wasn't an accident."

He had talked with Pam who said her brother "had just vanished." She had been down with him; Nicole had gone back up to the boat. When she came up, Jonathan wasn't there. Jack had also been on the phone with Greg Lambert, following step-by-step the details of the search and investigation. There was no trace of Jonathan's body. The area where he was diving was at the edge of Lighthouse Reef, thirty feet of water that fell suddenly to over three hundred feet. The prevailing current was strong right up to the reef. It was entirely possible that his body would never be found.

"Is there anything else I can do down here," Lambert had asked, "besides escorting the ladies back to New York?"

"Yeah . . . ask around. Jonathan had made arrangements with a bank and a couple of land companies. Make sure that there's nothing else. Nothing in her name, or that they jointly owned."

Alexandra was in a dark dress that looked particularly out of place on the sun-drenched patio. But that was her only concession to mourning. Her hair was styled and her makeup flawless. There was a box of tissues at her elbow but the wastepaper basket under the table was empty. She knew she would cry over the loss of her son, but that was something she would do in private.

Victor Crane had returned from Belize the previous night and had arrived at Rockbottom before breakfast. In his dark suit, and with the somber expression on his long face, he might have been an undertaker. But he had three associates in tow who seemed to be from sequential classes of Harvard, Columbia, and Yale. Their counsel had been grim, indicating exactly how well Nicole would do. "Fifty million, but that's preliminary. We'll need several days to assemble an exact figure." They had listed Jonathan's assets as only twenty million in themselves, the long-established trust funds he had come into just last year. But he was the owner of record of fifty million dollars parked offshore, and it would be counterproductive to claim that those funds were really untaxed profits of Sound Holdings. Then there were trusts of which Jonathan was the beneficiary, set up to avoid the possibility of estate taxes. Nicole would have a claim on their value. The legalities were, understandably, very complicated. But the overall picture was clear: as Jonathan's wife, and in the absence of a specific bequest, the courts would rule Nicole entitled to a minimum of one half his wealth. The other half would be contestable. Making matters worse, it would be quite difficult to minimize Jonathan's paper wealth. In setting up the Donner trusts, no one had imagined that Jonathan would marry without a prenuptial agreement, and then die before his affairs could be reordered.

"No one but Nicole," Alexandra had chided her learned counsel. Then she had raised the point of Jonathan's body: without the body there was no proof of death. So, there would be no inheritance.

Victor Crane was pursing his lips before she finished. Although still in his forties, he had mastered all the expressions and mannerisms of an older, more learned man. "Technically, you're right," he agreed. "But given the circumstances, the presumption of death is strong. It won't take her very long to get a death certificate. And, in the meantime, she has full access to everything he left behind. His apartment, the car, stocks and bonds, checking account . . . Mrs. Donner can live quite nicely while she waits."

Jack had growled impatiently at the details. "So what do we do?"

The attorneys paused and glanced from one to another. Then Victor cleared his throat. "In matters such as these . . . it's often advisable to settle privately."

"Never!" Alexandra slapped the table to drive home her point.

Jack folded his hands on the edge of the table in front of him. He was listening.

"We can drag this out for quite a while, and keep her in court for maybe a year or two. That, plus the possibility that she might lose, could be used as an incentive to take a lesser amount free and clear."

"Why should we agree to pay her anything?" Alexandra demanded.

"Because it's highly probable that in the end she would walk off with much more. And, during the litigation, financial arrangements would be brought to light that are best kept confidential." The lawyer focused on Jack who knew exactly what "financial arrangements" he meant. A thorough investigation of all Jonathan's affairs might involve Jack and Sound Holdings with the Internal Revenue Service, the Securities and Exchange Commission, and maybe the federal prosecutor.

"But wait until we have all the numbers and have done a tight review on the law involved. There may be a better way to handle this, and you'll want a decent interval anyway before approaching the widow with an offer."

THIRTY-TWO

Nicole and Pam landed at LaGuardia Airport and were met by a limousine sent from Rockbottom. The driver's instructions were to bring them both back to the estate where the rest of the family waited in mourning. But Nicole countermanded the instructions and had the car take Pam by herself. She took a taxi to Jonathan's Manhattan apartment. There she spent the evening unpacking her suitcases and moving her things into the master closet. Twice the phone rang, once with a call from Ben, the other a call from Jack. She let the machine handle both promising herself that she would return them as soon as she was settled.

There was a lot that she had to do. There would be a cold welcome awaiting her out on the North Shore and she had no desire to meet Alexandra face-to-face. On the flight up from Miami she had decided not to accept a room in the main house, or even use of the caretaker's cottage, but instead, to move into Jonathan's Manhattan apartment and keep her distance from the family. So, there were the housekeeping arrangements of closing down her own apartment, gathering her own things, and arranging for Jonathan's belongings to be delivered to his family home.

Then, there were the legal implications. She knew that there would be an avalanche of attorneys bearing papers for her signature, most of which she wouldn't understand. She needed to find a legal firm that wasn't on retainer to the Donners or to any of their business holdings.

Finally, there were the few allies she had won over in her brief appearances as Jonathan's woman. Pam, of course, could be her advocate within the fortress, and Ben Tobin might be her legal representative. Jonathan had told her she could always count on Ben, but she had to wonder whether his loyalty would survive the assault of the Donner millions. She would have to meet with both of them and find out exactly where they stood.

Nicole had to steel herself. It was going to be a long and difficult battle, in the courts, and probably on the society pages. There were volumes of information about her past that would be dug up and used against her. There would be moments when she would welcome the chance to run off and hide in her previous obscurity. She had to be strong.

It was two days later when she called Rockbottom to announce that she was coming and then drove out to the North Shore in Jonathan's convertible. Her attire was intentionally toned down to her basic black without jewelry. The exceptions were her wedding and engagement rings, symbols of Jonathan's commitment to her. Her cosmetics were applied sparingly — a bit of lipstick and a hint of eyeliner. She didn't bring an overnight bag so she couldn't be coerced into staying.

She had a pleasant smile for Raymond, who offered his sympathies, and then she walked nearly the length of the house to Jack's study where she was told the family would be waiting.

Pam's greeting was emotional. She threw herself at Nicole, clutched her in an embrace, and burst into tears. They rocked in each other's arms for nearly a minute. Jack stood, crossed to her, and took her hand. They exchanged words of condolence. Alexandra remained seated in a leather chair that had been designed for a men's club. She had a cup of coffee balanced in her lap. Nicole went to her and bent to kiss her cheek. There was no response from Jonathan's mother. It was as if she had kissed a statue.

Jack began the conversation with random remarks about the tragedy and the great loss that they all shared. He had been demanding of his son, he admitted, but that didn't mean he hadn't loved him. "I was excited about his plans in Belize. He promised to share the details with me and I was looking forward to partnering with him." Then he mumbled assurances that Nicole was part of the family, and asked her if there was anything she needed. "You're welcome here, of course. But if you prefer the city . . . or Newport . . . just let us know."

Pam begged her to move into the caretaker's cottage. They had so much to talk about. She had lost her brother and wanted to be sure that her new sister didn't just drift away.

Alexandra got right to the point: there were legal matters and property questions that had to be settled. It might be easier for everyone if Nicole spent a few days at the house so that all the issues could be discussed. Nicole was noncommittal. She would give it some thought, but for the present, she wanted to be in Manhattan.

She was "between lives," and needed time to sort things out. Perhaps she would settle back into her old job and reclaim the career that she had just put aside.

She walked with Pam down to the cabana, borrowed a bathing suit, and went for a swim. They sat on the edge with their feet dangling into the water while they reminisced over the plans that Jonathan had made for a diving service and a first-class resort hotel.

"Are you going ahead with it?" Pam asked.

Nicole shook her head. She didn't think so. "That was Jonathan's dream, not mine. I would have done it for him. But that's not the kind of place where I want to spend the rest of my life." Pam was buoyed when Nicole assured her that there were many things they could do together. "Maybe that gallery you were thinking about," Nicole said. "That would be more to my liking."

They toweled, dressed, and walked back up to the house. Alexandra was waiting on the patio. "Nicole and I have to talk," she said, dismissing her daughter and gesturing Nicole into a chair. She had a pitcher of lemonade brought out from the kitchen.

"You said you were between lives," she began after the servant had left them alone. "I can understand that. Everything happened so quickly. It must be difficult for you to imagine what role you could possibly play in our family."

Nicole nodded. "It is difficult. Particularly when you've already told me that I'm a danger to the Donners and Sound Holdings."

Alexandra was pleased at Nicole's frankness. It would save a great deal of polite evasions. "I still feel that way, and I think with a little effort that you will appreciate my viewpoint. Jonathan's presence might have spared you open criticism and derision. But with him dead, and given the suspicious nature of his death, I'm afraid all gloves are off."

"Suspicious?" Nicole's antenna was up.

"Well, unresolved," Alexandra conceded. "Circumstances that make it difficult to tell exactly how he died."

Nicole set down her lemonade. "I've told the police and your investigators exactly how he died."

"Yes, of course you did. But there were only two witnesses, and Pam brings up different details every time she talks about it. Add that to the fact that you are the major beneficiary of his death and I think you can appreciate the probability of rumor and insinuation."

Nicole stood and broke through her cover of respect for the older woman. "You're the only one who has insinuated anything. So, if there are any rumors, I'll certainly know who started them."

"Sit down!" Alexandra ordered.

"No thank you. I'm about to leave."

Suddenly Alexandra was on her feet. "Jonathan wouldn't have died in some godforsaken jungle if you hadn't taken him there."

Nicole went toe-to-toe. "I wouldn't have taken him there if you hadn't set out to destroy his marriage. And it wasn't my idea to get away from you. It was his —"

Alexandra's simmering rage exploded. Her hand slapped viciously across Nicole's cheek. Nicole's eyes widened in shock. But in an instant her own hand was flying, returning the slap with even more energy. The force of the blow knocked Alexandra back a step until she reached the edge of her chair. Then she fell back into the seat.

Nicole gathered her purse and stormed off, her heels sounding like hammer blows against the polished wood floors of the house. Alexandra sat perfectly still, her hand to her burning cheek, her expression bewildered. In all her adult life, no one had dared to defy her, much less slap her across the face.

THIRTY-THREE

Nicole wore dark sunglasses to her luncheon meeting with Ben Tobin. It would be easy to say that her eyes were red from crying. There was no point in getting into the slight bruise on her cheek and her altercation with Jonathan's mother.

They had played phone tag for a few days and finally connected the previous evening. Ben was sympathetic and solicitous, suggesting a meeting in a small downtown restaurant where they were unlikely to be interrupted by friends of the family. He had taken her arm at the doorway, escorted her to the table as if she might not be able to walk on her own, and seated her with the care and concern usually afforded to arthritic dowagers. She laughed when he suggested a glass of sherry. "Ben, I'm not frail and damaged. I'm going to be just fine." She ordered a Bloody Mary, and then got right to the point.

She needed him to recommend a lawyer. Alexandra didn't want her to have any association with the Donner family, would probably try to have her marriage to Jonathan annulled, and would certainly contest her inheritance. It promised to be a long and painful battle. He offered his own services and those of his firm. He knew Alexandra fairly well and thought he might serve as a bridge between the two women.

"Can you live without the Donners' friendship?" she asked. "Because they'll turn on you the second you take my side. If you have any financial stake with Jack, or obligations to Alexandra, you won't be able to help me."

He assured her he was an outsider. Jonathan had been his significant link to the family. He had escorted Pam to a couple of parties and one or two of Alexandra's charity affairs. And he was providing Pam legal advice on the terms of her trust fund and her hopes of launching a business of her own. His answers to her detailed grilling seemed to satisfy her. By the time luncheon was served, Ben knew that Nicole was a formidable woman in her own right, and wouldn't need any help cutting her filet.

"There are two dangers," Nicole said to her new attorney. "One is the legal matter of Jonathan's estate. I need advice on my chances in court as opposed to my settlement value." He nodded without looking up from his lunch. "The other is more immediate. I'll need protection in case they decide to avoid any financial entanglements and simply have me killed."

He dropped his fork. "You can't be serious . . ."

"Very serious," she said. "Someone has already tried."

She told him about the intruder who had invaded their island villa during the honeymoon, and showed him a copy of the police report. "It wasn't a typical burglary," she pointed out referencing the report. "It seems that the man came to get me. He knocked me down and tried to drag me out of the house. If I hadn't managed to make enough noise to wake Jonathan, I'm certain I would have been found floating near the dock." She explained how they took nighttime swims off their private beach. "It would have been easy to guess that I had gone out on my own, dived off the dock, and hit something in the water."

"But why Jack and Alexandra?" he asked, still flabbergasted by the suggestion.

"Because they had used detectives to find out where we were. Nobody else knew."

Then she got into her suspicions about

Jonathan's death. "We were wearing identical wet suits. Pam thought that it was Jonathan who had gone back to the surface. Suppose someone else made the same mistake. Someone who was out there stalking us."

"You think Jonathan was killed by someone sent to kill you?" He was openmouthed in amazement.

"He was a good diver, Ben. You know that. He wouldn't have made the kind of mistake that would get him killed. And no one down there wanted him dead. He was about to become a big investor. But underwater, in an identical jacket, he could easily have been mistaken for me. It's the one explanation that answers all the questions."

"Nicole, I just can't believe —"

"The next morning," she went on, "before anyone in Belize knew he was dead, Jack's detectives and lawyers were on the scene. How did they know there was a problem? They were down there with papers to cut me off from Jonathan's money. Neither of us was anxious to sign."

"Still . . . it seems so far-fetched . . ." Ben was mumbling into space.

"It wouldn't, if you had been the one being dragged out of the house. The

Donners want me out of the way as quickly as possible. They'll try to buy me out, but if that doesn't work . . ."

"Nicole, why would you be such a problem for them?"

"Order us a glass of wine," she told Ben. "There are a few other things that you're going to have to know."

They sat for another hour while she laid out all the gritty details of her past. Her modeling, her work for an escort service, her involvement with drug smuggling, her affair with a director who might promote her career. She held nothing back, giving Ben a vivid description of the photographs that would probably turn up as evidence, and a rap sheet that might be uncovered by someone who dug far enough. It was a litany that Alexandra wouldn't want recited in front of her family and friends. But kill to keep it quiet? Could she possibly do that?

Could Jack do it? He was known to be ruthless in his business dealings. And if he felt that his wife was in danger of being embarrassed, or that his company's reputation might possibly be tarnished, he would undoubtedly do whatever was necessary to solve the problem. He had threatened several men who crossed him with financial and social ruin and he had always delivered on the threat. But have his daughter-in-law killed? That was outside of Jack's definition of reasonable. He wouldn't know the first thing about hiring a killer in New York, much less than in the Caribbean.

Of course, there were the security people. Ben had met some of them at the gate to the Donner home, and aboard the huge yacht that they sailed out of Newport. Well groomed, impeccably if unimaginatively dressed, invariably polite. But in their eyes they were all business, devoted to doing whatever it took to protect Jack and Alexandra from harm. If Jack explained a problem and told them to take care of it, they would. They wouldn't talk about the details and Jack would never ask.

He suggested that he make the first contacts with the Donners. "I can make it less legal, less confrontational. They'll know that I'm serving Jonathan's interests. And Pam will certainly polish up my credentials." Then he put her in a taxi and caught his own cab back uptown to his office where he briefed the partners on the firm's new client.

THIRTY-FOUR

Alexandra wasn't waiting for the legal dialogue to begin. She had talked several times with Greg Lambert who was still investigating the details of Jonathan's death, and backtracking over all of Nicole's activities since she and Jonathan had returned to Belize. She didn't like what she was hearing.

First was the report that Nicole was a very accomplished diver. The dive boat operators didn't believe that she was the novice she claimed to be. "She has good technique," one of the captains reported, "and confidence. New divers don't have confidence." She had pretended to be a novice at her husband's other venturous hobby. Apparently it wasn't true this time, either.

Nor was it true that she had been sunning by the pool when Jonathan was off meeting with bankers and real-estate speculators. Housemaids remembered her dressing immediately after Jonathan left in the mornings and leaving through the lobby. The concierge said she had requested the timetable for the ferry to Belize City, and he recalled that a local dive operator of questionable reputation had asked for her. "Doesn't amount to much," Greg Lambert had admitted. "She certainly could have gone shopping and made inquiries about boats. But I asked at the better stores. They have no sales receipts with her name."

To Alexandra, it *did* amount to much. Nicole had complained about wasting entire days by the pool, one of the reasons that Jonathan had included her in his later business meetings. That was just one more lie in what she was beginning to suspect was a pattern of lies.

Then there was the police report that said Nicole had gone down with a full tank of air and come back up early. There was no explanation for the difficulties she claimed to have had with her equipment. So, why wasn't she swimming beside her husband?

Finally, there was the woman at the guesthouse where the police had put Nicole and Pam when they were brought to shore. She remembered Pam as being emotionally wrecked, but Nicole being very much in control of herself.

It was this last report that enticed

Alexandra to make the trip down to Belize. "I just want to visit the site," she explained to Jack. "Maybe put a flower on the water. And I need to know that the authorities are doing everything they can to recover the body."

He argued that his people could do those things for her. But Alexandra wouldn't be dissuaded. "I need some closure," she explained.

Jack hired a private jet and had Greg Lambert meet the plane. Greg was a good manager and a good investigator, but he was also a physically intimidating presence, with a chiseled physique, thick neck, and set jaw. Alexandra would be safe under his protection. Greg chartered an oversize cruiser for the trip out to the reef where Jonathan had disappeared, and watched Alexandra throw roses over the side. He brought her out to the island where the newlyweds had had their honeymoon cottage, and waited while she walked the grounds and looked out from the end of the dock.

"If you wanted to kill someone, this would be the perfect place," Alexandra remarked.

"She was the one attacked," the security officer reminded her.

"Wouldn't that be her alibi? An intruder tried to kill both of them."

Alexandra found an ally in the police officer. The incident out at the island had never made sense to him. A thief would have stolen and fled. A kidnapper could easily have carried her off.

From the police station they went out to the waterfront rooming house where Nicole and Pam had spent the night. The landlady remembered that, unlike Pam, Nicole had been very specific about the bag she wanted brought from her cottage.

"One valise?" Alexandra asked.

"Yes, there was just one bag that she needed. She described it very carefully. The other woman didn't care what they brought her."

Alexandra glanced at Greg Lambert. "She'd already packed for her ordeal."

Jack Donner didn't want any trouble. He didn't want his personal finances or his business affairs aired in a courtroom, nor did he want his daughter-in-law's trashy past publicized for the delight of his business associates and society friends. There was always an easy way to handle affairs of this kind. All it took was an agreement between two reasonable people.

He had nothing against his son's wife other than the fact that she had reached too far. Of course she should have used better judgment in her early years, but those were the kinds of mistakes you made when you were desperately ambitious. He'd made a good many of them himself and escaped them only by blind luck. Like the time he had used a client's money to leverage a huge buy in an iffy stock. Had the stock gone down he would have had to sell everything he owned just to cover it. And even that might not have been enough. But the stock went straight up, and he easily covered his theft with the profits.

There was a great deal of good fortune involved in surviving youthful mistakes, and there was seldom anything to be gained by bringing them up again. Nicole would have done just fine if she hadn't latched on to Jonathan. It was that effrontery that sent Alexandra delving into her past.

The point was that the marriage was dangerous for all of them. And there was no need for a bare-knuckle fight. The basic issue was money and he certainly had more than enough of that. All he had to do was find a number that was reasonable to Nicole and persuade Alexandra that it was a small enough price to pay for peace and security. That was what he had in mind when he telephoned Nicole at his son's apartment and asked her to come into his office for a friendly meeting.

Once again she wore unadorned basic black, with her rings the only jewelry. When she was shown in, Jack jumped up and walked around his desk with an unusual display of concern. He personally set her chair at just the right angle and took her order for a bottle of spring water. With all the courtesies observed he clasped his hands on the edge of his desk, looked into her eyes, and began. "This all has to be tough as hell for you. How are you doing?"

Nicole shrugged. "Well enough, I suppose. I still find it hard to believe that he's gone."

"We all do," Jack agreed. "Especially Alexandra. She's in a daze and really doesn't know what she's saying. I hope you won't hold her little flare-up the other day against her."

Nicole returned his steady gaze. "It wasn't a little flare-up, Jack. It was a cold, calculated accusation. She accused me of killing him!"

He winced. "I'm sure she had no idea what she was saying. She's just so . . ."

"I think she knew what she was saying because she's said cruel things before. She told me I was an unsuitable wife for Jonathan, that I would bring ridicule and disgrace to the family, and the best thing I could do would be to get lost. You and I have to face the facts. Your wife hates me and wants me out of the way."

"It's all been so hard for her," Jack tried.

"That's because she kept Jonathan on a very short leash. She needed him to be dependent on her. That's why she hates me. Because with me, he didn't need her anymore."

He looked annoyed. "That's way over the top, Nicole. She was concerned for Jonathan, but she didn't want him tied to her."

"Yes, she did. But she blamed you. She told me you were the one who kept Jonathan around for your amusement, and robbed him of his courage and independence. But that wasn't true, was it? You liked the idea of him setting out on his own. You were ready to back his business venture."

"Of course! I wouldn't have held him back . . ."

"She used you as her cover, Jack. But when Jonathan turned to me it wasn't you who tried to destroy the relationship. It was Alexandra, and she still intends to destroy it."

Jack mumbled a few excuses for his wife. Distraught . . . under too much pressure . . . in need of a long rest. But then he moved to his agenda. What was the best way to straighten everything out? What could he do to bring peace back to his family?

"I'm Jonathan's wife," Nicole answered. "I think we all have to accept that fact."

"You're Jonathan's widow," he corrected gently. "And you're too young to stay a widow. Your future isn't with his family. As you said yourself, you're probably going to reclaim your old life. So, the real question is: What can we do to help you with the transition?"

"Just accept me. I have no intention of causing any problems for you and Alexandra. I even have some ideas for working with Pam."

The conversation wasn't going the way he had intended. He had expected that after a few polite evasions they would get to the money and that she would suggest the amount she had in mind. That would be her first offer. The agreed amount would probably be half the number she mentioned. Or, if Nicole remained evasive, he had a figure of his own. Three million dollars ought to meet her needs. Even if she buried it in government bonds, she would still be comfortable. He would start at two million, go grudgingly to three million, and top out at five million. Even at that amount it would be less than what he might have to spend on litigation.

But Nicole wasn't on the same wavelength. She didn't seem concerned about money. What she wanted was acceptance. She wanted all the privilege and prestige of Jonathan's wife even though Jonathan was gone. That's the one thing that Alexandra would never give her.

Jack knew that this wasn't the time to press for a deal. Business and financial agreements came in their own time. Hurry them, and you run the risk of egos colliding like seismic plates and sending out tidal waves.

"I'll talk to Alexandra," he said as he rose from behind his desk. "Probably not right away. I think it's best to put some space between her and Jonathan's death."

He took her hand and kissed her cheek. "We'll have to talk again very soon. And remember, if there's anything you need, don't hesitate to call me."

THIRTY-FIVE

Alexandra came home with fire in her eyes. She laid out all her evidence on Jack's desk and took him through it piece by piece. Nicole had lied her way into Jonathan's life pretending to be a novice jumper and later acting like a beginner at scuba diving. She had never revealed her seamy past, and when confronted with it had lured their son into a quickie wedding. Then, when assured that her marriage wouldn't stand up, she had taken Jonathan to an isolated island and out in a lonely boat. There could be only one reason. She had to make certain that he would never sign her out of his life.

"For God's sake, Alexandra. She may well be on the make. But a murderer? You're beginning to sound crazy. You go repeating this stuff and you're the one who will end up in an institution."

But she pressed on. "What kind of business dealings did the girl have down there? Where was she going when she left the hotel each day? And, in the final moments, why did she rush back up to the boat even though she had a full tank of air?"

"You're beginning to sound paranoid," he cautioned. "Pam was with Jonathan. It wasn't as if she left him to the sharks."

Then she dropped her most telling clue: Nicole had already packed for her overnight stay at the rooming house. Why would she pack things that she would have needed that evening when they returned to the cottage? Unless she was pretty certain that she wouldn't be returning.

She repeated her thread of circumstantial evidence to the attorneys who gathered on the patio. They listened, nodded, and even asked questions. "If your daughter-in-law was already back in the boat, how could she have harmed your son?" Alexandra thought she must have done something to damage his diving gear. "But they all checked one another's equipment," another lawyer pointed out. Alexandra answered that of course Nicole wouldn't have done anything obvious.

When her eyes weren't on the lawyers, they stole glances at one another. Alexandra sounded as if she could use a long vacation. When she finished, Victor Crane apologized that he and his colleagues couldn't really act on her information. "What you're suggesting would be a criminal charge, which would have to be handled by the police and through the district attorney's office."

At that point Jack jumped in to lay down the ground rules. "We don't want the police involved and we're not interested in a criminal prosecution. What we want is to get this woman out of our lives. How do we do that?"

"We deal with her. We make a generous, one-time offer. Take it, and walk away a wealthy woman. Or stick around and fight in court for the next three years with no assurance that you'll get a penny."

"And if she says 'no'?" Jack asked, knowing that she had already shown little interest in money.

Victor sighed. "Then we have to face a long and nasty court battle. The fact is that she's Jonathan's widow and fully entitled to all the considerations due a wife. The law is on her side, and we'll have to come up with reasons to set the law aside."

"You're telling me that she could walk off with a couple of hundred million," Jack snapped.

"Yes," Victor admitted, "unless you want to explain why all the money in Jonathan's name doesn't really belong to Jonathan. And then *you'd* be the one risking criminal prosecution for tax improprieties."

"Jesus," Jack hissed.

"Not one cent," Alexandra said with quiet determination. "She murdered my son. She can't gain any financial reward for committing a felony."

"Once you go to the police, it's entirely out of our hands," Victor countered. "The prosecutors and her lawyers can subpoena any records they want. Your household liquor bill would become a matter of public record. Is that what you want?"

"I want her in prison," Alexandra said defiantly.

Victor glanced at Jack, appealing to his business sense. And Jack announced his decision. "Get to her attorneys and make the offer. Hell, they'll advise her to accept it just to get their hands on their percentage."

"I won't let her get away with murder," Alexandra promised in a loud voice.

Jack put his arm around her. "Please, Alexandra. We have years ahead of us. Let's just get rid of her."

Ben conveyed Jack's offer to Nicole. There would be a two-million-dollar payment for giving up all claims to Jonathan's estate. She would keep the Donner name until she remarried, keep the Manhattan apartment free and clear, and have full access to the Newport house. He was pleasantly surprised when she turned it down.

"Is it the amount?" he asked as they sat alone at a conference table that was surrounded by twenty chairs. "We certainly could negotiate for a higher figure even though they presented it as a one-time offer."

She shook her head and then glanced absently out the window and into a canyon of New York skyscrapers. "No," she said. "It's the dismissal from their company as if I were some dirty peasant being tossed out of the castle." She looked back at Ben. "Jonathan loved me. You know that, don't you?"

He nodded. "Very much!"

"And I loved him." She stood, walked away from the table, and then whirled back. "So, why are they throwing money at me and telling me to get lost? It's like asking, 'How much do you want to pretend you never existed?' I'm Jonathan's wife, not his biggest mistake."

Ben conveyed the message back to Victor Crane. "If she were after money, I'd be here suggesting a higher figure. Frankly, with your client's upside risk in the hundreds of millions, I'd be demanding a better offer. But it's not money, it's respect. She just lost her husband, and now they want to bury her with his body."

"What do you suggest?" Victor asked.

"Give it some time. Maybe we shouldn't even mention a financial settlement for another year. Doesn't time heal all wounds?"

Victor reported back to Jack and Alexandra.

"So exactly what does she want?" Jack demanded.

Victor let the air escape slowly through his pursed lips. "Probably more money. But I don't think we'll be able to find out over a conference table." He looked at Alexandra. "I think maybe you ought to invite her to dinner."

Alexandra balked at the suggestion. Later that night, when she and her husband were dining alone, he raised the topic, suggesting that it might help things if Alexandra and Nicole were at least on speaking terms. "How in hell are we supposed to have a civil conversation in the face of all these accusations and counter-accusations?"

Alexandra barely spared him a glance. "I want her out of my life, not sitting across from me at our dinner table."

Jack pleaded that a settlement with their daughter-in-law was critical and argued that there would be no agreement unless the two women talked with one another and found some common ground they could stand on. "Just to be at peace with Jonathan's memory, we ought to get his affairs settled," he said.

It was later at night, when he stopped in her bedroom to kiss her goodnight, that she showed the first dent in her armor. "I could meet with her, I suppose. Not for any substantive conversations, but just to agree that we have to get through all this."

He was buoyed. "Anywhere you say. Just the two of you with no lawyers, no seconds. I'd really appreciate that, and I think it would do a world of good."

Jack conveyed the suggestion in person, unwilling to have its innocence tarnished by their attorneys. He chatted with Nicole, said he had something personal to ask her, and wondered if he might stop by for a drink. He detected an instant's hesitation in her voice, but then she responded enthusiastically. "Is five o'clock good for you?" she asked.

"Perfect, and don't go to any bother. All I need is a shot of Jonathan's Scotch and a couple of ice cubes."

She was in jeans and a sweater, minimum makeup and hair pulled back. And she hadn't gone to any bother. On the coffee table she had arranged a bucket of ice, a pitcher of water, a new bottle of an expensive single malt, and two short glasses. The only extra was a bowl of peanuts. She sat while he went to work as bartender, commenting that it was Jonathan who had weaned him off his favorite blend and onto the single malt. Then he sat back, toasted to his son's memory, and leaned forward to touch glasses.

"I want to apologize for the way our financial proposals were presented," he began. "It may have seemed like 'take it or leave it,' but that certainly wasn't my intention." He explained that, unfortunately, there did need to be some resolution of Jonathan's affairs that were entangled with the firm. He added that he also intended to assure her financial future, and guarantee her independence from the family purse strings.

The provision inviting her to use the Newport house had been made in the hope that they would see her from time to time.

She listened patiently, sipping her drink while Jack poured himself a dividend. Then she asked, "Does Mrs. Donner still think that I murdered her son?"

His eyes flashed, but then they lowered humbly. "I want to apologize for that, too," he mumbled. "She's still in shock, and she's still looking for someone, or something to blame. If I could just get the two of you talking I think all these . . . suspicions . . ."

"Accusations," Nicole corrected.

"Yes . . . accusations . . . would stop. You've both suffered a loss. That should be something binding you together, not leading to . . . animosity."

"I think we said it all at our last meeting." Nicole wasn't letting herself get caught up in his enthusiasm.

"Will you meet with her? I know I can arrange it. I'm certain that everything would work out if the two of you could just get past the first five minutes." He hated begging like this. Jack's personality was more suited to lifting her up and dropping her out of the window. But he needed a settlement and he was willing to grovel for it.

"Let me think about it," she said. She tossed down the remains of her drink to indicate that their cocktail hour was over.

"I'd appreciate that," he said, following her lead, and finishing his drink. Then, as she was leading him to the door he confessed, "Alexandra is really the only barrier to our getting all these problems straightened out. If we could just get through to her, it would make all the difference in the world."

"Jack," she said in the doorway, "you keep making excuses for Alexandra. And she pays you back by blaming you for everything. You deserve better."

In the elevator, he found himself shaking his head. Was that bitch coming on to me? he wondered. She wasn't the first woman who had told him how much better he deserved.

THIRTY-SIX

The meeting was set for the next Sunday at two o'clock. Alexandra suggested the caretaker's cottage that Nicole and Jonathan had shared as neutral ground. They could meet there, just the two of them, and chat for a while. And then maybe they could join Jack and Pam aboard the yacht for a sunset dinner. Alexandra's voice sounded so genuine that Nicole found herself replying graciously. No, there was no need for Alexandra to send a car. She would enjoy driving herself. No, she wouldn't stay over. She had matters to attend to on Monday, but she very much appreciated the invitation. If it were to be a war-ending treaty, it promised all the cordiality of Appomattox.

On Sunday, Nicole took the car out of the garage at noontime, and left the parkways so that she could drive the back roads. She circled both shores of Manhasset Bay, window-shopped the great manors of Kings Point and old Glen Cove, and then took the winding forest roads that led to the Donner estate where the security guard waved her through. She checked her watch as she got out of the convertible next to the cottage. She was early. She started down the path that led to the cabana and then to the bluff overlooking the sound. There was no more pleasant way to spend the fifteen minutes she needed to kill.

At five minutes to two, Pam left her mother in the main house and walked quickly toward the garage building. She noticed Jonathan's car at the cottage and pulled up short. She hesitated, looked around, and when she didn't see Nicole, crossed the lawn to the cottage.

"Nicole!"

There was no answer. Pam eased the door open and called in again. The only response was a hissing sound of gas coming from the kitchen. "Nicole! Nicole, where are you? Are you in here Nicole?" She glanced about quickly. The bathroom door was open and there was no activity in the kitchen. She moved to the stove, checking left and right in case her sister-in-law had been overcome by the gas. All the burner controls were open, and she shut them off quickly. She thought of opening the windows, but the gas odor was overpowering. She took a quick glance around and then rushed for the open door. The last thing she remembered was pushing the "OK" button to deactivate the security alarm.

The explosion was like a thunderclap, echoing around the property so that no one was immediately sure of its source. Nicole had just reached the edge of the bluff when she heard it, and almost simultaneously felt the concussion, a thump against her back and neck. She turned just in time to see the fireball climb over the trees, and watched while a cloud of debris rose slowly and then fell like hailstones. A piece that looked like a window frame spun in a tight circle and glided off like a toy Frisbee.

The banks of mullioned glass along the facade of the main house rattled violently just as the sound struck. A few of the panes shattered and fell. Others cracked into spiderwebs. The concussion deflecting off the roof made the attics rumble like kettledrums and set the chandeliers rattling.

Alexandra, who had been about to leave for her meeting, dashed to a window and saw the debris cloud as it began to settle. Jack jumped up from his desk and ran out onto the grounds. He missed the fireball, but saw the smoke that began to rise, and heard the tapping of roof tiles as they fell into the woods. Instinctively, he raced toward the signs of trouble and was the first one to turn the corner of the driveway and see the shattered skeleton of the gardener's cottage. He also saw a woman's body, tossed like a rag doll onto the lawn.

The explosion had fired Pam out through the front door like a cork from a bottle. She had felt the impact, and the blast of heat that seared her blouse and burned the skin on her back and neck. She had no recollection of flying through the air for a distance of nearly thirty feet, or of crashing facedown on the lawn.

She had been stony silent when her father lifted her off the grass and carried her away from the fire. Her eyes had flickered and she had managed to smile when she recognized her mother and then Nicole. But she hadn't really awakened until she was in the emergency room at the hospital with both her parents bending over her.

"It was gas," she said unemotionally. "The cottage was filled with gas. It must have exploded when I was running out."

"Oh, God, I'm so sorry," Alexandra sobbed.

Jack wore a forced smile. "Everything is going to be fine. The doctors say you're okay. Nothing broken. No scars . . ."

"How did I get out?"

"Like a cannonball," he laughed. "And not a minute too soon. The only damage was to the cottage, and we'll put that back together again."

It was a week later and she was back at home, sitting up carefully to avoid aggravating the burns on her back. Superficial, the doctor had called them, describing them as not much worse than a sunburn. But when she accidentally rubbed against the gauze covering, they hurt like hell.

The fire inspectors had found the stove intact, stained by the heat and chipped by the debris, but still in working order. The burner controls were all in the "off" position. The gas line to the stove was broken, which the explosion could have caused. But it seemed likely that it had broken earlier, and the gas line was the source of the leak. An accident, plain and simple.

Alexandra had a different answer. Nicole had blown out the pilot light and let gas seep into the cottage. Then she had used the telephone to dial her own cell phone, establishing a link between her and the house. "She walked down to the cabana, waited until she heard someone inside, and then triggered some sort of relay."

Jack had rolled his eyes. "Some sort of relay? Is that what you plan on telling the police?"

"Well, I don't know how those things work. But I know you can send a signal to turn on the lights, or open a garage door. All she needed to do was cause a spark."

"Alexandra, for Christ's sake, she had just arrived. Where in hell would she get the time to rig up a remote-control detonator?"

Alexandra had given it a great deal of thought. "It would take her ten seconds to blow out the pilot. And how long to dial her own phone? Another ten seconds? She didn't have to install or connect anything. All she had to do was leave a device next to the phone so that she could set it off with a signal from her own phone. Maybe just punch in the number three or something."

"And she did all this . . . because . . ."

"She did all this to get me out of the way," Alexandra told Jack. "Pam wasn't supposed to walk into the cottage . . . I was. Remember how nicely you had arranged everything? Just she and I for a little private chat. A chance for each of us to retract the hateful things we'd said to each other. A new beginning. I was supposed to walk in there alone in another minute for a caring embrace."

Jack's anger flashed. "Stop it, damn it! You sound as if you've lost your mind."

But Alexandra went on. "She said she got there early so she walked down to the bluff. Why? Why didn't she go into the house and make herself comfortable? Or walk up to the main house to tell me she had arrived? Why would she go a quarter of a mile away from where we were supposed to meet? The only answer is that she wanted me to walk into the trap that she had set."

He took her hands and promised to investigate. He would have Greg Lambert bring in a team of arson specialists. Experts would go through the house. If the phone line had been active at the time, they would know it, and if there were some type of remote-control device they would find it. He expected precise, scientific answers to the questions about the cause of the fire.

"The fire inspectors found nothing," Alexandra reminded him.

"Alexandra, they're suburban volunteer firemen. They climb ladders and squirt hoses. They're not arson experts."

"Then you don't think it was just an accident," she challenged.

"I don't know. Pam doesn't remember if the gas jets were turned on. But if I find out they were, or if the gas was ignited over a telephone line, then I'll have serious questions for our daughter-in-law. But for God's sake, don't go mouthing off with wild accusations until we have the facts." He lifted her chin so that she was looking directly into his eyes. "Okay?" he asked.

"Okay," she answered reluctantly.

But she was far from satisfied. From the very beginning she had suspected that the thing Nicole found most attractive about her son was his fortune. That wasn't alarming in itself. Money was an asset, just like good teeth and a full head of hair. She expected it to attract women and had already watched two or three young ladies play their best cards. One was an accomplished horsewoman who would have brought a couple of promising race horses to the marriage. Another dressed in various degrees of nakedness, displaying her amazing sexual potential. And there was an artist whose painting was right on the verge of world recognition. Jonathan had paid twenty thousand dollars for one of her abstracts and then agreed with Alexandra that it was best hung in the attic. They were all ladies on the make. Their ambitions were obvious and their sincerity pathetic. She had never really worried that Jonathan would be taken in by any of them.

But Nicole was frightening. She had jumped out of an airplane just to attract his attention. She had made a virtue of her up-from-poverty autobiography. She had underdressed rather than flaunt her abundant assets. And she had kept a respectable distance, letting him do the chasing. Somehow, Nicole had convinced her son that he had captured an elusive treasure. Somehow she had made him believe that the thought of his money had never crossed her mind.

Worst of all, her whole life was a lie. Her time in Chicago was unexplained. In New York, she had lived as an escort on the edge of the law, carried drugs for a gangster, and tried to sleep her way to a stage career. The only thing this novice actress had struggled with was the clasp on her bra. She was subtle and evasive where the other fortune hunters had been obvious. She was dangerous while they had been amusing.

And this was the last person to see her son alive. The only witness to his mysterious death. The beneficiary to his sizable estate.

Was there any doubt that she was, in one way or another, the cause of his death? Then why was it so hard to believe that she would kill again to protect what she had killed for once before?

Alexandra made her own call to Greg Lambert. “Keep digging! Get all the details on every moment of her life.” There was a smoking gun out there somewhere, and Alexandra was determined to find it.

THIRTY-SEVEN

Nicole was on the edge of rage when she appeared in Ben Tobin's waiting room. She was in a skirt and sweater that seemed all business and with barely the essential makeup. Her eyes were fiery and she charged into Ben's office with a nearly athletic gait.

"Well, what do we do now? Just wait around until she kills me?"

Ben blinked. "What are you talking about?"

"You don't know what happened?" Nicole was stunned until she realized that a fire in a suburban outbuilding probably didn't make the evening news. "You don't know about the explosion?"

His expression told her that he didn't, so she dropped into one of his side chairs, poured herself a glass of water, and then gave him the full story. She began with her arrival at the caretaker's cottage, her realization that she was very early, and her decision to spend a few minutes down past the cabana. Then the explosion and her race back to the cottage where she found the building in flames and Jack bending over what seemed like Pam's dead body. "The security people came. One ran from somewhere on the grounds and another one drove up from the gate. And then the fire trucks and police cars followed by an ambulance. I was just standing there, maybe ten feet from where they were working on Pam. And all I could think of was that it was supposed to be me. I thought Pam might die and I knew that I was the one who was supposed to have been killed."

Ben was as critical of the charge as Jack had been with Alexandra. "Who? Who tried to kill you?"

Nicole explained the arrangements for the peace conference between her and Alexandra. "It was just supposed to be the two of us. Cookies and tea in the cottage. A chance to explain ourselves and iron out our differences."

Ben was nodding. That was exactly the kind of meeting that he had discussed with Victor Crane.

"If I had parked the car and walked into the cottage like I was supposed to, I would have been the one caught in the explosion. Kind of a scary coincidence, don't you think? The daughter-in-law they are trying to get rid of gets killed in an improbable accident? How many houses on the North Shore do you think have blown up in the past ten years? How many when the evil daughter-in-law had just stepped inside?"

"I don't believe this," Ben managed.

Nicole nodded. "Neither will anyone else. That's what makes it so perfect. Who would ever believe that one of America's great families would blow up a house just to get rid of their son's widow? So, if it had worked, I'd be out of the picture. And if it didn't, at least I'd know just how far they'd go to get what they want . . ."

"I guess I don't know them all that well. But, still, I'm completely stunned by what you're telling me."

"Maybe that's what makes the rich, rich. There's nothing they won't do to get what they want. Well, if they think I'm just going to run and hide, they're in for a surprise. I don't want a nice, quiet settlement. I want to make them pay!"

He still couldn't make sense of what she was saying. He had known Jack Donner for years. He was a tough boss and a ruthless competitor. If he had wanted to scare Nicole off, he would have done it himself. Jack didn't have to resort to murder to get what he wanted. And he knew Alexandra to be tough and demanding. "They like to recall that in the early days, when Jack was just getting started and Alexandra was his office manager, that clients and suppliers were more afraid of Alexandra than they were of her husband. People would call to complain about something, and if they got Alexandra they'd just hang up." He had to agree that she would have gone to any lengths to protect her son. But rigging a bomb? That was inconceivable.

"What's our next step?" Nicole demanded. "And don't tell me about friendly negotiations with the Donners. I'd be afraid to be in the same room with either of them."

Ben urged her to reconsider. The worst thing a client could do was get emotionally involved in her own case. If this were contested in court, the probate lawyers would gather around the case like vultures. It might take years before any real money was awarded. But now, if the explosion had really put Nicole in danger, then the Donners would be that much more anxious to avoid any kind of a public airing. It took him half an hour to get her agreement for him to take up the discussions with Jack's lawyers.

Ben discussed the situation with his bosses, repeating Nicole's story as accurately as he could remember it.

"Jack Donner in a clumsy bomb scheme," one of the partners laughed. "You've got to be kidding. Your client must be smoking the drapes."

"Don't even mention the fire," another advised. "Just get the biggest number you can without aggravating Jack. Let's try to get through this without making the Donners our enemies."

The consensus was that Ben shouldn't even meet with Jack. He didn't have enough experience and Jack Donner would eat him alive. "If he gets involved personally, one of us will handle it."

THIRTY-EIGHT

Greg Lambert's arson experts lifted every stick of the caretaker's cottage and scooped up every ash. They also checked the electric lines and gas lines leading to the structure, the gas and electric meters, and the telephone service lines. The report took ten double-spaced pages plus another eight pages of drawings and exhibits.

It confirmed that the household gas had been the source of the explosion, and that the volume of gas was extraordinary. Due to the porosity of the structure, the gas source needed to fill the building had to be much more than a doused pilot light. That amount of gas would vent out almost as quickly as it entered. But there was no way of knowing exactly what the source was. It might have been the broken gas line that was observed after the fire.

Telephone records showed that the phone line was not in use. In fact, no calls had been placed from the cottage in several days, nor had any calls been received. Most destructive of Alexandra's theory was that no phone attachment or other electronic device was found. The inspectors had to look elsewhere to determine the source of ignition.

There were several candidates. Pam might have created a static electrical charge just by running across the hall carpet in her tennis shoes. That could have been sufficient to ignite a high concentration of gas. The cause might have been the sunlight focused by a window pane. Even a momentary beam created by the sun's position could cause a hot spot within the house. But the weight of the investigation pointed to the security system. Once she opened the door, Pam had twenty seconds to push the "OK" button. At the end of that time the alarm system would assume that an intruder — unfamiliar with the alarm — had entered, and it would automatically send a telephone signal to the alarm monitoring company. The relay, the report stated in both words and diagrams, was burned from the inside, indicating that it had sparked. That spark, occurring exactly twenty seconds after someone entered the door, could certainly have ignited the dense atmosphere of gas. But this, of course, was only a possibility.

The conclusion was inconclusive. The

gas leak could be the result of failure of the old gas line or carelessness on the part of a housekeeper. There were many plausible explanations for the source of ignition but there was no evidence that it had been caused by an outside agent.

"I don't give a damn what it says," Alexandra snapped when Jack told her. "How do we know that she didn't come early just so she could go inside and turn on the burners? And she could have left a small candle burning or even a cigarette."

"How would the candle know when someone was inside the building?" Jack pressed. "Face it, Alexandra, she may well wish you were dead and buried, but she didn't plan the explosion. Nothing in her sordid background qualifies her as a bomb expert."

He was right. There was nothing. Alexandra had investigated Nicole from every angle for every period of her life. The girl hadn't even taken high school chemistry. No one could seriously accuse her of rigging the explosion.

In fact, if the evidence pointed anywhere, it would have to be toward Alexandra. She would have had any number of opportunities to enter the cottage and disconnect the gas line. She was also completely familiar with the security system, which was the same one used in the main house and throughout the property. She knew that twenty seconds after the front door was opened, a signal would be sent to the security people at the front gate, and a phone call would be placed. Did she know that either of those operations could prove deadly in a gas-filled room?

THIRTY-NINE

Pam was put in charge of the preparations for the traditional Newport party, one of the highlights of the town's social season. Each August, when the Donners opened their Newport house, they brought their Manhattan friends up the coast to Rhode Island for a gathering that usually rated a full page in the *Times* society section. Most came by boat, either their own yachts or hired cruisers. Some of the Hamptons crowd arrived by helicopter, setting down on the dock amid the masts of the gathering fleet. Those already vacationing on the Cape or in Maine made the trip by car. No one ever passed up the invitation.

It was a two-day affair with most of the guests sleeping aboard the boats while close family used the rooms in the house. The arrivals came in their vacation attire, and gathered around the pool for cocktails. Then they moved out to the great lawn for a clambake that featured the morning's catch from the coast of Maine. The day ended with a fireworks display.

The second day was spent around the pool with a long brunch that lasted into the cocktail hour. The guests left to dress, returning in a show of summer's hottest fashions, and were treated to a banquet under a tent. Then there was dancing to the wee hours of the morning.

The event had its legends. A middle-aged gentleman, still spending a fortune made in the railroad days, had smuggled one of the catering girls aboard his yacht. On seeing his wife returning in a launch, he had instantly tossed the young lady over the side. He dove in after her when he realized she couldn't swim, and then became an instant hero for rescuing a poor, deluded woman who was trying to commit suicide. The wife, of course, suspected the truth, and filed for a divorce as soon as they returned home. She was awarded the yacht and half the old railroad fortune.

Another year, a stray shell from the fireworks display had landed on the deck of a forty-foot ketch and burned the boat down to the waterline. The owner, who had already written off the yacht to his corporation and its shareholders, was among the revelers who toasted and saluted as the ship went down.

Most scandalous was the young Puerto

Rican boy from the gardening crew who had passed himself off as a South American polo player. He had had his way with two of the debutante daughters, and was halfway through the main course at the banquet, before being discovered. For obvious reasons, no one had come forth to press charges. Over the years there had been enough dalliances, pratfalls, and brazenly outrageous behavior so that guests came expecting some sort of scandal. In most years, they hadn't been disappointed.

Pam had invitations printed that included a photo of the burning ketch to remind most of the regulars of the event's checkered past. But she delivered Nicole's invitation personally so that she could explain the affair's history. She wanted to be sure that Nicole didn't simply decline what she might think was just another stuffy party, nor did she want her sister-in-law to break from the family. Pam still hoped that Nicole might join her in her plans for an art gallery.

Nicole's invitation had been Jack's idea, something he had discussed with Victor Crane without sharing with his wife. Negotiations for a settlement with Nicole were going nowhere, his latest final offer of five million dollars having been rejected. Nicole, according to Ben Tobin, was fully prepared to risk a court test of her inheritance rights, which would involve delving into exactly what the value of the estate was.

Jack didn't want there to be any suspicion that there even were issues. Everyone would expect Jonathan's widow to at least make an appearance so that there could be some expression of sympathy. It would be best if she were seen as a member of the family, and not as the fuse about to ignite another society scandal. He also wanted to hold out an olive branch, hoping that a sign of goodwill might make her negotiating stance a bit less contentious.

"Have you gone completely mad?" Alexandra had demanded when he launched the first trial balloon. "I'm supposed to give a woman who tried to kill me run of the house? Give Jonathan's killer access to all our friends so that she can spread her lies?"

He had countered that no one, not even their own investigators, supported Alexandra's theories and accusations. He reminded her how much worse it would be if all this rotten business were aired in court in front of tabloid reporters. "It would be the biggest thing since the Jack Welch affair," he warned, referencing the gleeful headlines when the great CEO's marital difficulties were made public. Then he reminded her that there was a lot to be gained. There could be no negotiations through a barrier of animosity and suspicion. They had to win their daughter-in-law's trust before they could hope to settle her claims.

Pam was aware of these deliberations. She knew that it was in no one's interest for her mother's hatred to drive Nicole into court, or in her own interest for Nicole to take all Jonathan's money and run. She wanted to keep her new sister-in-law close at hand.

Pam had a genuine concern that Nicole might not accept the invitation. For one thing, she was the widow of a recent tragedy and might think that it would be crass of her to be seen out socializing. For another, Nicole wasn't part of the Donners' social circle and wasn't all that comfortable with their style of merry-making. Perhaps she had heard some of the women's whispers about how much better Jonathan could have done. Pam had heard the backbiting from some of the young socialites who thought they were much more suited to be Mrs. Jonathan Donner. There were any number of reasons why it would be easier for her to stay away and avoid all the hurts that the other guests might inflict.

So Pam carried the invitation personally, inviting Nicole to join her for lunch. They had met on other occasions in the city, and had twice discussed Pam's idea of opening a gallery for new artists. That was the topic with which they began their conversation at a small, trendy French restaurant.

Pam bubbled about how exciting it would be, and how much fun they could have working together. Her overblown position at the Philharmonic was interesting, and provided all kinds of opportunities for her to further her education, but basically she was just a marginal cog in an incomprehensible machine.

Nicole advised her to stick with it and develop the required contacts. The problem, as she saw it, was that neither of them had a talent for judging art or projecting its value, nor were they knowledgeable in the highly specialized art market. But Pam wasn't impressed by the harsh reality. She thought they should begin looking for suitable space in the high-rent district uptown.

Then she presented the invitation, and began selling it even before Nicole had a chance to read it. The boat fire was depicted as "the funniest thing you've ever seen." She went into detail and laughed merrily at the thought of the owner saluting as his own yacht settled into Rhode Island Sound. She recounted some of the other legends and then added her own tales of midnight rendezvous and infidelities that the young people had observed on their way to clandestine meetings of their own. It would be, she promised, a fun weekend.

Next she hinted at Nicole's obligation. As Jonathan's wife, she was part of the family, and as a member of the family she really should attend. People would be looking to meet her if only to express their condolences.

Her final sales point was convenience. Nicole could share her room at the house, which meant that she could slip away whenever she needed, and that the consolation of a true friend would always be available. She could find refuge with the younger crowd when the older folks got boring, Pam promised.

Nicole listened to it all, smiled at the enthusiasm, and then handed back the elaborate invitation. "I shouldn't go to this," she said, "as delightful as it sounds. It would cause problems for . . . your parents." Pam found the notion ridiculous, and promised a full-hearted reception. Nicole had no choice but to explain why she wouldn't really be welcome.

She chose her words carefully, avoiding mention of her face-to-face confrontation with Alexandra, and never elaborating on the accident at the caretaker's cottage. But she made clear that Alexandra didn't consider her a suitable mate for her son, had dredged up all the sins of her past, and tried to bribe her out of the marriage. "She never wanted me to join the family, and now that your brother is dead, she wants me out as soon as possible." Pam agreed that Alexandra was difficult, but was sure that she could be won over. Then Nicole got to the subject of the negotiations. They were offering money. She wanted acceptance. They were threatening. She was remaining faithful to Jonathan's memory. "I don't blame your parents for wanting to settle all the issues, and close the door on Jonathan's mistake. But I don't think that I was a mistake. I want them to accept me as his wife." With gaping differences in their viewpoint, Nicole concluded, it was highly unlikely that they would ever come to an agreement. "I think we all know that we're headed for court, and I don't think your parents want me socializing with the jury."

Pam said she was horrified at the thought of them going to court. She repeated, "The party would be the perfect way to put the family back together again. The way Jonathan would have wanted." But Nicole stood firm.

FORTY

Pam placed the blame for the split entirely on her mother. "Why are you trying to drive Nicole away?" she demanded angrily after storming into Alexandra's home office.

Alexandra was patient despite her daughter's juvenile outburst. "She wasn't completely truthful in her dealings with Jonathan, and she hasn't been truthful in dealing with us," Alexandra said. Then she added, "I'm not surprised that she's given you a completely one-sided version of what's been going on between us. But I'm disappointed that you've been so easily taken in." Nevertheless, Alexandra went on, she had agreed with Jack on the propriety of inviting her. She had extended the olive branch, but she wouldn't try to hide her delight that Nicole had chosen not to accept.

Jack took the next step in extending the invitation. He asked Nicole to join him for cocktails at a Park Avenue hotel, and was waiting in the lobby like a concierge when she came through the revolving door. He directed her to a table in the lounge with nearly fawning consideration, and ordered a bottle of outrageously priced champagne when she asked for just a glass. She listened patiently while he rephrased the invitation that Pam had presented.

"What does Alexandra say?" she asked.

"Do you think Pam would have invited you if Alexandra objected?"

"I'm sure she knows you're asking me. But I can't believe she's looking forward to seeing me, or that she likes the idea of my mingling with her friends."

He had his answer ready. Alexandra was stunned over the loss of their son. True, she had been against the marriage, but she certainly would have come around in time. He was sure that they would have come to an understanding if they had met at the cottage as planned. "The fire," he said, "was tragic for more than one reason."

Nicole tilted her head and looked at him suspiciously. "Jack, you don't really think that explosion was an accident . . ."

"Of course it was an accident," he answered instantly. "The fire marshal investigated it and I had my own experts go through it. There was a break in the gas line and something caused a spark. Probably the security system after Pam opened the door."

Then Nicole laid out her reasoning, starting with the attack during their honeymoon when an intruder had tried to carry her off. She, too, was able to quote an official report in which the police doubted that it was an ordinary burglary. She took Jack's hand when she brought up her suspicions over his son's death. "I think I was the one who wasn't supposed to make it back up to the surface." When he started to protest, she put a finger to his lips, and made him listen to her theory about the wet suits. She and Jonathan had identical gear and attire. "Down deep, where the surface light faded, you wouldn't be able to tell them apart from twenty feet."

Jack was shocked. "You don't think it was an accident . . ."

"Jonathan was an expert diver," she reminded him.

"But to have someone go down there to . . . kill you? You can't be serious?"

Nicole was quietly determined. "If I had any doubts, they were blown away by the explosion. Pam wasn't the one who was supposed to go into the cottage for a meeting. *I* was."

Jack put his champagne aside and called

the waiter to order a Scotch. He certainly couldn't agree with Nicole, but her line of argument wasn't completely foreign to him. He had already admitted to himself that if anyone had set a trap at the cottage it was more likely that it had been Alexandra. Now he had to consider that Alexandra might have also been responsible for Jonathan's tragedy.

But he had to defend his wife. "Would you please at least consider," he asked Nicole, "that your suspicions are unfounded? Alexandra might well have tried to block your marriage, and even to break it up. But I can assure you that murder is beyond her. It's completely out of reality . . ."

She nodded in respect to his opinion. But then she ventured, "If it were just you and I, with no interference from Alexandra, do you think we'd be having these problems? What would you have done with me? Just let me join the family and stay as long as I wanted?"

He had to agree. That was exactly what he would have done, but not for the reasons she supposed. He would have eased her out gracefully over time, letting her spend what she wanted until she met someone else. Then he would have sent her off with a fantastic wedding present.

But it wouldn't have been out of affection for her, or consideration for his son's memory. He would have done anything to keep her out of court, and to prevent her from searching through his business records and family finances.

"That's true," he said modestly.

"So, then, I'm not the problem . . ." Nicole prompted.

Jack smiled. "I never thought you were."

The subject got back to the party, with Jack repeating that her presence would go a long way toward satisfying Alexandra and getting them to an agreement. He threw her own reasoning back at her. If Alexandra were the problem, then didn't it make sense to try to at least neutralize her?

They parted in the lobby with Nicole agreeing to reconsider the invitation. Jack extended his hand, but she pulled him close and gave him a friendly kiss on the cheek.

FORTY-ONE

Greg Lambert was still digging and reporting his findings back to Alexandra Donner. He had spoken to half the taxi drivers in Belize and traced down all the addresses that Nicole had visited. None of them were unusual — stores, tourist sights, even a movie theater. There were two visits to a resort hotel owned by one of the international chains. But she had never registered or stayed overnight as a guest.

Her telephone calls were even less eventful: local taxi companies, several of the dive companies, five calls back to Rockbottom, probably placed by Jonathan, including one call to the guardhouse at the gate. There was a call to a beauty parlor, a jewelry shop, and several to the resort hotel that she had also visited by taxi.

Lambert had become suspicious of the resort hotel. Nicole had telephoned it once or twice before each visit. The pattern might indicate that she was meeting someone there, but a search of the guests yielded no names. There was no one who was registered each time she had visited.

He had checked at her community college, and confirmed that she left before graduation, anticipating that she would complete her remaining courses during the summer. Then he had gone on to her various addresses in Chicago. He could prove the obvious details of her life — her addresses, her employers, and the names of a few of her friends. But none of the friends had left a trail so there was no way to interview them. Nor was there any way he could establish what kind of work she had actually done. Some occupations don't do a great deal of record-keeping.

New York was more informative because the history was more recent. Friends and associates could still be found and interviewed. Records hadn't yet been carted off to the archives. But there wasn't much more than what he had already learned in the first investigation he had done for Alexandra Donner. Nicole was certainly no angel. She had done what she had to do to survive and become involved with nearly anyone who could further her theater ambitions. Call it tawdry, if you liked. Or compliment her for clawing her way ahead. She wasn't the first girl to give away favors.

The most damning relationship she had

formed was with a club owner, drug dealer, and small-time hoodlum named Jimmy Farr. Nicole had danced at one of his clubs, entertained several of his high-spending customers, and run a few errands for him, including one that had gotten her arrested on drug charges. Nicole had been released because no illegal substances had been found in her possession. But none of the drugs had ever reached Farr, which left him out a great deal of money with no recourse to his suppliers.

"Yeah," one source had told Lambert, "I remember her. Jimmy was really pissed and told her she had to make good. But she settled him down and got herself off the hook. How? How the hell would I know? That was between her and Jimmy."

Alexandra had jumped on the intelligence. "Find out if they still have any dealings," she demanded of Lambert. "Maybe this Farr person still has his hooks into her." Lambert did whatever the Donners asked of him. They had never once questioned his invoices.

Despite her suspicions, Alexandra agreed with Jack and her daughter that if Nicole accepted the invitation she would be welcome at Newport. She knew that the evidence didn't yet support her charges and that Jack was beginning to doubt her sanity. Best to agree with him, she thought, and wait until Nicole's past caught up with her.

Pam's party arrangements were extraordinary, proof that she was ready to take her place among the very rich and the landed gentry. First came the yacht accommodations. She wanted boats to moor right off the cliff where the Donner property fell down to the sea, and where guests would be able to take a tender in to the property's dock. She arranged with a boatyard to plant twenty moorings, anchored in blocks of cement, within five hundred yards of the dock. Each would be inscribed with the name of an arriving yacht. Then, she hired a tender and uniformed crew to bring the guests ashore.

A local aircraft leasing company came to the house to establish a helicopter-landing pad. They inscribed a ring on the lawn, just above the boat ramp, planted a windsock, and installed a microwave approach beacon. The pad was given its own call sign so that all the approaching choppers had to do was establish communications and lock onto the approach frequency. It was a better accommodation than most professional heliports offered.

She hired three musical combos, one each for the cocktail party, the clambake, and the late-night dancing. Two of them had platinum records of their recordings. There was a string quartet from Lincoln Center to play during the Sunday brunch, and Billy Joel was performing after the banquet.

The caterers were from the Culinary Institute of America. They would arrive with three refrigerated trucks, their own stoves, two master chefs, four chefs-in-training, and fifteen waiters. The tents would be large enough to house a circus. One would be devoted to the needs of the chefs, a second would be ready to rise over the swimming pool at the first sign of bad weather, and the third would be outfitted as a grand banquet hall, complete with chandeliers, fountains, and live floral gardens.

Lobsters for the clambake were chancy. So Pam had ordered twice what she might need, spreading the order over three separate lobstering fleets. Refrigerated trucks had been hired to whisk the catch from the docks to the Donner party.

The people who did the fireworks for New York City were to provide the pyrotechnic display. A barge, moored in Hempstead Harbor, was being outfitted with over two hundred rockets, shells, and starbursts, and a tugboat was standing by to tow it up to Newport.

The house staff had started work in mid-July. There were new linens on all the beds and new bath towels in all the bathrooms. Windows were cleaned, drapes and curtains taken down, laundered, and reinstalled, rugs dry-cleaned, and floors polished. The chocolates were ready to be placed on every pillow.

Pam had pushed aside the estimates as they arrived and gone right to the contracts. Bills were beginning to arrive covering deposits, down payments, security fees, and binders. The payables, tallied by Jack's accountants, were already at two hundred thousand. The final figure would easily slip past half a million dollars.

Every invitee had responded with their delights, even two couples who would return from touring the Great Wall of China, and then rejoin their party in Bangkok. Only the invitation to Nicole remained open. It wasn't until the fireworks barge was taken in tow, and a flotilla of yachts departed from Long Island and Connecticut ports, that Nicole called Pam to accept. She admitted, confidentially, that she had grave misgivings. But in the final analysis, she thought it was the right thing to do.

FORTY-TWO

She drove herself up from Manhattan, pausing in downtown Newport to catch her breath over a cup of coffee before confronting the family. Pam was there to meet her and hustled her to her room. Best, she thought, to allow Nicole to mingle with the guests rather than force her into a private audience with Alexandra.

Jack knocked on the door as soon as he heard she was in the house, took her hands, and looked into her eyes as he thanked her for coming. "I want you to relax and enjoy yourself," he told her. "I hope this will be the beginning of a completely new relationship."

"I'll try," was the best that Nicole could promise.

She saw Alexandra out on the lawn when the flotilla of guests appeared on the horizon. They exchanged glances and then forced smiles but neither made a move to cross to the other. Alexandra's implied excuse was that she was busy with arrangements for the champagne service that would greet guests when they stepped ashore. Nicole pretended that she simply didn't want to get in the way.

As the boats drew nearer, Nicole could count the masts. There was a gaff-rigged schooner, looking like an eighteenth-century coastal trader, and maybe half a dozen two-masted ketches and yawls. Surrounding them were giant sloops, multidecked cabin cruisers, trawlers, and a European-style motor yacht that would have been a capital ship in half the world's navies. Apparently seafaring pretensions were one of the diseases that could be caught from too much exposure to money.

As the fleet moved to within firing range, the air force made its appearance. A Jet Ranger helicopter made a deafening approach, and scattered a storm of paper napkins as it settled on the lawn. The two couples that climbed out were in chic casual costume, and they smiled and waved like arriving politicians as they scampered under the rotors. Another chopper circled as it waited for the landing pad to clear and then made its noisy arrival with four more people that had flown down from Maine. Jack, Alexandra, and Pam were immediately involved with their guests.

Horns sounded as the first cruisers

reached their moorings, and the launch set out from the dock to fetch the passengers. They came ashore in nautical chic with brass buttons, gold stripes, and jaunty caps that had been instantly aged by soaking them in brine. The sloops dropped sails and motored to their moorings, ketches and yawls maneuvered with their mizzens, and the schooner dropped lines to its own tender. From the first appearance to the final landing, the entire invasion took less than three hours. D-Day should have been planned as well.

They gathered around the pool in a display of casual wear that was startling even to the photographers from *Vogue* and *W.* At first they were assembled in clusters that constantly rearranged themselves to accommodate new arrivals. Ranks were quickly established with the famous, the scandalous, and ordinary billionaires serving as the focal points of the various gatherings. But gradually the younger guests drifted off to cabanas and rooms and changed into bathing suits. The more reckless among the young ladies simply stepped out of dresses to reveal the cutting edge of swimsuit design. Then the rock group struck up, blaring string sounds through amplifiers that caused waves on the swimming pool. The party began to gyrate to the beat, with some guests in and out of the water while others were back and forth to the bar.

Nicole made her appearance alone, but was quickly attacked by Pam and her friends who brought her to their table. She wore a white, one-piece suit designed more for swimming than sunning, and made modest by a colorful sarong. But still, she turned heads and caused a clatter of camera shutters from the press corps.

Her reception at the table was mixed — warm from those who were sympathetic to her loss and chilly from those who blamed her for stealing Jonathan out of their clutches. But she smiled at all, nodded to acknowledge murmurs of sympathy, and laughed at stories that she didn't quite hear. She accepted gratefully when one of the young men asked her to dance, but toned down her performance to eliminate any hints of abandon. With that lead, others came over and led her to the dance floor and she found herself genuinely enjoying the affair.

Most of her conversations began with an expression of sympathy. "Terrible about Jonathan. But, you know, that's the way he would have wanted it to happen, while he was involved in one of his adventures." Or, "Sorry for your loss. Jonathan took too many risks, but I suppose that was what made him so exciting." Many of her partners offered advice for her future. "Don't hurry into rash decisions. Take your time. These things are not easy to get over." A frequent suggestion was that she should travel. "Just get on a boat and don't get off until you've been everywhere." Another advised her to "Take a house in the south of France. Most beautiful place in the world!"

Jack brought her to the dance floor. "Please tell me you're having a good time because you seem to be the belle of the ball."

"I'm having a very good time," Nicole answered, "even though I'm not the belle of anywhere."

He commented on how well she looked, and how tastefully she was dressed. "I've been told a hundred times how extraordinary you are. Everyone is beginning to appreciate why Jonathan was so taken by you."

"Everyone?"

He dodged the question. "Absolutely. And particularly me. If there's anything you ever need, I'll be standing by and ready to help."

When the music stopped she asked, "Is this a good time for me to join Alexandra at your table?"

"Of course. No time like right now!" He put his arm across her shoulders and led her to the table that he and Alexandra shared with assorted guests. Nicole recognized a musical legend who had been guest conductor at the Philharmonic. With a white belly peeking out between his shirt and his shorts, he appeared more a plumber than an artist. Then she was introduced to the chairman of a large bank and his sultry Middle Eastern wife who was about Nicole's own age. The banker was in a Tommy Bahamas sports shirt. His wife wore a bikini and see-through gown over a perfectly sculpted body. There was a Dutchman, introduced as a ship owner, who smiled at everything but said nothing in reply. His wife was a bit too beefy, and was said to be a pretender to some long forgotten throne. A Swiss banker stood when he was introduced and clicked the heels of his Birkenstocks. The woman next to him was introduced as his niece. Then there was Joe Tisdale, the real-estate developer who seemed to be Jack's constant companion. He jumped up, stole a chair from another table, and placed it right beside his own.

Nicole walked around to the head of the table and was surprised when Alexandra got up to greet her. They leaned together exchanging cheek kisses. "You look lovely," Alexandra said. "I'm so pleased that you decided to join us."

Nicole returned the compliment, lavishing praise on the party and giving particular note to Alexandra's outfit, a simple naval jacket over white duck pants. The sleeves showed the rank of rear admiral. There was an awkward moment of smiling silence. Alexandra broke through with her hopes that they would have a few minutes to chat over the weekend. "Maybe this time we won't be upstaged by an explosion." Nicole had to admire the aplomb with which her mother-in-law could make light of an attempted murder.

They were all experienced actors. Everyone at the party played roles that even theater critics would admire. The men were knights of the round table, powerful champions of finance and industry, fearless in the defense of market values. Their yachting costumes were worn to signal that, for the moment, they had taken off their armor. They partied confidently, knowing that when they got back to serious business, they would still be on the top of the heap. The women wore many costumes to disguise insecurity and to present themselves as worthy consorts, like the Dutch woman who pretended to royalty, indicating that she was important long before her boorish husband struck it rich. Or the banker's trophy wife who liked to flaunt exactly what her new husband was getting for his money. Obviously, a great deal of money.

She had noticed that the young men at Pam's table were remarkably self-assured. The pose was regal, based on an assumed right to rule, and at the same time casual to indicate that they weren't really caught up in their material excess. The J. Press shirts were worn as beach tops, open to the waist with the sleeves rolled back. Cars were discussed by their marques, with insinuations that even the best were beneath their standards. "The fucking Beamer is in the shop again. I swear I'm going to push that heap off a cliff." Names of European watering holes were dropped as if they were local fast-food stops.

The young ladies needed to prove that they were terribly sophisticated, a role that involved frequent references to their promiscuity, foul language, and a total disregard for money. They laughed hysterically when they splashed into the pool, ruining a designer original and showing their breasts through wet cotton. It was all "too fun," as they repeated like a religious mantra. Any show of purpose, or remarks that evidenced ambition, had to be avoided.

Nicole had been exposed to enough reality to know that only nitwits were indifferent to money, and that the girl who thought the ruin of her dress was funny was probably the same girl who had badgered her father for weeks to come up with the money for it.

And then there was Tisdale, who had arrived without his wife as guest on one of the destroyer-size motor yachts and wanted to take her out and show her the ship. His wealth and fame were certainly attractive to women, but he made the mistake of assuming that he was physically attractive as well. He made several suggestions of how he could be helpful to Nicole. "My real-estate contacts can get you any apartment in the city. And if they can't find the right one, I'll build it for you." He hinted that he could introduce her to all of the city's power brokers. He thought that she might join him in his box at the opera, and knew she would enjoy one of his after-the-performance supper parties.

Nicole glanced over at Jack who was listening carefully to Tisdale's advances. He rolled his eyes in comic despair. Even Jack had his stage part. He played the tough but fair, ruthless but honest, financial kingpin who slaughtered his opponents and then prayed for their souls.

Only Alexandra seemed genuine, a person who would say just what she thought to be true, and then let the chips fall. She wouldn't allow herself to be cajoled by flattery, or swayed by promises of gain. What was right for her family was, by definition, right, and had to be advanced. What threatened her family was wrong and had to be destroyed. That's what made her so dangerous to Nicole. Alexandra regarded Nicole as a dangerous intrusion into her household. She would go to any ends in order to keep her out, and if all else failed, she might even resort to murder. That was why the two of them were locked in a struggle that no one else could understand. Not Jack, who pretended and appeased. Not Pam, who wanted Nicole to join in her gallery project. Not even her attorney, who still advised that a tactful deal might be made. None of them, Nicole reasoned, understood Alexandra as well as she did. None of them understood why neither woman could compromise.

She went to Pam's room to change for the clambake, selecting jeans, sandals, and an oversize sweater. She was careful with her makeup and pulled her hair back in a simple ribbon. Pam bounced in, dropped her wet bikini pieces on the floor, and walked directly past Nicole and into the shower.

"Some blast," she said as she fiddled with the valves. "Hope you're enjoying it."

"It's a great party. You've done a wonderful job with all the arrangements. And, yes, I am enjoying it."

Pam's voice called above the roar of the water. "Hey, do you want to sleep out on one of the boats? A few of us are going out to that schooner for the fireworks, and then we're going to stay for the night. You want to come along?"

"I don't think so," Nicole shouted back.

"Why not? It's going to be wild!"

"That's why not," Nicole answered.

Tisdale was on her as soon as she entered the tent. He was going back out to the motor yacht for the fireworks. "Best place to see them. They're really exciting when they boom right over your head."

"I'm no good on boats," she lied. "I'd probably get seasick."

He moved his place card so that he would be next to her for dinner, and took her totally into his care. The anatomy of a lobster was suddenly his field of expertise. He explained the philosophy of getting all the meat out of the shell, and then took her plate so that he could do the shell-cracking for her.

"You know, that big yacht hardly rocks at all. In calm seas like tonight, there's no way you could get seasick."

She said that just the sight of a boat could bring on her symptoms.

"And the ride out in the tender," he went on, not allowing himself to be interrupted, "is only a few minutes. You won't have any problems at all."

Again, Jack was eavesdropping on the conversation, and grinding his cigar as he controlled his anger. Tisdale was hitting on his daughter-in-law as if she were just another young social climber. But Nicole was his to watch over, a desperate widow who had wandered into his castle and traded her freedom for his protection. No true friend would treat her as if she were in play. He waited until Alexandra was distracted with a housekeeping matter, and then eased around the table to sit on Nicole's other side.

"Jack," said Tisdale, unaware that his intentions could possibly bother his partner in greed, "I was just telling Nicole that the only place to see the fireworks is out on the water. Maybe you can convince her that she ought to join me out on one of the yachts —"

"No," Jack growled. "I asked her first. We're going to watch them from the porch of the house."

Tisdale looked hurt. Why would his friend spoil his chances to claim the prize of the party? It wasn't as if he were trying for Jack's wife, or his daughter.

"Isn't that right?" Jack asked Nicole.

She nodded toward Tisdale. "He did ask me," she confirmed, "and I really do get seasick on boats."

It suddenly struck Joe Tisdale that Jack wasn't just concerned with protecting the young woman's honor, or saving the widow from the evil advances of the real-estate baron. His friend was harboring his own secret lust. Jack was enamored with his daughter-in-law, a passion that he hid with gestures of fatherly concern. He might not be able to have her for himself, but he certainly wasn't going to share her with his friends. Why you dirty old man, he thought with amusement, and he became all the more determined to beat Jack to Nicole's affections.

FORTY-THREE

The lobster carcasses were carted off by the waiters and replaced with servings of Italian ice, scooped from a mold of the Statue of Liberty. Alexandra returned from her duties and signaled to Nicole that this might be a good time for them to sit together. Nicole left the two men staring at one another, both embarrassed that their feelings had proven so transparent.

"How are you enjoying Joe Tisdale's attention?" Alexandra asked as Nicole slid in beside her.

"He wants to take me out to sea so that we can enjoy the fireworks."

"Not very original of him."

Nicole laughed. "I accepted that invitation once, but I was only fourteen at the time."

"It's an annual ploy. A couple of years ago he got drunk and invited two women out to a yacht. His problem was that they were mother and daughter. It was the only time that he actually did see the fireworks."

They wasted a few minutes praising the party and commenting on the conduct of the guests. All in all, they judged, Pam had created a fantastic affair that promised to get even better as the weekend progressed. But then Alexandra got to the topic that both of them were waiting to address.

"We'll never really be friends, will we?" Alexandra asked.

"Too much blood already spilled," Nicole offered as the reason.

"Too much alike," Alexandra said as her counter offer. "We both have strong ideas about what we want, and we both open all the throttles to get there. There's no house big enough to keep us from crashing into one another."

Nicole sighed. "Mrs. Donner, I never wanted to live in the same house with you. I wanted to live with Jonathan. The closest we would have gotten was one Sunday dinner a month, and maybe a few summer weekends here in Newport."

"If only that was all that you wanted."

Nicole thought about jumping up and leaving, but sooner or later she would have to face down her mother-in-law. Maybe it would be easier here, at a crowded party, where she wouldn't want to make a scene in front of her friends.

"What *do* you want?" Alexandra added.

"Just what's rightfully mine."

"And exactly how much is that? More, I take it, than my husband has offered?"

Nicole thought about her answer. "Much more!" she decided.

"For what? A few weeks of your time? You must be very good at what you do."

"Your son thought I was priceless. So you see, it's not just more. It's different. The more money you put on the table the more insulting it becomes. Is it possible for you to understand that?"

"Of course I understand. You want respectability. But I don't think that even Jack has enough money to buy it for you. That's something you sold a long time ago, and from what I'm learning, at a ridiculously low price."

Nicole shook her head in a gesture of despair. "Is this why you asked me here? To drive us even further apart?"

"No. As a matter of fact I didn't know what I was going to say to you when we met. That's why I warned Jack that it would be better if we didn't meet. But now I think I do know. I think I ought to warn you that I have investigators working in every place that you've ever been, turning over every rock that you've ever lived under. And I'm getting closer. It won't be long before I'll know just who you are and exactly what it is that you're after. So, if you hope to get anything, I wouldn't waste another minute. I'd take the money and run."

"God but you must truly hate me," Nicole answered.

"Worse than that," Alexandra finished. "I truly know you."

Jack had wandered off pretending to check on the timing of the fireworks. Actually, he had slipped down to the dock and told the launch officer that under no circumstances was his daughter-in-law to be taken out to any of the yachts. He brought the launch officer with him to the edge of the tent so that he could point out Nicole, but he arrived just in time to see her storming away from the table.

"What in hell did you say to her?" he demanded of his wife when he reached the table.

"Say to whom?"

He leaned over her. "To Nicole. She fired out of here like she was shot from a cannon."

"Just how much I was enjoying getting to know her. She's quite unbelievable."

There was a sudden clipped explosion,

and the sky instantly turned a deep red. The barge had just fired its warning shot.

Jack walked toward the house, the direction where Nicole had seemed to be heading. He caught a glimpse of her on the porch steps and then saw her silhouetted against the light from the front entrance. She opened the door and went inside. He went after her moving past the guests who were rushing to the water's edge to watch the fireworks.

He glanced about the ground floor that seemed vacant. Even the servants had gone out on the porch to watch the display. Then he started up the steps, hesitantly, until he saw the light under Pam's door. He continued up to the hallway, listened for a moment outside the door, and then tapped gently. When there was no answer he knocked again, this time a bit louder. He turned the handle and eased the door open. Nicole was standing at the window, looking out at the gaily lighted party but holding a handkerchief to her face to stifle her sobs. She wheeled around when Jack stepped into the room. There was a smear of makeup wiped across her eyes.

"Oh God," he said, his despair coming through clearly. He rushed to her and caught her as she fell into his arms. "Jesus, what's the matter? What's wrong?" He already knew the answer.

"Alexandra . . ." she managed to get out through the aftereffects of crying. Before she could say anything more she was crying again.

"What did she say? What did she tell you?"

Nicole was shaking her head as if it was too terrible to repeat. Jack clutched her even tighter. He could feel her body blend into his embrace.

"She's crazy," he said. "Her grief has pushed her over the edge." It wasn't an accusation, but rather an explanation. Then Jack felt his own eyes welling with tears.

"She said awful things," Nicole managed. "That I was just a whore . . . asking too much . . . for . . ."

"Oh God," he groaned. He raised her face and kissed her cheek. He saw her eyes close and felt her face press harder against his. He closed his own eyes and brought his lips to hers. He felt her pull closer and return his kiss with soft, yielding lips. She seemed hopelessly vulnerable, totally dependent on him for her very next breath.

The windows flashed with light from a salvo of starbursts exploding over the water. There was a loud gasp from the guests gathered along the shore. Jack and Nicole held their embrace, winding it ever tighter. A rocket whistled outside and then flashed into white light. There was applause from the onlookers and shouts of excitement.

Jack loosened his grip, and backed away a half step. Nicole seemed suddenly frightened at being left alone. He backed up to the door, never taking his eyes off her. She drifted over and then slowly sunk to the edge of the bed. She was still focused completely on him. He reached for the door handle and pressed the lock. He waited, perfectly still, watching Nicole as if he were staring down a deadly jungle cat.

She slid along the edge of the bed toward the night table, reached out and turned off the bedside lamp. For an instant the room was total darkness. Then it flickered brightly as another round of shells exploded in the sky. He could see her plainly as she fell across the bedspread.

God, but she was gorgeous. And he was the only one who could save her. He went to the bed, sat beside her, and with his fingertip traced the line of her face. In the flicker of the fireworks he could see fresh tears. In the moments of darkness he was aware of her breathing. His hands moved slowly, almost as if he were lifting the wires from a terrorist's bomb. They touched her breast. The sky crackled and the room filled with deep blue light. He settled down next to her into the darkness.

They made love with great need, discarding clothes along the way. And then they lay in each other's arms, oblivious to the artillery raging just over their roof. It was the quiet at the end of the fireworks display that suddenly alerted them. Jack got up quickly, fumbled for his clothes in the dark, and then bumped his way into the bathroom. Nicole tucked herself under the sheets. She heard water running, splashing, and flushing before Jack stepped out, dressed as before in slacks and shirt, his yachting blazer over his arm.

"Nicole, I . . . I think . . ." In his entire competitive career, Jack had never been at such a total loss for words. His body was leaden and his mind was flooding with guilt. He had just denounced his wife as a madwoman, and taken his son's wife in his daughter's bed.

"I have to go and be with my . . . guests." He couldn't bring himself to say "wife."

Nicole held out a hand for him to take but he made no move toward it. Instead, he edged around the foot of the bed toward the door. "We'll have to . . . talk," was all he was able to get out.

"Jack, thank you. I would have died if you didn't love me. I was so desperate. So alone."

He opened the door a crack so he could peek out into the hall. He listened to be sure there was no one on the stairs. Then he stepped out, glanced around furtively, and walked quickly to the back steps that led down to the kitchen. He didn't want anyone to see him coming down from the second floor.

Nicole showered, put on her pajamas and got back into the bed. She lay awake, realizing the import of what had just happened. Jack Donner, the iron-handed master of the financial world, had left himself completely vulnerable.

FORTY-FOUR

Jack came out of the house, trying to hide the guilt that seemed more obvious to him than any of the starbursts or skyrockets. As he passed his guests, their smiles seemed more like knowing leers. "Great show!" someone said, patting his back. Jack wheeled angrily until he suddenly understood that he was being complimented for the fireworks.

"Where'd she go?" It was Joe Tisdale's voice. "I've been looking all over for her."

"I don't know," Jack said, sure that his lie was transparent. "Might have gone with Pam and her friends."

Tisdale winced. "She wouldn't be wasting that magnificent ass on some college boy, would she?"

Jack's fist shot out from his side and hit Tisdale squarely on the jaw. The builder blinked in disbelief and dropped to his knees, then toppled sideways at the feet of the onlookers who gathered instantly. At the moment Tisdale began to fall, Jack had realized, to his horror, what he had just done. He fell to the ground and lifted his friend's head off the grass. "Joe, I'm sorry. I didn't mean it . . ." Tisdale's eyes opened but they looked in different directions.

"What happened?" a new arrival at the circle asked.

"Jack just coldcocked Joe Tisdale," a voice answered.

A woman gasped. "Is he all right?"

A man's voice wondered, "What started it?"

"I don't know. Tisdale came up to Donner. They talked for a second and then POW!"

The real-estate developer was recovered now, more dazed from the amount of alcohol in his system than from the minor concussion. "Jesus, Jack. That's a hell of a way to treat a friend," he said. His fingers brushed across his mouth as he felt for missing teeth.

"Joe, I can't tell you how sorry I am. I lost my head."

Jack helped Tisdale to his feet and put a steadying arm around him. "Let me get you a drink," he offered.

"Sure," Joe agreed. "And pour one for my lawyers. I'll be calling them in a minute." He laughed stupidly and provided even more entertainment for the crowd. Jack felt ridiculous. He had just defended the virtue of a woman whose virtue he had just sullied. What was the matter with him? Was he losing his mind?

He jumped a foot in the air when Alexandra came over and touched his shoulder.

"Oh, hi! Joe and I were just having a . . . conversation."

"I heard," she told him. "Some of our guests want to manage your boxing career." Then she leaned solicitously to Tisdale and studied the discoloration that was spreading across his jaw. "Are you going to be all right?"

"I'm not feeling any pain at all," he said and then laughed at his own joke. Alexandra turned her attention back to her husband.

"Where have you been?"

"Where? Here, of course. Where else would I be?"

"I mean during the fireworks. Several people were looking for you. No one could find you."

"Oh, then," he said, pretending to remember. "I was up at the house looking for Nicole." He quickly switched the topic. "Whatever you said to her sent her off in a hurry. What exactly did you say?"

"That I understood her perfectly," Alexandra answered. Then she got back to her question. "Was she at the house? Did you find her?"

He said that he had. "She told me she was leaving. I asked her to stay. She was pretty shaken, but I think I got through to her . . ." He winced at the inappropriateness of his own metaphor.

"And then . . ." Alexandra asked.

He pretended to be oblivious to her point.

"*Then* where were you?" she persisted. "You didn't spend the whole time asking her to stay?"

"Damn it, I don't know. We talked and then she went up to Pam's room. I watched from the house for a while and then I came down here."

Alexandra looked around. "I haven't seen her either. She didn't come back with you?"

"I don't know. Maybe she left. Or maybe Pam came back and got her. But for God's sake, what did you say to her that got her so . . . unhinged?"

Alexandra leaned closer. "She's a hustler, Jack. Be careful with her."

His eyes widened. He hoped he wasn't giving himself away.

FORTY-FIVE

Nicole was early to brunch, and found her own table by the edge of the pool. But Pam, who was just home from the party out on the schooner, joined her.

"Coffee . . ." Pam begged, and took the cup in both hands to steady it. "You missed some kind of blast. Do you believe that those people brought their own band along on the boat?"

Nicole nodded. She was ready to believe anything.

"I hope you're not mad that I stood you up. I mean you didn't wait up for me or anything?"

Nicole assured her that she hadn't been inconvenienced and that she had gotten a good night's sleep.

Jack came down with Alexandra and immediately spotted Nicole sitting with Pam. "Ah, she did stay," he said with mock surprise. He nudged his wife and nodded to the table across the pool. "Now for God's sake, say something friendly to her."

"I'll try to think of something," Alexandra promised.

Their guests were arriving in various stages of recovery, again dressed for the cameras but looking less like beautiful people. Tables filled, but there was an edgy silence until second cups had been poured. Then the conversation sputtered and started like a long-neglected motor.

"I'll see how she's doing," Jack told his wife when he had her seated with a group of friends. He wandered around the pool, exchanged greetings wherever he saw signs of life, and ended up in a chair across from Nicole and his daughter. Pam was in the middle of describing the party aboard the yacht, and went back far enough in the tale to get her father up to speed. The highlight of the evening seemed to be when the CEO of a chemical conglomerate started home, turned at the bottom of the companion ladder to blow kisses to the ladies, and then stepped off a few seconds after the launch had departed.

Jack listened patiently, nodding and laughing, but hoping that Pam would find some reason to leave so that he could have a moment alone with Nicole. He was feeling foolish, guilty, and compromised, all at the same time. He needed a chance to apologize and he hoped to hear Nicole's assurance that their secret would remain their secret. But Pam's recollections seemed endless. Then, when two of her friends joined them, Jack gave up. He wandered back to his wife's table, now carrying a plate of eggs Benedict and the requisite Bloody Mary.

"How did she survive?" Alexandra asked.

"She seems in better spirits. Didn't say anything about leaving . . ."

"I meant your daughter."

Jack reddened. "Quite a night out there! Did you hear Jay Johnstone missed the launch and went overboard?"

"That's what everyone is talking about," she answered. "That, and you punching out Joe Tisdale. So far, those are the most memorable events."

Jack wished that they were. What he couldn't forget was falling into bed with his daughter-in-law. His recollections of their sexual rumble were delicious. He could feel the excitement of opening her buttons and pulling her clothes away. He was still tingling from the silky touch of her skin. But his thrilling memories of conquest were buried in a gloom of self-loathing and the fear that his crime would surely be discovered. If only he had the evening to live over again he would never have followed her to the house or climbed the stairs.

Then it got worse. Joe Tisdale came over, his face obviously misshapen. Unlike the affable drunk of the previous evening, he was sour and serious. There was no hint of mirth in his swollen chin.

"Jesus, Joe, I'm sorry," Jack said. He stood to help Joe find his chair.

"You should be," Tisdale snapped. "Taking me by surprise, like that. What in hell got into you?"

Jack shook his head and threw up his hands. "I don't know."

"All I did was ask where Nicole was. We were going to watch the fireworks together."

"Joe, there's no excuse. I don't know what I was thinking."

But Alexandra was beginning to understand. She knew that Tisdale wouldn't have asked in exactly those words. "Where's Nicole?" was probably his most self-serving spin on "Where can I get my hands on that piece of ass?" and she was sure the colorful starbursts wouldn't have been the fireworks he alluded to. Joe Tisdale liked to play the dangerous lover.

And that would be what her husband took exception to — a dirty remark about his daughter-in-law. Jack was feeling protective toward Nicole, hardly the state of mind he needed to drive a hard bargain. Could it be that he was changing sides?

She played the gracious hostess, meandering from group to group, joining briefly in conversations, and throwing her head back in laughter. But she kept herself aware of her husband and kept looking for signs of his defection. The plan had been to make peace and win Nicole over to a more accommodating position in the negotiations. She was beginning to suspect that Jack was the one who was being won over.

For his part, Jack's entire focus was on getting a moment alone with Nicole. He avoided her scrupulously whenever she was with someone. But even as he chatted with his guests and endured the teasing about his first round knockout of "Canvasback Tisdale," he kept an eye on her. On several occasions he had spotted her alone but had been unable to disengage from a conversation. Once he had begun his approach only to be beaten to her side by one of Pam's young men who had set out to monopolize her.

Other guests returned from their rooms

in swimwear. Another of Pam's gold label rock groups arrived and blasted out an even more deafening sound. The party mood returned, banishing the alcohol-stunned stupor with which the day had started. As the mood swung, Jack's feelings began to change.

He hadn't been caught. No one had whispered in his ear that they knew his terrible secret. There were no smirks where there should have been smiles. At dawn he had assumed that everyone knew. Now he realized that no one knew anything. He was beginning to feel much less vulnerable and, for exactly that reason, much less guilty. After all, it wasn't as if he had forced himself on her. What was it that she had said? She would have died if he hadn't been there to love her. They were both consenting adults.

Not that the guilt didn't continue to raise its ugly head. "She's your son's wife, for God's sake," he reminded himself from time to time. "In Pammie's bed," was another recurring thought, as if his daughter still slept in a cradle. And there were stabbing pains whenever he caught a glimpse of his wife. "In Alexandra's house," he told himself, thinking of the sanctuary of a cathedral.

And there was fear. Now Nicole held all the power with just the possibility that she might reveal his indiscretion. A word from her could destroy everything he had built. She would be calling the shots when their negotiations resumed.

But as the day progressed, the arguments justifying their liaison became more convincing. Jonathan was gone and Nicole was a free woman, her need all the greater because of her recent loss. He had done nothing to hurt his son. So what if it had happened in Pam's room? His probably wasn't the only illicit sex that her bed had supported. She wasn't a child anymore. And it wasn't Alexandra's house. It was the open house that they used during one month of the year, sharing it with all who wanted to come and go. Best of all, he doubted that Nicole would ever want to talk about their night of fireworks. Wasn't she the one who had needed it desperately?

As the torments of self-hatred and fears of discovery began to fade, Jack started to recognize the familiar feelings of pride. It was like one of his financial takeovers where feelings of concern for the lives he might be wrecking and the people unemployed gradually gave way to the cockiness of being a winner. He had gone into battle and come out victorious. Why sully the moment with regrets for the bodies he had left on the field?

There were a hundred men at the party, probably more. Two-thirds of them were married to the women standing at their sides. Every one of them, Jack told himself, had licked his lips when Nicole stood by the pool. Every one of them would have gladly dragged her up to Pam's bedroom if they thought they could get away with it. What had stopped them wasn't moral rectitude, or concern for the rights of others. What had stopped them was fear. None of them had any balls!

Except for him. He hadn't been afraid of the risks, or hesitated in the face of danger. He had followed her up the stairs, charged into her room, and locked the door behind him. He had claimed the prize of the party for himself. So why was he whining about the few bruised egos he might have caused? He had triumphed. He shouldn't be hiding his victory with an innocent face and a fawning demeanor. He should ride out with his conquest tossed across his saddle so that everyone could see the spoils of war. What the hell was there to apologize for?

He jumped when Nicole was suddenly

standing beside him, and let the story he was telling tail off into meaningless words. "Hello," he said, and then panicked when he couldn't think of anything to add.

"So, this is Jonathan's wife," one of the men in the group said, coming to his rescue. "Terrible thing, losing someone like that. You have my deepest sympathy."

Jack found himself in time to introduce her to the group, and then ask if she was having a good time. She showed a full smile, and laughed easily as she joined in the praise of Pam's efforts. It was obvious to everyone that just a word of sympathy was enough. Nicole Donner had no intention of wallowing in her widowhood.

She has no regrets, Jack told himself. She likes being near me and she doesn't care who notices. His spirits lifted to an even higher level.

Alexandra looked up just in time to see them standing together, holding court before a group of the country's outstanding citizens. She watched as Pam joined in, putting her arm around her sister-in-law's waist. It was a perfect domestic moment. Except she was missing. As Alexandra watched, she could feel her family changing sides. Her husband and her daughter were going over to the enemy, and she was being left alone to defend all that she held dear. A current of renewed determination shot through her body, tensing her muscles and heightening her senses. Nicole had to go, and the sooner the better.

FORTY-SIX

Jack finally caught Nicole alone as she was walking back to the house. He had seen her take her leave from a cluster of Pam's friends, and then start off on her own. He had set his drink on someone else's table, and taken a roundabout route to follow her.

"Nicole!" He was short of breath as he ran up behind her.

She turned as if she had expected him to follow her. "Jack, I've been looking for a chance to talk to you since this morning."

He glanced around furtively. There were guests everywhere, but they were all involved in one another. His approach to Nicole didn't seem to have attracted any attention. "Where are you going? I'll walk with you," he said, flashing his most innocent smile for the benefit of anyone who might happen to notice them together.

"Just to get my things together. I'll be leaving right after the banquet. But I do want to talk to you."

He fell in beside her. "I know I should apologize for . . . last night. And if that's what you want to hear, then I'm sorry for mistaking your feelings."

"You didn't mistake my feeling," she said.

But Jack wasn't listening. He had a rehearsed speech that he was determined to deliver. "But the fact is, I have never been more attracted to anyone than I am to you. You said that you needed me, but *I* needed *you*. I know that makes me ridiculous, but I don't really give a damn. Last night was wonderful, and I'm glad that it happened. So, what does that make me, a liar or an arrogant bastard?"

She squeezed his hand and he loved it, until he realized that someone might be watching. He pulled his hand away. "Jack, I'm not sorry either. But we've created one god-awful problem for ourselves. I don't know where to go from here."

"I'll call you," he promised. "As soon as we're back in the city we have to get together and talk. There are a lot of things that we have to straighten out, and I don't think that there's anyone who can help us."

Nicole squeezed his hand once more as if it were a secret code that no one else would be able to decipher. "Yes, call me. You and I will be able to make sense out of all of this. We'll get it right."

He saw her again at the banquet. She came in just as all the guests were taking their places, and went to the table where Pam was sitting. She wore a summer pastel that showed her neck and shoulders, and a simple chain of silver. Her hair was loose, turning in above her shoulders in the latest fashion. She had done nothing extraordinary, but still she took Jack's breath away.

"Now don't hit me again," Joe Tisdale said to Jack for the benefit of the table, "but Nicole is one fine-looking young woman."

"Very lovely," Jack answered, stealing a glance at Alexandra to see if she were paying attention elsewhere. She seemed to be involved with another guest, so he ventured, "Very lovely, indeed."

The dinner was served; beef filets or swordfish steaks, with the appropriate sauces and vegetables. The wines were collector items, uncorked and poured to individual tastes. Billy Joel appeared and visited the key tables before he took his place at the piano. The Donners' summer affair began winding down to a perfect conclusion.

Pam pressed Nicole for a commitment. As they ate together she kept bringing up the art gallery, explaining the concept to her friends and enlisting their support. "You see, everyone thinks it's a great idea. We'll find people who know the art market. What will make us different is our willingness to take a chance on new talent." Nicole promised to continue the discussion in the city and told Pam to give her a call. She took her leave from the others at the table and then worked her way across the lawn to where Alexandra was holding court.

"Thank you for having me," she said to Alexandra. Alexandra accepted the compliment and expressed the hope that they would get everything taken care of in short order. There were no hugs or handshakes.

The men were standing and Tisdale repeated his offer of an evening at the opera. She promised to take him up on it. The Swiss banker clicked his heels. Jack took both her hands in his. "We'll talk," he said, hoping his tone would convey special meaning that only she could understand. "We will," she answered and then added, "I can't thank you enough."

"Delightful girl," one of the wives said to Alexandra. "Will we be seeing more of her?"

"I don't think so," Alexandra answered.

"I'm sure she has her own agenda."

Nicole walked back to the main house where one of the servants had already loaded her suitcase into the trunk of her car. She passed by the security people as she drove out through the gate and crawled through weekend traffic in Newport. She had crossed the bridges over Narragansett Bay and was headed west along the meandering roads that crossed behind the Rhode Island beaches when she realized she was being followed.

FORTY-SEVEN

She couldn't remember where the car had fallen in behind her. In the twilight, with the roof down, she had been enjoying the color in the sky ahead. It was only in the darkness that she became aware of the steady glare of headlights in her mirror. Nicole eased to the right lane and slowed a bit, but the car showed no intention of passing. Then she picked up speed, driving well over the limit. The car faded at first, but soon reappeared, taking a new position a little farther back.

She pressed on until she reached the interstate where the heavy flow of traffic gave her a sense of security. But the car stayed behind her. She watched it pull out around cars that she had just passed. Her lane slowed behind a climbing truck, and she kept her focus on her pursuer as cars flashed past. The car came abreast of her, a plain sedan with two men in the front seat. It passed by, and disappeared around the truck ahead. Nicole breathed easier, and found a music station on the radio.

She stopped for gas, and pulled to the

side of the parking area to raise the top. No one seemed to be paying any attention to her. But as she started out on the ramp, a pair of headlights flashed on in the truck area. The same car pulled out behind her and took up its position.

She could no longer deny her fear. Somehow, the car had slipped back behind her and followed her into the rest stop. The two men had sat in the darkness, watching her while she refueled. She realized how vulnerable she had been when she had gotten out of her car to raise the top, and how vulnerable she would be again when she left the highway. She had to get away from them.

She pulled into the left lane, pressed down on the gas, and accelerated past a line of slower cars. In the mirror, she watched a pair of headlights pull out behind. Nicole kept moving past the traffic until she came abreast of another truck. Then she slowed down, holding her position, so that the car behind was caught in the outside lane, blocked in front by her, and on the right by the line of cars following the truck. She waited until she saw the signs for an exit, timed her approach, and at the last second accelerated around the truck. An air horn blared as she turned sharply into the exit ramp. The truck blocked the sedan from following her.

She had escaped, but she sensed that she was still in danger. The car could slow down or find an on-ramp where it could sit and wait for her. She could go north to the state parkway but that would entail traveling on dark and deserted back roads, exactly the kind of situation where she couldn't let herself be caught.

She picked a secondary road that paralleled the interstate, and stayed on it for half an hour. For the most part, it was lighted and busy, and it allowed her to check the interstate's on-ramps as she passed them in sequence. There was no sign of the car waiting for her. After passing three entrances, Nicole pulled back onto the highway and moved at the traffic speed, careful not to do anything that might attract attention. She kept checking for any signs of a car maneuvering in behind her, and looked carefully at any sedan that she was overtaking. There was no sign of them, and as the minutes passed, her anxiety began to calm.

She had lost them and in the flow of Sunday night traffic it would be hard for them to find her. If they really had been following her. Maybe it was her imagination. Maybe the car that had pulled out of the service area wasn't the same one that she had seen earlier. She tried to convince herself that her fears had been ridiculous.

The Manhattan skyline finally came into view, a dazzling light array behind the dark silhouettes of the bridges. Her spirits lifted as she exited into midtown, and she nearly laughed in relief when she pulled into the garage under her building and parked in Jonathan's space.

There was another anxious moment while she was waiting for the elevator. Another car entered and moved slowly through the parked cars, turning at the end of the aisle and then heading back toward her. To her relief, she noticed a woman passenger inside and breathed easily when the car turned into its assigned space. The elevator door opened, and Nicole waited for the woman and her husband to join her. She had their company all the way up to her floor.

In her apartment, she double-locked the door behind her, and then walked from room to room, turning on lights. She felt ridiculous, almost like a child who's afraid of the dark. Of course there was no one here. Probably no one had been following her, and if someone was it was most likely that he had given up hours ago. The two men who had passed her in the sedan were probably coming home from a day of sailing or from some sort of sporting event.

She unpacked, showered, and slipped into a comfortable T-shirt. Just before climbing into bed she went to the window, opened it a crack, and tipped open the blinds. In the street below, a sedan was parked with two men sitting idly. It was directly across from the entrance to her building.

FORTY-EIGHT

Alexandra had new reports from Greg Lambert. In Belize, the police had arrested a small-time crook on a mugging charge and encouraged him to talk about his past activities. One of his botched crimes had been a break-in at a private guest cottage out on an island. The dates matched the time when Jonathan and Nicole were attacked during the night.

Someone had hired the thug, but he didn't know who it was. "Just a man in a suit. He gave me five hundred, and promised me five hundred more. There was a young couple staying in an island cottage. 'Very rich,' he said. I was supposed to rough the lady up a little bit. Not break anything. Just throw a scare into her. And if there was anything valuable lying around, I could help myself." He had rowed an inflatable dinghy over to the island from Ambergris Cay, circled behind the house and entered from the outside shower. But just as he had gotten inside, he saw the woman returning from the beach.

He thought that he could knock her out before she could make a sound, take whatever jewelry he found on her fingers, and then make his escape.

"She fought back," the thug had told the police. "The lady was tough, and she raised a racket. When I tried to get away, she held on to me."

"Who do you think hired him?" Alexandra asked.

"Hard to say," he answered. "Who knew that they were down there?"

The next bit of news came from New York. Lambert's agents had found another past acquaintance of Jimmy Farr, the club owner Nicole had worked for. Farr had held her personally responsible for the drug money he had lost when she had failed on her last assignment. Nicole had spent two years paying off the debt.

"So she has been dealing with this . . . gangster," Alexandra said.

"She was, but that seems to have been quite a while ago. And it's not all that damning. She wouldn't be the first theater-wannabe to get involved with the wrong kind of people."

"No," Alexandra agreed, "but she's certainly the first one to try and move into my family."

The information only furthered her opinion that her daughter-in-law was a scheming con artist, and made her even more determined to be rid of her. But she still hadn't found the smoking gun. Nicole could admit all the questionable things she had done, and all the sleazy people she had been involved with. It all could be seen as proof of her courage. She had repented her crimes and set herself on a more honorable path.

More troubling was the low-life's claim that someone had paid him to "rough up the lady." Who? Jack certainly had the connections to have it done without getting his own hands dirty, but Jack seemed to be on Nicole's side. Wasn't he advocating that she be paid off even if the price was outrageous? Or maybe it was one of Lambert's security people, some overzealous commando trying to move things along to curry favor with Alexandra. She suggested to Lambert that he take a good look at his own people.

Or was it possible that Nicole had arranged the affair herself to prove to Jonathan that his family wanted her out of the way? But it was a man who put the money on the table. How could Nicole have any contacts in Belize?

As she grilled herself, Alexandra's thoughts kept coming back to Nicole's drug-runner friend. She had to look at her notes to remember his name, Jimmy Farr. Lambert thought that Nicole had paid off all her debts. But what if she hadn't? What if Farr had raised his interest rates to take into account her newfound wealth? If that were the case then a solution might be simple. Just ask Nicole, "How much do you need?" But, of course, if she were being pressed by the underworld, she would have taken her payment as quickly as possible. She wouldn't be holding out for "acceptance."

There were so many possibilities, but there was really only one answer: get rid of the girl as quickly as possible by any and every means.

"Damn it, now she's having me followed," Nicole snapped at Ben Tobin. She was in his office for an update on the negotiations. Ben was explaining that the other side was in disarray with Jack trying to be generous while Alexandra was offering nothing more than a token payment. "She's trying to frighten me into giving up."

He was keenly interested in her detailed

account about the car that had followed her all the way from Rhode Island and then spent the night outside her door. "That's stalking, and we can get the court to put a stop to it," he told her. But as he pressed for more information he began to suspect that she had no idea who was following her. Certainly there was nothing to prove it was Alexandra. The car outside her house might not have been the same one she thought was following her. And the car could have been nothing more than two men interested in an attractive woman, driving alone, in an expensive convertible.

After he had calmed her down a bit, he raised a question of his own. He had spent Sunday upstate at a skydiving center, and had once again run into Harry Gillman, the man who remembered jumping with Nicole. "I'm only asking because this is something that might well come up if we have to go to court. Gillman says you were a very accomplished diver, not a novice who could forget to check her equipment. I told him he had the wrong lady, but he described you very accurately."

"Well, I couldn't begin to describe him," she said. "I don't remember anyone by that name." She conceded that she had taken some lessons upstate and that

Gillman might well have been one of the other students. "But I didn't get certified up there, and I was a long way from being accomplished."

He probed as to how she happened to find the jump center in western New Jersey. It wasn't well publicized, and there were other schools with better facilities. "Oh, I don't know. Someone may have mentioned it. I know I got lost the first time I went looking for it. Why? Is it important?"

Ben explained Alexandra's assertion that Nicole had insinuated herself into the family. "Almost as if you had stalked Jonathan to win him over."

"That's ridiculous! You were there. He spoke to me. I didn't come on to him. And even if I had, so what? Is it illegal for a woman to introduce herself?"

He laughed, but explained his concern. In cases like this, courts had great discretion in deciding fair and reasonable amounts. A distraught wife could expect to do much better than a calculating gold digger.

"Is that what you think I am?"

He waved away the suggestion.

"If that were true, why would I have turned down more money than I could ever hope to have in a lifetime?"

"I'm sorry," Ben cut her off. "That's not what I think, and it might not be important at all. It's just that if we're going to court . . ."

"It won't go to court," she snapped, and then seemed surprised at her own certainty. In a milder tone she added, "I think the Donners have much more to lose in court than I do."

FORTY-NINE

Jack Donner's voice on her answering machine was a raspy whisper, almost as if he were afraid to be overheard. "Hi! It's me. Just thought we ought to get together . . . for that . . . little talk. I'll try you later." There was a long pause as if he were trying to think of something else to say. Then he clicked off.

He was right. They had to get together and be very clear on where their encounter was leading. If he wanted to say "a terrible mistake" and blame a lapse in judgment on too many drinks, she would have to take him at his word. At least his feelings of guilt might hurry a settlement. How tough a line could he take with a woman he had used? But if he really meant that he needed her, and that she was the most exciting person in his life, then they would be facing problems that would dwarf her own battle with Alexandra. The scandal wouldn't be limited to the supermarket tabloids. And the property settlements in a three-way battle that pitted them all against each other might drag on for years.

That wasn't something she wanted to get into.

He called again, just after she returned from her meeting with Ben Tobin. Maybe he could stop by for a drink? Nicole checked the window to make sure the car that watched the apartment the previous night hadn't returned. But then she considered that the two men might have settled in for the long haul, maybe in an apartment across the street. "Jack, let's meet outside. Someplace public. I'll tell you why when I see you."

He picked the hotel where they had shared champagne, and met her there at 6:00.

It was a busy cocktail hour, and he felt sure they would blend invisibly into the crowd. And even if an acquaintance did spot them, what could be more innocent than taking his mourning daughter-in-law out for a drink? This time he didn't play with the bubbly. He ordered his Scotch and she asked for a flavored martini.

"I'm being followed," she announced, and then she went through the turns and taxi changes she had used on the way to their meeting, just to be sure no one was tailing her. Jack's shock seemed genuine, although it was still possible that he was the one who had put detectives on her. Maybe to protect someone important to him. Maybe to keep an eye on a woman who was suddenly in a position to destroy him. Nicole took several minutes to describe her ride home from the Newport party, interrupted only by the arrival of their drinks. She told him how she had managed to escape the car, only to find it parked outside her apartment. "Who would be doing it?" she asked. "Could it be Alexandra?"

"Of course not," he said instantly, but then he took a moment to reconsider. "At least I don't think so. I know she's been accumulating quite a dossier on you. You know, like getting hold of your yearbook. So she's certainly been asking around. But having people follow you? She wouldn't do that. It would leave her . . . vulnerable."

"Jack, why does she hate me so? What's wrong with the fact that Jonathan fell in love with me? Why does that make me evil?"

"I don't know. Maybe she wanted him to fall in love with one of the girls from our own social set. Or maybe she didn't want him to fall in love at all. She thought his money made him a target for all kinds of phonies. People who would win his confidence just so they could sell him the Brooklyn Bridge. Or marry him so they could clean up in a divorce. I guess it was natural that she would check you out. And then . . ." He decided not to finish the thought. Instead, he lifted his drink.

"And then she didn't like what she found," Nicole said, finishing the sentence. She looked down sadly. "I guess I can't blame her. I don't like what she found either."

"That was all years ago," he said, coming to her defense.

"Still, it was pretty sleazy. Not the virtues she would expect in Jonathan's choice of a wife."

Jack shook his head. "That's not it. The problem is that Alexandra has no experience. She's never had to take chances in order to make something of herself. I took the chances. Coming to work for me was the only risk in her life, and even then the worst was behind me. I was starting to make money. And when she married me she was pretty sure that I was going straight to the top.

"She never even met anyone like you. Half the people at our party were born with money. The other half had the connections to get to where money was being made. None of the men had to scramble through night school to get a degree. And none of the ladies ever waited on a table. Our sons start in the mailroom and then get promoted to vice president. Our daughters spend more on a pair of shoes than you probably paid for rent. How can she possibly understand what you had to go through? What you had to put up with?"

"But you understand?"

"Because I was there! I got scholarships to put myself through school. And I busted my ass to get my first customers. Believe me, it was no gentleman's game. If someone wanted to dig into my past they'd find lots of things that I'm not proud of. There were a half dozen times when I could have been bounced permanently out of the business. There were even a couple of deals that could have gotten me sent to jail. So I understand that you can't always tiptoe through the tulips. Sometimes you have to wade in the filth. I did what I had to do. So did you. So I'm not going to take cheap shots just because you posed for a couple of pictures. Alexandra never had to pose. It's easy for her to brag about what she never would have done."

Her hand went over his, and Jack had no

inclination to pull his away. Screw the onlookers, he thought, and if he had any close friends in the room, screw them, too. She was a wonderful young woman who had fought her way up just as he had. Why would he be afraid to hold her hand?

"You're a brave man, Jack," Nicole told him. "You're taking chances all over again just to help me. No wonder I need you."

He took another sip, this time for courage. "Can we . . . be together . . . tonight?"

"They may still be watching Jonathan's apartment."

"I have a place up on the East Side. There's no one there."

They finished their drinks and Jack paid the bill.

His place was a brownstone with the lowest floor sunk halfway below street level, and a flight of stone steps leading up to the parlor-floor entrance. It was wide open and furnished sparsely. An architect had erased the walls that created a row of rooms from front to back. A decorator had brought in minimalist furniture groupings in bright colors and then painted the walls in off-white. There was a fair-size art collection hanging in the front sitting area. Certainly enough work to launch Pam's gallery. The rear area was a library with walls of books, a giant screen television, and stereo stacks with private-label speakers. French doors opened out to a brick terrace that was covered with a vine-laced arbor. Between the two areas was a bathroom that could have been a Broadway dressing room. There was a vanity big enough for three women to tease their hair. The men had a separate door leading to facilities that Nicole could only imagine.

"Most of these places have been broken up into apartments," Jack explained. He gave her a quick tour down the closed staircase to the kitchen and dining room, the pantry and wine cellar. He selected one of the dusty bottles and carried it back upstairs. Then he followed her up the open steps that led to the bedrooms and watched while she glanced into the front and back rooms and the private bath that joined each of the rooms. The front room, with twin poster beds, had a feminine feel and its bath was done in decorator tiles. The rear room was plainly Jack's, masculine in chrome and light leather, with an enormous bed raised up on a step. The bathroom had a steam shower, a sauna, and a Roman shower in place of a tub. In a mirrored area there was a treadmill and a set of free weights.

He lifted the top of one of the night tables and swung out a miniature bar. There were wineglasses and the tools he needed to open and decant the treasure he had carried up from the cellar. A button on the stereo stack filled the rooms with a Beethoven adagio, vibrant in texture, but so soft that it could barely be heard. When he turned, he found that she was standing right at his side.

"I haven't thought of anything except you," he said. He leaned forward and kissed her lips over the tops of the wineglasses. "I can't believe what's happening to me."

She put her hand on his shirt and stroked the curve of his shoulder. "I was afraid that you'd want to forget me. I don't want to be a problem for you."

He touched her hair. "I'm not thinking about problems. Just that I've missed you every minute since you left the party."

She set down her wine. "Just give me a minute." She brushed another kiss across his lips and then slipped into the bathroom.

He was already in bed when she returned, wearing his terrycloth bathrobe. "Not the most alluring costume I've ever worn," she smiled.

"Yes it is," Jack said. He pulled back the sheet and Nicole dropped the robe as she slipped into his bed.

Jack was gone when she woke up but he had left a note tucked into the corner of his bathroom mirror. "Sorry. The European calls start coming in early. There's no staff in the house so you can stay as long as you like. I'll call you."

She showered, dressed, and then went down through the house to the kitchen. She made coffee and toasted a muffin that she ate standing over the sink. All the while she kept thinking of Jack and the unexpected complications that he was loading onto her life. Not that his advances were unwelcome. For one thing, he was handing her a knife already pointed at his heart, compromising his ability as a negotiator. How could he be anything but generous to a woman who could ruin his life simply by revealing their affair? He was also a doting companion and a surprising lover. If his interest in her were genuine, then joining him in his globe-trotting lifestyle would be glamorous and exciting. It would also be the ultimate victory over Alexandra.

But there was always the danger of discovery. Little mistakes like the note he had left on the mirror, or the coffee grounds she had almost left in the pot. Or the people who had tried to follow her, most likely Alexandra's investigators. Sooner or later they would succeed in following her, regardless of her twists and turns. If Alexandra walked in on them then her position as Jonathan's widow would be fatally compromised. And the probable divorce battle between Alexandra and Jack could tie up the Donner estate for years.

What she needed was to get the negotiations finished, take her settlement and get started on her new life. Jack's interest in her would encourage him to be generous, and if he wanted to see more of her, so much the better.

She looked carefully from the top of the front steps. The street was lined with parked cars but there was no one in any of them. Pedestrians marched by purposefully without sparing her a glance. She felt safe hailing a taxi, but still kept glancing out the back window to be sure no one was following. When she reached her apartment she was relieved that the suspicious sedan was nowhere in sight. She glanced up at the building across the street. There seemed to be no one in any of the windows.

At the lobby desk there were no messages, and she was relieved that no one had been asking for her. She relaxed in the elevator and had no apprehensions when she opened her door and turned to lock it behind her.

"Hello, Nicole!"

FIFTY

She wheeled away from the door and was stunned to see Jimmy Farr standing in her living room. "Jimmy . . ."

He smiled. "You don't seem happy to see me."

Farr had shed the trappings of his past. At one time he was open silk shirts with medallions on heavy gold chains, and rings big enough to serve as brass knuckles. Now he was in an olive-colored summer suit, a button-down collar, and a conservative tie. The teased wave of his hair was gone; it was now cut short with an Ivy League part.

"I'm happy to see you," she lied. "And surprised. You don't usually show up until there's money to be had. I'm still the penniless widow." She walked past him into the living room, and glanced around in search of the leg-breaker who had always accompanied Jimmy. There was no one else there. "Where's Steve?" she asked, referring to the bodyguard.

"In Attica," he answered with a chuckle. "He went out on his own but didn't do very well." He made a great show of taking in the apartment with its obviously expensive furnishings and decorations. "Not nearly as well as you seem to have done. This place must have set you back a bundle."

"It's my husband's apartment," she answered, "and it's still tied up in his estate." She walked into the kitchen. "I'm going to put on a pot of coffee. Would you like a cup?"

"A drink would be better," he answered stepping behind the bar. Then he raised his voice to reach the kitchen. "I heard about your husband. Tragic! I want to express my sympathy." She didn't answer.

Farr carried his whiskey and soda into the kitchen and leaned on the counter beside her. He raised her chin with a casual finger and slowly studied her figure from top to bottom. "I'll bet he died a happy man. You must have brought a lot of joy into his life."

She pulled away, took down a kitchen mug, and poured her coffee, feeling his eyes on her every second. She sat at the breakfast table and gestured for him to take a chair. "What do you want, Jimmy?" she asked.

"Want? Me? Don't be silly, Nicole. I just

stopped by to pay my condolences and to congratulate you on your newfound fortune. You've come a long way from posing in that bed in Tommy Hilburton's garage. What did you get for those shots? Five hundred?"

"Three," she answered. "And once he didn't pay me."

"And I'll bet the escort service wasn't much better. By the time everyone took his cut there couldn't have been much left for you . . ."

"What do you want, Jimmy?" she repeated.

"Just to see you," he said. "In our telephone chats you've been cold and unfriendly. Almost as if you're ashamed of your old friends now that you're in high society. You didn't even invite me to the wedding!"

"The Donner money," she said, getting to the point, "is tied up in trusts. It will be years before everything is settled, and there won't be much coming to me. Not enough to interest you."

"You know something, you're right. At first all I thought about was how much it would be worth to you to get back some of your old photographs. I figured the guy you were balling was probably worth twenty or thirty million . . . half for you and half for me. But the guy you're doing now! My God, do you know that Sound Holdings is one of the biggest investment banks in the world?" He enjoyed the shock that registered in her eyes. "Do you have any idea how much those guys handle every day? Let me tell that next to Sound Holdings, your dear departed husband was just pocket change. Daddy Jack really knows how to break the bank. When it comes to stealing, he's the best."

"Jack Donner wouldn't do anything illegal," she countered.

"Who said anything about illegal? Hell, those Wall Street outfits own the government. They write the laws. The way they steal is perfectly legal. Pick up a company for pocket change . . . kite the stock . . . and then dump it on all the fools who work for a living. It's perfectly legal. Hell, the government even gives you a tax break for doing it."

"And you think you can make money on Sound Holdings?" she asked sarcastically.

"Sure. With you on the inside, why not? And it isn't like I'd be asking you to get your hands dirty. Just suppose, for example, that you let me know what they were buying before they bought. I could get in on a good thing, like knowing how a horse race is going to turn out before the horses even come out of the barn. It costs you nothing. It doesn't cost Daddy Jack anything either. It's perfect."

"Except that I could end up in jail."

Jimmy laughed at the thought. "Nicole, you could go to prison right now for some of the things I've got on you. Besides, those guys never go to prison. Hell, they raise the money to build the prisons. That's where they put the people who get in their way."

The threat was obvious. Farr probably had lots of evidence of her past wrongdoings.

"I like your suit," she said to Jimmy. "But you're still the same rat."

He shook his head slowly. "I hate to hear you talk that way, Nicole, because I've really found religion. Adult entertainment is just a sideline with me. Now I'm into stocks and bonds. Sort of an investment adviser. I figure if you want to make real money you have to go where the money is. So we're really very much the same. We've both gone on to better things."

"Like blackmailing people," she fired back.

He wasn't at all angered by the charge.

"That's just business as usual. Your Wall Street friends do it all the time, and at City Hall it's a way of life. I think they call it Human Resources — getting the right people to do the right job."

Jimmy got up and set his empty glass in the sink. "And you're the right person for this job, Nicole. You're living right where they keep the horses, on the inside."

She told him he was crazy. She had been in Sound Holdings offices only for short visits with her husband. She had no idea what their business plans were and no way of finding out.

"Nicole," he said, when she had finished her argument, "I've invested a lot of time and effort in you. And it's not as if I was trying to cut into your action. All you have to do is join the firm and keep me posted on what they're up to. Is that so big a deal?"

"And how am I supposed to join the firm?"

"Just mention it to Donner some night when you're visiting his town house. He won't turn you down."

He smiled as he walked out of the kitchen and let himself out the front door. Nicole didn't try to stand up. Her legs felt terribly weak.

FIFTY-ONE

Pam had someone for Nicole to meet. William Kimes was a representative for several Midwestern galleries, a certified insider in the fine arts market. He was also anxious to move to New York, but had turned down several number-two positions hoping to launch his own venture. Best of all he was well polished and strikingly handsome, attributes that made him an ideal partner for Pam.

"I heard about him at work," Pam told Nicole in the taxi on their way to the cocktail party where Kimes had promised to be waiting. "My boss had met him at a gallery the day before and was planning to join him at an auction. I sort of hustled my way in."

"And he's interested?"

"Interested in what?"

"In your idea about starting a gallery."

"I think so. But we didn't get into details. I didn't want the word to get around that I was thinking of doing my own thing." She stuffed a wad of bills into the cabdriver's hand and stepped out into traffic, causing a blare of horns and a screech of brakes. "But I told him that I thought there was a real opportunity for a gallery offering new talent," she continued as she joined Nicole on the sidewalk, "and that I had a friend who was interested in starting one. I told him you would be putting up the money."

Nicole stopped short. Pam went on another step before she turned to face her.

"Well, you do have money and you'll be getting a lot more. And I want to be an owner, too. It's just going to take a while before I can pay my own way."

Nicole shook her head. "No wonder he's so anxious to meet me."

The party was in a West Side loft, over a huge automobile dealership. It was an art crowd; louder, younger, and more diverse than the financial types who had been in Newport with the Donners. Lots of black shirts and jackets, and hair colors that looked as if they came off an artist's palette. Kimes was easy to spot. He was one of the few in business attire, and he was being fought over by artists and agents. He excused himself when he recognized Pam and came across the chaotic room to join her. He bowed slightly when he was introduced to Nicole. "Don't go near the punch," he told her. "There are enough amphetamines in it to stock a hospital. And the wine would be an insult even to a jug. Stick with the bottled beer."

He led them to a corner where a windowsill offered a bit of seating and apologized for bringing them to such a trashy affair. "There are two artists here that are really going to make it big," he explained. "I want some of their work but I'm playing hard to get. So if we could stick around for a little while, I promise you a respectable supper in about an hour."

He was good to his word and took them uptown past Lincoln Center to a modest place that he promised "does great Italian." Then he got right down to business by asking Nicole how much she was planning to invest. Nicole glanced at Pam. "Whatever it takes, I suppose."

"Maybe five million," Pam filled in. Nicole tried to look blasé.

They talked through dinner with Pam hanging on his every word. Occasionally, Nicole interrupted with a question, and once or twice Pam added to something that Kimes had said. But it was his show, and his knowledge of the market was detailed and far-reaching. What disturbed

Nicole was how easily Pam was taken in. She was already in business with Kimes and they were lions of the art world. Whatever else she did, Nicole would make sure to get her sister-in-law a good lawyer. William Kimes might turn out to be a saint, but in the meantime someone should be looking out for Nicole's interests.

Jack called her early the next morning. He was already in the office taking the European calls, and claimed he just wanted to hear her voice. He hinted broadly that he would be late in town the next night, and would probably stay at his town house. "I've sent you something," he said. "It will be coming by messenger. If you don't want it, just throw it away. I'll understand."

She used the moment to tell him about Pam's plans to go into business. "He seems like a nice guy," she said of Kimes, "and he'd make a terrific partner. But you might want to give her some legal help if she's putting up the money."

"What money?" he grunted. "Pam doesn't have any money."

She had just finished her breakfast when the concierge called to say that he was sending up a package that had been delivered. When she opened it, she found a key to the front door of the town house.

FIFTY-TWO

Ben Tobin couldn't believe what he was hearing. Both sides in the bargaining over Jonathan's estate were caving in. He might be able to put together a settlement right on the spot.

First, it had been Nicole Donner. She was suddenly in a hurry to get the deal done. "Forget the apartment and the Newport house," she had called to tell him. "And I don't want the family name. All I want is to get out of this mess as fast as I can." She asked him where they stood on the money, and he told her it was at five million. Still too low, he advised her, considering the family's potential liability.

She had asked him about confidentiality. Was there a way that the agreement could be handled without anyone knowing about it? Difficult, he had explained. It need never make the newspapers but there would be papers filed in court to close the matter of Jonathan's estate. Then she had asked about offshore bank accounts. Could the money be deposited someplace where no one could get at it? More problems, he had explained. There were tax considerations. Once the money was hers she could put it wherever she wanted. But the government wouldn't let her take the money and run.

"Whatever is fastest," Nicole had urged. "Right now, getting away is just as important as getting every possible dollar."

"Nicole, what's the matter? Something has obviously happened. Tell me what it is."

Her answer was evasive and even bordered on being rude. "Lots of things have happened, and there's nothing I really want to go into. Just do the best you can to wrap it all up quickly."

Now he had Jack Donner on the phone, calling him directly without going through his army of lawyers. "I want to get this over with now, Ben," he had announced to his son's good friend. "Give me a reasonable offer. It doesn't have to be the cheapest, and it damn well better not be over the top. Just something that I can agree to without looking like a complete fool."

He couldn't believe he was talking to Jack Donner, the tightfisted, utterly unemotional tyrant who usually dictated what was fair and demanded a signature.

Not quite at gunpoint, but as close to it as he could get away with. When Jack presented a deal, he also presented a list of all the disastrous consequences that would beset an opponent who didn't sign. Sometimes the threatened ruin involved not only his adversary, but also the adversary's children and children's children. Yet here was Jack Donner begging an inexperienced junior not to make him look like a fool.

"Jack, I'll do everything I can," he said, hoping he didn't sound too obsequious. "I don't want to see Jonathan's name in the papers any more than you do."

When he hung up, Ben pondered his alternatives. Give Jack a deal that he would obviously appreciate, and then sell it to his troubled client. Or try to stiffen Nicole's courage and go for broke. One way, he might win Sound Holdings' business for the next generation. The other way, he could pull in a truly astronomical fee.

Alexandra thought she had found her smoking pistol, and there wasn't the least doubt in her mind that the evidence was genuine. Nicole had received two telephone calls from "that creep she was involved with," one the day after Pam's party, and the other while she was down in

Belize. One of Lambert's men had simply called Farr's cell phone service and talked to the clerk about alleged overcharges. Lambert didn't have a paper record, but one could be subpoenaed if necessary. The only conclusion, Alexandra believed, was that this Farr character still had his hooks into Nicole. The Donner fortune was just another opportunity for the two of them to make money.

But Jack didn't see it that way. All the calls proved was that someone from her past had tried to reach her and, whatever his motives might be, it said nothing about Nicole's motives. "Maybe the guy saw her name and figured he could blackmail her. He probably has the same old dirt that you dug up. And maybe she told him 'You're too late, pal, the family already knows.' All that's behind her, Alexandra, and I wish you could get past it yourself!"

Alexandra was taken aback by the vehemence of his defense and his refusal to even harbor a suspicion concerning Nicole. But then she remembered them chatting together at the party and Jack's long absence when he went to persuade her to stay. He likes her, she realized. Or, at least, he feels sorry for her. Or maybe he's sorry that he was never close to his son and he's trying to make it up. But whatever the reason, she knew she couldn't count on her husband to get rid of the girl. Jack wouldn't drive his typical merciless bargain where Nicole was concerned.

She was nearly as surprised by Pam's attitude. Her daughter was furious that Alexandra was still trying to find evidence that indicted Nicole and she wouldn't even discuss who might have called her or what the calls might mean. "Do you have any idea how mean and petty you are, hiring motel watchers to spy on Jonathan's wife? And why? All to save some money in the property settlement. Damn it, she's entitled to whatever Jonathan would have given her."

Pam had gone into her dealings with Nicole. "Jonathan's wife at least treats me as an adult," she said. She was Pam's confidante, and would soon be her partner in business. The news was a further shock for Alexandra. The girl had wormed her way into the lives of both her children. And with her gangster connections, she could be just as devastating to her daughter as she had been to her son.

It was no longer just a matter of money, nor simply a case of casting damaged goods aside. Alexandra realized that she was on the defensive. The girl was trying to take over her life, and it was beginning to look like she was succeeding. She had lured away Jonathan, and led him to his death in some Central American hellhole. Then she had captured her daughter into an empty-headed business deal where she might end up controlling Pam's money. And she had won over Jack. She had turned a shrewd, hardheaded trader into an old fool who was pleading her cause instead of cutting her throat.

Why was she the only one who could see through this girl? How could she be the only one who was aware of the danger? Alexandra understood that she had let Nicole call all the shots. But now she had to fight back. She had to take up the steel that her husband had cast aside. If he wouldn't get rid of her for good, then she would have to do it herself.

FIFTY-THREE

Jack was in no mood to quibble. Nicole was dangerous, able to destroy him with a simple reference to their affair. But he couldn't avoid the danger. He was drawn to her like a moth to a flame. He had to move her out of his life *now.*

"Twenty-five million," he told Ben Tobin, "paid out over five years. Five million a year."

Victor Crane sputtered into the water he was sipping. "You don't mean that Jack, do you?"

Jack looked daggers at his attorney. "I mean what I say, Victor. I want all this over with."

Crane asked Ben Tobin if he might have a word alone with his client and fidgeted with his papers until Nicole's lawyer was out of the room. "Jack, will you please explain what's going on here? I'm trying to keep the damage under ten million, afraid that you'll have my head if it gets even that high."

Jack grunted. "No one's blaming you.

You're doing your job —"

Crane interrupted. "It was their side that asked for this meeting. The young lady is collapsing. Ben Tobin was sent here to take what he can get." His hands went up in despair. "You're giving away twenty-five million dollars. Why?"

"That was Jonathan's legacy. When you clean up all the dummy transactions, that's about what he was worth. And she was his wife!" It wasn't easy for Jack to put too much sincerity into Nicole's rights as his son's widow. In the time he had spent in her bed he had taught himself not to be disturbed by thoughts of his son.

"She was his wife for less than a month. What could she do to earn that kind of money in a month?"

"Watch your mouth!" Jack flared. His eyes narrowed and his face contorted. "I don't want you talking about her like that!"

Victor Crane cringed before the onslaught. He had seen Jack explode on many occasions, usually when circumstances had denied him a financial victory. It was never a pretty scene. But Jack's rage vanished as suddenly as it had appeared. He shrugged, deflated, and settled back into his chair. "I'm sorry, Victor," he apologized, which was unusual enough. But then he went on to blame himself. "This . . . whole affair . . . has drained the life out of me. Since Jonathan's death, I've lost Alexandra and maybe even Pam. Nicole is even more . . . destitute . . . than I am. She's the only one I can talk to . . ."

A sudden flash of clarity jolted Crane. Jack and Nicole were no longer adversaries. They were on the same side, both hollowed by Jonathan's death and both terribly alone. Jack didn't want to be rid of Jonathan's wife. He wanted to take care of her.

"Let me handle this, Jack," he said in the solicitous voice of a friend. "I'll do right by the young lady, and right by you and Alexandra."

"That's what I was trying to do," Jack answered.

"You're so emotionally involved, it has to be impossible for you to stay objective," the attorney consoled. "Trust me! I'll get it right."

Jack nodded, got up from the boardroom table, and walked slowly through the side door into his office. "Thanks, Victor," were his parting words.

Now it was just the two lawyers who sat across from one another. Crane took off his suit jacket and hung it over the back of a chair. Ben pushed his chair away from the table, and leaned back with a writing pad in his lap.

"We have twenty-five million on the table," he said.

"Jack is distraught," Victor Crane answered. "The number has no meaning. Let's get down to business."

Crane said he was willing to agree to seven million right at that moment. It would be a one-time, one-payment settlement in return for Nicole giving up any future claims against the family. Tobin pointed out the enormous gap between the twenty-five million when he left the room and the seven million when he returned. "You don't expect me to give up on that amount just because Mr. Donner isn't feeling like himself."

Tobin guessed that Nicole would be happy with the seven million dollars. Based on her instructions, he didn't want the day to end without a deal, but he knew there was more money to be had. The problem was guessing just where Victor Crane's limits were.

FIFTY-FOUR

Nicole knew that she was running out of time. On one side, Alexandra Donner was digging for the information that could disinherit her. On the other, Jimmy Farr was expecting a lifetime of financial service. She needed to take the money and run.

That's exactly what she had done several years earlier when she broke away from Farr. Only then, the money had been pocket change — one packet of bills totaling five thousand dollars.

She had been on a mission for Jimmy, bringing cash to the Caribbean. Her assignment was simple. Check into a beachfront resort and enjoy the facilities while waiting to be contacted. Someone would approach her, identify himself, and give her a suitcase to pack. In return, she would turn over an identical suitcase that had cash sewn into the lining. Unpack one valise, and repack into another. She never even had to look at what was being bought and sold.

But then the police caught the man with

the cocaine and touched off a frantic search for the money. The drug people came looking for the cash. The police wanted to run down the other end of the transaction. And Jimmy Farr was telling her to catch the next plane back home. Nicole knew exactly what Jimmy wanted her to do. Keep his money out of the hands of the police and the grasp of his suppliers, and bring it back through already alerted customs officials and drug enforcement agencies. If she made it, he would tell her what a great job she had done. If she were caught, he would deny that he had ever heard of her.

She cut open the valise, took out one packet of money, and packed the case with some of her clothes and all the magazines and promotional flyers that had come with her hotel room. She had the bell captain pick up the bag and ship it to an address in Jersey City that served as a blind mail drop for Jimmy's interests. At the airport, she bought perfume in the duty-free shop, and put her money into the protective packaging. The perfume would go around customs and bypass the gate check. It wouldn't be returned to her until she was safely out of the country.

It seemed to go off without a hitch.

Nicole's perfume had been given to her in New York with all the proper documentation. She was able to give Jimmy Farr the receipt for the shipped suitcase, which won her a word of thanks and a pat on the fanny. But then the suitcase was seized by customs along with the cash inside. By the time Jimmy learned that the suitcase had been captured, Nicole had taken her money and disappeared. First, she used the money to lay low until Jimmy was just a bad memory. Then she made a new beginning as an apprentice in the brokerage business.

She had already moved up in the firm when Jimmy found her. By then, he had learned that the cash in his suitcase had been short five thousand dollars, and accused Nicole of helping herself to his money. She had suggested that the custom officials had probably taken a commission before turning the money over to the government, which was certainly plausible. But Jimmy couldn't shake down the government so he held Nicole responsible. She had paid back the money, with interest, over the next two years.

This time the money would come with legal papers to prove its authenticity. No one in government would be looking for it.

As far as the law was concerned she would be in the clear. But Jimmy didn't want her to run. He wanted her inside of Sound Holdings. Of course, once she left the family, his blackmail threat wouldn't hold much clout. But Jimmy Farr had never learned how to lose gracefully. If she crossed him, he would come after her.

That was why she was taking such precautions. The money, when received by her New York bank, would stay there for just the few moments it took to transfer it to Switzerland. Ben Tobin was making the arrangements for her settlement to go to a secret numbered account.

Then she had to disappear and become just as impossible to trace as the money. She had reserved a coach airline ticket under the name O'Brien, which was her maternal grandmother's maiden name. Then the Irish consul in New York had given her the application forms for an Irish passport, a courtesy the republic extends to descendants of Irish emigrants. The theory is that anyone who left Ireland must have been a political refugee because no one would leave of his own accord. The consul had checked the authenticity of the original O'Brien in Cork, and with no further ado, issued the document. It was already packed in the side of her suitcase. All that remained was Tobin's assurance that her inheritance had been deposited. Then she would head for the airport, and put an end to an affair that had turned into a terrible nightmare.

But the money wasn't coming. According to the call she received from Ben Tobin, he and Victor Crane were still far apart on the amount. Ben had heard Jack Donner say twenty-five million and, while he was prepared to accept that the figure was an emotional outburst, he wasn't prepared to take seven million instead. He was mindful that Nicole had told him to accept anything but, like Victor, he had a duty to protect his client from her moment of weakness. He had kept arguing for a number that would at least split the difference between them, and had decided that fifteen million would be a reasonable outcome. But the other attorney wasn't budging. Finally, Crane had announced they were at an impasse and had suggested they adjourn for a day or so.

"Are you going to be more generous in a day or so?" Ben had asked sarcastically and then suggested, "Let's get Jack in here and tell him where we are. Maybe he can come up with a solution."

Victor had put down the idea quickly. Too quickly, Ben thought, catching a hint that the enemy camp might be divided. That was when he had stepped out into a private office and phoned Nicole.

"I'm getting nowhere with Victor Crane," he told her. "But I think I could do better going directly to Jack Donner. What do you think?"

"Yes," she answered. "I think you would."

He read the situation accurately. Jack had reason to be very generous to Nicole, more generous than his handlers would allow. He had to get Jack alone in a room and get the deal done.

"Nicole, is there anything else I should know about? Any reason why Jack is vulnerable?"

She hesitated a bit too long, and then answered with platitudes about Jack's fatherly concern that she be treated fairly. "Alexandra drove both Jonathan and I away," she explained. "Jack wants to make it up to me."

He knew she was lying. Jack Donner didn't treat anyone fairly unless it was in his own interest, and he wouldn't easily cross his wife. There was something very different about his relationship with his daughter-in-law. What he suspected was nearly unthinkable. But then again, what was more unthinkable than Jack Donner giving away twenty-five million dollars?

Ben returned to the conference room and insisted that Jack be brought back into the meeting. Victor flatly refused. Ben picked up his papers and packed his brief-case. Then the other attorney made a fatal mistake. He raised his offer and announced he was ready to initial a nine-million-dollar deal right on the spot. All he succeeded in doing was to convince Ben that there was much more to be had by talking with Jack. He hoped it was fatherly affection, but he guessed that the hard-hearted banking baron was very much taken with his son's widow.

FIFTY-FIVE

Greg Lambert had pushed his investigation using Donner money in place of court subpoenas. Where federal detectives and local police could use the courts to compel testimony, Lambert had used bribes. Money had attracted witnesses that government agents wouldn't even have known about.

He had conferenced with Alexandra every day, even if he had no answers to share but only more questions. First, he had run down the exact nature of the relationship between Jimmy Farr and Nicole. Jimmy had taken her in when David Hanna, the director, had dumped her, and Nicole was at the very end of her resources. He had made her the chaperone to his adult dancers, most still in their teens, given her a cut of the tips, and lent her an apartment that he borrowed back on occasions. Then he had promoted her to courier in his drug trade, the position she filled on her ill-fated trip to the Caribbean. As far as Lambert could learn, Nicole had never been Jimmy's woman, although he might have taken advantage of her presence in his apartment. Basically, Jimmy wasn't interested in women except as a source of income.

David Hanna, on the other hand, had flaunted her as his personal and totally submissive property, even lending her to visiting Hollywood dignitaries. Her reward was his occasional attention, promises of important parts in upcoming plays, and access to his stash of cocaine. In many ways, Hanna had been more abusive than Jimmy Farr.

Lambert had run down roommates and boyfriends all the way back to Nicole's arrival in New York. "She was really trying to make it in theater," he reported to Alexandra. "But the general impression is that she would do whatever it took to get by." He had added photographs, bank records, and receipts, all supporting the picture of a young woman living on the edge of the law and even closer to the edge of decency. There was certainly more than enough ammunition to drive Nicole out of the family and back into hiding.

But Alexandra was past all that. Sordid living in the past was no longer enough. She needed hard evidence that Nicole was still involved with underworld types. She needed proof that would convict the girl of murdering her son and conspiring to steal the family fortune. It was that kind of information that Greg Lambert thought he had found.

"Phone records," he said, laying photocopies in front of her. "Farr phoned Nicole's apartment twice the day after Pam's graduation party. That would be when her picture appeared on the society page. Then Nicole phoned him from Belize City. She was in town filling out police forms about the break-in at their honeymoon cottage."

Alexandra smiled as she examined the records. "Where did you get these? From Nicole's apartment? Or from her gangster friend?"

"Actually, from his wireless company," Lambert smiled, enjoying a moment of self-congratulation. "Their network guru needed five thousand dollars."

"Nice going," Alexandra said. She gathered up the papers. Now even Jack would have to admit that Jonathan's wife had never severed her low-life connections.

She laid everything out for Jack and Pam later that evening. Jimmy Farr was the thug who had dominated Nicole's past. And here they were still chummy before, during, and after Jonathan's death. But Pam sprung instantly to Nicole's defense. The phone calls proved only that they had talked. "Nicole might have been telling him to get lost."

"They had several conversations," Alexandra countered. " 'Get lost' is only one short call."

"Maybe he was blackmailing her. Threatening to expose all the dirt that you've enjoyed playing in," Pam fired back. "And just who is this creep anyway? How do we know that he ever had his fangs into Nicole?"

Alexandra handed her the folder of Greg Lambert's reports. "There's a lot about your new big sister that you should learn."

Jack didn't want to hear any of the information. As soon as Alexandra mentioned new evidence, he went into a tirade about her using the security people to pursue her private vendetta. "Damn it, our son is dead! Why are you still trying to smear the reputation of the woman he married?"

"Because I think she may be involved in his death. I think she was scheming for his money right from the beginning."

He immediately sided with Pam. The telephone calls proved nothing. Alexandra was the one who had been scheming right from the beginning to break up the relationship. Jonathan had found a wonderful woman who would have made him happy. Just as important, she would have made him into a man. Hadn't she given him the courage to defy his father, and start out on his own business venture? Nicole had understood the problem. She had warned him that Alexandra couldn't bear the thought of Jonathan leaving home. She had been right on the mark when she said that Alexandra was blaming him for their son's insecurity.

When Pam stormed off with the evidence clutched in her hand, Jack was able to calm himself. He apologized for the attack on his wife. Then he begged her, "Let it go, please. She'll be gone in a few days. We're that close to ending all her financial claims. Then we won't ever have to think about her again."

He knew that wasn't true. Even as he said the words he knew that he would continue thinking about her. His fondest hope was that she would settle comfortably somewhere and then welcome his visits. His business took him all over the world. He could meet with her no matter where she went.

He was alone in his study when Ben

Tobin called on the telephone. Jack mumbled a greeting and then asked how things had gone after he left the meeting. Ben answered frankly that they were at an impasse.

"I'll talk to Victor," Jack said. "Give me a chance to talk to him before you two get together again."

Ben answered, "I think it will be better if you and I get together, Jack. I don't think Victor has any idea of how much you want to do right by the woman. He's treating her as an adversary. That's not how you think of her, is it?"

"No . . . no. Of course not."

"I'm sure that you and I can wrap everything up in an hour. Why don't I stop by your office in the morning? We can agree on the broad picture and then Victor and I can fill in the details."

"Sure," Jack agreed. "In the morning . . ." He hung up while he was still talking, before they could even set a time. He stood and went to his bar, poured a Scotch over ice, and then wrapped his big hands around the glass. Adversary, he thought. How could he think of her as an adversary?

She was trouble, no doubt about it, and he would be much better off to be rid of her. What would Alexandra do if she found out? Drag him through a year of humiliation while she broke his empire into little pieces? Leave him as a public fool. Or even worse, go right on living with him so that he would shiver with guilt every time he felt her eyes on him. And Pam? What would she think when she found out that her father was screwing her brother's wife? Who would she blame? The new sister who had brought independence and courage into Jonathan's life? Or the dirty old man who had seduced and ravaged her?

As much as he hated the thought, Jack knew that he needed a clean break. He needed to agree on an annual stipend to be paid with the proviso that she never have any further contact with him or his family, and that she agree to live in another country, across the ocean, or anywhere where their paths would never cross. How much money? What did it matter? The biggest price was that he would be living the rest of his life without her. The rest was just pocket change.

FIFTY-SIX

As she turned the corner toward her doorway, Nicole saw Jimmy step out of the car. It was a big sedan, less conspicuous than a limousine, and he held the rear door open as if he were a chauffeur welcoming a rider. "Nicole, what a coincidence. You're just the person I was looking for." He took her arm in a vise grip, making it clear that he wanted her to get into the car. She went easily, pretending that she didn't mind being plucked off the street.

There were two men in front of her, both making a point of staring straight ahead. Jimmy settled into the soft leather of the rear seat, and Nicole moved against the far door, keeping as much space between them as she could. The car pulled into traffic, made a westbound turn to Fifth Avenue, and then entered Central Park. Farr looked out the window as if Nicole wasn't even there.

"Where are we going?" she asked when she couldn't stand the silence.

"That's what I'm wondering," he said

sparing her a glance. "Exactly where are we going? How close are we to being inside the Sound Holdings boardroom?"

"We're a long way off. I've dropped a few hints, but the subject hasn't even come up. Jack Donner doesn't like women handling money matters."

Jimmy smirked. "We both know what Jack Donner likes. The question is how is he going to pay for what he likes. Does he give you a position because you tell him you're interested? Or does he take you on board because I tell him what will happen if he doesn't?"

"Be careful, Jimmy. Jack has all kinds of connections. You won't be able to frighten him with your muscles."

"Who said anything about muscle? All I have to do is tell my friends in the tabloids who he's sleeping with." He had to laugh at his own brilliance. "Bet he'd hate to have his wife see your pictures while she's checking out at the supermarket."

Nicole shook her head. "You haven't changed a bit. Still the same rat!"

"I get what I want," he answered.

She turned in her seat so that she was facing him. "Not if you try to blackmail Jack Donner. You might ruin him, but you'll end up in Attica with your friend,

Steve. Two past mayors, the police commissioner, and the federal prosecutor come to Jack's parties. If they can't find a crime to jail you for, they'll make something up."

He frowned. "Okay, then. What do you suggest?"

"Patience," she answered instantly. "I can't just walk into a board meeting. It's going to take time to get invited."

"How much time?"

"I don't know. A few months. Maybe longer!"

"A few months?" He leaned forward and pulled a newspaper out of the seat-back pouch in front of him. The paper was folded to an article that had Sound Holdings in the headline. "Did you know about this?"

She glanced at the first few lines and shrugged. "He took a position in some bio outfit. So what?"

"Yesterday, Sound Holdings bought fifty thousand shares of BioLabs at thirty. This morning the stock opened at forty, and jumped to fifty-five. That's a profit of three-quarters of a million on one stock in one day. Do you know what that can add up to in 'a few months'? Do you have any idea how much we could be making if you were inside, telling me about the next

BioLabs before Jack Donner puts up his money?"

"It will take time," she answered.

"Nicole, I'm not going to sit quietly and miss out on opportunities for a few months. I want you inside in a few weeks."

There was no point in arguing with him. All she really needed was a few days to move the money and then move herself. Jimmy wouldn't know how to look for her in Europe. And once Alexandra figured out that she was gone forever, she wouldn't even bother looking. "I can't guarantee when it will happen, Jimmy. But I'm working on it, and I'll push as hard as I can without turning Jack off."

He reached out and pinched her cheek. "That's the Nicole I used to know," he said with a smile. He touched the driver's shoulder and the sedan pulled to the curb. He reached across and pushed open her door. "Remember, I'll be looking in on you from time to time."

She hailed a taxi and rode back to the East Side. As she got out in front of her building she glanced at the windows across the avenue. Then she walked to the side street and looked for the car that had followed her. Ridiculous, she told herself. Like all the city's side streets, this one was a row of cars parked bumper to bumper. Jimmy could use a different car each day, so what was the point in looking? There were a hundred windows looking down on her from across the street. Prying eyes could be behind the curtains in any one of them. Hell, Jimmy had even let himself into her apartment. It would be just as easy for him to have someone watching her from one of the other apartments. She had to accept it as a fact that Farr had her under around-the-clock surveillance. Maybe he was even tapping her telephone. She decided to walk around the block so that she could use her cell phone to call Ben Tobin.

"What happened?" she asked when he came on the line.

"Nothing. Jack Donner never showed at his office. I spent over an hour cooling my heels in his waiting room."

"What does that mean? That he's done talking with us?" She was frightened at the thought that her deal might be falling through.

"I don't know what it means," Ben admitted. "But it isn't just me he's ducking. The people in his office don't know where he is and they're plainly worried. Victor Crane hasn't heard from him. Nobody has."

Jack was waiting in Nicole's apartment. He had spent the previous evening weighing his choices against his responsibilities, and had reaffirmed his decision to send his son's wife into exile. On his ride into Manhattan he had decided that he and Nicole didn't need to be talking through lawyers. They could settle things themselves. He would admit how dearly he loved her, but would simply present the evidence that proved he could never have her. Too many others, people he truly loved, would be hurt.

Then, he would tell her what he wanted. She could go anywhere she wanted and live in whatever style suited her. All he needed was her agreement that it would be best if she never came near him or his family. That he would find unbearable.

He had left his driver at the door to his office building, walked through the lobby and hailed a taxi. Then he had gone to Jonathan's apartment expecting to find her there. He let himself in when she didn't answer his ring, and sat in silence waiting for her return. He hoped she hadn't gone to see her lawyer. He didn't want any more legal entanglements.

When the phone rang he knew he shouldn't answer it. There was no reason for him to be in Nicole's apartment. He let her machine record the message. When he recognized Pam's voice he sighed in relief. Thank God she hadn't discovered that he was with his daughter-in-law.

Pam didn't speak at her usual breathless pace, with words tumbling in half finished sentences. This time she sounded all business. "Nicole, we need to talk. William Kimes and I have our studio. It's an ideal space in a great location and I can't wait to show it to you. We want you in with us as a partner. Also, there's something I have to show you. It's information about you that my mother's snoops have dug up. It's stuff that could cause you problems. Call me back. We really need to get together soon!"

Jack was left staring at the machine when his daughter's voice clicked off. What studio was she talking about? And who the hell was William Kimes?

FIFTY-SEVEN

William Kimes had been slow to realize what a wonderful thing was happening to him. The blond art groupie that wanted to open a gallery had turned out to be one of the richest women on earth. And she was coming on to him as if he were a rock star instead of an art dealer.

He had agreed to meet her friend who supposedly was the investor. The friend hadn't been all that interested, and Kimes thought that the lure of an investor was just a line to get a date. Clever girl, he had thought. It was a better approach than asking his astrological sign, or wondering if he would take a look at her stereo system.

"Love to talk more about your project," he had said when he packed her into a taxi. "I'm in town quite a bit. I'll call you." It was a routine promise, but one that he thought he might keep. After all, she was certainly attractive and pleasant company even if her enthusiasm could become tiresome. What was her name again? Dasher? Dander? He found the card she had given him when he was undressing back at his hotel. Pamela Donner. Donner, that was it. He slipped the card into his wallet. Maybe he'd call her to set up a date when he was returning to New York.

He had been taking his morning shower when he remembered where he had heard the name. Donner was the lady who was on the board of one of the museums. The money was her husband's, some tycoon from Wall Street. Who in hell was he? Kimes dropped the soap when he remembered. Jack Donner from Sound Holdings! Could she be? He shook his head. No, it couldn't be. He laughed at himself for even considering such a ridiculous idea.

But when his phone rang it was Pam. She was bubbling with excitement and anxious to get started. "Maybe you could do some scouting. You have a much better idea of what we'll need and where we ought to be. I'm sure whatever you pick will be perfect."

"What am I scouting for?" he asked, his confusion obvious.

"The gallery. We'll need show space and storage space. We were talking about it last night."

"Pam, do I know you? Your name seems familiar."

"Probably it's my mother that you know. She's heavy into art. She raises all sorts of money for museums and galleries. She probably hit you up for a donation or something."

"Yes, I've heard of her. And your father is . . ."

"A financier. He owns Sound Holdings."

He was staring wide-eyed at the telephone long after Pam had hung up.

Kimes had called the desk and canceled his checkout. He called Indianapolis and told his office that he would be staying on in New York for a few days. Then he started down Park Avenue to visit some of his associates who owned galleries.

He and Pam had been together every evening, marching through the Upper East Side art district until everything closed, and then stopping in small restaurants for light dinners. Pam, he discovered, had excellent taste both in art and in properties. She also had an unlimited budget or, more accurately, absolutely no idea of what a budget was. She was sold on locations before she even asked the rent, and even the most outlandish figures failed to alarm her. She talked decoration and design as if she were furnishing a dollhouse.

In the course of conversation, Pam had

let slip little hints of the kind of money she might bring to the party. She referred to a desk as being like the one her mother had in the Newport house, and a picture was like a painting in the entrance gallery of the North Shore house. She didn't care for seascapes. There were too many of them hanging in the family yacht.

Carefully, he had probed these revelations, expanding them to their full significance. "It must be a big house?" was an innocent enough question, but it elicited that there were thirty-eight rooms at Rockbottom — not counting the cabanas. "Oh, and how do you like Paris?" was an inoffensive way of asking how often she went and where she stayed. As the evidence mounted, the size of her potential investment became enormous. Kimes realized that she might be able to buy any painting in the world, and that just one of the great ones could make their gallery the talk of the art world.

There also had been suggestions of romantic possibilities. Twice when he had dropped her off, Pam had asked him up for the requisite drink. She was probably just being polite, but there was a chance she was announcing her availability. And that was both a glorious opportunity and a dangerous hazard. Romantic involvement might become the glue of the business involvement, giving him endless access to both the girl's charms and financial treasure. But the same scenario could well be described as the seduction of Jack Donner's daughter intended to lay claim on Jack Donner's money. In his indecision, Kimes handled her like a bomb that might explode at any moment, afraid either to set it down or to toy with its wiring. The safest course was to toss it in one direction and run in the other. But to the handsome young art buyer, beauty and money were an irresistible combination.

They had settled on a location, a second floor on Madison Avenue, east of the Guggenheim. It was a new building that could easily be partitioned into separate galleries and office areas, and it had its own walk-up entrance from the street. It was at that point that Pam admitted she didn't have the money to put down, but it would be coming shortly. Her father would be delighted with her initiative, and would certainly cover the renovation costs. And then, her sister-in-law whom Kimes had met, would be bringing more money to the party. The funds were there, and there was no reason why they shouldn't plunge ahead. She had even brought him to meet Ben Tobin, her attorney, who had drawn up the agreement of partnership.

But the money wasn't coming and, while there were further hints of romantic interest, he was no closer to becoming Pam's lover. Gradually, it began to dawn on him that while he thought he was coming into a fortune, the fact was that little Pam Donner was picking his brains and marketing his expertise.

Pam signed the lease, paying the deposit out of her pocket money while he put up the advances due to the contractors. Then she and William began renovating the space. She concentrated on remodeling and decorating, while he searched for the artists he hoped to involve. But he balked at putting up any more money. What about the investor she had introduced him to? And where was Jack Donner's fatherly support? He began to hint that he might have to reclaim his old career, and return to his offices in Indianapolis.

Their romance started accidentally. A carpenter drove a nail into a new water pipe, and the water pressure pushed out the nail. Pam arrived after work to find part of the ceiling on the floor and workmen from three different unions trying to argue in unrelated languages. Kimes came upon Pam in tears, took her in his arms to console her and ended up making love to her on top of soggy drop cloths. They needed paint thinner to wipe off the stains of olive and white, and then showers to wash off the paint thinner. With that much intimacy already behind them, Kimes had no second thoughts about moving from his hotel to her apartment, hoping that the money would follow soon.

FIFTY-EIGHT

Jack was sitting with his face in his hands when he heard Nicole's key turn in the lock. She was stunned to see him but recovered quickly. "Jack, what a pleasant surprise."

"It's been a morning of surprises," he answered. He nodded toward the answering machine. "I just heard my daughter tell you that she was opening a gallery. She seems to be counting on you to become her partner."

She offered food, coffee, and then alcohol, but he waved them all away. "There's something I have to tell you, and it's not easy for me. I need you to just sit here with me and listen."

"I don't like the sound of this," Nicole answered, but she settled onto the edge of a chair directly across from his place on the sofa.

Jack spoke without emotion, just as if he were reviewing the pros and cons of buying into a new issue. His eyes were fixated on his hands that he kept folding and unfolding. Only occasionally did his glance flicker up to Nicole.

It was the story he had rehearsed. In the beginning he had assumed that she was just another of Jonathan's friends, classier than most of them and certainly more attractive than any. But he had quickly grown to like her and perhaps even envy his son's good fortune. "I love Alexandra," he assured her and himself as well, "but you had . . . have . . . this electrical attraction. I was certainly taken in."

He had never agreed with Alexandra's paranoia for protecting Jonathan. He had certainly never supported her snooping into Nicole's background. He knew that Jonathan was happy with his choice, and he was happy for his son. Oh, sure, he had his concerns. All parents do. But there was nothing that would have prompted him to oppose the wedding.

Then Jonathan died, and he was shaken to the soul. Despite all his bluster he loved his son, and the loss left him hollow and emotionless. He thought he recognized the same emptiness in her, and that was what had drawn him to her.

"I had no right . . . no right at all . . . to touch you. But I would have died if it hadn't been for you. And then I realized how much . . . how deeply . . . I loved you.

That's what I acted on. That's what I'm still acting on."

He made his case as to why he had to break off the affair, hoping that she would understand and not hate him too much. It would destroy Alexandra who, despite her irrational dislike for Nicole, still didn't deserve to be treated shabbily. It would drive away his daughter. It would certainly tarnish the empire he had built, and in financial empires tarnish was every bit as fatal as rust is to iron. His business was held together by confidence in his integrity. Scandal would gnaw away at confidence.

Nicole listened sympathetically, acknowledging that their relationship would always be a danger to him. What he was putting at risk was magnitudes more than anything she stood to lose.

Jack got down to his proposal. There had to be a wide and permanent separation between them. She had to leave the orbit of his life or otherwise he would always be moving toward her, even when he thought he was moving away. But he wanted her to live just as Jonathan would have wanted. He wanted her to have everything that their marriage would have provided, and the wealth and security that he himself would have given her.

"I don't want our lawyers and accountants arguing over you as if you were a commodity, or as if there were some price that would precisely match your value. So I'm going to settle it myself. I'll have a check ready for fifteen million dollars. Just sign the damn papers they put in front of you, and take the check. Try to think of it as an expression of affection, and not as a settlement."

He fell into a silence that she had to interrupt. "Jack, that's very generous of you. I'll never forget you . . . or Jonathan . . ."

Jack stood. "I'll say my good-byes now. I don't think I should be at the meeting. I couldn't fake a simple handshake." He took her in his arms, held her close for just a second, and then turned to the door. Nicole stood watching until he was gone.

FIFTY-NINE

"Fifteen million." Victor Crane shook his head. "It's a hell of a lot of money, and just because Jack can make it back in a few weeks, doesn't make it cheap."

"Cheap compared to the twenty-five million he wanted to pay her," Ben Tobin answered. "And when you figure how easily she might have tied the family fortune in knots, it's probably a bargain."

They were in Victor's conference room going over the details of the agreement. There were documents for Nicole that waved any future claims against the Donner estate, her surrender of the right to use the Donner name. There were also tax forms that recognized liability for the taxes involved, and agreements for Jack, Alexandra, and Pam, acknowledging the payment and giving up any future claim to the money. The two men read together, stopping to debate words and phrases and send secretaries scurrying back to their word processors.

Nicole arrived in a dark suit, befitting

the assumed dignity of legal proceedings. She signed without reading, simply glancing at Ben and acting on his nod. She took the check as casually as if it were payment for Girl Scout cookies, and handed it over to Ben for processing. Then she stood, shook hands all around, and left the office, her heels clicking on the hardwood floor of the lobby.

"What was she worth six months ago?" Victor wondered aloud.

"A few thousand. Less than ten, I think," Ben answered.

"A very fortunate woman!"

"She just lost her husband," Ben corrected.

Victor smirked. "A very fortunate woman," he repeated.

Nicole went back to her apartment, dressed in jeans and a sweater, and gathered her luggage. It was a minimal burden for the concierge — one medium-size valise with wheels and a handle, and an overnight bag with a shoulder strap. "When will you be coming back, Mrs. Donner?" he asked as he helped her into a taxi.

"In a few days," she lied. "A week at the most." That was the message she had left on her answering machine. She would be visiting out on Long Island for a few days and then would be back home. Jimmy would be pleased at the thought that she was worming her way back into the Donner household. She didn't want her absence to alarm him.

She directed her driver up the East Side and then across one of the East River bridges. Her head turned constantly, looking for cars that might be following. Once on the Queens side she directed the driver to return by a different route to Manhattan. When she was sure that no one had hung behind her, she gave her real destination, a busy tourist hotel on the West Side, only a ten-minute walk from the apartment she had left.

But the maneuver had effectively opened light years between her new life and the life she was leaving behind. Jack, for all his resources, wouldn't be able to find her. Jimmy Farr would spend a week watching her empty apartment. Pam, in her new venture, would have to fend for herself. And Alexandra would have no one to accuse no matter how much evidence she gathered. The woman they all thought they knew had vanished from the landscape. When she reappeared, it would be in totally new surroundings.

All Nicole had to do was wait a day or so, check with Ben Tobin, and make sure her check had cleared. Then the bank would be able to tell her when the funds were safely tucked away in her Swiss account. At that point, she would walk out of her hotel to a rental car agency, and take a car up to the airport in Boston. A transatlantic flight would carry her to France where her Irish passport would gain her easy entry. And then, with that passport giving her unquestioned access to any of the European countries, she would find a home suitable to a woman of her newfound wealth.

Jimmy would go crazy, a thought that brought a smile to her lips. He'd watch the Sound Holdings offices, probably even phone to find out if she had already moved in with the senior executives. He'd watch Jack's town house and check the residences on Long Island and in Newport. By the time he realized that she was gone her trail would already have turned cold. Maybe he'd find out about the settlement, and realize that she had already made off with more money than he had ever been able to pocket for all his wheeling and dealing. Nicole would love to see his reaction when he knew that his dancing girl had outsmarted him, but that was a pleasure she had to deny herself.

And Jack! Poor Jack! He was a decent man despite his tough-guy personality. He truly would miss her much more than any amount of money he could have paid. But he had made the only decision possible — the decision she had expected since the first moment she caught him ogling her. Too bad, because he would have made a great traveling companion.

She thought that she would like to see Pam again. She knew that Jonathan's sister would feel betrayed by her abrupt departure, and hurt that Nicole hadn't said as much as a good-bye. Probably Nicole would be able to follow her career in the art sections of the newspapers. It would be fun to drop in from nowhere at one of her European events. But that wouldn't be possible. Like the joy of watching Jimmy Farr go into a tantrum, it was a pleasure that she could never allow herself. She had to vanish completely and permanently.

Alexandra would be apoplectic when she learned that her daughter-in-law had made off with a fortune. Not that she couldn't spare the money but rather because the girl that she wanted to crush had slipped out from under her shoe. And there was no deniability in fifteen million dollars. That was more than her daughter-in-law would have cost her in a lifetime. Nicole was afraid to ever see her again. Alexandra, she knew, was perfectly capable of killing her.

She knew that Alexandra hated her and thought that she had killed her son with all the cold detachment of a psychopath. Jonathan's mother wasn't sure exactly how she had done it, but she knew that Nicole had caused her son's death just to lock in her claim to the Donner fortune. Jonathan's life traded for Nicole's financial security? Alexandra could easily have pulled the trigger.

Nicole walked two blocks from her hotel before using her cell phone to call Ben, and even then she talked as if someone might be listening. "It's me!" she announced. "Just calling to see how everything is going. Any hitches?"

He recognized her voice. "No, just the accountants setting up our fee and computing the set-asides. Looks like about nine going into your account now and maybe another three after the taxes clear."

"When?" she asked.

"Maybe late tomorrow. Certainly by Friday. Where can I call you to tell you when the money is yours?"

"My cell phone. But I'm keeping it turned off, so I'll be hard to reach," Nicole said. "I'll call you Friday. And Ben, do what you can to make it happen. I don't want to wait around over the weekend."

"Nicole, what's the matter? Is something wrong? Are you in some sort of danger?"

"People are looking for me," she answered. "It's best if they don't find me."

He searched his memory. "You mean Alexandra? Are you still worried about Alexandra? Because she's not your problem anymore. If she doesn't like the arrangement she can take it up with Jack."

"Alexandra will always be my problem," she answered.

Ben thought she sounded confused. "Nicole, you have nothing to worry about. If you want, you can come to my place. You can stay there until everything clears. . . ."

"Thanks, Ben," she answered. "I'll call you on Friday."

SIXTY

"The negotiations are over," Jack reported to his wife when he returned home that night. "You won't have to worry about her anymore."

"She agreed? With no future claims?"

"She agreed to everything."

Alexandra squinted suspiciously. "How much did she get?"

Jack rolled his eyes. "Nothing we can't afford. It was a good deal all around."

"Two million?" Alexandra speculated.

"Oh for God's sake," Jack snapped. "Isn't this what you wanted, Jonathan's wife out of your sight forever? Well now you have it. She's gone! Banished!"

"Jack, we have all the evidence we need to get rid of her. We don't have to pay her."

"Well, we paid her, and she's gone. So now we don't need to keep digging up evidence. We can stop all this and get on with our lives."

"It was more than two million, wasn't it?" She recognized his habit of trying to disguise a bad deal.

"Yes, it was more."

"A lot more," she prompted.

"I gave her fifteen million, which was less than half of what Jonathan's estate might have come to . . ."

Alexandra stared blankly and then began to chuckle. "Fifteen million? Exactly what did she have on you?"

His fists clenched as he struggled for control of himself. He turned away abruptly and stormed into his office, slamming the door behind him. In his humiliating retreat she knew she had guessed correctly. The bitch had seduced him, making it impossible for him to stand up against her.

SIXTY-ONE

Jimmy Farr was beginning to understand that a fortune was slipping through his fingers. He had been puzzled by Nicole's absence but not alarmed. Her recorded message, saying that she would be away a few days, made perfect sense. Probably playing house with Jack Donner, he figured. That was her surest way into his boardroom. Or maybe out at the North Shore mansion, trying to make peace with Alexandra.

But she wasn't anywhere. She hadn't come home, and there was nobody at the town house. Jack Donner was showing up at his office and taking his limo home at night, so they couldn't be off someplace together. And his watchmen hadn't seen any sign of her around the family mansion.

Nicole's absence could mean only one thing: she had been paid off! All her claims had been settled and she was footloose with a few million of the Donners' money. She had double-crossed him, even outsmarted him, and that was something that he couldn't allow. Whatever she had gotten, he was entitled to his share. And if she tried to hold out on him, he would take it all.

He started with the airlines. He had one of his exotic dancers call them, one at a time, claiming to be Nicole Pierce, and then Nicole Donner. She had lost her ticket and reservation. Could they help her? They couldn't, the girl was told over and over again. Not without a reservation number, or the date and destination of the flight.

He called the airports. He had requested a seat with Nicole Pierce or Donner. He wasn't sure which name she might have used. No, he didn't know the flight. Could they please help him out? They couldn't.

Then he tried the hotels. There were a thousand of them in New York, not counting all the Holiday Inns and Best Westerns in the suburbs. And who could be sure what name she might have used to check in? New York hotels didn't ask for a passport, and chances were that she paid cash. He struck out enough times to know that it was hopeless.

There was no way that he could find her. He simply didn't have the manpower to stake out all the places where she might be. All he knew was that she had walked out of her apartment and disappeared. Probably after she had received a couple of million dollars from the Donners to do just that. "Here's your money. Now get lost!" Easy for them to say, but it had cost him the best opportunity of his lifetime. He had almost been inside one of the circles that fixed the ups and downs of the market. He was guaranteed great quantities of easy money as long as Nicole kept acting like a daughter-in-law, or kept Jack Donner smiling in his town house bedroom. But it was all gone. She had disappeared without a word.

There had to be some way he could get at her. There had to be some inducement he could use to get her back. Maybe threaten to expose her affair with Jack Donner? But what would she care? She had her money, and if Donner's wife kicked him out, that wasn't her problem. Or perhaps leak that she had murdered her husband in cold blood. That would get her picture circulated and send a lot of people out to look for her. But, if she were caught, Jack's money would simply go back to the Donners. None of it would find its way into his pocket.

What he needed was a way to get her attention. Something very public that would follow her no matter where she went, so that even in Europe or South America she would realize that her game was up and that she had to come home and pay off her friends. But what? How? If she were already gone with a few million dollars, what could possibly bring her back?

He found the answer on the arts page, a page that he almost never read. It was a photo of Pam Donner with a soft news story on her new gallery, her partners, and the artists they were trying to attract. Nicole was mentioned as one of the partners. The opening was still weeks away but the article gave the Madison Avenue address.

Stake out the gallery, Jimmy thought. If Nicole is a partner, sooner or later she'll show up. He concentrated his attention on two places — the gallery and Jack Donner's town house.

SIXTY-TWO

Greg Lambert was taking a different tack. When Alexandra had ordered him to "find that girl before she gets away," he had started with the money. How was it being paid? When and where were the transactions taking place? At some point, Nicole would have to make a personal appearance and that was where he would lock on to her. He expected it to be very simple.

His first disappointment was that Victor Crane was already out of the loop. "We got the papers, and she got the check," he said with a shrug. "We won't know where she cashes it until the funds clear. Hell, it's her money now! It's none of our business what she does with it." Crane suggested that he talk with Ben Tobin. "He's the one who's getting paid by her. I don't think he'll let the money out of his sight until he collects his fee."

Tobin, as Greg Lambert had guessed, had no reason to be helpful. "I can't tell you anything about her plans, and I certainly won't discuss any financial arrangements she's made." He had hardly sat down when he was back on his feet to end the meeting.

"It would be a favor to the Donners," Lambert said. "I think you know just how grateful they can be."

It was terribly tempting. If he brought a piece of Donner business into the firm he'd be able to shake his reputation as a gofer, and maybe get back on track for a partnership. He sat back down again.

"The Donners could have talked to her any time. Jack could have walked into the signing and sat down next to her. So, what's changed?"

"It's not Mr. Donner. It's Mrs. Donner who wants to see her."

Ben remembered Nicole's fright the first time she had come to him for help. She was certain that Alexandra had tried to have her killed in Belize, and she had no doubt that Alexandra had tried again at the cottage. He hadn't taken her fears seriously. He had been Jonathan's guest at the house on many occasions and more recently Pam's. Even though he was hardly an intimate, he thought he knew Alexandra and Jack well enough to be sure that they would never kill anyone. But Nicole was calling him from her cell phone and talking in abbreviated sentences. There was no doubt that she was still afraid.

"Nicole calls me from time to time," Ben admitted. "I can get a message to her. I can tell her Alexandra wants to see her and even pass on a time and place."

"You can ask her where you can reach her," Lambert pressed. "Give her some reason why you have to get together, and then set up a meeting."

"I'm not sure she'd go along with that. Besides, I'd be setting her up for a confrontation she probably would want to avoid. Ethically —"

"Alexandra Donner really wants to see her," Lambert said, overriding Ben's ethical concerns. "It can be right here in your office. You can stay through the meeting. Mrs. Donner just wants to ask a few questions about her son's last moments. And, she has information that she needs Nicole to confirm."

Ben thought for a few seconds, his fingertips touched to his lips as if he were in prayer. "I'll put it to her in exactly those words," he offered. "But the decision has to be hers."

"Whatever you think best," the security officer said, rising from his chair. "But Mrs. Donner really wants this meeting. I know she'll be most appreciative if you can make it happen."

In the elevator, he weighed his chances. There was no doubt that Ben had understood the connection. Set up the meeting and Donner business will follow. The question was whether he was truly committed to a client that he might never see again, or to profitable opportunities that could last a lifetime. Generally, it was best to bet on the money.

But, just in case, he put one of his best men on Ben Tobin. "Follow him into his building and then watch the lobby. When he leaves, follow him wherever he goes." He handed over a photo of Nicole. "If he meets with this woman, then follow her. She's the one we're looking for."

SIXTY-THREE

In the morning, Nicole took her shower and then left a towel over her shoulders when she went to the sink. She opened a package of dark brunette hair coloring and read the directions as she mixed the ingredients. Carefully, she applied the color to her scalp and began combing it out through her hair. She could watch the transformation in her mirror. As her hair darkened, her complexion seemed to color with it. Even the blue of her eyes looked deeper.

When she had dried her new color, she brought her Irish passport into the bathroom so she could compare the photo with the image in the mirror. Close enough, she decided. She had used the same hair rinse when she had gone for the passport photo. The new version was a bit darker, but not enough to raise the tired eyelids of an immigration officer. And with her new look she could walk right past Jimmy as she boarded her plane without even turning his head.

She had bought new clothes to go along

with her new person. A pair of pedal pushers cut for a tourist. A blouse with more color than she generally wore. A straw hat with a brim that turned up in the front. Tennis shoes. And finally, mirrored sunglasses. The ensemble would suggest "tourist" when she walked through the airport, but it would speak in a soft voice. Not so loud that she would stand out and attract attention, but loud enough so that anyone looking for Nicole wouldn't even spare her a glance. She posed in her complete disguise and turned around and around in front of a full-length mirror. She was ready.

In the street, she blended in easily with the Manhattan crush, this time walking uptown before calling. Ben came on the line almost immediately.

"Nicole, where are you?"

She ignored the question. "Has the deposit been made?"

"Yes, it has."

"And the transfer?"

"Nicole, I have to see you. I have to know that it's really you."

She laughed. "Even I don't know that it's really me."

"Where are you? Where can I meet you?"

"You can't. Just authorize the transfer. The bank has the account number."

Ben paused. Then he answered, "I'm not doing anything with the money until I'm sure it's you. For God's sake, I can't send ten million dollars into oblivion on the basis of a phone call."

"Okay," she agreed. "Where do you want to meet?"

"My office?"

"No," she snapped immediately. "How about the fountain in front of the Plaza. One o'clock?"

She hung up as soon as Ben agreed, even though she felt uneasy about the meeting. What had changed? In their earlier meetings he had never been concerned about forwarding the money. It was her U.S. bank account. Ben had set it up for her so that wasn't the problem. The money now belonged to her. And he had arranged the numbered account. So, he knew perfectly well that he wasn't sending "ten million dollars into oblivion." Then why did he need a face-to-face meeting? It didn't make sense and more important it was dangerous. A meeting with anyone she knew would compromise the new persona she had carefully engineered. Why was Ben changing signals? Could Alexandra have bought him over to her side? Or maybe Jimmy had threatened him?

She went downtown and turned east through the park. Then she headed down Fifth, well across from the fountain. She started to window-shop, watching the fountain in the window reflections. Whenever she left a store window, she took a quick scan of the pedestrian traffic. The faces rushed by with no one taking any notice of her. She checked her watch. Ben should be arriving at any moment.

She saw him across the street, dodging in and out of shoppers and tourists as he rushed to the meeting. Carefully, she searched behind him. There was another man, someone she had never seen before, darting through pedestrians in an effort to keep up. Who? One of Jimmy's goons? Or a soldier in the Donners' private security force? It didn't matter. Both were dangerous.

Nicole walked away quickly trying to blend in with the flow of people. Across the street, Ben arrived at the fountain and checked his watch. He looked in every direction and then circled the fountain twice. The man following him went to the steps of the hotel, a vantage point where he could watch Ben and still keep his distance. She kept moving, watching the traffic lights until she saw a chance to cross back to the park. It was there, in the middle of the street that she recognized a familiar face. Greg Lambert was walking directly toward her, a tall figure in a summer suit, obviously in a hurry. She turned her head away, kept walking, and felt him rush past her, on his way to the fountain. Her makeover passed its first test.

But she still wasn't out of the woods. Lambert was the Donners' man. If the Donners had turned Ben Tobin, then it was equally likely that they had gotten to her banker. What would it take? A comment that they would be very grateful to learn if she came in to transfer her funds? A few words to imply that Sound Holdings was looking for a new banking connection? She was money being withdrawn. They were money being deposited. Which side would a banker want to be on?

What were her alternatives? Leave for Europe and have the Swiss bank transfer the funds? That was risky. Any sort of glitch would leave her broke in a foreign country. Or walk into the bank and sign the transfer herself? That would put her face-to-face with a banker who had seen her before and who would certainly be fascinated by her new appearance. Maybe he could refuse to act based on the claim that he didn't recognize her. And he could probably give a very good description of her as a dressed-down brunette.

One thing was certain. Her position wouldn't get any safer over time. Delaying just meant more opportunities for Alexandra's detectives and Jimmy's thugs to find her. She had to keep to her time schedule, and that meant taking her chances with her bank.

SIXTY-FOUR

Nicole phoned Ben from a park bench. He was breathless when he came on the line. "Nicole, I just got back. You never . . ."

"Did you know you were followed to the Plaza?"

There was a long pause. "No . . . who followed me?"

"A man I didn't recognize. He was running after you up Fifth Avenue. But that's not what bothers me. I saw Greg Lambert, Alexandra Donner's house detective. He was coming from the other direction and he nearly knocked me over on his way to the meeting." Then she asked, "Do you have any idea how he found out you were meeting me?"

An even longer pause. Then Ben said, "They must have me under surveillance."

"Are you helping them, Ben? Have you switched sides?"

"God, no! Lambert asked me to arrange a meeting with you and Alexandra. I told him I'd propose it, but it was entirely up to you."

"You know damn well I don't want to see her. I don't want to see anyone."

"Pam needs to talk with you," he said. "Nicole, you can't just vanish. There's too much unfinished business."

"What does Pam want?"

"You were going to back her in a gallery."

She gave a long sigh. "That's her fantasy. I never promised anything."

"She thinks you did."

"Ben, she's not a child. And she has much more behind her than I could ever bring to the party."

"Nicole —" he tried to interrupt.

"I'm leaving, Ben. As soon as you transfer my money to Switzerland."

He paused, breathing exasperation into the phone line.

"You are going to transfer my money, aren't you?"

"Nicole, the Donners will toast me. I can't help you get away."

"Is that what Jack said?" she demanded.

"No. It's Alexandra. And maybe Pam."

"Ben, talk to Jack. Because if I talk with him and tell him what's going on, you're really going to feel the heat."

Another pause while Ben thought his way through the problem. "You're right.

I'll talk to Jack. Call me back in an hour."

She took her time going back to the hotel. She was already checked out and her single piece of luggage was with the bell captain. She was in no hurry to get anywhere until she confirmed that her money was in Switzerland. Then she'd be gone.

Had she won her battle with Alexandra Donner? Not yet. Alexandra had stood in the doorway and blocked her entrance into Jonathan's world. If she just could have gotten past Alexandra! She hadn't even gotten the financial settlement she deserved. She had settled for much less than her husband's material worth. And still, Alexandra was hanging on.

Alexandra had seen through Jonathan's new love interest right from the start. She had been right when she accused Nicole of stalking her son like a big-game hunter, right about the guise of reluctant virgin she had used to bring him down, and right again in charging that Nicole engineered a hasty wedding before her background could be exposed. Still, Nicole had been able to back her into a corner, strip away her allies and, in the end, even compromise her husband. She had won at least part of what she had set out to achieve. All she needed now was for Alexandra to let go. Then she would be free. Free from her less than spectacular youth and from the restraints of small town America. Free from her troubled past with its seamy dance halls, sleazy photographers and doped up managers. Free from the taunts of a society she wasn't good enough to join.

She had a drink in the cocktail lounge, surrounded by exhausted tourists, scheming businessmen, and dating yuppies. She checked on her luggage and told the bell captain that she would need her rental car from the garage. She stood in front of her hotel to make her call. It was safe now. If someone traced the call and worked their way back to the hotel she would already be long gone on her way to Boston. She would overnight in a motel using an alias. The next afternoon, she would be off to Europe.

Ben picked up instantly. "It's me," Nicole said. "Everything taken care of?"

"No, there's been a complication."

"Damn it!" she snapped in anger. "Did you talk to Jack?"

"Nicole, it's not about the money. It's about Pam. She's been kidnapped."

The anger vanished from her voice. "What?"

"Pam has been kidnapped. Your old friends want to trade her for you."

The punch in the stomach drove the breath out of her. She tried to digest the implications of what she had just heard. "I don't believe it," she managed even though she already knew it was true.

"You're the only one who knows these people. Alexandra's security guys want your help. They need to know where to look and what kind of deal they should try to make."

"They should get the police," Nicole said.

"Not until they take their chances on a quick private recovery. They don't know whether your friends would really hurt her."

She leaned back against the building. "I'd like to help," she said. "But if Alexandra got her hands on me she'd trade me for her daughter without a second thought."

"Nicole, you know these people. How much danger is Pam in?"

"They're not nice, but all they're ever after is money. Tell Alexandra to offer them some of what she should have given me."

"And if that doesn't work?" Ben asked.

"Then it will be Alexandra's chickens coming home to roost. This never would have happened if she didn't drive me out."

"What should I tell her?"

"Tell her it's time to pay the piper. And, for Pam's sake, wish her luck."

She stood against the building for a few seconds after she hung up, trying to compose herself. Jimmy Farr was one of the world's great bastards, she thought. She hoped that Greg Lambert would help him pay his debt to society. Then she started back to the hotel where her freedom was waiting.

The money was hers, safe in her account with attorneys paid and taxes deducted. The Swiss bankers would welcome her deposit. If anyone tried to derail the transfer she would have to talk to Jack. She had a much better chance with him than she would walking into her New York bank and trying to transfer the money herself.

In the car, she drove north until she picked up the thruway. Her plan was to drive upstate to Albany where she could spend the night. Early in the morning she would pick up the Massachusetts Turnpike, and cross the state to Boston. And then, the plane to Switzerland. Her money would follow in just a few days.

"Poor Pam," Nicole said to herself, shaking her head in the process. She certainly was the innocent victim. It was hard to imagine that she could have had any dealings with Jimmy Farr, or anyone like him. And Jimmy had no interest in her. Her only sin, Nicole thought, was that she had gotten too close to her new sister-in-law. Nicole had vanished, and Pam was living out in the open, in plain sight. Jimmy had grabbed what was available, thinking that she would come to the rescue.

His mistake! She would call his bluff. Nicole had no intention of giving herself up just to make things easier for Pam. It was too high a price to pay for her freedom. And when Jimmy figured that out, what was he going to do? He had nothing to gain by hurting Pam. He wouldn't want to get into long dangerous negotiations for a ransom. All he could do would be to bellow and let her go.

Pam wasn't in any real danger, Nicole thought. Oh, of course her young friend was frightened out of her wits. But that wasn't reason enough to turn her car around and give up her escape.

SIXTY-FIVE

Greg Lambert blasted through Ben Tobin's front door the instant Ben opened it, sending links of the security chain flying. He pushed Tobin back into his living room, and then Alexandra Donner came in behind him.

"For Christ's sake . . ." Ben protested.

"Where is she?" Lambert wanted to know. He pushed Ben into a soft chair so that he towered above him. "We're out of time, Ben. We need to get Nicole now. So, where is she?"

"I don't know," Ben pleaded. Greg grabbed his shirt collar in one hand and made a fist with the other. He was ready to beat the information out of Nicole's attorney.

Alexandra put a hand on Greg's arm, restraining the punch he was about to throw. "Ben, please. You know that Pam's life hangs in the balance. If you have any idea of how we can reach Nicole . . ."

"She's gone," Ben interrupted. "I told her about Pam and that we needed her help. But she said she was leaving. She never told me how she was traveling or where she was going."

"She just said, 'no'? That was her only comment. Nothing more?"

" 'No' was the only thing that mattered," Ben answered Alexandra.

Greg pulled his cocked fist free from Alexandra's grasp. "Damn it! What did she say?"

Ben looked from the fist to Alexandra. "She said that none of this had to happen." Alexandra looked puzzled, and Greg seemed about to attack. "She said that none of it would have happened if . . . you . . . had accepted her." He was looking straight at Alexandra. "She said it was your chickens coming home to roost."

Greg took a step back. "Jesus," he blurted out.

"My fault?" Alexandra asked. "She blamed me?"

Ben writhed in his chair. "No, she was shocked. They were just words."

"But she was determined not to help," Alexandra concluded.

Ben answered, "She was determined to disappear. She just . . . ran."

Alexandra looked at Greg. "Then Jack is

right. It's all my fault. Jonathan, Pam, I destroyed them both."

Jack was sitting in his New York office staring at the phone. His words were rehearsed. "We can't trade one person for another, but we can give you more money than Nicole could have given you. I have five million dollars right in front of me. It can be yours in a matter of minutes. All I want is my daughter returned safely. There are no police. Nobody is going to try to trap you. On that I give you my word. It will be a clean exchange. You can take the money and walk away. I'll leave with my daughter and call it even."

This was the role that he could play; the grief stricken father anxious to pay anything for his daughter. Alexandra had chosen the other course of trying to find Nicole and trade her for Pam. As a third part of the plan, Lambert's men were watching every move that Jimmy Farr might make. Jimmy, they were sure, knew exactly what had happened to Pam and where she was. But if they threatened him, his best response would be to destroy the evidence. They hoped that he would soon lead them to the girl, but no one wanted to do anything that might threaten him.

Jack was distraught, nearly paralyzed with guilt. He was the one who had bought off Nicole and asked her to vanish. And it was apparently because of his solution that Pam had been taken as a hostage. He couldn't bring himself to blame Nicole. All she had done was try to outlive her past. She had wanted more than eking out a living in a backwater town, more than bit parts and commercials, and even more than the company of a famous director. Jonathan had been the answer to her prayers, but just when she finally had everything, it was all snatched away from her by Jonathan's death. By Alexandra's intransigence. By his own weakness.

Nicole hadn't meant to put Pam in jeopardy. Pam was her friend, her adopted younger sister. How could you blame her for the characters of her past who were determined to drag her back?

Jack knew that Nicole had been told about Pam. Like Alexandra, he thought that the right thing for her to do was come back to help win Pam's release. But he was the one who had sent her away. He had even paid her handsomely to have no further contact with him or his family. So how could he blame her for disappearing? It was as much his fault as it was hers.

The important thing was not to place the blame, but rather to get Pam back. And he had the money to buy her back, if only the damn telephone would ring.

SIXTY-SIX

The kidnapping had been discovered only a few hours earlier. A messenger who didn't ask for a signed receipt had delivered the videotape to Jack's office. "Could you make sure that Mr. Donner gets this," he had said to the receptionist. "And tell him to look at it right away. It's important." The woman had watched the messenger leave and then put the tape into her in-basket. It was over an hour before a mail clerk picked it up and delivered it to Jack's executive secretary. He was on a conference call and had left word not to be disturbed. Later in the afternoon she brought the tape into his office. "You look at it," Jack growled without even reading the label. "If it's important, let me know." The secretary was back in his office only a minute later, holding the cassette in trembling hands. "Mr. Donner. You have to look at this."

He gestured impatiently to the corner of his desk.

"No," the secretary said. "Now! It's about your daughter."

"Put it on," he snapped. He followed her to the credenza and watched as electronic static illuminated the television screen. Pam suddenly appeared, looking straight out at her father.

She was sitting in a straight wooden chair in front of a blank beige wall. She wore jeans and a simple white blouse. Her feet were flat on the floor, one in a slip-on casual shoe, the other bare. Her hair was a bit disarranged and she had lost one of the buttons from her blouse. But these were just details, to be recognized as Jack ran the tape over and over again. What he noticed instantly was the look of terror in his daughter's eyes.

"Daddy . . ."

Her voice was hardly a whisper.

"Louder!" a man's voice snapped from off camera.

"Daddy!" This time she was shouting. Her eyes glanced to the right, and squinted a bit as she tried to read from a cue card. "I'm being held by people who mean me no harm. They haven't hurt me, I'm comfortable and I have food. All they want is to talk to Nicole. As soon as Nicole comes here, they'll let me go. They say she owes them something and they have no other way of getting her attention.

"Don't go to the police. That will only cause problems and put me in danger." Pam stopped to lick her lips. Her eyes stayed on the cue card. "Don't tell your security people because they might do something foolish. I'll be fine as long as Nicole comes to meet them.

"Tell her she has to come alone. They'll know if anyone is with her. She should call her 'old friend.' She'll know who to call. Then she'll get instructions on how to get to me.

"Tell her I really need her. Because if she doesn't come, these people will just put me in a closet and leave. You might never find me."

Pam turned to the other side of the screen and looked anxiously. "Was that okay . . ." The camera cut off her words and the screen returned to static.

"Who brought this?" Jack demanded.

"It was on my desk," the woman answered.

"Well find out how in Christ it got there. Then call my wife and tell her I need her here in the city right away. Tell her don't get dressed, just come in whatever she's wearing. And get Greg Lambert on the line . . ."

She rushed off to do his bidding. Jack rewound the tape and started it again. He stood transfixed, watching his daughter deliver her message. She was frightened out of her wits. He could see it in her expression and hear it in the mechanical cadence of her speech. But she hadn't been hurt. There were no bruises on her face. Her hands weren't tied. All he noticed were the missing shoe and the button pulled off her blouse. Probably she had struggled when she realized what was happening to her. The button could have popped when she tried to pull out of someone's grasp. The shoe could have been lost when she was pushed into a car. Probably she was under guard in a house somewhere. All they had done was sit her in a chair in front of a blank wall and aim a camcorder at her. Her captor was probably pointing at words on a writing pad. When she was finished they had probably locked her in a bedroom.

Still, she was in danger. There was no telling what a bunch of thugs might do if they thought she was a threat to them. "Don't do anything silly," Jack said to the figure on the television screen. "Just sit tight and do what they say. I'll come and get you . . ."

His desk phone buzzed. "Greg Lambert, Mr. Donner."

"Greg, that son of a bitch from Nicole's past has kidnapped my daughter."

"Pam?"

"I just got a video. She seems to be okay, but the bastard is holding her and wants to exchange her for Nicole."

"You think it's Jimmy Farr?"

"I don't know his fucking name! The gangster that Alexandra keeps trying to connect with Nicole."

"Yeah, that's Farr. He wants to trade Pam for Nicole?"

Jack was sputtering. "That's what she says on the video. Nicole owes the prick something. So we've got to get him fast and find out how much he wants. Can you do that?"

"I'm on it," Greg said. Then he added, "I'll start with Nicole's lawyer. He's still got her money so he damn well ought to know where he can find her."

Alexandra was on the line as soon as he hung up. He told her about the tape, assuring her that Pam looked fine and had not been hurt. "I'm going to do whatever it takes to get her back right away," he promised his wife. "Then I'm going to find this fucker and break him and everything he owns."

"He wants Nicole," Alexandra said, reminding him of the information he had just given her. "Can we find Nicole?"

It was a loaded question. First, did Jack know where Nicole was? He had told his wife that she was gone, but had he really let her go without knowing where he could reach her? And second, if he did know where she was, would he put her in danger to save his daughter?

"Nicole is gone," he repeated. "If she owes this guy something I'll cover her debt. Then, when Pam is safe, I'll destroy the bastard."

SIXTY-SEVEN

Nicole tossed in her bed. It was 4:00 a.m. and she still hadn't been able to get to sleep. It wasn't the bed, or the rattling air conditioner. She was still arguing with herself, and she was losing the argument.

She had spent the entire drive up the thruway from New York thinking about Pam. She would be fine, she kept insisting. Once Jimmy knew that Nicole had escaped, he would have Pam released and would distance himself from the entire affair. Jimmy was no fool. He was probably not even close to where Pam was being held, and probably had at least two intermediaries between himself and the victim. Like Alexandra Donner, he knew all about deniability.

But she wasn't convinced by her own reasoning. Any number of things could go wrong. The ones actually holding Pam could be unreliable. People who owed Jimmy a favor tended to be lowlifes. Those who took his money were often feeding a drug habit. It wasn't as if she were being cared for in a convent.

Or the Donners might leap into action. Jack could turn his security army loose with orders to find Pam and get her back. They might shoot up a building and kick down the doors. It was easy to imagine some frightened dolt using Pam as a shield. And Alexandra could decide to face down the scum who had dared lay hands on her daughter. Nicole could picture her threatening to track down the kidnappers and see them in jail, just the kind of threat that would encourage them to bury the evidence.

She knew that she and Jimmy could solve the whole problem in a minute. "Jimmy, they've kicked me out. I'm not going to get anywhere near Sound Holdings. You can bellow and whine, or pull my hair if it makes you feel better. But it's over. I've already been given my walking papers."

Somewhere in his fit of rage, Jimmy would realize that Nicole certainly wasn't leaving the Donner household empty-handed. "What did you get? And don't lie to me because I can find out —"

"Five million dollars," she could lie. "Three after the lawyers took their cut, and we sent a share to Uncle Sam."

Jimmy would demand two million. There was no way he would ever take the short end of a deal. She would offer one, arguing that she had taken all the risks. They would settle on an even split.

She could have the money wired to one of his banks in the Caribbean, or even to the savings and loan that he kept in Staten Island. Then Pam would be set free and she would be on her way.

But, of course, it really wasn't that simple. Suppose he already knew exactly how much money she had? He would try to clean her out. Or suppose he felt so betrayed that he wanted revenge more than he wanted money. She would take one hell of a beating. She might even end up in a landfill.

So what should she do? Pam wasn't her problem, but then in another sense she was. She had no intention of hurting the girl, but wouldn't she be just as guilty if she stood by idly while someone else hurt her? It was risky to go back and confront Jimmy Farr, but would she ever be able to forgive herself if something happened to Pam?

Alexandra was another problem. She had spent weeks trying to run Nicole into the ground because she had stolen her son. If she were responsible for something happening to Pam, Alexandra would chase her to the ends of the earth. What kind of life could she have with Alexandra's detectives pounding at her heels?

Ben had told her that she was needed. The abductors had demanded her in exchange so she was the one most likely to be able to win Pam's quick release. And Ben knew Nicole's situation and why she had legitimate reasons to fear for her life. He would be up-to-date on where things stood. Maybe Pam had already been released and she was no longer important. Ben was someone she could talk to. She took her cell phone to the window and dialed his number.

There were several rings, and then the recording. "Leave your name and number . . ." She hung up and then thought of Jack. She had promised never to contact him. The ink was hardly dry on the agreement. And yet who could have foreseen that she might suddenly become Pam's best hope of staying alive? Nicole hesitated for an instant, and then dialed Jack's office number.

He answered before she even heard the telephone ringing. "Hello!" He was alone in his New York office in the middle of the night, answering his own phone. The situation had to be dire.

"Hello," he repeated. "This is Jack

Donner speaking on a secure line. Do you have a message for me?"

"Jack, it's Nicole . . ."

"Nicole? Thank God. Where are you?"

"On the road," she answered. "Have you heard from Pam?"

"No, nothing! That's what I'm waiting for."

"Can I help, Jack? What should I do?"

He didn't answer. She could hear his breathing so she knew he was still on the line. "Jack?"

"Do you know these people, Nicole?"

"I think so."

"Would you be safe with them?"

"I'm not sure. I should be, but —"

He interrupted her. "I'll go with you, Nicole. I'm not trading you. I'm not handing you over. If it's money they want, I have enough for both you and Pam."

"It will take me two hours to get there. Maybe three in traffic. Where should I meet you?"

"Do you have the key I sent you?" She said she did. "Then go to the town house and call me. I'll be waiting right here until I get your call."

She stayed by the window. Had she done the right thing? Or was she just playing into Jimmy Farr's hand? Nicole could see the turnpike. She could be in Boston at the airport just as fast as she could be back in New York. She was so close. Did it make any sense for her to turn back? Did she have a choice?

SIXTY-EIGHT

"I need to talk with Jimmy Farr," Greg Lambert said to the tuxedo-clad bouncer who was standing in his way.

"Who's Jimmy Farr?" The man answered with a smirk. He flexed his shoulders and stretched his neck as a reminder of his size and girth.

"Your boss. The guy who owns this place," Lambert said.

"Club Platinum is owned by a corporation." His tone was polite and informative, but indicated that he had no idea what a corporation was.

"Jimmy came in here about an hour ago, and he hasn't left," Greg said. "So will you please tell 'the corporation' that we're ready to make the exchange."

"Are you with the police?"

"No, I'm Jimmy's link to several million dollars. And I'm getting tired of being jerked around in the doorway. Could you just ask him if he's ready to make the exchange? He'll know what it's about."

The bouncer thought for a moment and

then nodded. “Hey Eddie,” he said to the small button on his lapel. Then he pressed a finger to the receiver in his ear while he waited for a response. “Gentleman here wants to see Mr. Farr about some kind of exchange. You know anything about it?” He pressed harder against the receiver. “Yeah, okay.” He smiled at Greg. “They’ll see if they can find Mr. Farr. You can wait at the bar if you like.”

Club Platinum was an upscale topless dance hall that catered to the credit-card crowd. Admission was steep, the drinks were overpriced, and the average tip to a dancer was fifty dollars. The dancers were stunning, all aspiring models and showgirls who were making more money than successful models and showgirls. Even now, after midnight, the clientele included law partners, bond traders, fund managers, and successful stockbrokers, all with their best clients and customers. A fire in the building would cause a global financial panic by morning.

The bartender, nearly as big as the front-door bouncer, was in a dress shirt and black tie. His grooming was impeccable. He served a tall drink on a cloth napkin, and set a silver bowl of cashews beside it. The place had illusions of being an Edwardian gentlemen’s club.

Greg waited, unable to ignore the near naked women who danced on strategically placed stages. Lighting effects made their movements even more provocative. At the service bar, there were three bartenders working furiously with three credit-card terminals. Lights were blinking as drinks were registered and credit-card accounts were sacked. Jimmy has himself a gold mine, Lambert thought.

A man eased up next to him, again in a tuxedo. "I'm sorry, but Mr. Farr has gone for the day. His assistant suggests you try tomorrow early in the evening."

Lambert nodded, and finished his drink. "You might leave word for Mr. Farr that the lady he's looking for has left the country. But she did authorize me to pay off her debts. It's a tidy sum."

He spun off the bar stool and reached back for a handful of cashews. "I'm sorry I missed him."

"Why don't you have another drink?" the man suggested instantly. "Maybe someone knows where he can be reached." Greg climbed back onto the stool. The bartender was already pouring a refill.

A few minutes later he was following his guide upstairs, past lounges set aside for private parties. They stopped in front of an inconspicuous door. "Would you mind?" the man asked. "No need," Lambert said, reaching around his back and producing a pistol. "It hasn't been fired in years." The guide pocketed the pistol. "It's really recorders and microphones that we object to," he said. Greg raised his arms while the man patted him down.

Jimmy Farr was leaning back in a swivel chair behind a large executive desk. On the wall next to him a bank of color monitors showed views of the club at the bar level and from the private lounges. There was one focused on the lobby where the bouncer had blocked Greg's path, and another panning the street outside. He gestured Greg to a chair without taking his eyes off the screens.

"So what can I do for you?"

"I'd like to get Pam Donner back. I thought you might be able to help."

"Never heard of her," Jimmy said. "Does she work for me?"

"She was kidnapped yesterday. The family received a video from her saying that she could be exchanged for their daughter-in-law, Nicole Pierce. The family would gladly comply, but Miss Pierce left the country sometime yesterday. They have no knowledge of where she is and it may be several days before they hear from her. So, they simply can't make the trade."

Farr showed no reaction. He raised his hands, palms upward, indicating that he was still confused. "Where do I fit in?"

Greg leaned closer. "We hoped you might be able to locate the people holding her and persuade them to accept money instead. You'd handle the cash, and be paid a commission."

"What makes you think I can find her?"

"The woman they want to trade for used to work for you. We thought there might be some connections you could exploit."

The true nature of the bargain was plain to both men. There would be no allegations of kidnapping, nor any implication of Jimmy Farr's involvement. Both sides would honor the fiction that he had nothing to do with it, but was simply the intermediary to an unnamed third party. The payment given to Jimmy was intended for the third party, even though both men knew the money would never leave Jimmy's hands.

"How much should I say you're offering?"

"Two million," Greg answered. "And then there's a half million fee for you."

"Is that enough?" Jimmy wondered aloud.

"It's more than the woman they want to

swap for got. They'll make more money than they can get out of her with none of the effort."

"I'll see what I can do," Jimmy decided. "How do I reach you?"

Lambert handed over his card. "This has to be a fast deal," he said. "Once the word is out that their daughter has been kidnapped, these people will have to work through the police. That's what's expected of them."

"A couple of hours," Jimmy said. "Unless the people I'm thinking of aren't the right people. But either way, you'll hear from me."

Lambert left the room, pausing for a moment to get his gun back, before he walked down the stairs. The ladies were dancing and the credit cards were being processed, both to a fast rock beat. Jimmy was just like Jack Donner, Lambert thought. They both made money without lifting a finger.

He used his car phone to call Alexandra who was waiting in Jonathan's apartment, the other logical place where a ransom call might be expected. Greg explained the arrangements he had just worked out. He felt sure that Jimmy Farr would go for the money and that Pam would be free the next day. Then Alexandra added some hopeful news of her own. Jack had informed her that Nicole was on her way back. "She knows these thugs," she said. "She's one of them."

Greg was going back to his office to await a call from Farr setting up the exchange. "Don't do anything until I call you," he asked. "If Nicole is going to talk with them we need to get our stories straight."

Alexandra wasn't comfortable with the idea of Nicole returning. Not that she was against the girl putting herself at risk. Maybe the kidnappers would take her money. There would be poetic justice in that. Or maybe some figure from her violent past would bring her to a violent end. Alexandra wasn't prepared to shed any tears over her daughter-in-law. Nothing had changed her conviction that Nicole's interest in Jonathan was economic, and that she had rushed the wedding in order to get the money before Alexandra came up with the damning evidence. She still suspected that Nicole might have been implicated in her son's death, and was still convinced that Nicole had somehow arranged the explosion in the cottage. So, how was she supposed to greet this woman who had murdered and shattered her family just to become wealthy? Thank her for coming back to save Pam, or condemn her for bringing people like Jimmy Farr into her household? How was she supposed to be sociable with someone she would rather see dead?

Or maybe, as Nicole had told Ben Tobin, all this was her fault — her chickens coming home to roost? If she had embraced Nicole with open arms then she would probably be planning a wedding right now instead of struggling to save her only living child. Jack kept insisting that Nicole's only crime was trying to leave her past behind. If he was right, then why had she insisted on dredging up all the girl's youthful sins?

SIXTY-NINE

Nicole let herself into Jack's town house, went downstairs to the kitchen and used the wall telephone. "I'm here," she said when he answered. He promised to be right over.

She hardly recognized him when he stepped through the front door and into the dimly lighted sitting room. His shirt collar was open far enough to show his undershirt, and the hair that fringed his bald pate poked out like thorns. His eyelids sagged, showing too much white.

"Thank God you came back!" He accelerated to her and gathered her into his arms. The embrace wasn't at all passionate, but more like relatives meeting at a funeral. As he rocked her he gulped for air, fighting back the crying fit that was just beneath his throat.

"I had to," Nicole said. "I couldn't just leave her . . ."

"Do you know where she is. Where they'd keep her?"

"No, but I think I know who has her. The same bastard who was threatening me."

He pushed her back. "Threatening you?"

She nodded. "You're not going to like this, Jack."

Nicole gave him a capsule version of Jimmy Farr's Wall Street ambitions. She told him how he wanted her to ingratiate her way into Sound Holdings. "He knew about you and . . . me. He threatened to tell Alexandra and take our . . . affair . . . public."

"Oh, dear God . . . I've condemned everyone I care for . . ."

"No you haven't. It's not your fault." Then she admitted, "It's probably all mine. I should have taken Alexandra's advice and . . . just left."

Jack pulled her back into his embrace. "I've made such a mess of things."

But when he let her go, his mood changed. "Now, what do we do? How do we get Pam back?"

"I've got to meet with him. And I'm going to have to give him money. I think that will do it. He's too smart to hurt Pam. He'll be glad to turn her loose."

"How do we get to him?" Jack demanded, his zest for action coming to the surface.

"*I* get to him," she answered. "And I offer him a cut of *my* settlement. Taking it from me gives him more satisfaction and less money."

He was surprised at her initiative. "How well do you know these people?"

"Too well," she admitted.

Nicole lifted the telephone and dialed while Jack watched over her shoulder. "It's me," was all she said when the phone was answered.

Jimmy stood up from his desk, his phone cupped to his ear. "Well, well. I heard you had left the country."

"Not even close," she lied. "I've been right here in town. That's how I know you're keeping a friend of mine as a house guest."

"There's no one staying with me," he said for the benefit of anyone who might be eavesdropping on the call.

"So, how do we make this happen?" she asked.

"Where are you?"

She glanced at Jack and then back to the phone. "I'm at the town house."

He laughed. "Walk to the Park Avenue corner at noon. Just you! Nobody else. I'll pick you up."

"I'll be there."

Jack tried to stop her from going. "I'm not going to let you walk into a meeting with a gangster. Anything could happen!" He insisted he was going with her.

"If you're there, he'll just drive past. We won't get anywhere," Nicole argued.

She kissed his cheek as she left for the meeting. Jack sat with his face in his hands for a few seconds. Then he called Alexandra, told her that Nicole had arrived and had gone to meet with her friends.

"Jack, we have an agreement. Greg is waiting for a phone call right now."

"Damn it," he yelled. "Why didn't you tell me?"

"I didn't know when you last called. I thought you'd contact me when Nicole arrived."

They mumbled explanations and apologies, none of which made any difference. The fact was that Jack and Alexandra were in competition to set Pam free.

Nicole stood back against the building until she saw Jimmy's sedan turning from the northbound lane. The door opened as the car was stopping and she stepped quickly inside, sliding into the seat next to Jimmy Farr.

"How nice to have you back, although I hardly recognize you. What have you done with your hair?" He was about to launch into a flourish of small talk, but she interrupted him with her prepared statement. "I've been kicked out," she began. Then she told him that there was absolutely no way that she could penetrate the inner workings of Sound Holdings. "They're paying me off with an agreement that orders me to get lost. So it's over, Jimmy. All you can get for holding Pam Donner is a jail sentence."

"I'm not holding anyone," he said with a wink in case she was recording the conversation. "But weren't you just a guest in Jack Donner's town house? That doesn't sound as if you've been kicked out."

"I had to meet him somewhere," she answered. "He told me about Pam. I offered to help get her back."

"Who's Pam?" he repeated.

"Oh, for God's sake . . ." She pushed to the edge of the seat. "I'm not wired. Search me so we can get this settled."

He did, carefully rather than provocatively. When he had satisfied himself, he grabbed her by the hair and shook her violently. "What the fuck did you think you were pulling, Nicole? Did you think you were going to outsmart me?" He banged her head against the windowpane. "Nobody plays me for a fool. Nobody!" His free hand slapped across her face and then backhanded her. "I ought to leave you in a garbage Dumpster." He slapped her again venting his pent-up rage. He was breathing hard when he let go of her and settled back into the corner of the seat.

Nicole touched the blood from the split in her lip. "What do you want?" she asked.

"All of it. Every fucking penny they gave you. I want it all in my hands right now."

Nicole rolled her eyes. "I don't have it with me."

"Then we'll have to visit your bank, won't we?"

"I told you, I've been cut off. There's not going to be any more money. I have to keep some of it. A million is all I can give up."

He laughed. "You think I give a damn about your problems? I said all of it, every last penny, if you ever want to see your friend again. You understand?"

She shook her head. "No deal, Jimmy. Just drop me off anywhere."

"I'll drop you out of a window, you bitch!"

"I'm talking about a million dollars with no one coming looking for you," Nicole told him.

"I could have done that much in an hour

if you had gotten inside Jack's company. So, a million won't cut it. It's all or nothing, and 'nothing' gets you and your friend work in a Colombian whorehouse."

"And it costs you a fortune. So why don't you play it smart? Let the girl go, and I'll split with you. That's half of three million."

His eyes narrowed. Three million. Was that what she got? Or was she bluffing? Could he squeeze more out of her? He decided to try. "Two million," he announced.

"That's more than I get to keep," Nicole protested.

"You get to keep breathing. And you get your friend back."

Nicole winced at her choices, letting Jimmy enjoy the hard bargain he was driving. "Okay," she conceded, her tone indicating that she had no fight left in her.

He smiled, savoring the joy of his victory for a few seconds. Then he took a business card from his breast pocket and held it in focus while he punched in the telephone number. He lifted the receiver. Nicole had kept her eyes on the card and read Greg Lambert's name. The Donners' detective. Why was Jimmy Farr calling the Donners' detective?

"It's me," Jimmy said, indicating that his

call was expected. "We've got a deal, but it has to be right now. Where can I pick up the money?"

He listened, his expression going from pleased to angry. "What guarantees? These guys aren't going to jump through hoops. If I give them the money they'll give me the girl. I'm taking a chance. They might get the money and shoot all the witnesses. We're all taking a chance. So what's it going to be? If you don't need me, I'm going home. I've got a business to look after." He listened again. He smiled. "Yeah, I know the place. Is that where the money is? Okay, in twenty minutes."

"You have another deal," Nicole yelled at him. "You bastard. You were just shaking me down."

"That doesn't change a thing. The price for little Pamela is their money and yours. I'll get their money up front. So it's still up to you to save your friend's ass."

SEVENTY

Jack was already at Jonathan's apartment when Greg Lambert arrived with the news. "It's all set," he reported. "Jimmy Farr is on his way over." Jack grimaced, his lips pulled tightly over clenched teeth. "I swear I'm going to kill the son of a bitch!"

Alexandra was more in control. "There's a problem, Greg," she said. "Nicole has already gone to meet him. She's the one he asked for, and she's trying to make a deal for Pam."

Lambert was stunned. "He didn't mention Nicole. Maybe she never found him."

"She found him," Jack insisted. "She phoned him from my . . . office. Then she left to meet him. That had to be an hour ago."

Alexandra sneered. "Very enterprising. He's going to let both of us pay ransom."

"No. Tell him we want Nicole back here," Jack said.

Alexandra took issue. "He'll deny he knows where Nicole is. Then what are we going to do?"

Lambert watched while the two of them argued. "He'll be here in a few minutes. How do you want me to handle it?"

Alexandra answered instantly. "Give him the money and get our daughter back. Then we'll worry about everything else." Jack started to protest, then fell silent.

Nicole realized where they were heading as soon as the car turned onto Park Avenue. She sat silently trying to make sense out of what was happening. Jimmy was heading to Jonathan's apartment to pick up Pam's ransom money. Greg Lambert was meeting him there to make the payment. Why would Jimmy be putting himself at such risk, exposing himself and his identity? Unless it didn't matter. Unless someone in the Donner household was working with him. But who? Was Greg Lambert, the loyal and resourceful servant, striking out on his own? Not likely! Or had Alexandra decided that her daughter's kidnapping would be a sure way to force Nicole's return?

They pulled to a stop directly in front of the building, making no effort to hide Jimmy's identity. The driver got out, exchanged a word with the doorman, and was welcomed inside as if he had been expected. Whatever Jimmy was up to, someone inside Jonathan's family knew about it and was involved in it.

"How did you get to meet Alexandra?" she asked, hoping to catch him off guard.

"I've never had the pleasure," he answered, keeping his eye on the door as he awaited the driver's return.

"Then why is Lambert helping you?"

Jimmy Farr chuckled. "We're both anxious for Pamela's safe return."

The driver reappeared, pausing while the doorman opened the door ahead of him. He carried a heavy satchel to Jimmy's door and lifted it onto the seat. Jimmy opened the zipper and Nicole was able to look inside at the neat bundles of cash. Jimmy hardly spared the money a glance before zipping the bag closed.

"Aren't you going to count it?" Nicole asked.

"When you're dealing with gentlemen, there's no need to count," he answered. "But when we leave your bank, I'll count very carefully. Now why don't you give the driver the address?"

They parked across the street from the bank entrance. Nicole reached for the door handle, but Jimmy's hand was on her shoulder. "Make a wire transfer," he said. He handed her a check with the account data encoded at the bottom. The account name was one of his phantom corporations. "Then come back here. We'll call my bank together and make sure the money has made it across."

"What about Pam?"

"When I have the money, I'll make a call. Then I'll give you an address."

"How do I know you'll let her go?"

He patted the satchel of cash that rested at his feet. "When I have what I want, why would I keep her around?"

"And if I don't come back?"

"Then neither will she." He reached across her and pushed open the door.

Nicole tried to look confident as she crossed the street and went through the revolving door, but her legs felt weak and the taste of fear was welling up in her throat. Someone inside the family was working with her former boss, and he was enjoying the rush of power. He had millions at his feet, still more about to fall into his hands, and he was bubbling with confidence. She was his to order about, nothing more than a pawn in someone's strategy. But whose? Who had brought her back from her escape and turned her over to Jimmy Farr? And why? With all the Donner resources, the money she was about to pay for Pam's release was a pittance. Obviously, her return was Jimmy's price for joining the conspiracy, but whom was he conspiring with?

Alexandra was an obvious choice. She was still demanding punishment for Jonathan's death. There was no way she could allow her prime suspect to get away, and with a sizable chunk of the family fortune as a bonus. Greg Lambert was the one who had run down her links with Farr, and he could certainly be the contact between the haughty grand dame and the vermin she would be reluctant to touch. But how could she ever deal with someone who had kidnapped her daughter?

Jack's situation was exactly the opposite. Nicole had no trouble envisioning him mixing it up with a lowlife like Farr. He seemed to delight in his up-from-poverty background and even bragged about his less savory deals. But he was trying to distance himself from his affair with her. Why would he ever want to bring her back? No matter what price Jimmy demanded, Jack would want Nicole kept on the other side of the ocean.

She gave her name to the platform receptionist and asked for the officer who had handled her account. She watched the girl walk to one of the back desks, saw the officer jump to his feet, start toward her and then stop abruptly. He seemed suddenly confused. Of course! He had never seen her before in her dyed hair and cruise attire. It took him several seconds to recognize her through her changed appearance.

"Ah, Mrs. Donner. Please have a seat. It will take me just a second to bring up your records." He began pecking at his keyboard, looking up at the screen after every stroke.

Maybe Lambert, Nicole thought. Wasn't it possible that the tireless and faithful bulldog had decided to freelance for himself? He was the one who was supposed to be protecting Pam, so he would be in the best position to take her and hold her. He would also be the logical intermediary between Jack Donner and the kidnappers. But why would he need someone like Jimmy Farr? And why would he insist that she be prevented from escaping the country?

The cell phone in her pocket vibrated against her leg. "Excuse me." She reached to turn it off, but then changed her mind. She was adrift in a sea of confusion. Maybe someone was calling with some answers. "I have a call, is there some place . . .”

The banker was on his feet. “Use my desk. I’ll be away for a moment.”

Nicole glanced around and lifted the phone to her face. “Yes?”

“Nicole?”

She recognized the voice instantly. “Pam?”

SEVENTY-ONE

"Nicole, where are you?"

"Back in New York . . ."

"Oh, thank God. You came back. Nicole, they're going to kill me!" Pam's voice was shrill, almost hysterical.

"Who, Pam? Who's going to hurt you?"

"I don't know. It's you they want. And if you don't come here right now they're going to kill me. Please, Nicole. I don't know what this is all about . . ."

"What about the money? The ransom?"

Pam shrieked. "They don't want money. They want you. I don't know why. They just want you."

They don't want money? But someone had just handed over a fortune. And the one who wanted her back already had her. He was waiting outside in his car knowing that she had to return.

"Where are you, Pam? Where do they want me to go?"

"I'm at the Newport house. They'll take me out to sea and dump me if you don't come."

Holding her in her own house? It *had* to be someone inside the family.

"I'll start up right away," Nicole said with all the determination she could put into her voice. "I have a car. It should take about three hours."

"Please hurry. They keep talking about a deadline. And for god's sake, don't tell anyone. Not Daddy, not the police, no one. Just come, and make sure you're not followed because they're watching the bridge and the road. If there's anyone with you . . ."

She sounded terrified, only seconds from mindless screaming.

"All right, Pam. Tell them I'm coming alone. I'll be there as fast as I can . . ."

The line went dead.

Now nothing made sense. Someone was paying a ransom that the kidnappers didn't want. And the people who wanted Nicole didn't know that Jimmy already had her. The only thing certain was that Pam was frightened beyond imagining. Whoever was holding her had gotten inside her head and convinced her that she was going to die.

Could Jimmy free Pam? If she transferred the money and went back to the car, would Jimmy be able to end it all with a phone call? If he could, then why would Pam be calling her? Wouldn't Jimmy have already called Pam's keepers and told them that he already had found Nicole? The only explanation was that someone else was holding Pam. And who, beside Jimmy Farr, would have demanded that she turn herself in as the ransom? Again, Alexandra seemed the most likely.

"Ahem!" The bank officer settled back into his chair and looked across at her expectantly. "You wanted to make a transaction?"

Nicole looked over his shoulder at the back door that opened out onto the next street. "No, not right now. I'll have to come back."

She glanced at the door she had entered. There was no sign of either Jimmy or his driver. She stood and walked out the back, paused for just an instant and then hailed a taxi.

Her car was parked near Jack's town house, but that wouldn't be a problem. There was no reason why anyone would be watching Jack's residence, nor did anyone know the kind of car she was driving. She could just pick it up and head for Newport. But she should tell someone where Pam was being held. If something happened to her Pam might still need to be rescued. Or, if she really was about to be swapped for her sister-in-law, then her own safety would depend on someone knowing where she was.

But whom could she trust? Certainly not Alexandra. And certainly not Greg Lambert. She knew for sure that he was the one that Jimmy Farr was dealing with. Maybe Jack. He was the least likely to be involved in a scheme that would bring Nicole back into his life. Unless he was afraid that Europe wasn't far enough and had decided to bury his problem permanently. God, could the money Jimmy had picked up be Jack's payoff for getting rid of his mistress? Jack had protested when she said she was going to meet Jimmy. But he hadn't stopped her from leaving the safety of his apartment and getting into Jimmy's car.

She paid off the taxi a block from where her car was parked and walked slowly down the other side of the street. No one seemed to be waiting in the vicinity and there was no one sitting in a nearby car. Nicole crossed the street, strolled past her car, then doubled back and unlocked the door. She pulled out quickly, cutting off a truck that was plodding up the street. If someone were waiting behind her, the truck would give her a moment to escape. And it would block anyone ahead of her who tried to pull out and follow. She rounded the corner and pulled to the side. No one turned in behind her. Satisfied that she was alone, she drove east toward the highway and the bridge that would start her to Connecticut. Three hours, she had promised Pam. She would need all of that even if the traffic kept moving.

SEVENTY-TWO

"She's taking too long," Jimmy Farr announced after he had waited for more than twenty minutes. "See what she's up to." His driver climbed out and dodged through traffic to the bank entrance. A minute later he appeared, his expression anxious. "She's not inside. There's a door out to the next street."

Jimmy screamed in pain. "The little bitch. She screwed me! She fucked me over!"

The driver was back behind the wheel. "Where to?"

"How the fuck would I know where to? She could have moved her money anywhere. And now she's on her way to join it." He shook his head. "She's a hustler, but I didn't think she'd throw her friend to the wolves." He sat silently, weighing his options. Then he looked down at the satchel of cash that rested beside him. He shook his head and smiled. "The hell with her. Let's just go back to the club."

He had two million in cash plus the half-million fee that Jack Donner had paid for his services. And Jack Donner was supposed to be the world's toughest wheeler and dealer. Wouldn't Jimmy love to see Jack's face when he finally understood that he'd been played for a fool? But that would have to come later. Right now he needed to go along with the game. Just waste a few hours so that he seemed to be earning his money, then call Greg Lambert and tell him where he could pick up Pamela Donner. Sure, Nicole had put one over on him. But their paths would cross again. In the meantime, having two and a half million fall into his lap was more than enough salve for his injured feelings.

Nicole was on the Connecticut Turnpike going as fast as she dared without attracting the attention of a policeman. She might look like the photo in her passport, but there was little resemblance between her new look and the photo on her license. She could lose hours if she were pulled over.

She still hadn't called anyone to tell where Pam was being held and where she was headed. There was no one she could trust completely. She had thought about William Kimes, Pam's partner. He had seemed genuine when she met him. But Kimes was interested in the kind of money that would make a spectacular impression on the art world, and Pam wouldn't be able to deliver that kind of money for several years. Maybe he had found a faster way to tap into Pam's fortune. That would also explain why she was part of the ransom herself. She was the other investor.

She had also thought about Ben Tobin. Jonathan had told her that she could rely on Ben, and he had represented her well in the negotiations with the Donner lawyers. But she knew that Tobin was under surveillance by Lambert's detectives and, worse, that Alexandra might have turned him. Hadn't he suddenly balked at transferring her funds abroad? Wouldn't he need her on hand if he planned on retrieving the money from her account?

Everyone seemed to be tainted. She could make a case for any one of them kidnapping Pam, or at least pretending to kidnap her in order to keep Pam's sister-in-law from escaping to Europe. But even as she ran the possible scenarios she knew how ridiculous they sounded. Jack Donner didn't need to set up an elaborate scheme. All he had to do was pay her off which was exactly what he already had done.

Alexandra would never stoop to dealing with the likes of Jimmy Farr even to rid her family of her unwanted daughter-in-law. Nor could she see Greg Lambert betraying his years of loyal service. William Kimes was an art dealer, hardly the credentials needed to pull off such an elaborate scheme. And Ben Tobin was a successful lawyer who would be risking everything if he became involved with kidnapping and extortion.

She had to trust someone. Nicole couldn't take the chance that she might vanish along with Pam. But who? Of all the players, which one had the least to gain by luring her back and collecting a ransom? That thought made her decision easy. She picked up her phone and keyed the number of Jack's town house. The phone rang a few times and then an answering machine picked up. She broke the connection and then dialed the private line at his office. Again, ringing but this time it was a secretary who finally picked up. "Mr. Donner's line. He isn't available right now . . ." Nicole hung up before the secretary could finish.

There was one other place she could try — Jonathan's apartment where Jimmy Farr had picked up the ransom money only a few hours earlier. But she knew that Greg Lambert was there, and probably Alexandra. The odds of getting through to Jack were slim. She decided that the town house was her best bet and dialed it again. She waited through Jack's message and then spoke quickly. "Jack, it's Nicole. Two things you should know. First, Jimmy Farr is working with Greg Lambert. He picked up a satchel full of cash at Jonathan's apartment. I hope you know what it's all about because it sounds as if someone on your side might be involved in the kidnapping. And next, I got a call from Pam on my cell phone. She's being held at your Newport house. She said if I didn't show up they were going to kill her, so I'm on my way there. I should make it at about five o'clock. I'm not supposed to tell anyone. Pam says the people holding her are watching the bridge and the roads, and they'll kill her if they see anyone with me. So be careful, Jack. You can't come barging in." Nicole closed with words that she immediately regretted. "I'll talk to you as soon as I know something . . . if I can."

SEVENTY-THREE

Jack paced the confines of the apartment like a caged animal, circling around the sofa where Alexandra sat in silence. Occasionally, he veered over to the chair next to the telephone where Greg Lambert was keeping vigil.

"How much longer is this going to take?" he demanded for the third time in the past half hour. Alexandra didn't even favor him with a shrug. Lambert repeated that it was hard to tell, but that it was probably too soon for them to be concerned. Then he got up and poured himself another cup of coffee.

They were all working with incomplete information. They knew that Jimmy Farr had arranged the kidnapping. Who else would want Nicole to turn herself over as ransom? They knew he had agreed to take money instead, using the ruse that he was only a messenger. They knew the ransom had been paid and that there was no reason for the thug to harm Pam. He had gotten more from the family than he ever would have gotten from Nicole. They also knew that Nicole had contacted him and gone to meet him, and that she was out there someplace trying to arrange her own deal for Pam's release. What they didn't know was whether Nicole's arrival on the scene had fouled their deal. Was Farr now looking for more, perhaps the money Nicole had gotten in her settlement? Was Nicole balking? Or did Farr have issues with her that went beyond the ransom? If Greg Lambert had known that Nicole was coming back, he never would have cut a deal with Jimmy. And if Nicole had known that Jimmy had agreed to a ransom, she never would have returned. It was the fact that two different plans were operating that posed the greatest danger to Pam's safety.

"Jesus," Jack growled as he made his turn at the window, "if he's the one holding her all he has to do is make a phone call. What in God's name is taking him so long?"

Alexandra couldn't take it any longer. "Jack, will you please sit down. You're driving me crazy."

He dropped onto the sofa beside her, but in a second he was back up and hovering over Lambert. "Isn't there someone you can call? You don't just turn over a few million without knowing where it's going."

Jack wasn't completely sure of Greg Lambert. It had been Lambert's idea to contact Jimmy Farr with the ruse of Jimmy serving as messenger to the kidnappers. He had, in effect, offered Jimmy the ransom without Jimmy admitting that he held the victim. If Greg were so inclined, it would be the perfect way to pocket a bit of the family's money without leaving a trail. Greg was the one most familiar with Pam's movements, the one responsible for protecting her. It would be easy for him to have one of his operatives take her, and for him to make it look as if Jimmy Farr was the kidnapper. Jimmy would get a half million for his services, and Greg would leave with two million.

In fact, he wasn't even sure of his own wife. Alexandra would do anything to bring Nicole back and strip her of the settlement money. Could this whole kidnapping be something she cooked up with Pam? Was he being played for the fool?

He snatched up the telephone. "Someone must know something," he announced.

Alexandra winced. "Who are you calling?"

"My office!" He dialed the town house. If Nicole had tried to reach him that was where she would have called. He listened to his machine and heard Nicole's voice. Pam was alive at the Newport house and that was where Nicole was heading. Greg Lambert was working with Jimmy Farr. He already knew that; they had all agreed to pay Jimmy the ransom. Don't contact the police. Pam's captors would know if anyone were closing in.

"What is it?" Alexandra had watched him as he listened and had seen the confusion in his expression.

"Nicole . . ." he said absently. "Pam is being held at our Newport house. She's on the way there now."

Alexandra jumped to her feet. "Pam is all right?"

Jack nodded. Then he rambled on in a stream of consciousness. "Nicole must have been with Farr when he picked up the money. She knew all about it. Then later, she heard from Pam who was still being held. So Farr never called his people." He turned to Greg Lambert. "He has our money and he still has our daughter . . ."

Greg returned the look of confusion. "If he had Nicole, why did he let her go? And if he let her go, why is she heading for Newport where his people are waiting?" He threw up his hands. "None of this makes sense."

"What makes sense," Alexandra said, "is that we have to get to Newport."

Lambert made a phone call to arrange for a helicopter. They would be picked up at the Fifty-ninth Street heliport. The flight to the Newport house would take only an hour. Then he told his people to contact the police in Newport who could be on the scene in a matter of minutes.

"No!" Jack cut him off. "No police. I don't want Pam in the middle of a shootout. And we can't land on the lawn. We have to land away from the house and then get there in an ordinary car. Something that won't look like us. That will at least get us onto the grounds. And then call your fucking friend Jimmy Farr. Tell him we're heading up and that Pam better be in good shape when we get there."

"Remember how we're playing it," Greg cautioned. "Jimmy doesn't know the people who are holding her."

"We're not playing games anymore," Jack answered. "Tell him that if anything happens to Pam, I'll kill him. Tell him that I was a thug when he was still stealing little kids' lunch money."

SEVENTY-FOUR

Nicole reached the top of the bridge with its stunning view down the east shore of Narragansett and out into Rhode Island Sound. But her focus was on the road immediately ahead and, with a glance to her mirror, on the road behind. One last check to be sure that no one had pulled up behind her, and then a slow search ahead for whoever might be waiting. Pam had been clear: they were watching the bridge and the road down to Ocean Drive. Her captors would know if she brought reinforcements.

She had kept a sharp lookout ever since she left the city in order to be certain that she wasn't being followed. Greg Lambert might well have been watching where her car was parked. Or Jack, once he understood that Farr hadn't released his daughter, might well have called in the police. People following her would think they were coming to Pam's rescue. But if Pam were right, they would be sealing her fate. If they saw police, they would get rid of the evidence.

Now, as she turned off the bridge in

Newport, Nicole had a new concern. Someone might not want Pam rescued. She was still baffled by the ease with which Jimmy had collected from someone in the family, and still surprised that he hadn't ordered Pam's release. Jimmy, she figured, wasn't alone in the kidnapping and wasn't completely in charge. Someone else, with a different agenda, might be calling the shots.

What was obvious was that Jimmy had never expected Pam's phone call. He had Nicole under his control and was about to take away what he thought was most of her money. The last thing he would have allowed was for Pam to change the signals. So, it seemed likely that whoever was holding her had no idea of what Jimmy was up to. But if not Jimmy, then who? Who else would bring her back and then entice her to a closed house on a secluded coastline?

She saw no one. Not a single suspicious character lurking along her route. Not one car in the nearly empty street behind her. And there was the house ahead of her, the gate thrown wide open with no one guarding it. Nicole slowed and drove past, peering through the gate and up the driveway. There was nothing, not even a parked car.

The house seemed to be deserted. She doubled back and looked in again. No one was there.

She turned through the gateposts and rolled quietly down the driveway. Slowly, the entire house came into view. Only a few weeks ago the grounds had been crowded with guests with giant tents set over improvised banquet halls. Now, the property seemed to have been abandoned. Down the hill she could see the dock where the launches had landed from the yachts moored offshore. Now there was a single yacht, a large cruiser with an enclosed pilothouse and saloon tied to one of the moorings. Its tender, a small outboard launch, was tied to the dock.

Nicole stopped in the driveway and then carefully turned the car so that it was pointing toward the gate. Then she got out and went up the steps to the house. The door was locked. She hesitated, then walked around to a window. The inside was in darkness with just the beams of light through the western windows offering illumination. There were dust covers on the furniture. Paintings had been taken down from the walls. The Newport house's short season had ended and the house was closed until the next season began. But they still might be inside, waiting for her. Nicole tried the doorbell and then listened at the intercom. There was no response.

She turned on the porch and saw the yacht floating peacefully no more than fifty yards offshore. She remembered that when she first came to Newport, with Jonathan in the off-season, that there was no boat. He had told her that the Donners' northern fleet wintered at a marina. If the house had been closed, then the yacht should have been gone. Nicole kept her eyes fixed on the boat as she walked down the hill to the dock.

The launch was an open whaler, lightly tied with just bow and stern lines. There was a red fuel can under a seat, with a fuel line leading back to the engine. The key was in the ignition switch on the console. The whaler, like the yacht, was still in use. Someone had been riding back and forth between the dock and the mooring. That meant that someone was ashore, probably in the house and looking down at her right that instant. It also suggested that Pam was out on the yacht, probably being held captive by another member of the team. She had said that if something went wrong, all they had to do was take her to sea and drop her overboard.

She looked up at the house trying to

catch a shape in a window or the movement of a curtain. There was nothing. She turned back to the yacht, swinging innocently as it pointed toward the offshore breeze. Nicole stepped down into the whaler, turned the key, and heard the engine catch instantly. She slipped the lines off the dock cleats and brought them aboard. Then she eased the throttle ahead.

There was no one moving about on the yacht and there seemed to be no one in the pilothouse. But the gangway was down, sloping from the deck to a small landing platform. Apparently, she was expected. She eased the whaler in close, cut the engine, and threw one of the lines over a cleat. She tied off the second line and then made her way slowly up the ladder, expecting to see a face peering down at any second. But no one appeared. When she stepped across onto the deck she seemed to be boarding a ghost ship.

"Anyone aboard?"

No response. All she could hear were the waves lapping against the side. She made her way aft, then opened the door and stepped into the saloon.

The interior was finished in teak and wood tones. She was in a lounge with a sofa and two deep upholstered chairs surrounding a table. There was a bar to starboard with bottles and glasses behind the shelf rails, and a television console was to port. Ahead was a dining table surrounded by eight chairs.

"Pam!" She heard her voice echoing forward, past the galley and into the pilothouse. "Pam!" she called again.

"Here," came a muffled response. "I'm down here."

SEVENTY-FIVE

The helicopter lifted gently and then swung out over the river. Greg Lambert sat next to the pilot and was on the radio making arrangements for their arrival in Newport. Jack and Alexandra were in the rear seat, each staring out a window, each lost in private thoughts. The copter moved east, crossing the river and continued inland to avoid the LaGuardia flight patterns. It climbed as it made its way past the Long Island bridges, and then east out over the Sound. The pilot aimed it directly at the Rhode Island coast.

Greg leaned back over the seat. "Okay, we'll be landing at the police compound on the far side of the peninsula. It's about a mile east of the house. The police have an unmarked sedan for us, but the driver will be one of their officers. They have a SWAT team standing by, but they won't approach the house until we're inside the gate."

"Damn it, I said no police!" Jack snapped. His temper was at an explosive edge.

"They're not going near the house unless we call for them," Greg told him. "But damn it, Jack, they can't just let a bunch of civilians wander into a crime scene."

Jack growled, but he didn't argue.

Alexandra didn't join the conversation. She leaned to one side, her chin resting on the back of her hand, her nose pressed to the window, seemingly fascinated by the passing Connecticut coastline. But her thoughts were ahead to their landing at Newport and their arrival at the house. She had no doubt that Pam was there. Nicole had no reason to lie about where she was heading. Jimmy Farr had reached them in their car with the address where Pam would be found. It was their Newport house. But that was all that she was sure of. Whoever was holding her daughter had no knowledge of Jimmy Farr's involvement. And the motive for the kidnapping wasn't money. The motive was her daughter-in-law. So who would have planned it, and what did they hope to gain? Those were the questions that tormented her.

She was also confused about Nicole. All the evidence she had run down pointed to a lowlife whose only interest was money. The girl had lied her way into her son's life and lured him off to his death, just to get her hands on his fortune. Then she had compromised her husband to assure a generous and swift payment. She had done exactly what Alexandra had predicted. She had taken the money and run.

But then she came back. With everything she wanted within her grasp, she had turned around and put everything at risk. Why? Was it only because Pam was in trouble and needed her? Because that didn't fit the profile that Alexandra had so carefully drawn. There had to be something else. Some other reason. And if Jack knew, he wasn't letting on.

The radio crackled and a distant voice asked for Greg Lambert. Greg took the handset. "Yeah . . . what . . . when did that happen?" He listened anxiously, his expression alternately pleased and disappointed. "I thought we had an agreement . . ." He hunched his shoulders. "Yeah . . . I understand . . ." And then, in a loud voice, "No! Don't do anything! We'll just have to hope that this doesn't matter."

"What the fuck is going on?" Jack demanded.

Greg held up his hand while he signed off. Then he said, "The police picked up some guy who was watching the houses on Ocean Drive. They thought he might be casing a house for a robbery."

"Jesus!" Jack slammed his fist on the seat back. "I thought the police —"

"It was just a patrol car. The police chief didn't tell everyone on the force about our problem. This guy just happened to spot someone loitering in a car and did what he's supposed to do. But here's the important part: the guy works at Jimmy Farr's club. One of the bouncers."

Jack's eyes widened. "Then Jimmy did have her!"

"Looks that way," Greg said. "Probably called his people off and left Pam where we could find her. Then he told us where to look."

"Well, then let's land right on the property. If they've left her there then there's no one to stop us."

Greg nodded in agreement and turned to the pilot.

"No, wait!" It was Alexandra suddenly involving herself. "None of that explains why Pam called Nicole. Pam said she was in danger long after Farr had picked up his money."

Jack thought, and then answered, "Pam probably doesn't know that they've left . . ."

"Even when she was free enough to make a telephone call? And if there were no one with her, why would she have called Nicole? Why not you, Jack? Or me?"

"I don't know," Jack admitted, and looked to Greg Lambert.

"You've got a point," Greg told Alexandra. "Maybe we better leave things just as they are. We'll go in quietly without the police."

SEVENTY-SIX

"Nicole, in here."

She was halfway down the steps to the cabin level, but she still couldn't pinpoint the voice. Pam was in a cabin, behind a steel door, and her voice was echoing through the empty passageway.

"I'm coming," Nicole called. "Keep talking so I can find you."

She reached the bottom step and turned into the passageway. She was face-to-face with Ben Tobin.

The sun was low in the west when they flew past the mouth of Narragansett Bay. They stayed well out over the water until they were past the house. Then they turned inland, crossed over the coast, and settled down into a cloud of dust that obscured the waiting police cars. Greg took the lead, running directly to the ranking police officer and then introducing Alexandra and Jack. They could scarcely hear one another until they were away from the landing pad.

"We're holding the guy who was watching the house," the police lieutenant explained. "He hasn't called anyone, so we're pretty sure that no one knows we've got him."

"Any activity at the house?" Greg asked.

The lieutenant shrugged. "We've been keeping clear, just as you asked. But we've got a SWAT team aboard a bus waiting to roll, and there's a police boat just around the point. So if there's anyone in there, he's not going to get away."

They slid into the car, a midsize sedan painted medium gray. The driver was a police sergeant wearing a sports shirt, looking completely innocent except for the sawed-off shotgun on the seat next to him. There was a tiny microphone pinned to his shirt collar, and he wore a receiving button in his ear.

"We're just going to drive up to the house, and through the gate. There's a parking area by the garage where you can let us out," Lambert instructed. Then he turned to Alexandra and Jack in the backseat. "I think you should stay in the car with the officer. Give me a few minutes to look the place over."

"I'm going with you," Jack insisted. Lambert argued that he might just get in the way but Jack would have none of it.

"It's my daughter they're holding."

They drove along quiet streets, with the driver naming each intersection into his microphone. They turned onto Ocean Drive and after a few minutes the gate came into sight.

"We're there," the police officer intoned. "The gate is wide open. We're going in." They rolled through the open gate and started down the driveway. Within seconds, they saw Nicole's car, parked in the driveway and pointed straight at them. "Someone's here," the officer reported to his commander. Then he asked, "Anybody recognize the car?" No one did.

They stopped in front of Nicole's car. Jack and Greg got out. The policeman slid from behind the wheel and stood between the two cars, the shotgun hanging at his side. Lambert climbed the porch steps and went around to the window. The room inside was dark. He moved slowly around the side of the house, pausing at each ground-floor window. The furniture was draped in dust covers. There wasn't a light on anywhere. He went to the front door and tried the handle. Then he used the key from his collection of keys to all the Donner properties.

Inside, he moved cautiously. He circled

the ground floor and then went up the stairs and tried all the doors. There was no one in the house, and no sign that anyone had been there recently.

Jack was waiting at the front door. "They must be out on that boat," he said, pointing out to the yacht that was beginning to disappear as daylight failed. He and Lambert started down to the dock. The police officer followed at a distance, hiding the shotgun along his leg. Stealth wasn't really necessary. No one on the boat would be able to make out the men much less the policeman's weapon.

There was no launch at the dock. They stood helplessly staring out at the outline of the yacht that showed no lights.

"Whoever came in that car has to be out there," Greg said.

"Yeah," the officer agreed. "A woman named Nicole Pierce. That's the name on the rental agreement."

"Nicole," Jack said, sounding surprised. But then he remembered that she had gotten a good head start on them. "It could be her," he agreed.

"Then they're all out there. Pam, Nicole, and whoever took Pam," Greg concluded.

"Did . . . Nicole bring ransom money?" the officer asked. "Did she bring something that the kidnappers wanted?"

"They wanted her," Jack told him.

They stood silently, watching the night envelop the yacht. Greg and the officer made eye contact. They both knew something had to be done quickly. Greg took on the task of telling Jack.

"They've got Pam and now Nicole, Jack. If they have what they want, it may be time for them to get rid of the witnesses."

Jack understood clearly. "Then we can't just wait them out, can we?" He focused on the policeman. "What do you have in mind?"

SEVENTY-SEVEN

"Ben?" He was the last person Nicole expected to find. "Where's Pam?"

"Behind you. The last cabin." He pointed down the passageway.

"How did you get here?" she asked.

Ben took her shoulders and turned her around. "The last cabin," he repeated.

She walked ahead of him. "Is she all right?"

"See for yourself." He reached around her and pushed open a cabin door.

Nicole stepped in and found Pam seated on the edge of a bunk. Instinctively she rushed to her and threw her arms around her. "Are you okay? Did they hurt you?" She heard Pam stifle a laugh. Then Pam's hands were on her shoulders, pushing her away.

Nicole turned to Ben who filled the cabin doorway. "Is she all right? What did they do to her?"

Ben looked past Nicole to Pam who was still seated on the bunk. "She still hasn't figured it out," he said with a satisfied grin.

"Not a clue," Pam answered. "Ben was worried that you'd just keep running. But I told him you'd come back. Isn't that what big sisters do?"

Nicole stared at Pam. "You were never kidnapped . . ." She was finding it hard to believe what she was beginning to understand. "You faked it, to get me to come back."

"Very good!" Pam complimented. "You got it on your first try. I've been living aboard, working my way through the pâté and the champagne."

"And you, Ben. You've been helping her. So this must be about the money I was given."

"The money you extorted," Pam snapped, jumping to her feet. "The money Jonathan was going to invest in my gallery until you came along and played him for a fool."

"I loved your brother . . ."

"Save the sob story, Nicole. Mother had you figured right from the start. You found a mark with a billion dollars and you screwed it away from him. An easy mark, because Jonathan couldn't resist a great piece of ass. He was a made-to-order chump. Well who's the chump now, Nicole?"

Nicole was beginning to assemble all the unknowns. Pam's money was five years away, and Jonathan had had his already. But she couldn't get her hands on Jonathan's by killing her brother. Her brother had just taken a wife who was automatically his heir . . .

"I was the one you wanted to kill. It wasn't supposed to be Jonathan who drowned over the wreck."

"Very bright of you Nicole. Too bad you were so damn stupid out on the boat. I rigged his regulator and your tank was half Valium. He was supposed to retreat back up to the surface and you were going down to the bottom. Only you mixed up your tanks."

Nicole staggered and sagged into a chair. She could remember the horror of that evening off the reef in Belize. But what was most clear to her was the expression of shock she had seen on Pam's face when the younger woman pulled off her mask and saw who was in the boat. She had been expecting it to be her brother, and she had probably rehearsed the sympathy she was going to shower on his recently departed wife. It would have been difficult for her to act grief stricken because Nicole's lien on Jonathan's fortune would have vanished along with Jonathan's interest in building a diving resort. Pam would have a hard time suppressing a smile, much less shedding a tear.

"And the explosion?" Nicole asked through her hands. "I blamed Alexandra . . ."

Pam laughed. "So did everyone else. Mother made no secret of hating your guts. She knew you stole her son and she was pretty sure you had killed him. Everyone knew she wasn't going to let you walk off with a fortune.

"And it was so easy. Just turn the gas on and wait for you to arrive. You wouldn't know about the alarm signal, and that you had just twenty seconds to push the reset. You'd run around trying to turn off the gas, and you'd probably run up the stairs to be sure Alexandra wasn't trapped inside. When the time was up, the alarm would send a signal to the gatehouse. The spark from the switch would have blown you out of my life. They probably wouldn't have even found what was left of you."

"But I didn't go in," Nicole said, filling out the ending of Pam's story. "I went down to the bluff to look out at the Sound." She looked up, puzzled. She could tell that Ben was just as confused as she was.

"So, how did you damn near blow yourself up?" Ben asked.

"A mistake," Pam answered. "I saw Nicole's car and thought she had gone in without tripping the alarm. If she was in there, I wanted to be sure that the gas had gotten to her. When she wasn't, I knew I had to call the whole thing off. I turned off the gas jets and turned off the alarm. The 'off' switch must have caused its own spark."

Nicole fixed on Ben. "You were part of all this."

He raised his hands innocently. "Not me. I was just an adviser. Oh, I did show her how to foul the air regulator. But blowing up the cottage was too crude for my taste."

"That's why you wouldn't transfer the money," Nicole concluded.

"I did transfer the money, but not to your account. You would have found out when you tried to bring it over to Europe. So we couldn't let you get away. Sooner or later you'd tell Jack, and he would find out where your money had gone. So, you see, you became the insurmountable obstacle in an otherwise perfect plan. Until we came up with the kidnapping!"

"That was Ben's idea," Pam said. "We

kidnap me, and make it look like it was your old thug friend who wants to get his hands on you. So when you vanish, everyone goes after him. No one thinks about us. And they assume your money is in some foreign account known only to you. So, no one goes looking for the money."

Nicole could hardly get her words out. "You did all this . . . for money? Killed your own brother?" She shook her head in disbelief and then said to Ben, "He was your best friend. How could . . ." She swallowed hard and couldn't manage to finish her thought.

Ben looked away from her. He seemed to be talking to a memory when he said, "Jonathan wasn't very bright, and he certainly never worked very hard. But he had all that money and he loved to flash it around as if he had earned it." He looked back at Nicole. "It was never easy being the monkey on the end of his string. I didn't like being his court jester. I'm too smart for that."

"Jesus . . ." Nicole stood slowly. "I think I'm going to be sick."

"Poor dear," Pam mocked. "You probably need some fresh air." She nudged Ben. "I think you ought to take her for a boat ride."

SEVENTY-EIGHT

Jack climbed aboard the police launch and reached back to help Alexandra. Greg was already aboard, standing near the control console and going over plans with the captain. He came aft and sat across from Jack. "They're not going to show the boat," he explained. "We'll loiter on this side of the point, as close as we can get to them without being seen. Then the police are going to put two divers into the water. The divers will get close to the yacht, ready to go aboard."

"That's too risky," Jack barked. But a second later, in a much less authoritative tone, he asked, "Wouldn't that be dangerous for Pam and Nicole?"

Lambert nodded. "Yes, there are dangers. But the divers won't be attacking. They're just getting close, in case anything crazy starts happening. They can be aboard before we even round the point."

"If they have Nicole, why don't they release Pam?" Alexandra asked. "That was what they demanded, wasn't it?"

"Nicole has already been aboard for an

hour," Lambert reminded her. "But we'll wait. If they send Pam ashore, great. But if they head out to sea, we'll have to stop them."

"Why, if it's dangerous for Pam?" she wondered.

"It's like a hijacking," Lambert explained. "You can't let them take off from one airport to another. That just postpones the inevitable. Sooner or later you have to take the chance and face them down."

Alexandra looked at her husband. "I hate to force a showdown."

Greg answered. "The police think their best chance is right here. And under cover of darkness so they can't see us coming."

The deck hands took in the lines, and the police boat headed away from its dock. They could see the light tower blinking ahead of them, a half mile off the headlands. But they were staying inside it. They weren't heading out to sea, but hugging the shoreline instead. They were getting the divers as close as they could without exposing themselves and alarming Pam's captors.

Alexandra shivered. The night sea air was cold and she wasn't prepared for it. Lambert got blankets for both her and Jack.

"I don't like this," Jack told him. "We're taking chances with Pam."

"I don't either," the security officer answered. "But I think it's all we have. Let's just take it one step at a time."

The divers were waiting at the rail, two muscular men in dark wet suits. One of them gave Jack a thumbs-up sign of encouragement. Jack returned it. The boat slowed just fifty yards off a rocky outcropping. The divers waited, watched the speed of the wake, and then dropped over the side.

SEVENTY-NINE

Ben Tobin jammed the barrel of a pistol into Nicole's side. "Let's go!" He eased her out of the cabin and then to the foot of the steps. "Take it nice and easy. I'm right behind you." She moved up the stairs into the saloon and hesitated at the top. Then she felt the gun in her back. "Keep going, out onto the deck, and then down the gangway."

She moved slowly, glancing from the corners of her eyes in search of some route of escape. But the gun kept bumping against her, reminding her that if she should bolt away she would probably never live to take a second step.

"Why are you doing this?" she tried.

"Keep walking." He wasn't going to be deflected by conversation.

"You have a great career. Why are you throwing it all away?"

He laughed softly from the back of his throat. "Ten million dollars," he said.

They were out on the after deck. Ben took her arm. "This way." He aimed her around to the starboard side where the gangway led down to the boat.

"Ben, for God's sake, don't do this!"

He nudged her to the top step of the gangway.

"Please. You can still walk away from all this. You haven't hurt anybody."

"I will walk away, with my cut of the money to go wherever I want and do whatever I want. Isn't that what you planned to do?"

They reached the bottom and stepped onto the landing where the boat was tied. "You first!" Ben ordered. "Climb in at the bow and sit next to the anchor."

Nicole knew the plan. He would take her out a mile or so, far enough so that no one would hear the gunshot. Finish her with a single bullet in the head. Then tie her to the anchor and throw her over the side. She would probably never be found. And, if by some accident she should wash ashore or be hauled up on a lobster line, Jimmy Farr would get all the credit.

"I'm not going Ben," she told him. "If you're going to kill me you're going to have to do it now."

He took her arm and twisted it behind her. "Get in the boat!"

Nicole fought back and let out a piercing scream.

"Damn you!" Ben cursed and he raised the gun over her head like a bludgeon. Nicole held his arm with her free hand and screamed again. Ben pushed her back and ripped the gun hand out of her grasp. He raised the weapon again and was about to crash it down on her head, when he heard a splash. Something had lunged out of the water at the edge of the platform. He wheeled just as a hand locked around his ankle. His foot was pulled out from under him and he staggered wildly trying to find his balance. Then he was falling over the edge. The gun fired harmlessly into the air and he splashed into the sea.

"Jesus," Jack screamed when the sound of the pistol shot reached him.

"Let's go!" Greg snapped at the captain who was already reaching for the throttle. The boat jerked itself up and skimmed out around the point. Within seconds, the dark outlines of the yacht came into sight against the background of lights on the land. It looked so close, yet every second seemed an eternity.

"They wouldn't kill her," Alexandra said to no one in particular. "Why would they kill Pam? They have the money. They have Nicole. It couldn't have been Pam . . ."

Jack squeezed her hand, but his focus was locked onto the yacht. He was hoping that he would hear more gunfire. More shots would indicate a battle with maybe the police overcoming Pam's captors. The single shot sounded ominously like an execution.

They turned around the stern of the boat, slowed the engine, and made for the gangway platform. At the last second, the captain saw something in the water and veered away. A searchlight snapped on and lit up the platform as a black-suited diver hoisted himself out of the water. Another appeared next to him, and together they lifted a struggling figure up between them. Ben Tobin held up his hand to protect his eyes from the glare.

"Ben?" Jack was openmouthed. He gaped mindlessly as the boat made its landing behind the launch. Police were onboard instantly, taking Ben away from the divers. He came face-to-face with Jack.

"Ben, what are you —"

"It's Nicole, Jack. I followed her here. She came to kill Pam . . ."

Jack was bewildered. He looked around to see if the others had heard what he had heard.

"She's up there now," Ben continued,

"looking for Pam. You've got to stop her."

One of the divers stood awkwardly. "You were the one trying to kill someone. You were trying to drag a woman into the boat."

Ben flustered for only an instant. "That was Nicole. I was taking her ashore to turn her over to the police. Now she's back up there! For Christ's sake, Jack, you've got to stop her!"

Ben pulled free from the hands that were holding him and started up the ladder. Policemen with assault rifles were right behind him. "She's armed," Ben warned. "She's gone crazy!"

Nicole had caught only a glimpse of the diver, and had stood transfixed while Ben gyrated and fell over. The gunshot had sent a jolt of fear through her that kept her frozen for another few seconds. But as Ben disappeared under the lapping waves, she had turned and raced back up the ladder. Even with Pam still aboard, the yacht seemed a safe haven from the struggle that was taking place at her feet.

She hesitated when she reached the deck and looked fore and aft. What she needed was a place to hide. A place where Pam wouldn't find her and where she could wait until the man in the water showed his hand. She hoped he was a rescuer sent by Jack, but he might also be from Jimmy Farr.

She ran forward and tried a hatch that led into the yacht's galley. It was locked from the inside. Then another hatch atop the crew's quarters. It too had been locked. She ran aft and pushed open the saloon door that Ben Tobin had just brought her through. The room was dark but she remembered the lounge area with its soft chairs. She crouched down and felt her way into a corner hidden by a chair. Then she sat in the darkness. She guessed that Pam would be coming up from below. She must have heard the pistol. She would certainly know that something had gone wrong.

There was an engine sound, still at a distance Nicole guessed, but growing closer. Then she could hear the pounding of a boat against the water. Someone was coming. Probably whoever had sent the diver. But who was it? The police, called by Jack when he finally heard her message? Or Farr's people, who had followed her from the city, or who had been watching the house?

The boat landed. Nicole could hear

people jumping onto the landing and the sound of voices. She couldn't recognize any of them, until one voice broke out of the confusion. It was Ben Tobin's. There were suddenly footsteps pounding up the ladder, and then Ben was warning the others that she had a gun. That she was crazy.

The cabin light flashed on, a startling blast coming out of the darkness. Nicole blinked and risked a glance around the chair. Pam was walking toward her with a small chrome pistol clutched in both hands. She hesitated an instant to look behind the first chair. Then she took another step and pointed the gun over the second chair and right at Nicole's head. Nicole sprang up, pushing the chair ahead of her and into Pam's face. Pam fell backward but kept her balance. When Nicole came toward her she was staring at the muzzle.

Ben, with the armed police at his heels, had just reached the deck when the lights in the saloon flashed on. Shafts of light fell from the windows and instinctively the men dove for cover, Ben flat on the deck and the policemen up against the superstructure. Greg Lambert came up and threw himself down next to Ben.

"Get in there. Shoot her before she kills Pam," Tobin whispered frantically.

Suddenly Greg's gun was in his face. "You stay right here! Don't move!"

"But we have to save Pam . . ."

"Just don't move a muscle."

The policemen were already edging forward, each covering the other as he moved. Greg got to his feet and walked directly to the stern, past the assault team and the open windows.

"Get down," a policeman cautioned in a whisper.

Lambert kept walking to the open cabin door. On the way, he pushed his weapon into a holster that hung on his back. "Pam!" he shouted, and then, "Nicole! You can come out now. It's all over."

"She has a gun," Nicole's voice shouted back. There was a crashing sound, followed instantly by a gunshot. Lambert stepped through the doorway only to be pushed aside by the rushing assault team.

Nicole was on the floor, next to the toppled chair. Pam was standing over her, pressing the tiny chrome weapon against Nicole's head. The assault team pulled up short.

"It's over, Pam," Greg announced. "Give

me that damn thing before you get yourself into real trouble."

"Get back," Pam said ferociously. "I swear to God, I'll kill her. She and I are leaving, and no one better try to stop us."

"You'll do no such thing!" Alexandra pushed the police aside and stepped into the cabin. Pam's hard expression suddenly turned uncertain.

"You look ridiculous with that thing," Alexandra said. She started toward her daughter. "Give it to me before you hurt yourself."

Pam backed away, but she still held the gun, now raised toward her mother. "Stay back," she said. "I don't want to shoot you."

Alexandra's pace never faltered. "Of course you don't want to shoot me. Whoever heard of anything so ridiculous." Pam backed against the table. Alexandra kept walking right at the gun.

The police were frozen in place. They had a clear shot at the girl, but then Alexandra walked in front of her. It was too dangerous to fire.

"Don't come any closer," Pam said. It wasn't an order. It was a plea.

Alexandra reached out her hand. "I said, 'Give it to me!' "

Pam's eyes were locked on her mother's. Then the hand holding the gun began to tremble. Her grip softened. She turned the pistol on its side and laid it gently into her mother's hand.

She turned to Nicole. "And as for you young lady . . ." She saw the stain spreading across Nicole's chest and down the sleeve of her shirt. "Oh, dear God, she's been shot."

EIGHTY

A policeman used a dinner napkin to slow the bleeding while a wire gurney was brought up from the boat. Nicole was carried down the gangway, put aboard the police launch, and rushed ashore. Alexandra was at her side. Pam was kept in the saloon, watched over by the two assault specialists. Jack sat beside her, holding her hand. Ben Tobin was under guard out on the afterdeck. The police had tried to question him but he had fallen back on his legal training and remained silent.

Greg Lambert didn't need a confession to figure out what had taken place. Ben couldn't have come aboard the yacht to rescue Pam from Nicole. There was only one launch, and if Nicole was aboard she must have used it to come out from the dock. Ben had to have been aboard before her.

It was also obvious that Pam hadn't been kidnapped. She had to be the one who had provided the keys to the yacht, and moved it from its yacht club berth. She knew that a secure mooring would be waiting offshore because she was the one who had ordered it set for the party. So whatever they were into, they were into it together.

What he couldn't yet understand was the reason. Nicole had been paid off handsomely and, as he understood it, was leaving the country. Everyone wanted her to disappear so why did Pam and Ben go to such great lengths to get her back? Why did they want her dead when it was obvious that she wasn't bringing them any money? He had trusted the police diver's instincts when he said that Ben was trying to kill Nicole. And Ben's hastily concocted story that he was taking Nicole ashore to turn her over hadn't rung true. Wouldn't his first concern be to bring Pam ashore to safety? So when he had shouted that Nicole had a gun and urged Greg to shoot her, Greg had realized exactly what was involved. They needed Nicole dead, and even in the process of rescuing Pam, Ben had been more concerned with having Nicole shot.

The only thing he still couldn't comprehend was why.

The police launch returned around the point, this time with its lights blazing. The boat had come back to bring the prisoners and their guards to shore. Maybe then, in a police interrogation room, he would get the answer. Or maybe Nicole would be able to tell him. If she lived.

Alexandra waited in the hallway, sipping a terrible cup of coffee that had come from a vending machine. She had watched Nicole being rolled down the corridor, an IV held over her head by a nurse who had to run to keep up. She had disappeared behind swinging doors into the arms of a medical team that was already waiting. Then the parade began. A endless stream of doctors, nurses, and technicians had rushed in and out. Frightening looking machines had been delivered, along with plastic bags filled with blood.

Alexandra caught the arm of every person who came out through the swinging doors. "How is she?"

One nurse simply patted her hand and pulled away. Another mumbled that they were doing everything that they could. Then a doctor asked her, "Are you family?"

"Yes," she announced, surprised at her own answer. "Yes, she's my daughter." The doctor took her arm and led her inside.

Nicole was on a gurney, surrounded by what seemed to be confusion. Her face was hidden in a mask connected to a thick flexible hose. IV bags hung from posts, draining fluids into her arm and leg. Blood was dripping into the other arm. Wires seemed to come from every part of her body, connecting her to machines that showed graphs and numbers and beeped ominously.

There were three people hovering over her head, working on a gaping wound just under her collarbone. They moved spastically, using and discarding instruments at a frantic pace, grunting words that Alexandra didn't understand. Other figures in medical garb were lined up on both sides of the table, one holding a huge hypodermic at the ready, another feeling for a vein so that she could start another IV. Most ghastly of all was the blood that was spattered down the fronts of the gowns and was dripping from the edge of the gurney. Red-soaked gauze pads were scattered on the floor.

Alexandra could take only a few seconds of the brutal procedure. She turned her eyes away and then walked out the door. She was shocked that Pam's little chrome-plated pistol could have done so much damage. She paced for a while, and then stopped at the vending machine for another cup of coffee.

The doctor who had been working on

Nicole's wound came through the door, his mask hanging down around his neck. He seemed just a boy to Alexandra, and he was past her before she realized who he was.

"Doctor?"

He stopped.

"Will she make it?"

He seemed uncertain. "We've stopped the bleeding. But she lost a lot of blood. We're trying to get her stable, and then we'll get her up to surgery."

"Will she make it?" Alexandra demanded.

"I think so," he said. "But she's not out of the woods. Next hour or so will tell."

Alexandra nodded and whispered a word of thanks.

At the police station, Jack was already launched into damage control. He had noted Ben Tobin's example, and wouldn't let anyone talk to his daughter. He had called Victor Crane, given him a thirty-second summary of events, and told him to hire the best criminal lawyer he knew.

"Kidnapped herself?" Crane asked, his shock obvious. "I'm not sure that's a crime . . ."

"There may also have been extortion."

"Money? Who was she extorting from?"

"It's not that simple," Jack said. "We're going to need that criminal lawyer."

Like Greg Lambert, Jack had figured out the scheme. He had met Nicole in his town house, so he knew she couldn't have been out on the boat holding Pam captive. He had also figured out how Jimmy Farr was involved. Jimmy had been looking for Nicole and watching Pam figuring that Nicole might contact her. His people had followed Pam to Newport, and knew that she had taken one of the family cruisers and headed out. Then the boat had shown up at a mooring right in front of the Donner house.

Farr must have been stunned when Greg visited him with the news of Pam's kidnapping, and delighted that the Donners thought he was involved. All he had to do was collect the money and then tell them where their daughter could be found. If they thought the money had bought her freedom, they might still come after him. But how could he be charged with a kidnapping that had never taken place, or with extortion when he hadn't demanded any money?

Jack could understand Farr's motives. The man was driven by money and would stoop to any level in order to enrich himself. But nobody got away with cheating Jack Donner. Farr's reckoning would come.

What he couldn't begin to understand was why Pam was involved. Or Ben Tobin, for that matter. It had to be an effort to take the money that Nicole had just been awarded. But Pam didn't need money. In a few years she would come into a fortune much larger than anything she could take from Nicole. And Ben? Maybe he couldn't stand to hand that much of his friend's money over to a woman who had known him for such a short time. But he was an attorney with a promising career that would be completely ruined by his involvement in a crime. Why would either of them have risked so much? Self-interest didn't explain it. It must have been irrational hatred of Nicole.

Alexandra had watched as Nicole was taken from the emergency room and wheeled into an elevator. The glimpse she got was anything but reassuring. Nicole still wore the apparatus that breathed for her, and was still tethered to bags of fluids and electronic machines. She watched the elevator doors close and then kept track of the floors as they blinked above. Four, she noted, and then she stepped to the next elevator and punched in the fourth floor. She arrived only a few seconds after the gurney had been pushed into an operating room.

She sat staring at the door, amazed that Nicole's life should be so important to her. She despised the girl, still certain that she had played her son for a fool, still suspicious that she had compromised her husband. She hadn't wavered a bit in her perception of Nicole as a conniving manipulator who had invaded her family just to steal its wealth.

But she had come back! The girl had already won her battle and was carrying off her loot. Yet she had turned back to try and save a friend from a mobster's vengeance. She could be enjoying her first sip of champagne at a lush European resort. Instead, she was lying on a table, spattered with her own blood, and hovering in a grim zone between life and death.

She held no affection for Nicole. The girl was a shameless hustler, and any attempt to elevate her status would only blacken the reputation of her own daughter. If Nicole were the victim, then Pam was the criminal. She should be over at the police station with her husband and her daughter. But the guttersnipe had come back to save a friend, and the friend had tried to kill her. So just who was virtuous and who was depraved?

She wanted Nicole to live, and not just because that would make things easier for her daughter. She needed resolution. There was a fundamental flaw in her equations of good and evil, right and wrong. Nicole might be able to point to the error. If she died, Alexandra would never know where she had gone wrong. She doubted that she would ever be able to sleep again.

The door swung open and the attendants reappeared, now pushing a bed. There were still the poles and the IV bags and the electronic displays. But the bed was made up with fresh white sheets. The blanket was pulled taut and tucked in. The desperation seemed to have vanished from the nurses' expressions.

A doctor came out, glanced around until he spotted Alexandra and then came over to her.

"You're her mother?"

"Yes, I am."

"She's going to make it. The bleeding has stopped, her signs are stable, and the wound has been cleaned out. You won't be able to talk to her tonight. But she should be conscious in the morning. Is there someplace where we can reach you?"

"I'll be right here. I'll be waiting outside her room."

EIGHTY-ONE

Alexandra was nervous as she left the house and started down the path to the cabana. As she walked she rehearsed the words she would use, unusual for someone who simply spoke her mind. But this was going to be a difficult conversation. She was going to ask Nicole to help Pam stay out of prison. It was a favor that she had no right to ask and that her daughter certainly didn't deserve.

She had stayed at the hospital through the first days of Nicole's recovery, until the tubes were removed and the monitors were disconnected. She had thanked Nicole for coming back to rescue her daughter, and apologized for Pam's murderous behavior. Then she had gone to the administration office and made the arrangements for Nicole to be moved out to Rockbottom for her recovery.

Alexandra came home to find Pam in the living room, released into the custody of her father. Jack had called in dozens of favors, presenting a scenario of a ridiculous and childish scheme by his daughter. He had sent Nicole away, and Pam had plotted to bring her back. Why? Because she wanted her as a partner in her gallery.

What about the gunshot? The attempted murder? A terrible accident Jack's lawyers had argued. Did the prosecutors really think that his daughter had any hopes of holding off the police assault team with a purse-size pistol? The crime, they argued was entirely within the family, and no one in the family was anxious for prosecution. In truth, Jack's daughter was mentally ill and needed psychiatric care more than a stint in prison.

Ben Tobin had to be rescued if Pam's defense was to hold up. They couldn't have Ben on a witness stand explaining how Pam had rigged her brother's air regulator, and how they had brought Nicole back with the specific intention of murdering her and disposing of the body. So Ben was presented as simply the intermediary between the two women.

There was a great deal of contradictory evidence. A quick check of bank records showed that Ben had transferred over nine million dollars from Nicole's account to an account he shared with Pam. And, of course, there were police witnesses who could testify that Pam had a gun pressed against Nicole's head, and had promised to kill her sister-in-law unless the police let her escape. Negotiations between Jack's attorneys and the prosecutors had been going on all the while Nicole was in the hospital, and were continuing during her month of recovery at Rockbottom. It was because her daughter's fate was still in the hands of the district attorney's office that Alexandra needed Nicole's help.

When she reached the cabana she saw Nicole struggling with her laps in the swimming pool. She was making fine progress. When she had been released from the hospital she hadn't been able to raise her left arm over her head. Now she was able to stretch it into a swimming stroke and was regaining much of her lost strength. Alexandra had been impressed by Nicole's determination. The girl had politely avoided offers of special treatment and had plunged into the painful task of rehabilitation. She knew that Nicole wouldn't be satisfied with anything but a complete recovery.

But her admiration fell well short of affection. She and Nicole would never be friends, much less come to see themselves as mother and daughter. Too much anger and resentment had passed between them.

Alexandra was unshaken in her belief that Nicole had worked her way into her son's life only to lay hands on his fortune. She knew that she had tricked Jonathan into a hasty marriage. She suspected that the girl had even seduced her husband just to guarantee herself a hefty settlement. There was no doubt in her mind that if Nicole hadn't come along, her son would be alive, her daughter sound, and her family intact.

For her part, Nicole would never forget that she had been rejected out of hand and deemed "not one of us." She could probably never forgive the ruthless investigation that exposed every secret sin of her past. There was no way to ignore that Alexandra had openly accused her of murdering Jonathan.

The two women had not found peace but had merely accepted a truce. They could function together, be polite, share feelings, even admit their own vulnerabilities. But they were still a long way from a heartfelt embrace.

Nicole climbed out of the pool and retrieved her towel from the chaise.

"You're doing better each day," Alexandra called as she emerged from the shadow of the cabana building.

"Oh, thanks! It seems to be getting easier."

As she approached Alexandra couldn't help noticing the scars. Pink tissue extended out from both sides of the shoulder strap, stretched into ugly welts. The star-like pattern was as big as her hand, reaching from her collarbone to her shoulder, and disappearing into the top of her swimsuit. When Nicole had heard the police approaching the cabin she had made a sudden leap behind the toppled chair. Pam fired and the bullet punched a tiny hole in the back of her shoulder. But it had carried shards of broken bones out through her chest, tearing up muscles and arteries on the way.

"Is that scar fading?" Alexandra asked.

Nicole looked down. "Maybe a bit. It doesn't seem so . . . angry." She draped the towel around her shoulders so that it hung over the offensive wound. "The doctor wants me to see a plastic surgeon. They can smooth it and change the color. But that's for another time. Right now the plan is to get everything working."

She climbed the steps to the guest apartments above the cabana, Alexandra following at her heels. Nicole had moved down from the main house as soon as she was ready to begin rehabilitation. Alexandra had set up one of the rooms with gym equipment and decorated another as a permanent residence.

"I understand Jack has come to an agreement with Jimmy Farr," Nicole called from the bedroom where she was dressing.

"Yes, he did," Alexandra answered from the living room. "How did you find out?"

"He sent me a note telling me that Jimmy wouldn't be bothering me anymore. I hope he's right!"

"I'm sure he is," Alexandra called back. "Jack usually gets what he wants."

Jimmy Farr had scarcely banked the bogus ransom dollars when his troubles began. Banks bought up the mortgages to his properties and then were horrified that their investments were being used for illegal purposes. They called in the loans. Health inspectors went through his kitchens and found numerous violations. The clubs were shut down. Then tax agents charged unreported income, and had documents from offshore banks that were usually more discreet. Within a month, Jimmy felt the full power of Jack's enormous financial muscle. When Greg Lambert suggested that the Donners would be grateful if he returned the ransom money, Jimmy Farr jumped at the opportunity.

"Some spring water?" Nicole asked when she came from the bedroom, dressed in slacks and an athletic sweatshirt.

"Yes, I'd like that." She followed Nicole into the kitchenette and took a bottle of water from the refrigerator. The two women gestured a toast and then drank. They struggled with small talk until they were back in the living room, and then Alexandra drew a breath and started into her prepared speech.

"Nicole, I want to tell you where Pam's legal affairs stand. And then I'm going to be brash enough to ask for your help." Nicole crossed her legs and leaned back, showing that she was willing to listen.

"We're close to an agreement on a plea bargain. Basically, both Pam and Ben will plead guilty to extortion and receive suspended sentences. Ben will be disbarred. Pam will stay in the sanitarium until the doctors tell the court she's cured. I know this is a miscarriage of justice and that it basically ignores the cruelty you've suffered. But much as I detest my daughter's crime, I can't bear to think of her in a jail cell."

"I can't either," Nicole agreed.

"Thank you, but there's more that I have to say about my responsibility. Mine and

Jack's. We've both been arrogant and demanding, and in the process we seem to have crippled our own children. Jonathan never learned responsibility, and Pam has no concept of honor. Jonathan wouldn't do anything, which was his fatal flaw. On the other hand, there wasn't anything that Pam wouldn't do to have her way. Including trying to kill the person who had risked everything to save her. Our children should have been the center of our lives. But Jack and I have kept those positions for ourselves. That's been our fatal flaw."

Nicole interrupted. "I don't think that you have to blame yourself for —"

Alexandra held up a silencing hand. "What has occurred to me over the past few weeks was that you might well have been the salvation of both of them. As a wife, you certainly gave Jonathan ambition and courage. And as a sister, I think you might have taught Pamela that success is never easy . . . never assured. Unfortunately, I didn't give you that opportunity."

She swallowed hard, perhaps stifling a sob. Then she squared her shoulders, lest her apologies seem to be weakness. "I remember thinking that if it hadn't been for you I would still have my family around me. But, in truth, it wouldn't have been much of a family with two self-engrossed parents and two damaged children."

"What can I do for you?" Nicole asked.

"Join Jack and me in a fiction. Let Jonathan's death be an accident rather than Pam's stupid attempt to destroy you." She reached across and touched Nicole's shoulder. "Let this be the result of a stray round rather than a well-aimed bullet."

Nicole nodded. "All right."

"You can topple the plea bargain with just a word. And you have every right to scream that you were supposed to be a murder victim. What I'm asking is that you keep your silence."

"I understand," she answered. "And I hope as much as you do that Pam makes a full recovery."

Alexandra stood and straightened her skirt. "Thank you," she whispered.

She had opened the door when she turned with another thought. "Do you have any idea what you'll do when you're fully recovered?"

"Just what I was about to do. Go far away and start a new life."

"You don't have to leave. You'd be welcome here. At the main house. Or in Newport."

Nicole shook her head slowly. "I don't

think so. There have been too many hurts. I think we would always remind one another of our failings. It would be hard to forget all the bad moments. It's really best that I leave."

"I suppose you're right," Alexandra agreed. "But if you should ever change your mind, or ever need anything . . ."

"I'll be fine," Nicole said.

Alexandra stepped into the doorway, but she couldn't leave without saying it. "You know, for someone with such a trashy background, you certainly have many admirable qualities."

The employees of Thorndike Press hope you have enjoyed this Large Print book. All our Thorndike and Wheeler Large Print titles are designed for easy reading, and all our books are made to last. Other Thorndike Press Large Print books are available at your library, through selected bookstores, or directly from us.

For information about titles, please call:

(800) 223-1244

or visit our Web site at:

www.gale.com/thorndike
www.gale.com/wheeler

To share your comments, please write:

Publisher
Thorndike Press
295 Kennedy Memorial Drive
Waterville, ME 04901